P9-EKJ-048

SNAKEWOOĐ

SNAKEWOOD

ADRIAN SELBY

www.orbitbooks.net

Copyright © 2016 by Adrian Selby

Cover design by Lauren Panepinto
Cover illustration by David Palumbo
Cover copyright © 2016 by Hachette Book Group, Inc.

Orbit
Hachette Book Group
1290 Avenue of the Americas
New York, NY 10104
orbitbooks.net

Simultaneously published in Great Britain and in the U.S. by Orbit in 2016
First U.S. Edition: March 2016

Orbit is an imprint of Hachette Book Group.
The Orbit name and logo are trademarks of Little, Brown Book Group Limited.

The publisher is not responsible for websites (or their content)
that are not owned by the publisher.

The Hachette Speakers Bureau provides a wide range of authors for
speaking events. To find out more, go to www.hachettespeakersbureau.com
or call (866) 376-6591.

Map illustration copyright © Tim Paul

Library of Congress Control Number: 2015956501

ISBNs: 978-0-316-30230-2 (hardcover), 978-0-316-30232-6 (ebook)

Printed in the United States of America

RRD-C

10 9 8 7 6 5 4 3 2 1

For Rhian

These, in the day when heaven was falling,
The hour when earth's foundations fled,
Followed their mercenary calling
And took their wages and are dead.

Their shoulders held the sky suspended;
They stood, and earth's foundations stay;
What God abandoned, these defended,
And saved the sum of things for pay.

Alfred Edward Housman,
Epitaph On An Army of Mercenaries

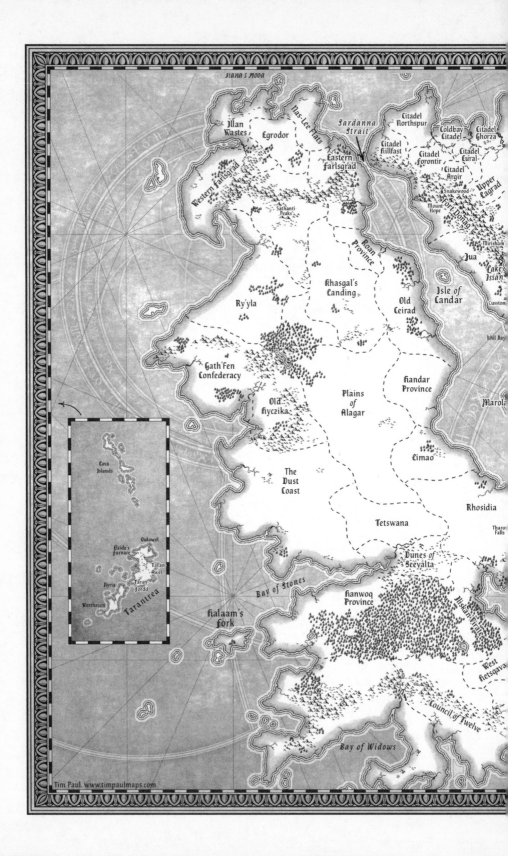

Tim Paul www.timpaulmaps.com

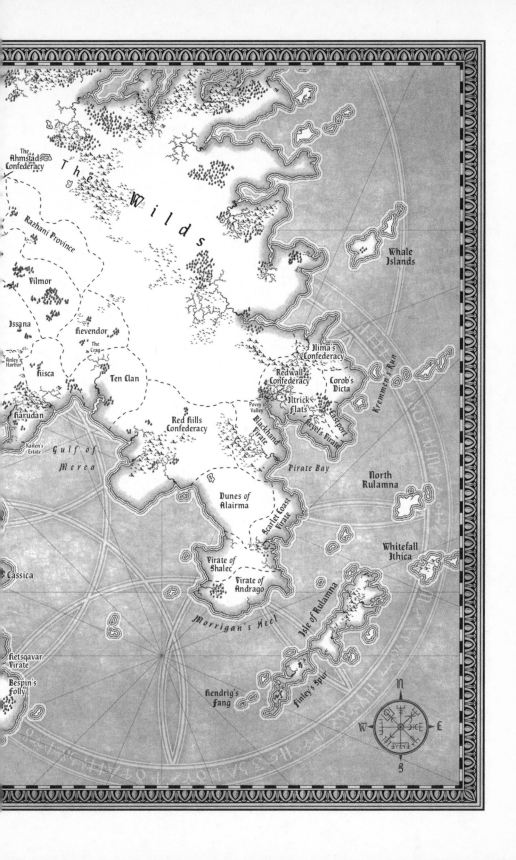

The Wilds

The Ahmstad Confederacy

Razhani Province

Vilmor

Issana

Hevendor

The Crag

Anley's Harbor

Hisca

Ten Clan

Harudan

Kailen's Estate

Gulf of Merea

Red Hills Confederacy

Ilima's Confederacy

Redwall Confederacy

Corob's Dicta

Ultrick Flats

Povey's Valley

Fastport

Keyel's Virate

Blackhand Virate

Whale Islands

Kremman's Run

Dunes of Alairma

Pirate Bay

North Rulamna

Scarlet Coast Virate

Whitefall Ithica

Virate of Shalec

Virate of Andrago

Isle of Rulamna

Cassica

Morrigan's Heel

Hetsqavar Virate

Bespin's Folly

Hendrig's Fang

Finley's Spur

N

W E

S

SNAKEWOOD

Introductory Notes by

Scholar Goran

I never knew my father. Not until the end.

It was my patron who brought him home to our tribe, mortally wounded and ready to die.

All of what follows is for him, Gant, and his last wish that a record be kept of what became of the greatest mercenary crew ever to take a purse. Kailen's Twenty.

The stories of them in their prime are few and far between all these winters later. I spent almost two years tracking down those who fought with or against them, but their downfall is, for me, the more compelling and tragic story, one I've been given the mandate to record by my patron, out of respect for my father and all those others who were killed by his failing them. I have put all these documents together in a way that I hope makes sense of the fate of the Twenty, and I include accounts of them in their prime, when, arguably, they saved the Old Kingdoms at Tharos Falls, when twenty men held the line and the line could not be crossed.

To tell this story I was given also the letters of the princess who waits to be returned to her throne, as well as the man whose loyalty to her was the beginning of the end for the Twenty. The man betrayed at Snakewood.

In the moments of his dying, my father asked us a simple question, and from the papers that follow, it is clear he did not ask the question of himself.

"Who ever got what they deserved?"

Chapter 1

Gant

My name's Gant and I'm sorry for my poor writing. I was a mercenary soldier who never took to it till Kailen taught us. It's for him and all the boys that I wanted to put this down, a telling of what become of Kailen's Twenty.

Seems right to begin it the day me and Shale got sold out, at the heart of the summer just gone, down in the Red Hills Confederacy.

It was the day I began dying.

It was a job with a crew to ambush a supply caravan. It went badly for us and I took an arrow, the poison from which will shortly kill me.

I woke up sodden with dew and rain like the boys, soaked all over from the trees above us, but my mouth was dusty like sand. Rivers couldn't wet it. The compound I use to ease my bones leeches my spit. I speak soft.

I could hardly crack a whistle at the boys wrapped like a nest of slugs in their oilskins against the winds of the plains these woods were edged against. I'm old. I just kicked them up before getting my bow out of the sack I put it in to keep rain off the string. It was a beauty what I called Juletta and I had her for most of my life.

The boys were slow to get going, blowing and fussing as the freezing air got to work in that bit of dawn. They were quiet, and grim like ghosts in this light, pairing up to strap their leathers and get the swords pasted with poison.

I patted heads and squeezed shoulders and give words as I moved

1

through the crew so they knew I was about and watching. I knew enough of their language that I could give them encouragement like I was one of them, something else Kailen give me to help me bond with a crew.

"Paste it thick," I said as they put on the mittens and rubbed their blades with the soaked rags from the pot Remy had opened.

I looked around the boys I'd shared skins and pipes with under the moon those last few weeks. Good crew.

There was Remy, looking up at me from his mixing, face all scarred like a milky walnut and speaking lispy from razor fights and rackets he ran with before joining up for a pardon. He had a poison of his own he made, less refined than my own mix, less quick, more agony.

Yasthin was crouched next to him. He was still having to shake the cramp off his leg that took a mace a month before. Saved his money for his brother, told me he was investing it. The boys said his brother gambled it and laughed him up.

Dolly was next to Yasthin, chewing some bacon rinds. Told me how her da chased her soak of a mother through the streets, had done since she was young. Kids followed her da too, singing with him but staying clear of his knives. She joined so's she could help her da keep her younger brother.

All of them got sorrows that led them to the likes of me and a fat purse for a crossroads job, which I mean to say is a do-or-die.

Soon enough they're lined up and waiting for the Honour, Kailen's Honour, the best fightbrew Kigan ever mixed, so, the best fightbrew ever mixed, even all these years later. The boys had been talking up this brew since I took command, makes you feel like you could punch holes in mountains when you've risen on it.

Yasthin was first in line for a measure. I had to stand on my toes to pour it in, lots of the boys taller than me. Then a kiss. The lips are the raw end of your terror and love. No steel can toughen lips, they betray more than the eyes when you're looking for intent and the kiss is for telling them there's always some way to die.

Little Booey was the tenth and last of the crew to get the measure. I took a slug myself and Rirgwil fixed my leathers. I waited for our teeth to chatter like aristos, then went over the plan again.

"In the trees north, beyond those fields, is Trukhar's supply caravan,"

I said. "Find it, kill who you can but burn the wagons, supplies, an' then go for the craftsmen. Shale's leadin' his crew in from east an' we got them pincered when we meet, red bands left arm so as you know. It's a do-or-die purse, you're there 'til the job is done or you're dead anyway."

It was getting real for them now I could see. A couple were starting shakes with their first full measure of the brew, despite all the prep the previous few days.

"I taught you how to focus what's happening to you boys. This brew has won wars an' it'll deliver this purse if you can keep tight. Now move out."

No more words, it was hand signs now to the forest.

Jonah front, Yasthin, Booey and Henny with me. Remy group northeast at treeline

We ran through the silver grass, chests shuddering with the crackle of our blood as the brew stretched our veins and filled our bones with iron and fire. The song of the earth was filling my ears.

Ahead of us was the wall of trees and within, the camp of the Blackhands. Remy's boys split from us and moved away.

Slow I signed.

Juletta was warm in my hands, the arrow in my fingers humming to fly. Then, the brew fierce in my eyes, I saw it, the red glow of a pipe some seventy yards ahead at the treeline.

Two men. On mark

I moved forward to take the shot and stepped into a nest of eggs. The bird, a big grey weger, screeched at me and flapped madly into the air inches from my face, its cry filling the sky. One of the boys shouted out, in his prime on the brew, and the two men saw us. We were dead. My boys' arrows followed mine, the two men were hit, only half a pip of a horn escaping for warning, but it was surely enough.

Run

I had killed us all. We went in anyway, that was the purse, and these boys primed like this weren't leaving without bloodshed.

As we hit the trees we spread out.

Enemy left signed Jonah.

Three were nearing through the trunks, draining their own brew as they come to from some half-eyed slumber. They were a clear shot so I led again, arrows hitting and a muffled crack of bones. All down.

In my brewed-up ears I could hear then the crack of bowstrings pulling at some way off, but it was all around us. The whistle of arrows proved us flanked as we dropped to the ground.

The boys opened up, moving as we practised, aiming to surprise any flanks and split them off so a group of us could move in directly to the caravan. It was shooting practice for Trukhar's soldiers.

I never saw Henny or Jonah again, just heard some laughing and screaming and the sound of blades at work before it died off.

I stayed put, watching for the enemy's movements. I was in the outroots of a tree, unspotted. You feel eyes on you with this brew. Then I saw two scouts moving right, following Booey and Datschke's run.

I took a sporebag and popped it on the end of an arrow. I stood up and sent it at the ground ahead of them.

From my belt I got me some white oak sap which I took for my eyes to see safe in the spore cloud. I put on a mask covered with the same stuff for breathing.

The spores were quick to get in them and they wheezed and clutched their throats as I finished them off.

I was hoping I could have saved my boys but I needed to be in some guts and get the job done with Shale's crew.

Horns were going up now, so the fighting was on. I saw a few coming at me from the trees ahead. I got behind a trunk but I knew I was spotted. They slowed up and the hemp creaked as they drew for shots. There were four of them, from their breathing, and I could hear their commander whispering for a flanking.

I opened up a satchel of ricepaper bags, each with quicklime and oiled feathers. I needed smoke. I doused a few bags with my flask and threw them out.

"Masks!" came the shout. As the paper soaked, the lime caught and the feathers put out a fierce smoke.

My eyes were still smeared good. I took a couple more arrowbags out, but these were agave powders for blistering the eyes and skin.

Two shots to tree trunks spread the powders in the air around their position and I moved out from the tree to them as they screeched and

4

staggered about blind. The Honour give me the senses enough to read where they were without my eyes, better to shut them with smoke and powders in the air, and their brews weren't the Honour's equal. They moved like they were running through honey and were easy to pick off.

It was then I took the arrow that'll do for me. I'd got maybe fifty yards further on when I heard the bow draw, but with the noise ahead I couldn't place it that fraction quicker to save myself. The arrow went in at my hip, into my guts. Something's gave in there, and the poison's gone right in, black mustard oil for sure from the vapours burning in my nose, probably some of their venom too.

I was on my knees trying to grab the arrow when I saw them approach, two of them. The one who killed me was dropping his bow and they both closed with the hate of their own fightbrew, their eyes crimson, skin an angry red and all the noisies.

They think I'm done. They're fucking right, to a point. In my belt was the treated guaia bark for the mix they were known to use. No time to rip out the arrow and push the bark in.

They moved in together, one in front, the other flanking. One's a heavy in his mail coat and broadsword, a boy's weapon in a forest, too big. Older one had leathers and a long knife. Him first. My sight was going, the world going flat like a drawing, so I had to get rid of the wiser one while I could still see him, while I still had the Honour's edge.

Knife in hand I lunged sudden, the leap bigger than they reckoned. The older one reacted, a sidestep. The slash I made wasn't for hitting him though. It flicked out a spray of paste from the blade and sure enough some bit of it caught him in the face. I spun about, brought my blade up and parried the boy's desperate swing as he closed behind me, the blow forcing me down as it hit my knife, sending a smack through my guts as the arrow broke in me. He took sight of his mate holding his smoking face, scratching at his cheeks and bleeding. He glanced at the brown treacle running over my blade and legged it. He had the spunk to know he was beaten. I put the knife in the old man's throat to quiet my noisies, the blood's smell as sweet as fresh bread to me.

I picked up my Juletta and moved on. The trees were filling with

5

Blackhands now. I didn't have the time to be taking off my wamba and sorting myself out a cure for the arrow, much less tugging at it now it was into me. I cussed at myself, for this was likely where I was going to die if I didn't get something to fix me. I was slowing up. I took a hit of the Honour to keep me fresh. It was going to make a fierce claim on the other side, but I would gladly take that if I could get some treatment.

Finally I reached the caravan; smoke from the blazing wagons and stores filled the trees ahead. The grain carts were burning so Shale, again, delivered the purse.

Then I come across Dolly, slumped against the roots of a tree. Four arrows were thrusting proud from her belly. She saw me and her eyes widened and she smiled.

"Gant, you're not done . . . Oh," she said, seeing the arrow in me. I might have been swaying, she certainly didn't look right, faded somewhat, like she was becoming a ghost before me.

"Have you a flask, Gant, some more of the Honour?"

Her hands were full of earth, grabbing at it, having their final fling.

"I'm out, Dolly," I said. "I'm done too. I'm sorry for how it all ended."

She blinked, grief pinching her up.

"It can't be over already. I'm twenty summers, Gant, this was goin' to be the big purse."

A moment then I couldn't fill with any words.

"Tell my father, Gant, say . . ."

I was raising my bow. I did my best to clean an arrow on my leggings. She was watching me as I did it, knowing.

"Tell him I love him, Gant, tell him I got the Honour, and give him my purse and my brother a kiss."

"I will."

As I drew it she looked above me, seeing something I knew I wouldn't see, leagues away, some answers to her questions in her eyes thrilling her. I let fly, fell to my knees and sicked up.

Where was Shale?

My mouth was too dry to speak or shout for him, but I needed him. My eyes, the lids of them, were peeling back so's they would burn in the sun. I put my hands to my face. It was only visions, but

6

my chest was heavy, like somebody sat on it and others were piling on. Looking through my hands as I held them up, it was like there were just bones there, flesh thin like the fins of a fish. My breathing rattled and I reached to my throat to try to open it up more.

"Gant!"

So much blood on him. He kneeled next to me. He's got grey eyes, no colour. Enemy to him is just so much warm meat to be put still. He don't much smile unless he's drunk. He mostly never drinks. He sniffed about me and at my wound, to get a reading of what was in it, then forced the arrow out with a knife and filled the hole with guaia bark while kneeling on my shoulder to keep me still. He was barking at some boys as he stuffed some rugara leaves, sap and all, into my mouth, holding my nose shut, drowning me. Fuck! My brains were buzzing sore like a hive was in them. Some frothing liquid filled up my chest and I was bucking about for breath. He poured from a flask over my hip and the skin frosted over with an agony of burning. Then he took out some jumpcrick's legbones and held them against the hole, snap snap, a flash of blue flame and everything fell away high.

There was a choking, but it didn't feel like me no longer. It felt like the man I was before I died.

Kailen

"Let's see it."

Achi flicked it across the table, a pebble across wood, but this stone was worked with precision, a stone coin, black and thick as a thumb. There were no markings on it, a hairline of quartz the only imperfection of the material itself. The ocean had polished it, my face made a shadow by it. It was the third I'd seen in the last few months.

"The Prince, from your old crew, his throat was cut," said Achi.

Achi drained his cup, leaned back in his chair and yawned, the chair creaking, not built for such a big man still in his leathers. He was filthy and sour-smelling from the weeks sleeping out.

"How are the boys?" I asked.

He opened his eyes with a start, already drifting away to sleep. I smiled at his irritation.

"Sorry, sir, all good. Danik and Stimmy are sorting out the horses, Wil went looking for a mercer, wants to get his woman something as we been away a while."

"Stimmy's boy is on the mend, I had word from the estate. Let him know if you see him before me."

Achi nodded and yawned again.

I looked again at the black coin in my fingers. Such coins were given to mercenaries who betrayed their purse or their crew. But who had The Prince betrayed?

We had called him The Prince because there was a time when he was in line for a throne, last of three, least loved and cleverest. His homeland chose its emperors in a way as ridiculous as any; which of the incumbents best demonstrated martial prowess. His sister won their single combat on the day their father died and was thus made

8

queen, but his sword wasn't what made him worthy of the Twenty.

The Prince did the politics his sister could not. War allows only two perspectives, yours and theirs, a limit his sister was not capable of seeing beyond. Nations require the management of more factions than cut diamonds have facets and I met nobody that could exploit his empire's *politic* more adroitly than The Prince.

I plucked a white grape from the bowl, milky and juicy as a blind eyeball. Achi peeled eggs, head bowed. The bargirl came in and cleared away my plate. She offered a quick smile before retreating to the noise of the inn below us.

I recalled the two other black coins I'd seen recently, as perfect as this one. The Prince had shown them to me in his cabin aboard one of the Quartet's galleys only a few months ago. The Quartet were an influential merchant guild across most of the Old Kingdoms, and it was as fine a cabin as I'd ever seen him in, satin cushions, exquisitely carved chests and lockers, some of them the work of masters I had had the good fortune to commission myself at my wife Araliah's recommendation.

I'd travelled to see The Prince after he'd sent an escort bidding me to return with him.

"These coins were found with Harlain and Milu," he said. "I will try and find out more."

"How did they die?" I asked.

"Harlain returned to his homeland, Tetswana, became their leader, the Kaan of Tetswana no less. It was the gathering before the rains. Leaders and retinues of nine tribes. Seventy or so dead, the black coin in his hand only."

Harlain would not join us at Snakewood, the last time any of the Twenty were together. He had wanted to leave us some time before the end. Paying the colour had taken from all of us, but it took his heart. It was only as we embraced for a final time and I helped him with his saddle that I realised I hadn't heard him singing for some months. I was glad he made it home.

"Milu?" I asked.

"He became a horse-singer out in Alagar. They found him lying at the side of a singer's pit. Someone had been with him, footprints in the sand around his body, the coin in his hand."

"Poison?" I asked.

"Almost certainly. No way of placing it."

Milu had also been at Snakewood, but stayed only for a drink and to buy supplies before leaving with Kheld. They had lost heart as much as Harlain had; no talk of purses or where in the world was at war; they did not discuss, as did Sho or Shale, how my name could be put to work to bolster the gold of a purse.

I never tired of watching Milu work, his grotesquely big chest and baggy jowls filling with the songs that brought the wild horses to his side, training them to hold firm in the charge. It seemed that he, like Harlain, had been able to let go of the mercenary life before the colour took everything.

"Their deaths are connected, Kailen. It must be the Twenty."

"You've heard from nobody else?"

"Only that Dithnir had died. He went back home to Tarantrea; one of their envoys that negotiates with the Quartet I represent knows me well and shared the news with me. I asked about a coin but there was none. Apart from that I keep in touch with Kheld when I'm in Handar, but the rest, no word."

I breathed deeply of the morning breeze that blew across the deck and slapped at the fringes of the awning we were beneath. Dithnir was a bowman, almost a match for Stixie, shy and inadvisedly romantic with whores, cold and implacable in the field.

"I remember Snakewood," said The Prince.

Our eyes met briefly. "No. That was dealt with." I'd said it more sharply than I'd intended. Why did I feel a thread of doubt?

He reached across the table, took the carafe and refilled our glasses with the wine I'd brought for him.

"Your estate is improving," he said, holding up his glass for a toast.

"Yes, these vines were planted two winters ago; they'll improve. I only wish for Jua's cooler summers, perhaps an estate nearer the hills. How is the Quartet? I hear you have brokered a treaty with the Shalec to cross their waters. Not even the Post could manage it. Have you considered lending them your talents?"

"Why would I toil through its ranks to High Reeve or Fieldsman when I can be a Partner with the Quartet? The Post – The Red himself – could learn something from the Quartet regarding our softening of the Shalec, but I'm glad he hasn't, I'm lining my pockets beautifully. Remarkable as the Post runs so much trade elsewhere. They can bid lower than us at almost every turn; we can't match the subs, but we can work with lower margins, give Shalec a fee on the nutmeg, a pittance of course. But every investor north of the Gulf believes the Post controls the winds."

"While the Post can sub dividends over fewer summers than anyone else, the flatbacks will flock," I said, "but enough of trade: congratulations, Prince, I'm glad to see things are going well; being a Partner suits you. Will you get a message to me if you find Kheld? It would be good to know he's still alive."

He nodded.

The Prince had been the difference at Ahmstad, turning three prominent families under the noses of Vilmor's king, extending the borders and fortifying them in a stroke. The mad king is still being strangled in the noose The Prince tied. His death proved that whoever of us was alive was in danger. I signed our purses. This could only be about getting at me.

Achi had fallen asleep.

I poured him some of the dreadful brandy that was the best The Riddle had to offer.

Shale and Gant were taking a purse only weeks south. If they were still anything like the soldiers of old I would have need of them. Achi's crew would be glad to be going back to Harudan. I needed good men with my wife, Araliah. Still, there was one more thing I needed to ask of Achi himself, one person I needed to confirm was dead.

The Prince and the Ahmstad

An account by a Fieldsman of the Post regarding Kailen and The Prince. Fieldsmen are the most elite Agents of the Post, from the ranks of which The Red himself, the head of the Post, is often promoted.

This Fieldsman was disguised as a bodyguard to the Ahmstad's "Ladus" (chief), present at the negotiation by which Kailen and The Prince secured a bloodless victory for Ahmstad over Vilmor, nine years before Snakewood.

Goran

Destination: Candar Prime, Q4 649 OE
Eastern Sar Westmain routed
CONFIDENTIAL FOR THE RED ONLY
Report of: Fieldsman 71

You are aware of Vilmorian expansionism under their King Turis. They have been amassing an army for assaults on two fronts, the Luzhan Province and Ahmstad.

A clan leader for Ahmstad brought a mercenary known as Kailen to their war council. To say the Ladus was displeased was to put it mildly. The clan leader, Hasike, asked that the Ladus hear him out.

What follows is a transcript of the meeting as best as I can relay it. It is evident that Kailen, and his fellow that he called The Prince, displayed a formidable understanding of both sides of the potential conflict. He is a most unusual mercenary and a compelling speaker, though of course this does not come across half so well in my approximation of the meeting.

"May I ask the Ladus the size of the army he is amassing?" said Kailen.

"The clans represented here have committed to me near eighteen thousand men and women. Do I speak right?" Raised voices, eliciting approval and some banging of cups.

"And what would the Ladus say losses of such men might be, were Vilmor to bring to bear an army estimated at twenty-five thousand?"

"Where do you get such numbers, soldier?"

The Prince speaks then. "We served with Vilmor, as you no doubt already know. They have seventy-six fiefs, variously providing twenty to two hundred men and women."

"With these numbers, in open battle, the losses would be?" This was Kailen.

"Far higher on their side." More cups were banged at this point.

"Ladus," said Hasike, somewhat frustrated, "who bears the brunt of their aggression? My clan. We are your border with Vilmor."

"As we border the Wilds," said another, "but we do not cry to the Ladus over it."

"The Wilds do not bring in twenty thousand men in front of a fortified supply line," said Kailen. "Bang your cups and brag if it pleases you, but you stand over a map that shows clearly where Vilmor will push, through Hasike's land and to the heart of Ahmstad."

The Ladus raised his arms to quieten the shouts.

"My council waits with bated breath for the wisdom of a Harudanian mercenary on its own affairs. You have disappointed me, Hasike, bringing to our gathering men paid to chop up soldiers when what we need is to outwit Turis's generals."

"You ought to consider Hasike wise, Ladus. I will gladly demonstrate why." Remarkably, the mercenary sounded angry. I had expected him to be run through at that point, for the Ladus enjoyed nothing more than disembowelling everyone from servants to his own family for sleights of honour or even dark looks.

"You have not begun to muster from your war communes, the

sheriffs and quarters are still securing your supplies: wood, cattle, grain. The men at this table await their levies, and the last time I fought Ahmstad I would not hold such hope for the weak and ill-equipped majority that are enrolled. Hasike's lands will be pillaged and burned, some fifth of your tithe in buffalo, a seventh of all your guira and ska crops." He had the room now, though the Ladus's fist was white as it gripped the handle of his axe.

Kailen swept the arranged blocks from the map and reset them. He laid out the routes the Vilmorian army would take, the challenge for the Ahmstad forces, and every way that he laid out their options they were to expect heavy losses, even in victory.

The room was silent, for each anticipated deployment and stratagem had been devised and its consequences presented soundly.

"I have a question," said the Ladus: "if we are likely to lose, why have you sold Hasike your services? Do you and your friend of some dubious royal lineage plan to defeat Turis with your own hands?"

"No. For one hundred and fifty gold pieces my friend of dubious royal lineage will explain why you need not raise a sword to defeat the forces of Vilmor, gain yourselves land and new allies and weaken Turis significantly."

The Ladus erupted with laughter. "If I'd wanted a fool I would have left my first consort alive. I suppose you wish to be paid before you share your grand plan with us as well?"

"Listen to him, for my people's sake," said Hasike.

The Ladus was always a big and intimidating man, easily a foot taller than anyone else in a room, and I'd seen him press and win, time and again, from Hasike more cattle for the northern Ahmstad clans he favoured. Hasike was desperate. The Ladus took a deep breath.

"Fifty gold pieces. If I like what I hear you'll get your hundred more, if not you'll swallow them and I'll cut them out of your belly." He turned his head slightly towards where I stood with his treasurer, and a nod commanded the treasurer to count out the coins. Kailen took the proffered pouch as calmly as a man receiving payment for food, suggesting that, uniquely in my experience, his purses were of a not dissimilar amount.

Kailen's man, The Prince, was, I learned shortly afterwards, called so because he was an heir to the throne of Old Ceirad. He had the Old Kingdoms aristocracy in every bone, an educated, persuasive speaker. He also used Ladus's map and his blocks to explain his argument.

"Vilmor, as I have said, is comprised of seventy-six fiefs. Your lands border eleven of those fiefs. Of those eleven there are three that matter. These three share a common ancestry with Hasike's clan. You will have noted how peaceful the border is there, compared to the Wilds and Razhani borders. Only Lagrad is more peaceful, and precisely because of your longstanding treaty.

"These three fiefs, comprising two clans, do not, shall we say, dine at the top table with Turis and the bigger fiefs. Indeed, he has seen fit to put to a vote the redrawing of the fiefdoms in favour of a cousin whose land lies behind theirs. His mistake, as I see it, has been to give his cousin the oversight and control of levies, in the name of Turis, to see to the construction of the forts that now press against your borders, in those three lands.

"As many of you in the room will testify, if the Ladus here designated Hasike or anyone else to command your own men to build forts in the Ladus's name, irrespective of the cost to your lands and your harvests, you would be displeased." This earned a few grunts of approval.

"Two castles have been built, at great cost to those fiefs, along with seven other wooden forts and the construction of bridges through some of the marshlands that edge your borders, giving Vilmor the advantage of which we speak.

"I would suggest that the hundred gold pieces not be paid now, as I summarise our plan, but upon its execution. Will you bind to that, Ladus?"

You now understand how interesting these two mercenaries are. The Ladus is a great warrior, but a vain and ridiculous man. They understood this, as they must have understood Hasike's position as well as the intelligence they had gathered on the border before they approached Hasike and the Ladus. I was struck at that moment by the thought that one hundred and fifty gold pieces was not as preposterous as it initially seemed. Nor did

Kailen's demeanour shift for a moment at this change in the agreement, as though it too had been rehearsed.

The Ladus looked about the room, and I noted Kailen's satisfaction. He had concluded much as I did that this gesture indicated Ladus did not have the initiative or command here. He sought the faces of his clan leaders for their view on this offer, though it would have been madness to refuse.

"Explain your plan," he said.

The Prince continued. "Enfeoff the three clans, give them freehold land, at the cost of one quarter of Hasike's own lands and four of his herds. Make also a gift to each clan of five hundred gold pieces, along with two hundred jars each of cocklebur seeds and the recipes for them. Commit also to fund a war commune there and give them a place on the council. In return . . ."

There were cries of "Disgrace" and others much more colourful, but The Prince continued over them.

"In return you have extended your borders, united four clans that Hasike will soon get control of, gained two castles and a number of forts, and weakened Turis considerably on this front."

Though the hubbub continued a moment, the Ladus raised his hand for silence.

"Hasike?" he said.

"I believe with some suitable marriages, the war commune in what remains of my territory and my family's lineage in respect of these clans, I and my sons after me will take overall control of these lands, though I expect, as The Prince has said, that they will accede to our offer willingly. I can commit from my own men enough, with Kailen's help, to secure the castles while we secure the lands."

The Ladus nodded. Hasike had improved his standing immensely. He took some time, looking over the map, lost in thought.

"Return with the agreements and I will have the payments ready, both for those clans and these two mercenaries."

The territory was duly won, Kailen and The Prince were proved right.

I understand from some of the soldiers that I'd questioned

regarding them that Kailen commands only a crew of twenty, and they have been making a name for themselves wherever they've signed. They have not yet signed a purse for a general that lost a battle.

I recommend an introduction, we may learn much from this remarkable man.

Chapter 2

Gant

Sunshine.

I was laid on a straw mat in a tent where men were either sleeping or yelling and babbling with whatever the drudha had forced down them or up them. My ass was stinging, I needed a shit. Bones were creaking from the brew as I paid for the measures I took with the usual spasms and headaches and sores. All these years on brews meant the down was harder and longer each time.

I didn't know how Shale got us back. I needed to eat and get my compounds on. I just managed to crawl on a bucket thick with flies and get out a few squirts when he come in, a shirt and breeches on him stinking enough to have been what he wore on the raid. He kept his head shaved so the grey coming through wasn't too obvious, but his skin was so weathered and dark from paying the colour it didn't help, for when you drink fightbrews they change your blood and how your skin is, turning it different colours according to how much you have or where it's from or its quality. You tell a soldier by his colour.

"You fuckin' woman. Blackhand sauce an' you din't put your guaia to it?" he said, helping me up from the bucket and giving me a wipe with the stick.

"I were killing or dead anyway," I said. "I killed me boys, lost us the ambush. Stepped in a fucking birds' nest."

He put his hand on my shoulder, sat me down and kneeled next to me. He stared at me, looking for something in my face, it seemed.

18

He shook his head a little, disagreeing with something. He set firm then, he was holding something back in his way.

"Did what I could wi' that wound, but it was a mess. Not sure you can, you know, be made up. We need some plant, good plant, but . . ." He took a deep sigh. He was trying to deal with what it meant. "It in't good, Gant. It . . ." His words wouldn't come out. He swallowed and bowed his head and I let him be.

I looked down at my side, wrapped up and cotton gummed to it. With your life all about killing, it was still something that hit like a mace; my guts felt the drop like I was on a ship at sea. He was straight up, though. I had weeks maybe.

"I'm going north then," I said, "see me sister if I can. I want to go back in the world at Lagrad. Near me da."

He had recovered somewhat. "In't a drudha goin' straight north from here to Upper Lagrad worth a shit, Gant. You won't make it home. Harudan High Commune, unless we can find some plant on the Hiscan Road an' a cooker whose kit we can use. We can get there in a few weeks, fix you up tight an' give you a chance to get up there. Good plant will slow the poison down a good bit. Fer now we get some decent brandy an' cheer usselves up." He kissed my head and stood straight.

"Harudan's over southwest, it's more than a few weeks. We go through Hisca," I said.

"A few weeks that way'll buy more 'n a few for goin' north."

"We won then?" I said, referring to the effect of our sortie on the Blackhands.

"Three o' the Red Hills hasts moved in from east an' pushed Trukhar's lot back north. Reckon they're cut off, but the confeds say we sit here an' fort. Wi' the caravan took out, we secured the border again."

The tent was getting into my nose. Who's going to empty the buckets unless they're shouted at?

"Need some air, Shale," I said.

He hauled me up off the mat I was on and got hold of a pike for me to lean on.

A middling breeze picked up as we moved away from the tents and workshops and up some slopes to a view across Mandrik's Hast, our

19

current purse. It was mostly bald dry bluffs and some scrub, hard living in summer for those about.

Shale got me some bread and cheese and unstoppered us a flask when we reached somewhere to sit. We took a few kannab pipes and settled back.

"I'll head up north wi' you," he said, "I in't gettin' younger. They had boys there pushin' me a bit. Seems more an' more it's tactics an' plant not muscle an' steel that gets me over the crossin'."

A boy come up the hill towards us. I see it now as clear as I did then, a moment polished up in my head. The start of it all.

He was a recruit, from seeing the scabbard bash about his legs and his skin still pale with the lack of fightbrews.

"Excuse. Captain Forthwald, he wants to see you. Says it's important."

Shale nodded and stared the boy away down the hill.

"What's he want?" he said.

"I in't in a fit state to be digging foundations."

"In't payin' us fer that either. Pack us another pipe, Gant, bit more o' the Rosie in this one before I got to help you back."

Like many captains, Forthwald was too good at the job with the boys to move up out of harm's way. He kept the hast-lords at bay and got the boys their due. There's a way only a few have that can talk crews down off brews or talk them up from a loss of a leg or their seeing. Kailen had it too.

Evening was setting a deep pink that smoothed everything out when we were stood at the Purse's tent with him. He had a few boys with him what helped keep an eye out while he was counting purses and scribbling out the inventories and that.

"With you in a second, boys." He had a table full of tally foils in piles. There was sweat on his head made me think he had been going through the weapon forms with the kids what had been sent by levy from the hasts.

He looked up then.

"Good work on the caravan, the pincer was sound. Shale told me what happened, Gant, but even when it went ass over, it drew the guard away from the main 'van. We'll be able to push their army back into the Wilds or their homeland. Some brandy?"

We nods, glad not to be hitting our own flasks so far from any decent refill.

"Dolly made me promise her purse goes to her da. See it does, Captain," I said.

"Of course, Gant, of course."

One of the boys in the tent then nods at him as he stood and moved over to a chest of drawers on which were a couple of bottles and some wooden cups. He splashes us out a good measure each as well as for himself.

"How long, Gant?" he said.

I nearly said it was a matter of weeks, my breath shortening with a thump as I faced what it meant again. Then I saw what he was referring to, how long before I could be back at it, earning the purse.

"About a week, Shale did some good work on me, guaia and rugara cleaned me out," I said, though it wasn't true enough. He nodded, and his eyes flicked from mine to over my shoulder, back out of the tent. They come back in a moment and he smiled.

"Good. Your purse sadly doesn't let you see out this awful heat guarding the fort. There'll be sorties in a few days and . . ."

"Got somethin' else to say, Forthwald?" said Shale, draining his cup. "Only there's a stream o' shit leavin' yer mouth much the same as what Gant passed into the drudha's bucket this afternoon."

Forthwald made to look shocked, but Shale wasn't a man that other men found easy to be near, or be clever with.

"It got a bit quiet a bit quickly outside the tent, Forth," said Shale, "and yer man here's sweatin' as bad as you are."

Forthwald nodded, nursing the cup in both hands. The two men with us put their hands to their hilts.

"Fuck," said Shale, "you boys are thicker than the wood o' that table. You'd be dead if it weren't for whoever our Captain has outside."

"I'm sorry for this, boys. What can I say? There's a bounty on your head so big that our Lord Olgin himself gave the order. An hour or two earlier and you might not have been on that ambush this morning. You're good men. You've been good for this company as well in your time with us, got the respect of the lads. Only sorry I never got to see

21

you and the Twenty in your prime. Come, let's get this shitty business underway."

He led us out of the tent, his two fearful guards behind us. There were a few pockets of men about, looking over at us, muttering, smoking and half naked in the evening. Between us and them was a circle of men positioned around the tent. Agents of the Post. They had the silver-grey leathers, a burgundy leather patch of the Post's sign, the outline of a Coldbay Tern, stitched into the larger shoulderpad on their defensive arms. Each had two fieldbelts, double slung on the shoulders, and they were already masked, bubbling with a half-brew suitable for this work. We both could hear their breathing, faster than ours, their bodies humming like kingfishers over a stream.

One of them stepped forward, short and heavy, old as we were from the look of him, his colour similar, a paler red to it, years of good mixes.

"You can drop your fieldbelts and swords and strip, or we can do it. One ends up with lots of bleeding."

I nods to Shale and we did it. Agents of the Post weren't like your regular Reds, they had some fierce training and access to the best mixes the Post could buy, which was saying a lot. Whoever hired these boys to bring us in was a wealthy man.

"Who's lookin' fer us?" said Shale.

"You'll find out. We're just to look after you, take you north a bit and wait for the lady. Usual procedure, I'm surprised you asked."

"Not that familiar with your 'procedure'," said Shale, "Post could never afford us, not for anythin' ordinary anyway."

I smiled, as did this little bear of a man.

"It's our procedure for moving people around, usually from their hiding place to those that paid us to find them. Men that have paid colour we strip; no belts, no leathers, no tricks. We could give you a sheet if it rained I suppose." He got a laugh for that, this being high summer in the Red Hills.

He picked up our swords, took mine out of its sheath.

"What do you call her?" he asked.

"Like I'm goin' to tell you."

"Patterning looks like Redwall steel, the finest. Might keep this one. What do you think, boys?"

22

"I'll have the other," said the one called Jador.

He picked up my belt then. He wore gloves of course, for we all pastes our belts and swords with a poison we've become immune to, stopping any casual thieves. He flipped open the pouches and pockets on it.

"White oak, rugara, raw betony. Think we'll get us some fair coin for that."

"What happened to yer Creed for yer conduct? Yer worse than wildmen," said Shale.

"The Farlsgrad Creed? Might matter to our masters, but we ain't paid enough."

One of the others picks up our necklaces then what we'd put with our shirts. "Gilgul," he says, addressing this cock what was winding us up, "they got Flowers."

"Well fuck me, Flower of Fates, and two of them! All sealed up." The caps on the tins were waxed and glued, needed snapping to open, the whole thing the size of a little finger. On them was etched the skull and two leaves.

"You seen 'em used?" he said.

I nodded. "Aye, we were defending Hevendor from Wildmen. They get organised from time to time, come in their thousands and had been pillaging at the borders and taking towns for themselves . . ."

"Fuck, I don't want an old nana's tale." This made his crew laugh.

"Well, I saw ten men use 'em. No more Wildmen come to Hevendor ever since, far as I knows."

He shrugged before putting the necklaces with the tins on them in his pocket.

There were eight Agents about us, and with us paying the colour right now, it was too much for us to try something as they approached to tie us. We would have to see what opportunities presented once we'd evened out a bit.

We were marched north that night, stopping only the following morning because I was bleeding badly from my wound.

"You've got to let me dress it," Shale said to them, "or he's going to be dead before you get wherever it is you're going. It's Blackhand poison in there."

"How did he not get his bark in it?" said Gilgul. He come up close to me, bending down to take a look at the cotton that was soaked to my skin. He tore it off and I had to let out a yelp, though I expected he'd do something stupid. A few of his boys laughed. I fell to my knees, the pain was something else.

He pulled the collar of his wamba down and I saw the bark in his neck, the sort that ended up being part of the skin, not the sort that broke up.

"Guaia's what you old timers swear by, but for that hole you'd want birch bark and balsam. You look a bit Lagrad, or Vilmorian, but there isn't a drudha up there worth shit is there, or it would be in your belt and saving your life, seeing as you've got so many of those trees up there. Though who knows why an old man like you's in the front line taking arrows anyway. Greedy I'm guessing." He started pressing the wound then, poking it to get a reaction, which he got I'm sorry to say. He was looking at Shale of course, trying to get him going. Shale was quiet, not looking over.

"Jador, best help keep this man's guts from spilling out, or the lady won't be happy. She's paying for that pleasure for herself."

They ate some rations, give us some durra sticks and water and after I was bound up we were led along again, hands and feet shackled and the sun a fucker for the next week or more as we crossed the stony ravines of the Red Hills. They were long, hard days on our feet and we burned a bit even with our colour. Purse seemed important enough they bound up the wound so's I could bear the miles we did.

Evening come along then one night, and they chose a bit of grassland that grew around the few crumbling walls of what must have been a fort once.

"Tie them to those posts," said Gilgul, "bit more water for our two guests, Jador. Well, we've arrived. How are you boys doing? I hope you got over your disappointment with losing a fat purse, well, your fieldbelts, swords, gold, horses and your fat purse. We just wait here for the lady now."

We didn't say anything, knowing it was the best way to get under the skin of those what are looking to wind you up.

"You know," he went on, "the boys are finding it hard to believe you two were in Kailen's Twenty and did something like Tharos Falls, fussing and shaking and scratching at yourselves as you have been this last week. A nice story though, eh? Suppose if I told enough people I had two cocks they might believe it too. What's the truth when a big purse is at stake?" There was a moment's silence then, but for the crack of an axe hitting a tree nearby as they were getting some wood for the fire.

"Nothing to say for yourselves, boys, your honour, such as it is?"

I had stabbing pains to fill my thoughts more than his rambling, needed my compounds and it's been a while since I didn't have them, forgot how bad my body gets without the plant it needs. He started barking at the others to hurry up the camp, perhaps reading their silence as a sort of challenge about what was next now we weren't taking the bait and giving him banter.

I glanced over at Shale, and he give the barest flicker with his eyes that he was enjoying himself.

The long walk and a bit of bilt and some nuts settled me enough to sleep through the pain the poison was giving me, a few hours perhaps before a sharp whisper woke me.

It was night, and more Agents were in the camp, stood over us.

One of them spoke to Gilgul.

"You brought their horses?" he asked.

"We'll be reporting this to the lady when we get there, and no, we left the horses, we were going to make these fuckers walk," said Gilgul.

"What's going on?" said Shale.

"Seems like the Post has a more pressing interest in you than the lady who hired the Post to bring you in," said Gilgul.

"It's wrong," said Ranad, who was one of Gilgul's crew, "Post don't take a purse then turn it over. You sure those papers is right and proper?"

"The Red hisself wouldn't doubt 'em. You saw the seal, they're from Candar itself." He turned back to the Agent what had come to claim us, stocky-looking man, not Gilgul's size though, but a richer, proper colour on him.

"But I take my orders from Marschal Laun," said Gilgul. "She's with the purse. She should approve this, not me."

"The seal and papers are all the approval you need. You've seen the High Reeve's signature and your own roll confirms it. You're to go to Guildmaster Filston's estate and await his return."

Gilgul looked him up and down. He smelled something was wrong, me and Shale did too, but whatever it was passed for their authority overcome it, the colour and the leathers were as proper as would be near impossible to fake.

"Get these men their clothes, weapons and belts, Gilgul. They'll be coming with us."

"Fuck that. Jador, get their things." He turned to look at me. "Hope to see you again. The lady will not be put off and I'd hate for that sauce to kill you before I did."

"Best give us those Flowers too, eh," said Shale. Gilgul give a look to Achi and he took out the necklaces and threw them at us.

Other than that we kept quiet of course, doing nothing what would stop us from getting those fieldbelts back. If they weren't emptied then we had a chance, though this new Agent wouldn't risk us with belts if he weren't speaking true.

It was a small crew that come to claim us, four in all. They took over the camp, got a pot on the fire that Gilgul's boys had going from before while his lot packed up and left.

One of the crew cut us free and Shale come over as I was sorting through my shirt and wamba. He dressed my wound, put a salve on it and some leaf in it and got it tight, then he helped me into my leathers and a cloak to warm me up.

The Agent helped him to get me over to the fire, where they had some cups of stew for us, oily, probably neck broth. It was plain to see they'd been drilled well, and their belts, leathers and masks were well used. They moved like us, in control of the plant. Each was quiet, looking to the man what had spoken to Gilgul. There was no grey in him, but his eyes had seen a bit too much, a stillness about him what good commanders and leaders have.

"I'm Achi," he said, "and for me and the boys it's an honour to meet you. This is Hau, this is Danik. Danik, fetch their clothes and belts. The big man here is Stimmy." Stimmy looked like he'd been breaking and lifting rocks all his life.

"We're most grateful to you," said Shale, "but we don't know you an' we got no powerful friends to speak of."

"No? Kailen sent us. But he's in trouble, you all are, the Twenty."

Kailen.

It was a shock to hear his name, all these years on, and for this

26

Achi to speak of us all, the Twenty, though we were all these winters on from when we broke up.

"Kailen? We in't seen him in a long time. What trouble is he in?" I asked.

It was a blessing to be free of the bindings, and Stimmy helped me and Shale with the cuts from them now my wound was sorted out.

"He's at the Crag. We don't know much more and I think that's his purpose," said Achi. "He found out a few of the Twenty had been killed recently, black coin. He'd learned you were in the Red Hills, and you can guess he was on terms with Olgin, head of the Starun Hast, or some of his quartermasters. Must've been him that confirmed you were taking a purse here."

"It were Olgin sold us out to these Agents," said Shale. "Forthwald told us there were a big purse on our heads. Don't get why. We in't done any more than our job fer many winters wi' no complaint from our paymasters or betraying our purses."

Achi nodded. "I couldn't disagree, but something is wrong, Kailen is convinced of it, convinced enough for us to seek you out, to do this. He was keen we find you and get you to head to the Crag to see him."

"You in't the Post then," I said. "Those leathers and whatever you showed that Gilgul looked real, but he din't trust you all the same."

"We aren't the Post, but you boys should know a bit about subterfuge and in particular what Kailen is capable of."

"He got a new crew now then? You and these boys?" I asked.

Achi smiled. "He drills us like we're a crew, but he retired, we work on his estate down in Harudan, we run his 'vans now, preserves, wines and the like. He's paid out."

Paid out was a way of saying that you had left the soldiering life, settled your account as it were with the fightbrews, and what they took from you, and you had moved on.

"So yer takin' us to the Crag?" asked Shale.

He shook his head. "He's asked my crew and I go back to Harudan. He's worried whoever is giving the Twenty a black coin might learn where he's living and he wants his wife and estate safe."

Good for him he got out of this shit.

"We headin' for the Crag in the mornin' then," said Shale.

"We'll come with you for a day or so, to be sure this Gilgul's convinced of us, then we're off south, well, my boys are, Kailen's got me going north."

"He called up anyone else from the Twenty?" said Shale.

"He has. You're the only ones that are able to go it seems, of those he found still alive."

"In't right," said Shale, "in't right at all, what we owe him."

"Where in the Crag is he?" I asked. "Been there only a few times over the years, not familiar with it."

"Slums. Don't know if you know the gangers there but he's with the Indra Quarter Crew. Find them and you find him."

It was weeks since we were marched out of camp and I was still angry that we had been forced to leave our horses there. Been with mine for two years and she was one of the best I'd had. The horses that Achi had brought along were good enough for the journey we'd need to make, however. Shale's seemed skittish with him but he soon got him under control. We both knew a bit of the horse singing and had mouthpieces for it. Some cured bacon and cold tea, oils and rubs and we rode with them northwest towards Hevendor.

A few days later we saw off Achi and his boys. Not much to tell of the journey to the Crag. We pushed northwest out of the Red Hill Confederacy and then west more directly into Hevendor. We saw nobody save some nomads we got some bread and wine from.

I did some thinking. We didn't speak much at all that week. He wasn't sleeping though. It'd been a long time since we give much thought to the old crew. I was thinking about my sister Emelt too, though. I sent her coin for years for the hast. She'd pass it on to the council and all, see that they could keep trading for iron and salt and what plant they needed if they didn't get the crops or livestock to trade. She had a boy too, Goran.

She been bidding me come back for years, no more the shame to my da now he was gone and Amila that I had loved now with that boy who must be on the council after all this time. I heard from Emelt the new council was practical, it needed swords. Trouble is, all around Upper Lagrad where I was born and raised there were chiefs and hast-lords needed steel and brutal doings, not least for the borders to the Wilds unmapped. My little sister got a viper's tongue for getting the council to listen to the herders and keep some peace in our lands. I missed her. There was often a stab of longing to get back to those fierce hills and cold forests. Now my guts set me for it.

But I did wonder about Kailen too. Kailen's Twenty must have split up near fifteen years ago. We were guarding the royals of Citadel Argir, the king and his two children. He was on his way out, the king, paid us off, and by then of course we were fighting each other, sodden with the brews, snuffs and drink. Kailen saw it – we were embarrassing, not tight with each other like we were before – so he called it.

There were ructions of course. Kailen got us all rich, got the victories, read the wars and leaders and picked us right for gold and glory. The crew went their separate ways, alone or a few together. Me and Shale banded up because we were tight from early when Kailen picked us up. Some stayed a while with Kailen but the stories from the Post and caravans dried up as our legend faded.

Seems like he went back to Harudan as I'd thought; he wouldn't have kept looking for a purse with shittier men when he had his gold and family connections at home with the aristos. He had nothing to prove; hand to hand he was unbeaten, though we were all unsure he would've beaten Shale. First time they fight, Shale landed awkward and Kailen waited for his foot to heal before they went at it again, which they did with nobody watching. He wasn't telling how it come out though, and Shale was the only other man I ever saw unbeaten with a sword, duel or otherwise.

Shale had been wondering about whatever was the cause of all this, our being taken by the Post and Kailen being in trouble, and spoke of it one night a few days out of the Hills as he prepped a rabbit.

"Don't know who could still be havin' a problem with the Twenty all these years on. How many of us are still warrin', Gant, takin' purses? You see the lifers fallin' down, only the gold we made could get us the prep an' strains from the best recipe books. Harudanian an' Juan drudharchs been preppin' all our mixes fer years. Most o' the brews out there just breaks soldiers up, sends 'em mad. Ibsey were mixin' up some fierce stuff fer us to rise on. Stixie Four, Digs, Sword Sho, Ibsey an' all, none could run the forms for the shakes an' drink. Fuck it, Gant, any one o' those kids we hit back on that ambush could have dropped more'n a few of us at the end, never mind now."

Said well. I couldn't even keep Kailen's weapon forms right these days; my knees were going, my back can only straighten out with a compound of black sugar oil or salmon oil and copper salts. I look in a bowl of water and I see only bits of hair between all the scars and burns and my skin's greening over my usual mash of colour, because of the compound. I look like I'm covered in mould. Pair of us got our ritual for the oils for each other. He's less fucked than me, but he needs the iridus oils dropping in his eyes and his shoulder needs treating when it flares up.

He did his best with the wound each day, cleaning and dressing it up. We got some maggots for it but all in all I could feel it creeping into me, sore like I been punched through.

We got to Hevendor and down through it peaceful. The Crag was a big riverport for the East-West passage, part of the network what made up the Hiscan Road. Old Kingdoms shinies, plant, wines and stuff went east; slaves, skins, metals and other plant come back. Not much went south with the river as it cut through the Ten Clan lands. They've been good purses on and off these last few years, mind.

We followed a caravan in, wagons of slaves looking at us with the light out of their eyes, only enough sense left in them to eat. They were on the Droop. Most had the shakes and were whining for it. None needs shackling when they're on the Droop.

It was only as we headed for the Slums to find some gangers that we saw the streets and alleys were full of militia, all over the roofs and all, with a thick pall of smoke over everything. A lot of buildings there had fallen down and burned, rioting had got widespread it seemed and I never saw so many soldiers except when a town or city was besieged. There was wreckage everywhere, stalls turned, bodies piled up or strewn about; the deadcarts and their hooded crews were overworked. A lot of Post were about as well, so we found an inn to put the horses with so we could go in on foot, quick and quiet. Whoever was after Kailen had called for a scorching, and if a scorching had happened we could see we'd missed it. Weren't good odds for him if he had militia and Reds against him and a few gangers, but he'd made it through worse, and I was looking forward to seeing him.

* * *

30

Destination: Candar Prime, Q2 670 OE
Eastern Sar Main routed
CONFIDENTIAL FOR THE RED ONLY
Report of: Fieldsman 84
Debriefing of: Marschal Laun. Guildmaster Alon Filston of
  Filston-Blackmore Guild.

Marschal Laun, assigned to Galathia, has reported a further mercenary killed, in the Virates, a place called Povey's Valley. It is
another of the long disbanded mercenary crew Kailen's Twenty.
His name was Sho. As previously reported, Digs and Connas'q
of that same crew have been pursued and killed through the
purse of Galathia's husband, Alon Filston.

Marschal Laun's report refers to an unknown individual present
at Sho's execution, that the Marschal suspects was there also to
kill Sho. Marschal Laun escaped with Galathia and the rest of
her crew, at the loss of an Agent Kolm and four Reds, as per her
duty to protect Galathia. This would-be assassin has not surfaced
since.

I reprimanded Marschal Laun and Alon Filston for indulging
Galathia, as per your instruction. Both were reminded of their
instruction to ensure Galathia's safety while we lay the ground-
work for her reinstatement to the throne of Argir. Marschal Laun
was reminded again that Galathia's pursuit of mercenaries once
of the crew Kailen's Twenty was explicitly forbidden.

She is clearly frustrated by our concern that Galathia is not
being kept safely enough. She requests recognition that judgement
of risk remains hers and she requests recognition that the pursuit
of targets of no political value accords with our overall goal,
while also asking that we recognise these targets are so important
to Galathia she believes it would be impossible to persuade her,
short of physical restraint, from pursuing them. She also requests
recognition through the accompanying field reports that her
targets were isolated and incapacitated before Galathia was exposed
to them. I made clear it was our view that the state of the Ten
Clan and Red Hills in high summer, particularly a summer our
Post Houses report is the worst they've witnessed, was a great

deal more risk than she should have been exposed to irrespective of the threat her targets posed as experienced mercenaries engaging in their own field operations.

Alon Filston was instructed to coordinate with his allied guilds, the Darrun-Luke Family of the Citadel Eural and our Reeves regarding signatures for a new ruling council and re-investiture of his wife Galathia and her royal line in Argir.

However, Galathia's pursuit of the Twenty continues. Gant and Shale of the Twenty have been captured by Agent Gilgul's crew, who were recruited by Filston via Marschal Laun. The arrest was made without incident in the northern Red Hills Confederacy (their purse was to counter a border incursion by the Blackhands). Kailen himself has also been identified at the Crag, Hevendor. Galathia's intention is to apprehend and kill them all, utilising Laun and a further complement of Reds, the additional fees covered also by Filston.

As instructed, I forbade the pursuit and apprehension of Kailen as a highly dangerous target. I have instructed Filston to broach the subject of her return to the throne and I have suggested how this may be done. I have instructed the Private Cleark to begin drafting a speech for such an occasion, as well as instructed him to engage Juan and Mount Hope metal workers to fashion gifts and prepare a banquet for the nobles she will be returning to.

Expecting, regarding Kailen, that my order may not be enforced, I have informed the High Reeve of Hevendor and Crag officials to give help where required. In all respects except for controlling Galathia's wilfulness, Marschal Laun has won her confidence and friendship and will be a close ally in steering her opinion in our favour.

Instructions to the High Reeve regarding Kailen, with a briefing of the Indra Quarter, have been provided.

Chapter 3

Galathia

I have constructed an account of the Princess Galathia's part in the downfall of Kailen's Twenty, using letters she had written to her brother Petir that my patron was in a position to secure transcripts of, and her subsequent account of these events to me while she was in captivity. Below are letters to her brother outlining her pursuit of Kailen's Twenty, and a statement she gave me of her part in the assault on the Indra Quarter.

Goran

Written 669 OE, regarding events 668–9 OE

Dear brother,

I wonder how you felt when you first drank a fightbrew? The training brews don't really prepare you for it, do they?

The first time I drank a full measure, I shivered in the desert winds of the Ten Clan steppe. It was to kill Digs, the beginning of my ambition to get us revenge on Kailen's Twenty. My husband, Alon, purchased the services of a Marschal of the Post, Laun, and her crew, to assist me. Laun has proved the Post's efficiency in gathering news of these old mercenaries. Digs was the first we'd tracked down.

We had led camels for two weeks into a drought in Ten Clan lands such as none of us had seen. The dead were littered across the main tracks. Men tried to sell their children to us for rice or coin, their women mute and dazed or throwing stones at us to forbid the trade with what little strength they had. We had no use for children. The nearer to the Red Hill borders the worse it got, the same lack of rains was causing their own starving to move into Ten Clan territory. Here were the nomads, long used to enduring the summers at the heart of the Ten Clan, now setting traps for refugees, their families waiting like statues as they traded water for some bilt. I saw many campfires where animals picked over the remains of whole families. The dead were burned in pyres where some remnant of community remained.

Digs and his crew were taking a caravan of grains and cured fish from the coast to the soldiers at their borders. It wasn't just the Red Hills refugees flooding in that needed to be repelled. The Wilds bordered on both territories, and the borders needed defending from their incursions as well.

I had learned that Digs had been on the caravans for a number of summers. It was unlikely therefore that he would have the answer to my inheritance, but like the others, he betrayed me, he betrayed you.

The nomads had traded us some knowledge of the trails through the Ten Clan heartlands. Digs's caravan had stopped on a ridge overlooking a stony plain ahead north.

I was given a set of Agent leathers and a belt, for me to understand better the drills and how to use the armour and its plant while in combat.

Laun and Midgie had dressed me, and then we dressed Laun. Her closecut promised blonde, the common colouring of Farlsgrad women. In another life she would have been a prize for any prince or lord, had she been born of any social status. I was a sufficient prize for Alon with my red hair and white skin. The colour the brews have given me since seeking my revenge had attracted open comment at the gatherings and feasts Alon's guild held or attended. I was not the plump gossiping jewel his peers required to reflect their status. I had drilled for years since my days at the Juan High Commune. He was considered to be too indulgent with me. He knew better, knew what I had been through. It had taken the death of one concubine to discourage his taking of others.

Laun had watched me drink my measure of the fightbrew. It was the texture of custard, an awful flavour of boiled weeds and soil, a dry chalk-like feeling that made it hard to swallow for hours afterwards, a coating to resist swelling if vapours or powders were inhaled. She would not give me the recipe of course, so I cannot pass it on.

There are moments then where the stomach curdles, a revulsion throughout one's guts, but it soon warms, then gets hot, hot even to touch the skin as it soaks into the body. Veins thicken, muscle thickens and then what some soldiers have called the song of the world, as one's head fills with the brew. This cold night soon brightened, all those points of light in the sky seemed themselves filled, a black fabric that held back some great light beyond, pregnant and about to burst. I cannot convey the speed of thought, the awareness, the sense all at once of every hair on your arms touched by the breeze, the breeze itself almost visible, its shifts and flow on the edge of prediction. We could feel something move far beneath our feet, water perhaps, and I could smell now the campfires of the caravan, the meat they were burning, the stink of their camels. Laun and Syle took my hand, I was dizzy with the brew, had been every time I had risen, so we chanted, mumbling as novice soldiers do the 'cants to focus oneself, to "stone the brew" as they would say, meaning to become still, without thought.

I followed them as we ran hunched over towards Digs's camp, a hollow and some thorn bushes providing cover within arrowshot of their camp. There were seven of us. Three of the caravan were on watch at the head of the ridge, two near us at the back. Laun signed for us to move forward, Syle and Omara making two perfect shots with their bows, the two guards falling silently.

Laun had guessed that the sound of our bows would alert the other guards, on mixes that heightened the senses. We needed to be at the camp before their own brews could begin to diminish our advantage. As we ran, Syle, Midgie and the others shot spore-bags at the camp. The camels started snorting and stamping at their ties and the camp was alerted. The bags were driven open by the points of the arrows and the dust spread. Men threw open their tents and brought their bows up to shoot. It was remarkable

35

how slowly they moved. They launched arrows, some getting masks on before shooting, but it would be too late for them. On the fightbrew I could see the arrows bend and leap from the bows, knew instantly if I needed to drop or keep running according to my judgement of their flight. We reached their camp and, as instructed, I held myself back a few paces. I would have expected to feel frightened, perhaps inadequate as we engaged, due to my only having held a sword in training, but the brew made me fearless, potent, perhaps for the first time in my life; the desire to fight, to kill, was thrilling. Two men jumped from a tent to ambush Syle, who was engaged with one of the guards alerted by our initial assault. Their brew hadn't given them their full vigour, they were breathing too hard, willing the rise, but, so much slower in movement and thought, I parried a swipe and got the first few inches of my sword into the chest of the first of them out of the tent. He staggered back in shock and in moments was wheezing, then choking. Our poison was a Farlsgrad recipe, known throughout the Post to have efficacy against the Ten Clan.

Syle spun in front of me and disarmed the other one before running him through, while I edged the guard who was on Syle backward, with a lunge intending to buy her that moment to focus on him.

Others came running, some having been sleeping on the wagons when we struck. None fitted the description of Digs, who was considered unnaturally tall. They had to have been waiting in a tent for the rise before coming out and taking us on. I ran quickly for the fire at the heart of the camp, an arrow flying inches behind my head as I moved, the whip of air pimpling the skin of my neck. I grabbed a branch, its one end charred red, a lick of flame on it. I ran from tent to tent and set them alight, determined to flush Digs and his crew out before they'd fully risen.

Laun's crew were more than a match for the mercs and clan driving the caravan. When Digs emerged with four of his men it was obvious they weren't prepared. One of Laun's crew, Prennen, saw them and took one down with his bow before Digs closed on him. I ran up from behind and ran through another of his men; the third turned and I managed to cut him. Then I lost the initiative for a moment as the fourth joined him and forced me back. It was

36

a defining moment in my life, once more at threat after so many years. I was thinking too much of what my training required of me, yet all the training had been about stoning the brew, unthinking. It was the difference between describing a flavour and tasting it. The song that soldiers spoke of was being sung; to think was to be deaf to it. I forced myself to just watch them and feel their movement, my mind ready to predict it. As one of them thrust I moved, a parry and counter, my blade slicing across his gut, a slight tug on my arm as it opened him, then a reverse cut into his leg. I saw the other's blade sweep down and put my own up to block it, a crack that went through me, my knees wobbling with it as I twisted and fell off balance deflecting its force. The moments froze as I tried to bring my now numb arm up for what I thought would be the blow to kill me, when he stiffened, Syle's sword erupting from his chest and vanishing back as swiftly as a snake's tongue. I would have been dead if they had risen fully on their own brew.

I turned to see Digs on his knees, shivering as he continued his own rise. His ankles and wrists were being bound together by Laun. He looked like a bull made man and I do not doubt that had he managed to rise fully before we ambushed them, our success would not have been so easily achieved. I had been told stories of his strength, his leadership of miners and sappers and knowledge of fortifications and their weaknesses. Kailen's Twenty had won through many of their purses because of his siegecraft. Now he was kneeling before me, risen. What force in a man? How fearsome must it have been to face the Twenty in their prime, if they were the equal or more of him? And how entitled they must have thought themselves, to betray my father's purse, to betray my brother and I, because of their power and their fightbrew.

"Agents of the Post?" he said. "Did we get lost between our last silk cushions and our next?"

"Fuck you," said Midgie.

"Enough!" said Laun. She glanced at me, a prompt.

"We came for you, Digs," I said.

He looked up at me. He would not recognise me masked, my hair bound.

"You should have just knocked. I got cock enough for all of you."

37

"I hoped that you could tell me where I might find any of the others you fought with in Kailen's Twenty."

"Kailen's Twenty? That crew is long disbanded, if not dead for the most part. I can see why you'd be looking for more from your purse than you're getting from this lot. If they were any good they'd be making real coin at war."

I stepped closer to him, a great urge on me to hurt him; I trembled with it. But I realised also it would be futile to hit him, for all my balled fist wanted to break his nose. I stretched my fingers, trying to release the rage the brew brings. His own brew would inure him to most pain.

"Bitch, it makes no difference to me if I knew where they were or not, does it? I don't know where any of them are except Connas'q. Most likely he's north and waiting for the Clans, being a Red Hills boy, and worse an Afagi. You had best start your torture, to satisfy yourselves I'm speaking the truth."

"I'm happy to brew us some tea to help with the fall," said Midgie, "while you start work. Or I can start on him if you wanted."

I believed Digs. Still I tortured him. I wanted to see this big arrogant pig cry and scream, suffering something of that which during his life he put countless others through for the sake of silver and gold. I took the skin of one of his arms mostly off, applied salt and here was a noise soldiers on a brew desired to hear. He had no more about the Twenty. Fingernails, then fingers, were slowly removed and he grunted and sweated through it. I did not have the art, of course, to find the extremes of his will. He had no answers for me, no lead beyond Connas'q. The Afagi, Connas'q's own clan, would have nothing to do with his own Morafan clan for historic reasons I struggled to follow, even taking into account his bellowing and shrieking as I undid him. The Ten Clan and the Red Hills had long been in and out of war. I was plucking at the muscle of his arm to get the reaction I wanted and I had considered starting on his scrote when I began to fall, to pay the colour. Midgie's tea helped, but my body was shutting down.

Digs's head was bowed, breathing hard as his own fall began, the pain of his torture increasing. I would have liked to keep it going longer, but I needed to rest, something he knew from his increased goading. He was trying to prove himself unbowed and also was attempting to expedite his death. I said nothing, just took up a sword nearby and swung it, slicing off his head cleanly. In this one respect he had beaten me and I cried immediately, uncontrollably. Laun came over and held me. I could barely stand. From my abandonment at Snakewood, to this point, the first of the Twenty killed, it all fell from me. Laun laid with me then till my body wearied enough of the fall that I passed out, my arms around my father's neck, squeezing him as he lifted me off my feet and all the while I'm bidding him follow us out of the palace.

The caravan's supplies paid handsome passage, with the seal of the Morafan clan, a thistle, right to the border of the Red Hills Confederacy. The fall and my subsequent sleep left me with a growing confidence as we pushed on to the Red Hills. With Alon's money and Laun's crew, I was now convinced I would hunt down these betrayers. That conviction was tested as we pushed into the mountains and valleys. Hunting Confederates in their own land required plant; healing plant, alka, more than poisons. Among these dry and stony hills there was little need for elaborate poison, and no clans here would be foolish enough to engage an enemy openly when they had knowledge of the passes and caves one could pass by the face of and miss.

One of our crew, Ry'le, was raised among these clans that roamed the heights with their small herds, and he knew that here, where the wealth from the coastal clans that dominated the Confederacy did not spread, there was little loyalty, a short-sightedness common enough in the Old Kingdoms. Connas'q's Afagi Clan were a major force in the Confederacy, their lands around the coast, far from the suffering here. Ry'le knew enough of the dialect, the customs of proper greeting and gifts, to assume leadership, for Laun's leadership here would be questioned, and without respect we would be hunted for the plant and weapons we carried. We had news from the last Post House on our route into the Ten Clan that Connas'q was leading scouts that patrolled the borders around Morsten's Peak.

These were lands long disputed, borders that soldiers interrupted from time to time to try and reset them in their favour, when those

39

who lived here managed such borders perfectly well. It was true, I suppose, that the clans that lived here on either side were closer to each other than they were to those that governed them. Debts of honour, the trading of plant, goats and sheep, the caches of supplies and knowledge of the trails were so necessary to survival that none here had the luxury of politics.

We had taken a pass winding up to highlands where snow still spilled from under outcrops and overhangs from the winter just gone. Eagles rode the sharp, bitter winds looking for movement in the shale of rocks strewn about a large and empty plain. Perhaps a lake was here once, long dried up, for I saw the bones of a fish as we crossed it.

"All armies will pass over Morsten's Peak, following this trail, to save leagues winding their way through to Abner's Plain beyond," said Ry'le. "If Connas'q passes through we should know."

Such mountains as I remembered from my homeland, the Citadel Argir, were covered in pines, impassable with snow until late spring.

We had reached the edge of the dried-out lake when Syle, ahead of us, stiffened. Almost as soon as she had seen movement ahead on the slopes we saw fifteen men and women approach us from either side, bows drawn. Their robes and headwraps were bleached the same grey as the stones. Some were thick with dust, now scattering in puffs from the breeze. They must have been in the shale, watching the basin.

"Afa'n il am Post," called Ry'le. He continued in this unfamiliar tongue, and I recognised the names of some of our plant, and "drusst", which I've heard some use for "drudha" when at Alon's feasts. Laun's drudha, a quiet and shy man called Tofi, took his recipe book from a pocket in his cloak and waved it. They lowered their bows, and called to each other as they closed on us. A few of them ran over the slope ahead, presumably to their camp.

I watched as Ry'le and their leader, silver hair braided into three tails woven with hoops — all others here had one or two — placed their hands on each other's shoulders.

The leader spoke and Ry'le repeated. Once or twice this was reversed, and by the time they had split from this, all negotiation on our gifts was done.

40

"The Afagi passed through two days ago. Eight scouts, Connas'q among them," said Ry'le as these herders led us to their camp.

"How will we find Connas'q?" I asked Laun as we took the bags off the donkeys and presented the plant and bacca supplies that passed for gold in these heights.

"You recall me telling you that Kailen assembled his crew to be able to join a force of soldiers and, in almost any situation, be able to drill, teach and lead them to victory. His men were the best at whatever they did. Our friend Digs back there was draughtsman and engineer for many stone forts, including the Razhani's Fort Zandar. Kheld was Lord Sailsman of a Handar flot, twenty-five ships. Connas'q assassinated three chiefs of the Ten Clan in their own pavilions. He specialised in being unseen, with a drudha's knowledge of life-sustaining plant encompassing lands from Mount Hope through the Virates. In his homeland we stand almost no chance of finding him if he chooses not to be found."

Laun pressed some bacca into her pipe, a stubby old clay that her grandfather passed to her father, eight etched symbols, one for each son or daughter in the line going back a hundred summers or more, representing a quality that this heir should demonstrate with each of the others in order to earn it. It was unlikely, with the fightbrews, that she could pass it on to children of her own. Women had little chance of giving birth after a few years as soldiers. We pay more deeply than men for most things in life. The colour is no different.

I shared the pipe with her, bacca and bejuco twisted with some kannab. At the camp we sat under a blanket at the mouth of one of the large tents. The herdsmens' leader had bid all of them to sleep us as guests.

"You must have thought of something, Laun. It's what I pay you for."

She smiled. "The purse is rich, but only equal to what you ask of us, never more so than here. Of course I've thought of something. Now take another draw, it'll help us sleep in this forsaken place. The days are hot and the nights will freeze you to death at these heights, you'll need to tuck into me."

*　　*　　*

41

Four days later, a few of the herders remained, a subterfuge to keep Connas'q from being suspicious.

Connas'q's crew threaded its way down through a channel in the cliffs and into the camp, calling the herders they saw.

Midgie, Ry'le and Fazen, another of Laun's crew, were hidden behind boulders or concealed in the scree of the slopes around the camp, masked and robed in the herders' colours. The rest of us were in four of the tents, Laun and I in one, one each in the other three.

Midgie said later that Connas'q had called for his men to run before we had been seen, guessing the camp's lack of children was what had alerted him to trouble. Ankle breakers had been dug around the tents and concealed. Two of his men fell foul of them, one outside our tent, and he began shouting to cause confusion for us as much as him being in pain.

I took some mouthfuls of Laun's "siege" brew, a diluted fightbrew that could be used over a much longer period of time. We heard arrows, so Midgie's lot must have risen from their concealed positions and started shooting bags at the scouts, the herders sadly caught trying to run for their own lives. There was a clang of blades in the next tent, then the grunt of someone dying. Two of the scouts opened our tent, blood on their swords. Laun had her bow raised and the first took an arrow in the chest. The other threw his limebag to the ground and the mat it landed on caught, smoke filling the tent. He left the tent, dropping the flap to keep in the smoke. I went to jump for the opening but Laun caught my arm and stopped me, finger to her lips. She pointed at the side of the tent, then the flap. There were two of them. Smoke stung my eyes as it reached me. She took her bow and put two arrows where she sensed the other scout would be, waiting for us to try to escape the tent from the other side. The arrow hit him with a soft thump, then she leaped to cut through the wall of the tent. The other scout heard us, and was on her a moment after she had cleared the rip. She backed away from him to better let me through the rip. I looked across the camp and saw what must have been Connas'q exchanging shots with Syle as Midgie and Ry'le were themselves shooting at one of the scouts, who had retreated the way they came. He shot well, a man easily over forty summers old, as calm as Connas'q, who had then spotted us and was signing to another of his crew.

I wasn't proficient with the bow, having spent the years I'd drilled with soldiers almost all with swords and knives, but I tried all the same to launch the sporebags I had at Connas'q, hoping the others could press the advantage.

The scout was a poor match for Laun. He lasted a few exchanges but was impatient, a problem some men had fighting women; unable, in some part of their mind, to believe they would not fold under their blows. Laun had been taught the supremacy of balance over strength.

The other scout had fled back from the direction they came. The rest then were dead or had themselves escaped. We closed in a circle on Connas'q as he dropped his bow and took up his sword.

He was a slight man, his colouring faded or disguised, but other than his white hair there was little that gave him distinction to the eye, a considerable advantage in his former role. He lowered the tip of his sword to the dirt and drew a circle around him. I had seen it before once, a man posturing to his enemy that he could stay within the circle and kill him without being forced from it. It was preferable to spitting or cursing I suppose.

As with Digs there was a temptation to remove my mask, to explain to him why he was about to die and what for. But he was about to die. Those moments would only be for me, and for me his death would be enough.

"Tell me about Kailen's Twenty? Where would I find Kailen?" I asked.

He gave it some thought. "You searched long and hard if you come to this peak in this awful summer, and you have come through the Ten Clan, judging by the packs on those nags. What could I have done to the Post to bring its Agents out here? And why would the Post be killing off my old crew?"

Laun and I looked at each other. He couldn't have known we'd killed Digs.

"Are more of you dead already?" I asked.

He took a small flask from his belt and with his thumb popped the stopper.

43

"I'll have a last drink before I die. I could think of worse places, when I think back on my life." He looked about us. The sky was a clear blue and a soft breeze filled the silence. He took a few mouthfuls before dropping the flask.

"Yes, young lady, is the answer to your question. You're dressed in Post's leathers but you're as much of a soldier as I am a woman. You must be the purse. I don't know you and can't imagine what I've done that you come out here to kill my crew and me but, hoping we can be reasonable, I will tell you that I received a note just prior to this patrol, from one of our runners. It had been written by someone that works for Kailen, telling me to take heed that somebody was out to kill us, that we should meet."

I did not know what to think. How could Kailen know about all this? I've heard much of Kailen over the years, stories that I'm sure grew with the telling; a man who knew what you were going to do before you did, who never lost a duel or battle.

"What I don't understand," continued Connas'q, "given we're standing here, is what any of us have done in over fifteen winters since Kailen chose to disband us that's getting us killed. We had an easy time with that sad old king, and could have won purses almost as rich after his own people put his head on a spike at the crossing with Eural." I flinched. I wanted to fill him with this quiver of arrows. "Instead, Kailen sent us on our way without a second thought for what we would do. Fuck him. Everything we went through and he called it over, like that." He clicked his fingers. "A letter like that just stirs it all up again. As though he gives a shit now all these winters later. I shouldn't be spun that it arrived so shortly before you. We made a few enemies I suppose, but not the Post. We weren't stupid. Which means you been hired yourself, lady, or I killed your family or something. I don't remember how many I've killed. I was a mercenary."

The breeze whipped the dust about from the ground around us. They were waiting for me to kill him.

"Well, I suppose it would be pointless telling me who hired you, then killing me. But that's hardly satisfying for any of us. Why don't you or one of your Reds step forward and try to get me out of this circle, and if you can't, you tell me who hired you? One of you must want a go against one of the Twenty?"

"Never fucking heard of this Twenty!" yelled Syle. "You're closer to sixty than you are twenty now though eh, you prick!"

"Leave it, Syle," said Laun. She stepped forward. I took a step as well but she raised her hand to stop me.

Good leaders challenge themselves to be worthy to continue to lead. Her crew were fiercely loyal, but I believe she felt it was important to reassert this authority, particularly when there was a challenge of single combat presented. Not to have stepped up would have damaged her, and this was Connas'q's intention, to divide the crew before him, and give himself a glimmer of a chance.

Laun approached and their first exchanges proved how formidable he still was. Twice he forced her off balance. She escaped with cuts to her leather only. She nodded to herself. The next couple of exchanges she didn't fully commit to. It was an examination of what he knew, what she needed to know.

It soon became apparent to those of us watching that she had decided to wear him down. She controlled the exchanges with caution; where she might have pressed a risky advantage she withdrew, joining swords again the moment he recovered.

Connas'q taunted her, mocked her for not taking advantage, until he realised what she was doing. She remained silent, seeing the feints, avoiding openings that looked too obvious. Connas'q was soon breathing hard, lacking her endurance. Time went on, her crew and I watching in silence but for the gasps and grunts and the clap of swords. I, like anyone else, could not be other than transfixed by a fight to the death, made the more compelling because for all his evident training, he was bound by his pride to remain in the circle, his disadvantage exploited with cruel precision. It was her youth and better condition that would beat him. She had chosen not a heavy blow or a winning thrust but the attrition of his stamina, goading him to end it, where the slightest mistake, as he tired, was punished with a cut, kick or slap. She had chosen to fight cleanly, no poison on her sword, for her cuts did no more than draw blood.

Soon enough his blood covered his hands, soaked his leathers already darkened with his sweat. He could not speak for breathing. She exploited a weak guard and hit his sword so hard and suddenly that it dropped out of his slick hand, landing outside the circle.

"Pick it up, Connas'q."

He stared at it dumbly, exhausted, before putting his hands to his knees to catch his breath.

"Step outside the circle and pick it up." Laun was breathing hard herself now, but she shone with sweat and triumph, at being able to answer this question she asked of herself.

He spat, but it too was weak, most of it falling back on his chin, hanging over his throat.

She looked at me and nodded. I raised my bow and put an arrow in his hip. I stepped forward and notched another arrow. He fell to his knees. These men were old, yet their past glories left them undiminished in their own minds. I put the arrow through his leg. He panted, unable to raise enough air in his chest to scream. I notched another arrow, gave myself a few more moments of his suffering. He stared at me then, the same way I remembered his stare in my father's palace. He was lying in the banqueting hall at dawn with the others, his hand rubbing his whore's breast as he watched me passing through, a thoughtful, absent look, as though this moment was beneath him.

The final arrow went through his head. I shouldered my bow, walked over to Laun and embraced her, kissing the sweat from her cheeks.

A subsequent letter to her brother, describing her continuing search for the Twenty.
Written 669 OE

Dear brother,

I cannot tell you how thrilled I was to receive your messenger, and to hear more of how your daughter is growing. I cannot wait to meet her, I'm sure as well she is not half the terror I was to our servants and our father.

Things are going very well for us. Marschal Laun has become most precious to me, a resourceful and capable commander. With her crew and the resources of the Post we have managed to find more of Kailen's Twenty. Three are dead, with two more captured, Shale and Gant, and Kailen himself discovered in Hevendor. We have arrived here at a place called the Crag, intending to trap him. He is holed up in some slum. It makes little sense to me why he would be in a slum but we know it's him.

I had written previously of our killing Connas'q and Digs. The latest of the Twenty to die was Sho. I recall at least, as you may also do, his scimitars, how he used to slice the thinnest parchment with them as though he were wielding a razor. I killed him myself but there was one aspect of our execution of Sho that I found both unexpected and troubling, as you'll see. I would have your thoughts on it.

We had tracked Sho to the Virates, a place called Iltrick, the worst part of which was a warren of ratty subterranean runs they called the Burial Chambers deep in Povey's Valley, cut down into the rock, dug to escape the sun of that desert-like Virate. Laun, Syle and poor Kolm, who didn't make it out of there, had received their direction from the Post's local Reeve, a man who was damp in every sense of the word. "Sword" Sho, as you might remember he liked to be called, was spending his purse in a khaat cooker's joint. Khaat was a big import into Iltrick, according to my husband, and it helped to further impoverish a lot of already useless men, chewing and mumbling their grievances and hopes, getting nowhere.

Despite his bulk and his uneasy shuffle from the door to the back of the alley where we waited, Sho still wore those two preposterous scimitars, stuck out from his belt at his hips like large silver feathers. We were in three nearby doorways, on the verge of entering the joint to get him out on a pretext. His appearance was a magist's blessing. He shook his head as he planted his hand on the wall for balance and fumbled about for his cock. His head slowly lolled forward and he almost fell asleep as he pissed against the wall.

Kolm drew a knife and stepped forward. I shook my head. A killing this easy I would do myself. As I drew my own knife and stepped out I instinctively glanced down the alley, only twenty yards till it forked away out of sight. At the fork stood a masked figure, cotton vest, loose leggings and a fieldbelt. He had paid the colour, the whites of his eyes standing out from a face mottled with colours too hard to make out in the half-light. I heard the stream of piss weaken and Sho mumble. I knew immediately that somehow this man was also here for him. I stepped forward, held my breath and stabbed Sho in the back of the neck, clean into his windpipe as Laun had showed me. Sho trembled briefly, but was gone in a moment, dropping to the ground.

"Move!" said Kolm, drawing his sword. The figure was running towards us. Laun threw a sporebag at him, I threw another at the ground between us and as I did Kolm grabbed my shoulder and pulled me back. "Get her out of here!"

I turned and ran, Laun ahead of me, following the route we'd agreed should something go wrong. They were Agents for a reason. The chambers were a maze of passages surrounded high on all sides by the buildings made from the stone the passages were cut through. We wove or pushed through the people who were out; families eating, cooking and shouting in and out of their doorways, beggars playing flutes, gangs of boys looking for opportunities and weakness. We ran up steps at the side of one of the houses, carved out to give access to the upper floors, and jumped from there to a nearby roof. Laun signed for me to flatten myself to the roof while she crouched and looked over.

"Stay here," she whispered, "I'm going to alert the Reds back at the square and come back for Kolm. Don't move until daylight, unless I return first." She slid off the roof and was gone.

I looked over from the roof I was on to the window of a room overlooking me, a candle somewhere inside offering a dull, wavering light and from it the sound of a woman singing to a child a rhyme of some sort. I did not understand the language, though parts of it were just notes her voice made. It cut through the echoing chatter of the people moving through the alleys below, cut through my trembling as I came to terms with the kill, and whatever story was being sung had moments of triumph and despair in it. I've longed ever since to know what she sang, for my own snatches of the tune were unfamiliar to anyone I've since met.

Then I heard shouting, a few alleys over, someone screaming and a commotion going up. The militia announced themselves, and there was a swell of noise as people in the buildings around us heard the shouting and gathered up to go and look after their own. This was a place of the desperately poor, and I knew well the law held scant respect for them.

A while later, the excitement of whatever had gone on gave way to the increasingly drunk or cooked soaks. Laun then leaped the gap to my roof. She startled me, and shushed me as I fumbled for my dagger. She was out of breath, wheezing, and she fell to her knees. She gestured weakly to her face and belt. Then she looked up, and I saw her cheeks and forehead were lumpy with white blisters, her eyes swollen.

"Fulva, pressed arnica." I knew what was needed; both to be mixed in water, making a jelly, which I rubbed into her face and neck. She was in some pain, her skin never fully recovering, despite the quality of plant we carried. We sat on that roof in silence for the better part of an hour while the mix soothed and drained out the blisters.

"Kolm's dead, four of the other Reds too. Even risen on plant we were nothing to him. If it weren't for one of his bags hitting a little girl that happened to run out of her door between us, we'd all be dead. A few of those nearby saw it happen and went for him. Five of us turned to fifteen in moments when she fell down screaming. Poor child, her own brother it must have been that ran her through to stop her agony. But he killed them all as easy as breathing, and the bag he put down sent most people back into their houses. Then some others started throwing stones and whatever else they could find at him, from windows above, and the militia heard it and joined. I tried to put a few darts into him but he dodged them, as quick to us on our brew as we are to those not on any brew at all. I gave chase, for I knew then that Kolm must have been killed, but there were too many, and I think, well, I think I would not have stood much of a chance against him, sword to sword."

"Why was he here? Why after Sho?" I asked her. I put more of the powdered arnica into an alka cream and worked it into her wounds as she kneeled.

She shook her head. "I don't know."

Below is an account Galathia gave me of the assault on The Riddle, the tavern where she believed Kailen himself was hiding out, at a place called the Crag.

Goran

I was with Laun in the slums at the Crag. Though I was paying her to do my bidding, she, with the command of seven Agents, had no qualms about disagreeing with me.

"Syle and Faré have not reported in. I'm concerned that our mystery assassin is here now, intent on killing Kailen. We barely escaped in Iltrick, this is much too dangerous for you to come in on."

"You've trained me for over a year, Laun, the gangers don't have the plant or the poisons to trouble us and I can control the brew. I have to see him. You have the command, I just want to help."

She looked down at the stone floor, conceding to me. "I must leave. The Crag militia's captain is going to get us all killed if I leave him in charge of his men. Those gangers, the whole Quarter, have been attacking militia and Reds on sight. If you come in with us, you will not engage anyone on a fightbrew. If you do I will knock you out myself."

"You worry unnecessarily, Laun, I have no intention of dying just yet, and certainly not in a slum."

She gave me the merest hint of a bow and left.

I picked at the spiced lamb on the table before me. I was nervous, though such nerves would vanish once the fightbrew got hold of me. I looked at the backs of my hands. My skin was no longer the white of my people, but grey, the once blue veins darkened by the training brews I'd been given recently.

The first time I paid the colour, my very first training brew, I finally understood why soldiers taunted each other so little, why among their ranks there was a commonhood, an intimacy that those of us more used to ordering them around than living with them could not possibly understand.

Laun and her letnant, Letnant Syle, had washed me and cleaned me as my belly burned and I lost control over my movements that first time I drank a brew. I was fearful of their mocking me, that their initiation had gone the better for their being soldiers. I feared also being naked with them, particularly the men, but as I drowned in the fever and shook myself to pieces Syle sang to me as my own mother or father never did.

"Galathia of Filston?" Someone at the door, a knock.

"Yes."

A boy entered, no more than ten or eleven summers, a limp and a way about him that told me his life was spent trying not to be noticed.

"What's your name?" I asked.

"I'm to give you this." He held out the letter, trembling and frowning at the floor, as though I was making his duty more difficult for asking questions. In the moments I took trying to catch his eye he dropped the letter on the table, desperate to be rid of it.

"I should give you some pennies. What do you think?"

He raised an eyebrow enough to glance at my boots, my legs crossed before him as I sat on the dining chair. A whipped dog might at least have wagged its tail.

"A copper sixpence." I rolled it along the table. He bowed, a short bob he must have been told to do for the woman that was once a princess. It looked like a spasm.

"Take some lamb, eat it before you get outside." This got more of a response, his eyes locked onto the plate as I slid it over. He pushed pieces into his mouth rapidly, a frenzied breathing through his nose as he crammed it down. I got another bob, his eyes tearful with the sudden pleasure. He shuffled out, curving inwards on himself. I recalled how it felt, that greasy hot rabbit meat that the old hunter gave me when he found me near dead, whispering what I thought were my last curses in the world, all those winters ago.

I picked up the note. "Shale Gant secure."

Good. Three more of the Twenty taken care of, once Kailen is beaten.

The sum he paid the Indra Quarter Crew must have been staggering, for they were dying rather than giving him up. Reeve of the Post Infis Kulam, the Post's chief administrator here at the Crag, waved away our concern over some regrettably over-cooked horsemeat. He knew the "scapos", as they called those who ran the gangs here; had favours to call in.

"This time tomorrow evening, we will be dining with the four scapos who run the slums. One of them has this Kailen. Your generosity could not be ignored even by men far more powerful and wealthy than these . . . brutes."

The following evening we dined alone, the slight to this Reeve making him an insufferable host.

Kailen had used the Post to put messages out across the Old Kingdoms and no doubt he had also seen the posters my husband had put out along the Eastern Sar coast, offering a rich reward for news of Kailen's Twenty. Kailen had also been looking for his old crew, and our contacts within the Post had alerted us. Alon, my husband, responded, saying we had information and that we would meet him here. I quietly expected that Kailen would introduce himself before long. Alon made sure his visit to the Crag was known, for it was him to which all contact would be directed.

The reason why the scapos did not show that night became clearer in the subsequent days, however. On the night we dined with the Reeve, two of the gangs lost some of their senior members. The following night all four main gangs lost men. While the Reeve's delight was obvious, I despaired. Laun and I were convinced that this was the assassin.

Then the Reeve lost an officer and three of his Reds. All were in the slums at his behest, looking to bring the scapos to heel. Of course, the Post looks after its own, and Reds came in from the Post Houses in the surrounding districts looking to help find the killer. The Reeve leaned on the Crag's Master Cleark as well, to ensure its militia focused on this.

So, the Reds and the militia started cracking heads together until the Slums clammed up and shut down.

Finally, yesterday, with the family of Scapo Darin in the cruel hands of the Crag's Master Drudha, along with two of his captains, he told us the Indra Quarter Crew had Kailen, holed up at a tavern called The Riddle, widely known to be where Scapo Ostler, head of the Indra Crew, held court.

This was at the back of the slums. The Reeve and Laun were pleased, as the Indra Crew's district backed onto the walls, and was cut off by the Alnar River east. Only two ways out.

The one captain of the Indras we managed to catch watched his woman die, before himself dying under torture without saying a word. Good torturers are harder to come by than one would think.

The Reds and the militia, however, saw a chance to strengthen their hand, if they could clean out the Indras and get a more amenable scapo in there. But I have seen how men and women fight when their children are threatened. The quarter was silent now, the other gangs leaving them to their fate. Soon we would go in, a hundred at least, to kill or clean them out until they gave Kailen up.

I checked over my belt again: waxes, pastes, leaves, sporebags, lime-bags, caltrops, powders, guni sticks and a knife greasy with poison; a fat, short blade given me by a man called Nielus. His gift had saved my life as a girl.

Laun returned then, Midgie with her.

"We found Syle and Faré. Beheaded, stripped bare and shit on," said Laun. She was breathing hard, determined to control herself in the face of our engagement at hand. "There's something wrong here, because together, there's nobody outside my crew in the Crag that could lay a hand on them."

Midgie, the only other woman left in her crew with Syle gone, had been crying. She wouldn't look at me. She'd always wanted to be tougher, unmoved and calm no matter what. She'll learn.

"I'm sorry," I said. I had come to know them too, I was shocked, but before I could make a gesture to comfort Laun she had somehow changed, and held me firm with a stare that I could not read, either an accusation (for this was my purse) or a grim resolve.

"It's time," she said.

I undressed. Laun and Midgie helped me with the cotton shirt and leggings from a satchel where they had been folded through with sheets of cork pregnant with alka, the cotton damp with it, to resist the spread of poison from any cuts that got through the leathers I would wear over them. As she prepared me, Laun whispered the plan to herself over and over.

She led us, the rest of her crew and the fifteen or so militia that her drudha had brewed up out of the inn I had kept us at, and up to the warehouses on the eastern edge of the Indra Quarter. We gathered at the back of one of the large sheds and waited for the signal to go from our spotter squatting on a roof ahead of us. He was waiting for the other Reds and militia to start their own assault from the far side of the Indra Quarter. Within a few minutes he signed for us to move.

The rest of the Post would be moving in from the west slums to the Indra Quarter, intending to use the force of numbers to get into the Linney Lanes, a warren of hovels famous in decades past for being the birthplace of two scapos of old. Our group would move in from the east, through the dockside wareshouses, towards The Riddle, the tavern at the heart of the Indra Quarter where the Quarter's scapo had his hideout and where Kailen was likely to be hiding himself. There were a handful of us, so any spotters for the scapo's crew wouldn't see a pincer.

We ran fast and quiet like a pack of wolves, putting a fright on any that saw us as we flew through the wagons and the few dock workers oblivious to what was about to happen. I understand how one might get addicted to this, to the brews, the jeopardy.

The wareshouses were built over two storeys. We hoped they would keep us out of sight of the Indra spotters on the roofs of the rows of hovels that stood between the wareshouses and The Riddle itself. A horn sounded, over west in the Linney, followed by another nearer, no doubt for those around The Riddle, who would be drinking their own brews and getting ready for them.

We ran along the side of the wareshouse nearest to the slum. Laun looked out to the hovels of the slum between us and The Riddle. All silent. She gestured the militia with her crew to cross the lane and get inside the houses there. They began running out, and I about to follow them, when bowshots from both ends of the lane and the open shutters of the hovels opposite struck three of the militia. Laun pushed me over as the arrows came in and they cracked and clattered about me as I scrambled back behind the wall of the wareshouse.

We heard whistling. A few of the Indra were communicating with their mouthpieces, the clicks and chirps their own sort of code that we would not be able to decipher.

The militiamen, now only twelve, looked to Laun. They weren't used to even modest fightbrew mixes, and they stamped and fussed with their blood up. She had given them their mix and as with any novice on the rise, the fear of it, the wrestle with it, makes one afraid to be far from one's cook, crew leader or drudha. We were quicker than they were due to the brew we were on, so Laun picked us to offer covering shots while the militiamen dashed for the houses to get in them and out of the killing zone of the lane separating us from the slum.

She led us out and as we cleared the side of the shed we each put arrowbags through the open shutters of as many of the nearby buildings as we could, not waiting to see which were and weren't occupied.

The twelve militia charged out and ran across the killzone. Three more took arrows but the sporebags had given those in the houses pause. The militia spread to four of the houses across the lane and those with heavy hammers smashed through the doors while we kept putting arrows into every open window we could. I heard screaming some way off, a rapidly spreading riot. A militiaman gestured for us to join them. We ran for the doorway. As we did so I looked up to the rooftops we intended to climb to better understand what lay beyond around The Riddle. He rose from a crouch, the assassin I'd seen in Povey's Valley, now in Agent leathers, and he shot twice while I raised the warning. Ry'le fell, along with another of Laun's crew. She must have seen or heard them fall, and judged where the shots came from in an instant, because, without breaking stride, she raised her own bow and put an arrow inches over his head.

As we burst through the door she turned to look back at the two of her crew lying dead.

"Fuck it! Fuck! Fuck!" She kicked the door shut and kicked it again so hard one of the hinges was ripped off and it sagged half across the doorway.

"The assassin, he's in our leathers," I said.

She nodded and signed for her crew to get upstairs and kill the resistance there. With a deep breath she pushed past me, bidding me follow. We now knew how Syle and Faré had died.

We walked through to the room at the far side of the house, a hearth, a shelf with some woollens and a few pallets of straw were all those dwelling here had, though they had fled presumably to facilitate this ambush. There was yelling as our men got to work on the gangers in the houses about us.

I gently teased open the shutter to the street beyond; another, wider street between us and the houses and The Riddle opposite. I saw, among its chimney stacks, half hidden, the outlines of men lying in wait. Laun looked out from behind me. Her eyes were full and she dabbed her thumb to them. Ry'le had been with her from the start.

"Stay here, shoot anyone leaving The Riddle. If they get within twenty yards get upstairs, do not, am I clear, do not try to take them on your own. Now my whole crew is brewed up properly, that assassin will not escape us. Once he's dead we wait for the main force to push through the Lanes to The Riddle on its far side and then we can approach it."

She left and ran up the stairs to the floor above, joining in the butchery. I closed my eyes, succumbing to the song of the world and what it could tell me. The militia were fighting people in the next house along, the floorboards echoing with running and stamping as we engaged with the gangers. I heard more shouting from outside, from the houses where we'd been ambushed moments ago.

I opened my eyes again to the street and the assassin was stood before me, filling my view, staring at me through the partly open shutter. The point of his sword was a hair's breadth from my eye. I staggered back as though I had been struck, for so aware was I of everything in the world when risen, so familiar is that state of all-knowing, that the silence with which he had descended from the roof was shocking. I could see only his eyes but it was obvious he recognised me from seeing only the part of my face not hidden by my own mask. He shook his head, as if to break himself out of a dream or some recollection, before spinning around and heading for The Riddle, from which smokebags were being dropped from the upper windows.

I tried to raise my bow to shoot him but something stopped me, the shock, I thought at first, of him appearing without warning only inches from my face.

As two shutters opened in The Riddle, from which a hail of arrows was aimed at him, some gangers from the nearby hovels and storehouses rushed out to stop him. I watched him turn and charge the men coming at him, knowing it would stop those in the houses from shooting, and I realised then what held my arrow. I knew him.

Kailen's Twenty and the Clan Razhani

I record here an account, from the current Razhani Clan leader Rhain, of how, after their success at Ahmstad and previous to that with her father, Rhain hired Kailen's Twenty. Kailen ensured her clan became both the principal clan of the Province and the nemesis of the Wildmen that plagued their borders at that time. This was eight years before Snakewood.

I am given to speculate that, with what has subsequently transpired with the Wildmen, Kailen may unwittingly have unleashed a great peril on the Old Kingdoms in the course of achieving success with this purse.

Goran

Kailen's Twenty, though they commanded a steep purse, did well for my da.

Talk around the clans at our Meets was all about what he did with the Ahmstad against that ass Turis. We was waiting for word that Turis was taking Ahmstad but it never come. Now our people that I put in and around his city says the word is he's killing those he sees are his enemies at his court, those critical of him for how he lost those clans to the Ahmstad.

My da had hired Kailen's crew once previous to that to help with Vilmor. They had been with Turis for a bit and knew what he had planned I think and from what Kailen had said to my da he didn't think much of Turis, which you couldn't say the same of his da, Torin, who had the respect of everyone, being a peacemaker, which us border-lands needs with the Wilds all around us.

When my da died Kailen and his men come to the Sending. While a few was a bit pissed at this, thinking him come to see what work was around while they was paying respects to him, he didn't approach me that week and was all set to leave when I was ready to see him. I admit I was a bit in awe of him back then, him and his crew, and this was as much because of his drudhas. We knew so little compared. Their colouring, how Kailen could read those of us he spoke to like he knew our minds, was fearsome enough. But worse I struggled a bit around him because I did find him kinny, which is a way of saying I wanted him, and whenever he was about I used to think he could see what I was thinking, eyes like mountain pools he had, and he was special to look at anyway because of some accident at the academy he trained at back in his homeland that turned his skin all mottled and callused, like snakewood.

Reason I needed him for a purse was that my da was ill for a long while, and word had got out. He hated me to see it at the end, when he was all shrunk and coughing and wouldn't have me nursing him though who else could do it right without our ma there that died winters before. He missed her fiercely. I suppose he could bear the servants even less than me to care for him and it was as much at his bedside as at the classes I was given that I learned what state-craft I could pick up about the agreements we had and who was fighting who and the troubles that all clans have with their under-clans.

While he was ill though, those herders and growers that paid goods by way of tithe for protection started slowing up with their deliveries and then those on the borders, the underclans, had Wildmen come in worse than they ever had and at Meets were demanding a new leader. I couldn't let it be my brother – he was a droop, fucking useless – but my da saw it too, and with my uncle and his other advisers, they said to give me the chain, this one I'm wearing now, that all leaders of the Razhani wear. We saw my brother off so he wouldn't cause me trouble and I got the Clanguard out into our bit of the province and letting them know that tithes was owed and I was leader and if they had a problem then the court was here at Heje.

After our fighting with Vilmor, we had troubles too among the clans. The Lorzh had been hit hard by it and there was a need for a clan to step up to be the Arch Clan because there was a few brothers in the Lorzh that was looking for that chain and instead they was making it all worse for their people.

Us Razhani had a way with the alka we got from our grain, of purifying it, a distillation our drudhas call it and we get a lot of trade from it. The Post and other guilds come out to us to buy it from all over the Old Kingdoms.

Kailen says he would look at what was needed to stop these Wildmen now they was looking to make slaves of my people and steal our crops, if we give him the secret of that distillation. He had this queer drudha Kigan, quiet, not the sack of tremors Ibsey was, his other drudha. Kigan had a sort of loneliness on him, always drawing in his book, and asking for animals or anyone we was putting to death that he could use. He was saying how he could use what we supplied to make the recipes we had much better.

My drudhas was fierce angry, that we would let these mercenaries look at our book, as you know out here the recipe book is what decides which clans rule and which are the underclans.

My da believed Kailen was different. Honourable if that can be believed. Still, I overruled my drudhas and let this Kigan and the other one Ibsey see the book and on this understanding Kailen give his service for free. And he never give the recipes away as far as I know.

Kailen did one simple thing that give us a victory against the Wildmen and made the Province the Razhani Province instead of the Lorzh Province. It wasn't simple looking at it the other way. He bid me put out for the levies from the underclans, and my Clanguard; got them all on parade on a plain near Heje. I was proud of them all there, a good turnout and all, according to our agreements, accounted for.

Kailen was troubled. Him and his men made them stand there while they went about them, his giant black Harlain, the sad-looking one Valdir, the one that was always cracking jokes and teasing Kailen that he called Bense. The others were quieter and didn't speak much. The two he seemed to confide in the most was one called Mirisham and another that was a prince from somewhere over the Sar. The three of them says to me that my army wasn't fit for the troubles we had. I took my captains about with them and learned a lesson about war as I did, when he showed me the state of their weapons, the chain and leather, the boys that shivered when they stood up close to them. These was just bodies.

"You put brews in them," he said, "and they'll fight of course, for the brews make you crave blood, but the colouring is poor, and if we took them through some forms now, I think you'd wish you could give the clan to your brother."

"What Wildmen could put out anywhere near eight thousand like this," I said.

He nodded. "You have six hundred horse, more than they could muster I believe. My men Bense, Gant and Milu are our best with horses. They think it's about all you can be proud of and they have work to do with them and their singers besides."

I waited. What was there to say? And none of my captains said much back either and it made me think that they all thought as much. I thought then that they could not have trusted me and this was a lesson to learn.

"Have you asked the underclans why they turn out men like this?"

I shook my head. Seemed obvious and I was too ashamed to say it.

"She's not been leader for long, Kailen," said my second, who was my uncle on my ma's side.

"Sshh, unc, don't matter, leader can't make excuses and I should've done it."

"And that's why your da made you leader," said Kailen's man Mirisham, who was a bit older than the rest of the Twenty. "A leader doesn't hide, they see a mistake, accept it and fix it."

"So how do I fix it?" I asked.

"When Ibsey and Kigan are done with your drudhas your recipe book will be the envy of the clans. You know war is about fightbrews, but you can grow a mouse this much, and a leopard this much." And he gestured as such. "You're better with half as many men coming here better armoured and with the same supply for their keep, and you'll have brews the Wildmen have no counter for. Your underclans can afford that levy better, because that's what I asked them as we inspected your army. I asked your leaders and they told me they struggled to meet the quotas. The levies are the very men that farm plant and food or raise children or keep herds. There aren't enough, or enough to bring the caravans without which they go hungry."

60

Mirisham spoke then. "Send half of these men back home, leave the other half with us, along with the best weapons and armour. A big walking army isn't the force you need for the hit and run the Wildmen are plaguing you with. You know this, Rhain. We take half the mice you've got out there and turn them into leopards. On a fight-brew they will be worth more than the half you've given back to your people, which will thank you the more for it."

I agreed the change in levy with the underclans, we drank on it and they left their captains and we put the men left in the hands of Kailen and his band.

Over the months that followed we hit settlements, went further into the Wilds than we'd been before, because as Kailen said, we needed to know more about what we was dealing with. We burned what we found, and his drudhas, the quiet one in particular, did things on those we found. Him and Kailen would argue, but he learned things from those he tortured and we found and captured the one that was leading the attacks that had become more organised and his name was Caragula, and a few summers younger than I was then. The tribes sent people for him, because he said he could deliver peace on our border and a peace was agreed. He give a lot of mouth while he was imprisoned. I think his lip got him a few beatings but the peace was on condition he was returned so, much as me and Kailen wanted to kill him, we let him go.

Kailen's man Digs and another called Kheld was put in charge then of getting forts put up and at the next Meet of the main clans word had got about of our brews and our victories against the Wildmen and in the matter of choosing the Arch Clan, Kailen asked me what I thought the Province needed, and how would I make it stronger. Seemed to me that Hevendor needed allying, as much because of Vilmor as of the Wilds, and our clan was best placed to secure that, and my da had always had a good settlement with them and trade was good for our alka. Kailen agreed and it was his man that was a prince took my uncle and my second and settled an alliance with the north of Hevendor on our common border with the Wilds. There was few could then dispute that with the Clanguard I had and our brews I could head up the Province's council, making it the Razhani Province, after my clan's name.

I learned a lot from Kailen, and have had sore need of him since, but his change to my levy, which seemed madness to me on the surface, give us a backbone we needed ever since, though nobody, not even Kailen, could have expected Caragula to come back like he has done.

Chapter 4

Kailen

"Kailen, old friend, you can give me a little can't you, bring me back all even?"

I looked to the drudha. Bense was lying on his bunk, I was sat next to him, and his fingers traced across my robe, looking for my belt, looking for a rise.

"You say there's betony in that?" I asked.

The drudha picking through Bense's shit in a pot near the door nodded.

"Colouring suggests it, shit's black. His lips are broken up, scabby, he's sweating hard. What do you think?"

The drudha was competent enough, though he had not realised the sores on Bense's skin suggested a far stronger and purer mix than a guard of this rank of lord could afford, or indulge if he was looking to keep his employment. It was obvious in his eyes, the discs enlarged, and how he trembled intermittently.

I had opened the shutters over his bed, in an outbuilding near the villa of his master; minor Juan lord, Lord Fesden, modest ranking, flatback (meaning newly rich), his father having made a great fortune from cargoes, his uncles drinking and smoking away the fortune as fast as it was being earned. Their banner was hastily conceived, three blue waves and a shield, as drab as the prestige of the three families that have so far pledged to it.

Bense started trying to open a pouch on my belt. I eased his fingers off, his skin like butter.

"Drudha, thank you, your expertise has been most valuable. Could you fetch over the jug of water before you leave?"

He handed me the jug and I waited till I could hear his footsteps on the stones outside.

From my saddlebag I took some caffin powder, tincture of betony.

I tipped out most of the water, shook it up with the mix and dribbled it into Bense's mouth. The gums were shrunk back, most of his teeth missing, a common problem rubbing betony or chewing khaat. He had been a great pitfighter, his legend drawing me out of my way to see him all those years ago when I was building the crew. He always had a problem taking orders from men who couldn't match him in practice, come his training. Even then it was clear he was addicted to betony, and in a land that was not tolerant of plant for anyone apart from its soldiery. Our single combat was a formality between him and the purses that would bring him the very finest plant east of the Sar. Once with me he showed a formidable talent in the cavalry, a natural with horses.

He had been a big man before the betony took hold, after Tharos. His and Milu's drilling of the cavalries of the Ahmstad were instrumental in cementing our reputation. But it is the past. We earned and spent the purses and with his he has destroyed himself, a shuffling skeleton.

Soon enough he was sitting upright. He seemed to be re-familiarising himself with the room and my presence in it. For a moment I suspected he was playing up a little more than he was letting on, but dismissed it. In hindsight I shouldn't have.

"Stixie said he saw you, Bense; he came here on his way to the Hillfast tourney. You look dreadful. Where did you get that betony mix you're on?"

"Kailen? What are you doing here? I saw Stixie. He comes through Jua, stops in, shares a few pipes. Getting fat and all."

"The betony, Bense, where did you get it? You're on a fierce mix, Fesden is thinking of letting you go."

"It's fine, it's fine. He knows I'm good. I, well, it's just Stixie give me a few coins, he wasn't short, and give me some raw betony, a three point block."

"He didn't look that rich to me to be giving out three points of raw b."

"Ask him."

He was full of shit. He seemed gone within himself for a time. The cavalryman who had more dirty stories than a docks brothel drudha and who could spin the dice like they were loaded was gone altogether.

"It's good to see you, Kailen, you're looking well, must be making a proper purse still eh? Not like the rest of us just making ends meet and we . . ." He trailed off, had become fascinated with the window. He kneeled up on his bunk and looked out.

"There's a girl, seventeen summers I reckon, bitties out here and comes into the estate from the farm that's, um, down there, the road, been down there, well, I like to watch out for her, they bring milk up, cheese as well. She always gives me a nice big smile, asks where I got my colour and I tell her it was with you. She never heard of you. Can you imagine that? Kailen's Twenty? No idea. I tell her how good a horseman I am, how I could pull her up on the saddle behind me mid-gallop and then ask her where I could take her, and she blushes and I know I will have to go there and meet her da, talk about a marriage."

He went quiet. A point of raw betony goes no lower than three silver at an emporium or from an Academy; I can get it for two going to the farm. Something wasn't right.

"Have you got more of this mix?"

He didn't turn around. "Buy your own. I'm joking, no, no more. Back to the tea, back to the bullshit."

"It's not bullshit, Bense; betony any purer than an eighth to the standard is going to kill you within months."

He shrugged. "Is that why you come to see me? You see Stixie and hear I'm a bit soaked and you get a heart and start caring for one of your old crew? Hey, do you need me back? I can come with you, I just need to get back on the Forms. Fesden pays nothing, not like when, how long is it?"

"You're fucked, Bense, you had barely the strength to shake my hand. I'm not taking a purse any more. I came because I think someone wants us all dead. I thought you should get warning."

"Can I get some soup?" I couldn't tell if he had heard me. He got to his feet. There was a small patch of piss soaked into his bedshirt. The blankets he was lying on were stained similarly.

"Have you seen any others of the Twenty?" I asked.

He sat back down, glanced at me again in the way that made me think he had only just recognised who I was.

"Have you seen any of us, besides Stixie?" I repeated.

"Not really. If you're going can you leave me something, not that shit you just give me, something to smooth me out. Tell Fesden I just need a day, put in a good word, eh? You owe me that."

I stood to leave.

"I'm going to find some soup soon, then I'll, I think I'll try some Forms. They come back quick enough." To him I was no longer there.

I heard him grunting and counting, warming up, as I walked down the stone steps, past the heavy-breasted girl from the farm with her arms around a stablehand, and over to Fesden's villa.

A crooked, greasy-haired grandfather led me at his own pace through to a courtyard of whitewashed stone and euca saplings. On an incongruously ornate marble bench Lord Fesden watched a child, his boy, struggle with a sheaf of papers. He was teaching him his letters.

The crooked man found a lower notch in his back and waited, bowing, until Fesden's son finished and smiled at his father, awaiting some recognition.

Fesden hadn't been listening, picking his substantial nose and staring at his silk slippers. The silence after the recital was what brought him to.

"*Pri amota, pri*. Excellent. Come the Elevens you will honour us all."

The boy left as a servant dismissed.

"You should bow when introducing guests, Haster, even mercenaries." He winked at me, while Haster, who rose a few inches more upright, turned and left without introducing me. I was long over the attempted indignities by which those who paid our purses aimed to disassociate us from them.

"My lord. As a mercenary I have no awareness or skill enough of words to speak cleverly in praise of you as a greeting. You will know I was once Bense's captain. I came because I happened upon an old friend of mine and Bense's, Stixie, the archer that I think entertains you occasionally, a blue feather in his cap and a white bow. He told me Bense was unwell, in some distress."

"Stixie, yes, remarkable bow, the arrows he shoots are only barely outdone by a javelin for size and weight. But Bense has been a problem, worse than most with the colour that we get here after the armies have spat them out. He had been a few days off duty complaining of some ailment that our drudha knew full well was betony. He is apparently mending well."

"That's good to hear. I see, however, that such betony, according to your drudha, was expensively bought, unless you reward your servants with silver pieces. I fear that he may have been subdued this way as a means of someone getting better access to you, that he has been bought, not to put it kindly, and would betray you for whoever it is has given him this plant. Do you have those who hate you, my lord?"

"My gains are another's loss, are they not? At least that would be the word in the fields and taverns where the peasants play."

I nodded, lowering my head to help him settle into the notion that he was in control of this conversation.

"I believe there is a way we can help Bense to recover himself and become once more the fearsome guard that fought at Tharos, as well as protect you. I can take him to the jailhouse in Cusston, I'm owed favours by the militia's captain. He can sweat out the betony there and recover himself, at which point your mercy will bind him to you while at his lowest ebb. He will reveal everything, if there is a plot of which he is a part."

"You speak well and wisely for a mercenary. You desire the purse to remove him to Cusston?"

"I will not take a purse for helping him. I would take a horse for him, however, and supplies, and will send the horse back with the Post."

"It's done. I would gladly take you on as a guard in his place until that time. What is your fee?"

"I no longer have need of purses. Thank you for your kind offer."

He stood up to face me. "How long will it take?"

"Six weeks perhaps, it's hard to say, but he'll be a different man, the betony's hold broken, and ready to serve once more. It would be wise to ensure that one of the guards at Cusston is willing to share Bense's progress with you. I will ensure the guards pay attention to anything he says while sleeping, no matter how unusual. I will try to make it this way again soon and would be most interested in seeing him well again."

I excused myself and over the journey to Cusston met a surprising resistance from Bense to leaving, under the pretence it was an errand for Fesden. His howling when they locked him up earned him a beating before I had left the jailhouse and I doubt his mood would have improved as the weeks became months. I hoped I had saved his life until I could return.

Now I'm at the Crag, Scapo Ostler stood before me, as capable as all of them of kissing his son with love as pure as rain and then slicing a man to red pieces in front of his own.

Scapo Ostler has offered his life and that of his crew for our bond of debt and I will take it, without telling him of the awful power that has found me, that may be a match for me. He has offered the lives also of those in the Indra Quarter who would not leave their homes.

The Indra Quarter had been a useful place from which to conduct my search for those of the Twenty who may yet be alive, away from scrutiny, with people who would recognise any stranger. Up until a few nights ago I had little fear for my own life, even when, a few weeks ago, a poster was brought to me, put up by the Post, from a guildmaster looking for information about the Twenty. I replied to it, and have prepared the slum for a meet with this guildmaster who I fully expect to be hostile, sure that he was the source of the killing of the Twenty. But now another killer has appeared, and I already have no doubt in my mind as to their being responsible for the assassinations. Yet this killer doesn't seem to share allegiance with the guildmaster. There is an interesting puzzle here that his actions have caused and yet denied me the chance to examine. I have indicated to the guildmaster that I can be found in the Indra Quarter, yet the killer does not appear to know this. The killings he's performing seem indiscriminate but he is searching for information. They may well have concluded his actions are of my conception. It may explain the haste with which the militia and the other scapos have turned their backs on the Indra Quarter Crew.

Horns sounded to the west. The Post and Crag militia, I predict near a hundred, will close on us from the Linney Lanes. These murders will have been too tempting an opportunity for the Crag's Master not to clean out a scapo and divvy up his quarter for the servitude of, and in accordance with the favour he bestows on, the other scapos. The act will be seen favourably by those who bother voting for him.

Meanwhile I had correctly anticipated that a force would attempt to arrive by stealth from the dockside, eastward in the opposite direction. The calls from the roofs that way counted fifteen or so, with Agents. I turned to Ostler, pasting his knife with a wax block impregnated with poison that I'd given him to pass around his boys in The Riddle.

"It begins. Tell your men to take their brews. The militia will force their way into the Linney, expecting most resistance on Blenner. It's too obvious. You will wait until the first of their men are smashing through the tavern and houses at the end before setting them on fire. Then they will come round to Blenner where you've got your bowmen. Your cap and his men will put down smokebags on Back Lane. They will shoot any coming through, nice and close. You've spiked the end of that lane anyway, a killing zone. Get yourself to Blenner. You'll be King Scapo by morning." I smiled reassuringly until he left.

I cannot fathom why the Twenty are hunted and killed now, after so many years; why so many in this slum are about to die in my name. Why would the enemies we'd have had back then have waited so long to exact a revenge?

I knew Scapo Ostler would help, would try to keep me safe while I guided my men to seek those of my brothers I had not yet found, while I determined who it is seeks to kill us all. I had hoped Achi would have brought Shale and Gant. Perhaps they will not come.

I told Ostler the other scapos would desert him and he would not believe me. How could he not see it? He introduced me to the other scapos the night I arrived; Darin, Reed and Andarin, organising a dinner for us. He believed it would increase his prestige with them, a mercenary of my renown looking to go dark with his help. Fifteen winters on, however, my name is on the lips only of soldiers now mostly retired or dead. As the song goes, "No song shall long their deeds proclaim". The other scapos were polite but ignorant of me.

Darin drank the most of the wine I had brought, but left our gathering without having thanked me for it, let alone recognised it as a

Juan vintage. I gave them a keg each as an offering, but he left his, a snub in these parts all the more ridiculous for its value. Ostler baited Darin over his relationship with the Crag's Reeve of the Post and Andarin said nothing despite having contracts with the Post himself. Ostler is thus ignorant and arrogant, Darin seething with antipathy, while Andarin despises Ostler and Darin. Reed remained above it throughout, the strongest of them all, but unwilling to help Ostler out of the mess I was creating for him. Three goblets of wine into the evening and I knew I would need to engage Ostler's captains if I was to get adequate notice of, or protection from, whoever might be killing the Twenty. Ostler was not running his crew, his captains were. The other scapos would carve up his quarter more readily than the hog on the table before us.

Ostler's sister waits on my wife, Araliah, and tells me she walks the orange groves and vines while I'm away, singing with the children and taking water to those that work our estate. My wife has the habit those born from the very wealthiest families all have, a grace gently forged from the lack of want, a guileless expectation of decency and a curiosity and compassion for those people's lives the hotter and more intimately joyous and cruel for the want that shapes their suffering and ambition. I miss her.

Ostler's family, and Ostler himself, were slaves of the family that founded my estate. When that family fell into ruin I took on its slaves and made them tenants. Ostler was a bully and a thief as a child, his mother a widow of a father that died at sea. He left the farmer's life to return to the Crag, where he had cousins. He was fifteen summers old and had no idea what the slums would be like. Perhaps the stories of whores and cheap plant he could get wasted on appealed more than the summers of Harudan. It's easy to overestimate a fool. Nevertheless he grew strong in the slums, a born fighter it would seem. At some point he discovered the notion of honour, and remembered how I gave his family back their own.

He has a family here now, his crew. Four days previously he lost two of them, one of them a captain. So did Darin's crew. The following night all the scapos lost men, and came to see us at The Riddle.

Each had five or six with him, mostly greenskins, only one with anything like the reds and blues that spoke of fightbrews. They wore their belts and leathers as though they were going to war, though the leather on all of them was too clean to have been used much. The scapos, for a gathering like this, came bare-chested, displaying their inks. Only Reed's inks spoke of children and his kills, none of his wealth. Here was the strongest scapo.

"What trouble are you in, Kailen?" asked Andarin.

"What trouble are you having?"

"One of my good boys, Elsin, was killed in front of his girl. She's told that more gonna die if Kailen isn't given up," said Reed.

"Debt of honour," said Ostler, "he gets me last breath if it protects him."

"Get him outside the Crag and protect him there, he's getting good people killed."

"Can't you protect your people?" I asked.

Andarin jumped up, jabbing his finger at me. "If you're supposed to be this great warrior, perhaps you get out there and show this Agent or whoever he is just that."

They all jumped up with him, except Ostler, hands on hilts, fingers in pouches on their belts.

"It isn't an Agent." I wanted to say it was worse. "I've put measures in place, with Ostler, which should help us show the militia, and this killer, what they're dealing with. I don't take unnecessary risks."

"And why should you?" said Reed. "When the likes of us take them for you. Darin's lost a captain, we all lost someone, including some Reds, so now Reeve Kulam's got a poker up the ass of the Master that runs the Crag and the militia are breaking bones."

Reed sat back down, the others followed.

Andarin spoke. "I had merchants from the Beney district and my people in the Ruvvies come see me today, along with militia and some Agents. They was asking about my agreements with the militia that was meant to favour them, and turns out the officer I had tucked up has himself a promotion to the Selvens, and they've got someone in looking to make a name, nobody to squeeze behind him. He's ignoring our agreements now and my people are losing their faith in me." By "nobody to squeeze" he meant no family he could threaten. Love compromises people.

"Did you say Agents are here in the Crag?" said Reed. He looked at Ostler and me an unspoken challenge. There wouldn't be a man among them could give himself good odds against an Agent.

"They want you to force me to give him up," said Ostler. "And I reckon any of you that was hiding someone would want me to protect your secret? Or sell you out? I lost men too."

The silence was telling. Ostler didn't have the respect necessary to win their favour, an opinion almost immediately bolstered by his misreading it.

"Exactly," he said. "I wouldn't sell you out. The quarters are running well, we got arrangements, peace for a few summers with each other's crews. Let's keep it."

"I'm done," said Darin, getting back up, nodding to his men.

"I have your word?" asked Ostler.

"Of course." He looked him in the eye as he said it, but blinked twice, rapidly, a clear enough tell. Darin was going to sell Ostler out, the kidnap of his woman and children by the Master Cleark the following day would merely expedite it. They would offer no resistance to the militia, allowing them to gather outside the Linneys, edge of his own quarter, with no dispute. This was the outcome I prepared for.

The scapos said their farewells and left The Riddle. Locals now started wandering in after being given the nod.

"That went well," said Ostler. One of his captains glanced to the floor, the other two staring into their cups.

"Preparation needs to be made." I said. "You've got good captains, we can get your quarter ready for the invasion of an army if you let me determine how it will be done."

I glanced at his left hand, fussing at the drawstring of his kannab pouch. His teeth were green, stained with a breed from Iltrick or the Scarlet Coast. It must have been mixed with an opia, probably threaded with Enla root, another of the Virates' great exports to the Old Kingdoms. He was looking for a rise, distracted by it when his own quarter was threatened.

"Give him your support," was all he said to his captains.

I drank the Honour. As I waited for the rise I prepared my belt and took my journals and the letters, bound up in a satchel, to the cellar. Em, one of The Riddle's serving girls, was waiting.

72

"Em, thank you. Does the landlord know you're here, does he know about the box?"

She shook her head. She was fretful as a mouse, hard-worked and dirty. She drew no comment with her coming or going, nothing that the eye could lay itself upon, and through her I managed to get word out of the Indra Quarter to my men searching the Old Kingdoms for the Twenty.

"You need to put these papers in this box. Tell no-one except Achi, who you met some weeks back, or two other soldiers, men of the colour like me, Gant and Shale. I've been expecting them, but they won't arrive in time to help me. Hide the box, then you get out of the Quarter until light."

She nodded and took the satchel.

A hot wave rose with a dizzying rush through my guts and chest. I began changing, growing with the Honour, and shoved at her to leave until I had my breathing.

I would not be hiding in The Riddle. That would be merely where the fight will end.

The lamps were snuffed out across the Quarter, from the Back Lane, Linney Lanes and Blenner. The noise of the women and children that escaped what was to come echoed over from the riverside. One of Ostler's caps, Senis, led a handful of his gangers with me across the Back Lane, all mist and mud, threading our way through the blades and ankle breakers that were dug in across the whole Quarter. Shouting had gone up at the end of the Linney Lanes. The houses between us and them were full of men, women and boys ready with bows, slings and sporebags. Senis led us up through a brothel that had been cleared out, though a cloying stink of petunia oil remained. I bid three men stay inside while he and a ganger joined me, climbing out onto the roof of the brothel, the tiles slick with damp, and darker here where these roofs nestled in the shadow of the great city wall behind them.

With the luta mix I had supplied to all those staying to defend their homes while I instructed them, we could see as bright grey outlines the men on the roofs further along the lanes where the militia were coming in, taking shots as the first sounds of smashing wood and clash of swords was on. The screams began, and both these men, on a brew stronger than they'd ever had, felt the surge that came with the sound of fighting.

I motioned us along the roof of the brothel to hop over to the next building. Senis would remain there, near this end of Back Lane, giving the signal to lay down the smoke when he was signalled himself to do so, an attempt to keep the militia and Post channelled into the Linney.

He made to jump the gap but as he did so he twitched, shot with a dart. He landed on the other side and one leg gave, the standing foot losing grip on the steeper side of the roof. He fell choking to the ground below. There were men on the roofs intersecting the Back and Linney lanes, all of which were lying flat, waiting with the smoke bags. A few lifted their heads up as they comprehended what they had just seen. I dropped to a crouch with the other ganger next to me, signed for him to check behind us. He leaned over the roof to look onto the Lane, then sat on his backside, before slumping back against the roof. A remarkable poison. I unshouldered my bow, considered the way they had collapsed, the line of the attack. The city wall. I span to face it. The figure up there was quick, my arrow vanishing past him. I didn't wait. With my mouthpiece I alerted the gangers still inside the brothel and those on the roof opposite. The clicks and whistles were loud and close in the silence of these lanes, sounding like the crafted metal birds that came from Tarantrea. They were a code to talk to each other. I used the mouthpiece to bid them be alert for the killer. I heard choking, looked over, saw the outline of two men holding their throats and smashing their fists against the tiles, their bodies spasmic, then falling still. I dropped from the roof, caught the edge of it with my fingers, kicked through a window shutter and swung myself into a room. I laid titarum seeds along the ledge and floorboards just inside. Crushing them and inhaling the spores would cause vomiting, working through most masks.

I walked out of the room and signed to the other gangers Senis and I had left in the brothel to take positions at the end of the long corridors on the ground and first floors. I waited on the second-floor passageway, closed my eyes and put my hands to the walls. Fully risen on the Honour, I absorbed through my palms the song of this structure. A whisper of a hinge, two rooms along to my left; someone was there. I had a vial of a mandrake decoction, counted to two and threw it at the doorway to that room. The floorboards beyond creaked, a step away from it. I ran along to the doorway and stabbed my sword through the wall as I approached, in case they were waiting, before throwing another vial into the room. The room was empty, just the odour of crushed titarum seeds mixing with the mandrake. Where had the assassin gone? It had not caused any choking, implying he or she was using some remarkable plant. I retreated back to the corridor before the mandrake and titarum got into me. There was a chirp of a mouthpiece downstairs, I ran to the stairwell, and one of the younger men gasped out Senis's name before hitting the floor somewhere below. I signalled to the others to put down sporebags and meet at the stairwell that threaded through the heart of the brothel. They were isolated in the corridors; they needed to stay in sight of each other. But I was too late, failing to appreciate what we were up against.

The sound of swords striking was sharp in this empty place, and another of the gangers was run through, a thick mukey gasping as a blade repeatedly stabbed him. Moments later the last ganger must have spat his piece, crying out as he ran to meet the killer. I leaped off the rail to the corridor on the first floor, and threw a limebag down the lower stairwell to hit the ground floor. The firelight was almost blinding with the luta mix in my eyes, an incandescent white rippling across the entrance hall, splashes of it sparking up and spreading along doorframes. The assassin had killed them all; we were alone in the building.

I threw caltrops either side of me, to cover the corridors to the left and right. He was on this floor, I could feel it, but I couldn't place him. The boards in the corridor were rigged with trips and loose floorboards, the rooms as well, all but one.

I backed into it and gummed over the door cloth strips of the titarum, that would rip if the door were opened. Then I readied my bow for a shot.

I crept to the window. I signalled out with my mouthpiece to those across the lane, to put smoke down as was the original plan. There was a step outside the door. I let the arrow fly, low and slightly off centre from the noise. It punched through the door and into the wall beyond. The next step I heard, a crack of wood bending against a nail, was in the room next door, remarkable for the silence and speed of his movement. He could smell the titarum, and that would mean he could smell me, knew exactly where I was stood. This was plant as good as any I had used. Could it be him? The flames were finding their voice on the ground floor, a heavy smoke rising as the building caught. I sensed his absence. I leaped through the open window behind me and into the smoke that filled the Back Lane. With my mouthpiece I called for support at the alley that separated Linney Lane from the Back and bade those near to keep an eye above them. He would be in no rush, despite how close he must have come to engaging me. He knew well enough to position and reposition himself until, like me, he felt he had the decisive advantage.

I called to those on the rooftops to mark the position of any Agent they saw, for none would be here yet except him, though he was no Agent.

Three more gangers approached. I signed for them to maintain a full view around us as I moved us away from the Back Lane through to Linney.

Bowstrings hummed above us, where the Linney lane came to a dead end, on the far side of which was The Riddle. The gangers up there signalled he was on the roof of the building that closed the end of the lane off. I signalled for four of them to make the jump to the rooftops towards him and I led my three into the first building on the left, aiming to get to its roof and follow them.

An old man was sat in a chair near open shutters as we entered. He had a broom across his lap, waiting to offer some defence of the place. He gave the boys with me a nod as we went through to the stairs leading up. Shutters opened out front and back of the hovel, so we split and climbed through each under cover of those moving about on the rooftop opposite.

The sound of shouting and screaming was getting louder, the far end of Linney was becoming a slaughter despite the defences slowing and crippling many who did not know where to step. For those who survived there would be a reckoning when this was over, because the other slums did not come to help them.

The first of the boys that got a grasp of the roof tiles and put his head up took an arrow in it. I was beneath him, helping him up when

76

he fell backwards, away from the shutter and into the mud below. To move would give away my position. Not to move meant the two on the other side of this hovel climbing out of the shutter there were also dead. I heard a man shout for arrows on his target, heard the shots pass through the air above me outside.

The one shouting began choking, then footsteps as one of the gangers with me had got onto the roof, the other side of its arch. He fell swiftly, hitting the ground below. The one remaining ganger came back through to the room I was in. I raised a hand to still him.

The assassin was in control. He had been so since he killed Senis. For the first time I could remember I had been outmanoeuvred, utterly. At every turn he had the ground advantage. He knew my position and positioned himself accordingly. I needed to change that.

I remembered the Agents that had been seen at the wareshouses on the riverside. They would be moving towards The Riddle where they believed I'd be holed up. There was the tactical advantage. Superior soldiers with better plant and, not being allied with the assassin, would be hostile to him. I needed to bring him close enough to them to cause him to consider them, dilute his attention.

There was a pall over the quarter now, from our smoke and the fires, obscuring the streets. Even with luta it would be difficult to see into.

I signed for the ganger with me to swap my wamba and fieldbelt for his jerkin, and for him to run for the riverside. He looked at me in shock as I handed it over, would have said something but for the urgency of my instruction, for I was leaving myself few options against such a foe as this without a belt. I kept back a couple of the pouches I thought I would need later. I would make it to The Riddle under the smoke that had now spread throughout the quarter.

He took my bow and we descended.

"Thank you," I whispered, "your family will be taken care of if you don't make it."

It helped him to hear it; he had been flinching with every sound, aware he was far out of his depth. He headed out to Blenner, attempting to make it across the avenue that Blenner and The Riddle intersected on, and past The Riddle's stables to the dock buildings.

The Agents would be busy there; at least forty men armed with bows were intended to slow them or finish them, a killing zone and most of the buildings rigged with trips.

As the ganger left I closed my eyes, feeling the world about me. There was a stillness that gave me the confidence the killer had taken the bait. I climbed up to the roof where he had just been and looked across to The Riddle, a rough but busy inn at this northwest edge of the riverport. I saw the smoke eddy where the ganger had run, I heard the slapping of someone running along tiles on rooftops just south of The Riddle, then saw the silver outline of the killer pursuing him. I had a shot, but a miss would turn the advantage the ganger had bought me. The killer moved over those tiles as surely as on grass, as fast as a horse. Once he'd dropped off the house out of sight, heading for the dockside, I dropped down myself. I had no gangers here, all dead. There was screaming from those injured or dying, the blast of horns from militia as they moved towards me and The Riddle, making their force seem larger than it was, but only a few of the Quarter remained to offer resistance now. The gangers had the best plant that could be concocted, but the sporebags of the Agents, the oilbags that gave off noxious vapours, easily overcame their masks and brews and they were dying in their homes.

As I approached The Riddle, I signalled to those on the roof of the inn and the heavy main door opened to admit me.

"What the fuck is this, Kailen!" said Ostler as I entered the bar-room. "My crew are being butchered by some Agent seems you can't lay a finger on yourself and my quarter is being butchered otherwise while Darin waits for his masters to clear us out." He had a captain with him, the rest of his men spread through the inn.

"Bar the shutters, no bows, lock us in. We gain the initiative."

"They'll burn it down," said his cap.

"No, they will want to know I died; they won't risk it."

"Fuck you, Kailen," said Ostler, "we're going, you can do this yourself. I'm not dying here at the hands of an army of Reds for some shit you did when I was swaddled."

"I'll be sure to tell your mother you ran."

His fist travelled a foot or so between us before I turned it out with my left hand, carrying through to punch him. The cap was on edge, loyalty with Ostler, respect with me. Ostler wavered on his feet, hurt

78

just enough to be stilled, but not enough to drop him. That would have been counter-productive. I glanced at his cap.

"The other gangers will bring you in, as one of Ostler's caps, but don't let me stop you."

He nodded immediately, with surety. Ostler was blessed with good caps. He turned and headed up the staircase, whistling the orders with his mouthpiece.

I heard someone coughing, disastrous in this situation.

"Help me, Ostler, we can't defend this bar, we need to control the staircase." I stood at the end of an oak table. He took a deep breath and lifted the other end. We turned it over against the main door and jammed another table against the door that went through to the coop and stable.

Men were running past The Riddle for the dockside. It was a rout. I followed Ostler upstairs. From the best room the inn could offer I dragged a bedstead out and pushed it onto the staircase, limiting access. Now there were two floors to control, bunkrooms that deck-hands and bargemen used on the long runs from the north.

The easiest access now would be the shutters of the window over-looking the roof to the stables. I waited in that room with the Cap and two of the defending gangers. The floor had spikes nailed into it behind the window, making it hard for anyone coming in to do so easily or quietly. There were calls out along Blenner as the militia and Reds moved up towards The Riddle. I could hear them pushing rakes, looking for the traps. The men on the roof above us began shooting. It lasted a few minutes. Then the banging at the bar door downstairs started. I went to the doorway at the end of this floor. At the opposite end, and in the middle at the second stairwell, gangers stood watching me as I pointed to the sounds of feet and hands scaling the walls and trying the shutters, the barest squeaks as they tested resistance. I could feel at least eight moving to the second floor. They signed the movement to the gangers in the upper rooms, who tapped the beams, messaging those on the roof.

Two on the roof were hit and fell. Then I heard swords, a thump as two grappled. More bodies hit the ground before it went still.

Downstairs there was a crack of wood. They were inside. Two gangers on the second floor were coughing, doing their best to muffle it but unable to stop. I realised then I had made a very serious mistake. I gave in to my rage for a moment, kicked a door nearby off its hinges.

I lifted my mask and as soon as I tasted the air I knew it. Aconite. These men had been in here for a few hours, the first symptoms a difficulty breathing, swelling of the throat. Which had to mean the assassin had been in here prior to that, coating the rooms. He'd thought of everything.

"Why are you smiling?" asked Ostler.

"I have met my match, and learned a lesson I have taught others many, many times."

"What does that mean?"

"It means I'm sorry, Ostler. The plan I conceived by which you could defend your territory with conviction, to succeed in it and send a message to your foes, it has been undone by whoever has been killing Reds and gangers alike. If they weren't killing Reds I'd think it was the work of a Fieldsman."

"They're the Post's top assassins, right? Reporting to The Red himself?"

"Yes. While I doubt it is a Fieldsman, I had not planned for an intervention of that calibre. The rooms around us have been coated with a poison, it's in the air. Take your men, shout down that we surrender, throw your weapons down as evidence. Your lives will be spared and you will see your families again, because if they kill you then they lose the other scapos not to mention the rest of the slums. Tell them I will be waiting in my room, take my sword as evidence of my intent."

"I'll be killed anyway," said Ostler; "these men won't follow me if I surrender to the fucking militia! You've given my quarter to Darin." He shook his head, on the verge of tears. It was good for his men to see this. It would mean a lot to them. I leaned close to him, so his men would not hear.

"Your family is safe and happy in Harudan, Ostler, I've given you that. As one of my academy masters was fond of telling us, everything changes. You have militia in the building and a killer hunting me that will make certain of your death if you resist. I told you that you would be King Scapo by morning, a platitude you may have thought, but in the few weeks I've been here I've discovered more about you feuding scapos than you have yourselves in the years you've been killing each other over a few muddy streets. If not King Scapo by morning, then a year at most.

"Darin is a puppet of the militia, but Andarin has been informing them about all Darin's crew's movements and thus Andarin was, until very recently, King Scapo. Reed, however, is your more deadly enemy. Andarin's dealings with the militia, now compromised by the removal of his lackey that he talked of the other evening, means he lacked the capacity or intelligence to spread his bet. Thus he is weak, particularly so now, as this assault on your slum will be painted as an uprising of gangers threatening order for their own greed. You need to look at Reed's quarter. He has a number of guilds with wareshouses there. Can you name the four biggest, besides the Post?" He shook his head. "No. I thought not. That will be your next move, when you have worked out how to overcome Darin and reclaim the Indra Quarter. Find out who those guilds are; you'll find out that they have influence over the Crag's Master, then find out what that influence is. Then you have the Master. When you have him, you will have Andarin and Darin, for they have no allies in power here, and you will be able to trade the knowledge of that influence to those in power to further your own end and simultaneously weaken Reed."

"How do you propose I do all that from a cell?"

"There is one other thing I will give you for free. This cap, these gangers, I've worked with them this past week, they are very capable men. I'm sorry you lost so many. You lean on them and they run things for you, but that is not the same as trusting them, nor do you support or listen to them. They are good soldiers, they've not deserted you or me and for this I promise recompense will come. Throw away that betony inla mix, find a kannab mix that weans you down but will keep you alert enough to make decisions. Win them back, as you won them to you on your way to Scapo. Start by taking at least half your stash, wherever it is, and sharing it among them for their families. In particular, there's one of Senis's crew, he sacrificed his life for me. He'll be dead nearby, wearing the wamba I had, the grey one, black stitching. These men will repay your kindness many times over in the years to come."

I gave him a few moments to absorb my advice.

"What are you going to do?" he asked. "You're not going to surrender."

"I'm going to give myself a quick and painless death, something I'll very much be denied by those downstairs. Araliah will run my estate, she's been doing it for years."

He nodded. "It was an honour." I shook hands with him and his men as they gathered at the top of the stairs that led down into the bar.

I closed the door to my room and sat on the floor, listening to the hollering of a negotiation.

The assassin would now know I was at The Riddle, and he had known I would be there at some point. The Agents from the docks will have converged also. There was no other way out, not with this calibre of ally and not without my fieldbelt and bow. I sensed the fall was coming too, the brew wearing off. And there would be torture. I had never been tortured deeply, though I knew enough of the procedure. I could not risk revealing what I knew of the whereabouts of any of the Twenty I had recently seen, Stixie, Bense, or the location of Gant and Shale, never mind my beloved wife and those other interests that of necessity were to remain private. From a pocket in my wamba I took a small vial, kept back from the fieldbelt I gave my decoy. It is a powerful mix that I have no time to outline the origin and rarity of. I confess that I wished to meet the man who had brought me to this, for instinct told me who it must be. I had so many questions for him, but not at this price.

And I was tired. I've been tired for such a long time. The years "brown and wither me" as the saying goes, and the world over which I've had some mastery has pressed me slowly into its history from its present. Until now. Perhaps now I can sleep.

I'm sorry, Araliah, my love. You deserved better.

Kailen and The Corner

An account, by General Lin of the Ten Clan, of how Kailen brought a potentially lengthy siege to an almost immediate and profitable conclusion, circa 641 OE.

Goran

I was lieutenant of a small crew and we were fighting at "The Corner", the stretch of our border with the Red Hills that also bordered the Wilds. Incursions from the Wilds were bad enough but those Red Hills shitholes would have a scorching and be leaving about signs enough to make it seem it was Wildmen. Then, when we send a force there we find there's Red Hills soldiers telling us they had killed the Wildmen and claimed the land for themselves, knowing a dispute over their actions would have repercussions.

There were a few years where the border was pushed back a fair way because of this, some four hundred square miles and some parts of the Hiscan Road, losing us the emporia and the levies we could charge. More than this, it was causing us a plant problem. We were using the calabar bean in our pastes. The southern Virates had recently been shipping it over after some of the guilds got Post backing to buy land over there. The calabar was effective against the Wildmen, and without it we were back on our own white narcissus, which they were getting a counter for.

We knew we had to take our land back, so three of the clans put word out for mercenaries to bolster our combined army, which I'm sorry to say was a bit of a shambles, infighting all over. I didn't know then Kailen's Twenty or any of the other mercenaries that were with

83

our column, one of four columns that the generals had decided on, and we were to reclaim two big forts that were once ours near the Red Hills border fifty miles south of The Corner. General we had at the time was a cock, fair at swordplay and cards but bloody useless at managing the army, so this mercenary who was hired, Kailen, took that on after a couple of the captains fell ill. He had his drudhas cooking our mixes. Fuck me, never risen like that before or since. I heard our Captain had let them have the run of our drudha tents but fewer come out of them than we would have thought and they were always arguing with Kailen, the younger one in particular.

Soon as Kailen took charge, seemed we all got paid on time and fed, and one of his crew, we ended up calling him Digs, he put the mining crews together and got them singing, getting the column's forts up and down faster than they'd ever done them on our march to the border. Then we hear him shouting at a captain; hard not to, being as the lieutenants' tents were near the captains. Seemed there were orders being given by the general that were contrary to what Kailen and the others were commanding. I heard then that Kailen went to the general and was giving him an earful. The general was saying that he'd never be lectured to by a mercenary. His captains were in uproar, not liking I think how these mercs were showing them how it was done, showing them up too, getting their ranks through their names and nought else. But the merc said he'd pay the general twice his purse if the siege lasted longer than four days. Couldn't back down then the general, he says yes. Then this Kailen spends a few hours talking to the soldiers that were camped up, his whole crew did and all, these mercs handing out brandy and some threaded kannab that their drudha worked up and the soldiers were happy to wag chins with him.

Then he gets us lieutenants together, tells us he thinks the captains and general are a pack of cocks who weren't fit to drink our piss and that we'd get this siege done and the fort taken the following night. His man Elimar was one for wine and he had a cask that Kailen's crew sat with us and drank and there wasn't a song they didn't know and they had a woman in their crew, Bresken, singing as dirty as the rest of them, a fair voice too what paired well with another of them, Bense. A fine night I can recall even now.

He then promptly goes off the following day and doesn't return until sundown the following evening, him and a few of his crew. We all thought him and his crew had done one on account of his bet, because the purse they took was big by all accounts. General had lost it by then, demanded a siege council to sort out a plan, and when he called Kailen to him he demanded they get working on his plan because he didn't need their gold just to get out of a bet they couldn't deliver; he was going to have their sweat and effort.

At this Kailen just makes the general another wager; had to know that he loved gambling. He says that if he can take the fort without a single drop of blood being shed the following morning the general was to swap out his captains for the lieutenants, and he named us, and he then told him he could be assured that his generalcy would be a glorious one if he did it. Would he accept it? The captains were all for cutting Kailen out of the purse at that point, but by then of course the quartermasters and us lieutenants piped up seeing as how we'd got fed and organised better since they came along and we had little time for the shower of shit the general surrounded himself with. The general laughed at him, conceded it to an approving roar from his captains and told us to prepare for the siege once we'd reached midday. The captains joined him as well in that, giving Kailen their opinion of his attitude and arrogance. I shut my mouth of course, the rest of us did, because we could see there was something in this crew, but the others couldn't see it; they said he was a man coasting on the excellence of his drudhas, and it may be that was true in part.

Kailen and his crew then proceed to get lashed and snore away the night. The next morning he rolls a parch on an arrow and his man Stixie puts it over the wall with that massive bow of his. Not an hour later out walks the castellan with a child in his arms, his own, and he's on his knees before the general begging for the antidote to save his boy's life. He's shaking, pale like he'd been vomiting.

There's a cheer goes up at that, the general is red faced, as furious as I ever saw him. Terms were accepted and the garrison is led out.

I got drunk with Kailen that night, me and the lieutenants that he had promoted, because we weren't letting those fuckers switch it back about somehow. I had to ask how he did it. He was dismissive, said he just asked all the soldiers he could who of them had hailed from these parts and if any had been to the fort, asked about the fort, when it was built, and he asked about the family lines in this district. Then he went looking for those living all about here that had been dispossessed of their land, living wild or enslaved or otherwise and asked them too, and some told him of the cave that was the secret entrance a mile or so out, as there was always one where a large fort on the borders was concerned and they told him also that the garrison had families that travelled with it after the initial occupation. Others that had traded in there before the occupation were able to give him the lie of it inside. Then he got a man in there on the secret way with some concoction of his drudhas strong enough only to put the children out and make the rest that ate that morning sick. All he had to do then was just put the letter over the wall describing to them what was happening and that we had the antidote and that the children would get worse and die horrible. He wasn't lying, for some did. But it was a poison that stopped the blood, so the bet was won after all, and many lives saved.

So if I became a general, and if the Ten Clan took back much of the land they'd lost, it was because Kailen taught me to ignore privilege and to understand, properly understand, the field of battle before committing a man or woman to it.

Chapter 5

Galathia

This continues Galathia's account of the events at the Crag. I've separated it because it concerns events immediately after Kailen's own account of the siege and its conclusion.

Goran

"Galathia, we could not expect to have had a chance to confront him," said Laun. "You saw what it was like out there. That assassin has killed as many of us as he has gangers. We did not have control of the assault."

"He's killed Kailen. Who knows what he learned of the Twenty before Kailen died."

"This ganger, Ostler, denies that the assassin could have reached Kailen," said Laun.

He could have been sleeping, except he was too still. It was some comfort to see this man, considered a legend by so many, dead in a ghastly little inn. It was fitting, although I understand Laun might not have been happy for me to say that, herself a mercenary. He looked older of course than when last I saw him as a girl, smaller, the way they all shrink once they're paid out, though he hadn't gone to fat, still must have led a disciplined life.

The bargirl was with us in the room, covering Kailen over with a sheet in preparation to wrap him and take him out.

"What are we doing to Ostler to ensure he has given us all the information he has regarding Kailen?"

"He appears to know very little," said Alon, who had the shutter open and was leaning on the ledge, looking out to the wareshouses.

"I suppose some gentle questioning was all that was required."

"Galathia, please, we must defer here to the militia and the Master of the Crag. This is their territory. Ostler is their prisoner."

"Not good enough. I want to see him. Laun, can the Reeve intervene?"

"We have lost many Reds and some Agents. The Reeve is aware of our request. I'm sorry, Galathia, but it appears Kailen had rigged the entire quarter against us, every doorway, sill, the lanes themselves. Bowmen everywhere. We could not get here sooner without losing more, and I was not losing any more of my crew today. Four dead since we arrived. Galathia, please, listen to Alon. I have men to bury and work to do."

She was shivering, the fall was building. She would need to rest soon, pay the colour.

I felt for her of course, I had known Ry'le and Ranz well, as I had Syle and Faré. Nevertheless, it was almost unheard of for a Marschal to lose so many of their crew, especially one of the best. I couldn't help that this frustrated me, that the situation couldn't have been anticipated better. Laun was a remarkable woman, Ranz particularly adored her I think, and she, of course, knew it.

A man entered, introducing himself as the proprietor of The Riddle.

"We has to take 'im," he said. "It isn't the custom 'ere for the dead to stay above ground overnight. Don't know what 'e took an' what infection 'e has neither." The proprietor kept his head bowed. Both he and the bargirl took an arm and dragged Kailen past us towards the door. A vial rolled away across the floor. Laun picked it up and sniffed it. It must not have been obvious what the ingredients were.

"Tofi?" she called. "Stand back from him, 'keep. His body isn't moving until my drudha has inspected it. It appears he might have poisoned himself."

"Will he have been infected with something we could catch?" I asked.

"You might get that kind of behaviour west of the Sar; Rhosidians or those savages in Cassica; but not here," said Alon.

"We should see the Reeve, I wish to see this Ostler," I said. I had no intention of letting up.

"Leave it, woman!" Alon had some colour in his cheeks it seemed, almost as much as the last time he was underneath me.

"What's bothering you, husband?" I asked. I enjoyed his outbursts.

"You. Everyone here is trying to protect you. Over a hundred dead, I'm sure, from the piles of bodies they've been carting off to the fields. You've almost had your own head taken off through your sheer bloody refusal to stay away from bloodshed and you have the temerity to criticise the Marschal paid to protect you on your travels about the hell-holes of the world looking for some of the most dangerous mercenaries that ever lived."

"You're paying the bills, you agreed to it. You know how important this is, to revenge my father and our family."

"I know it better than you do, it seems, or you wouldn't be dressing up to play as an Agent."

He was being ridiculous; he knew full well what I had endured in the years following my exile from Citadel Argir.

"Come now, Alon, the reason we were here is Kailen. We cannot leave until we've learned everything he's shared with those that had chosen to put their lives down for him. They aren't going to share if they're not going to be punished."

"You sound like you wish to apply the irons yourself."

Tofi, Laun's drudha, came in. He had a second fieldbelt over his shoulder, his hands were covered in blood from treating the wounded outside.

"Can you tell if there's anything in this room we should be worried about?" asked Laun. She gave him the vial that had been on Kailen.

He sniffed the vial, then took a small flask from his belt, swigged, spat and poked out his tongue.

"Cannot tell what this vial contained, but you need to get out of here, now. The air is thick with aconite. That explains why some of those gangers were coughing up blood. I thought it was spores. Downstairs, we'll have the shutters open please, throughout the inn."

"Can we take the body now?" said the bargirl.

"Yes," he said.

The bar was full of militia and Reds. There were two boys at the serving table, one crying as he served the men cup after cup, some fresh loss being endured while he worked.

"Laun, fetch us a bottle of wine. We should sit over here, this booth will allow us to talk freely."

She went behind the serving table to one of the crates of wine and brought a bottle and three cups back, first folding some coins into the tearful boy's hand. Then she gestured for three of her crew to sit near us. The assassin was unaccounted for.

"Aconite is a very powerful poison, is it not? Very rare?"

"Yes, Gala. It puzzles me why it is so thick in the air if The Riddle has been closed off to all outsiders for at least a day. We shouldn't be affected after this short time."

"This proves my point," said Alon. "Galathia, I have been tolerant of your wish to discover what happened to the Argir Book, containing the royal recipes, and your heirlooms, but you forget that these things do not confer your right to rule as does your blood. Your people, the people of Argir, there is a mood there, a dissatisfaction with the council that administrate its affairs. Taxes have been raised, but promises have been broken. There is call to establish your royal line again, the line of Welvale."

"How do you come by this? What business have you with my homeland that I do not know?"

"Many of our caravans, our merchants, explore supply up through Donag and Hope, turning Post merchants themselves on the make. They would not be doing their job if they did not listen to these merchants and the traders coming south with whale bone and oil. I would prefer, now that this Kailen is dead, and this mystery assassin of yours is taking care of the rest, you focus on your homeland, your birthright. I am in a position to help you significantly more with the political matters of Argir."

"And when did you imagine you'd tell me all of this, husband?" I admit I was angry. I was perhaps still overcome by seeing Kailen again, the man who did so much to influence my father to keep the Twenty by his side, bleeding us dry. Now my husband, my dear Alon, talking politics when he had only previously talked of profit.

"You are adept at multiplying coins, Alon, but affairs of state, the court and nobles, they speak a quite different language."

"All language, however decked in the blossoms of honour, right and wrong, all is reduced in the end to commerce. The latter begets the former. You need to put down your sword and let me help you. You told me the Post was likely to have been behind the coup that saw those other Citadels and Argir's guilds remove your family, the line of Welvale. The Post wanted control of the North Passage and its trade; Argir was key to it. The agreement must have favoured them then but they and their allies in those guilds have been abusing it since. I know well the dissatisfaction with the Post and those it has placed in the administration there."

"They must believe that Petir and I are dead, after so long."

"There are rumours to the contrary." He looked satisfied with himself, as men often do when they believe themselves to be in control.

"I asked you once and I'll ask you again: when were you going to tell me that you were speaking of these things? Of my life and my people? Because you certainly did not speak of them over our cups, as much as you like to think I'm bored by you."

"I imagine, Gala, you were preoccupied with planning your adventures in the Virates, or in the Red Hills and Ten Clan, sleeping rough with your mercenary friends. You chase a bunch of old men while your kingdom is being torn down from within and without. Incursions from Upper Lagrad are making things worse."

"It was what was done to my family by this council, my being left for dead, these things have been unpunished. If I cannot have justice for myself, how can I seek it for my people?"

"Now there's a fine sentiment, there's the princess that would be queen."

"What did you marry me for, Alon? Was this commerce? This vatch, this bosom?"

His teeth clenched and he stood up. "You know full well. We will need to discuss how we should proceed, because I can no longer support your pursuit of these mercenaries, not after today, and certainly not if this assassin is going to kill Laun's crew, paid to protect you, without any even remotely effective retaliation. I can and will support your return to the throne of Argir and my guild are working to that end with allies in Argir, some within the council itself. Laun, we're leaving, I don't wish to be in this slum any longer than I have to be.

Enough of these people have died over this foolishness, enough of ours as well."

Laun kept her head in her cup a moment before looking at me. Alon knew I had little time for these displays of his. I knew him well enough that the answer wasn't a confrontation. It would be more wine, a show of contrition, a fuck and then the application of reason when he was clear. I would have to tease out what he knew of Argir. I admit I was surprised by how I felt to hear that the Citadel and its people were struggling. Alon couldn't have been more surprised than me to hear me say "my people". It was all I could do to manage the swell of feeling that came with those words, but I wasn't ready to admit that to him, I needed time with it. Strange how the one memory of my mother comes back when I think of home.

I gave my husband a smile, affected some humility and stood to leave with him.

Across from our booth, through the militia getting rowdy with their ales, sat the assassin. He was smiling, waiting to catch my eye. There was no mask or leathers, just a filthy apron, such as a blacksmith would wear, over a vest and a skirt. His eyes were almost fully amber, warm and distant as the sun, his colour an exotic mix of blue and red and only a fuzz of grey about his head.

"Laun!" I hissed. Just then a group of men came in, a couple of them with their arm around one that must also, like the lad serving, have lost someone he loved. I lost sight of the killer.

"What is it, Gala?"

"The assassin, he's over there."

She stood up, hand on her sword hilt.

"Where?"

"Blacksmith's apron, blue and red colouring."

She stepped forward, sword now free of its sheath, its poison dripping on the floor. The bar went quiet, the men that came in parting before her. I stood, looking through the gap she'd created, but he'd gone, of course. I looked about, ran to the shutters and looked out into the street, but there was still smoke, and a mist rising with the evening that obscured the world outside.

Chapter 6

Gant

Looked like miserable work. Raining, and the militia and some Reds were cussing as they were raking the mud. They were digging up blades and caltrops and such, and we guessed it must have been Kailen what had set it up for a siege. They had stretchers out and there was a fair mob what were mouthing off at the militia as they made the streets safe to walk down.

Rain was good, an excuse for our hoods and so our colour wouldn't be too plain.

We found a woman and a dut in her arm, head down and trudging through the mud, no shawl on her but on her baby and it crying.

"Silver piece fer the whereabouts o' The Riddle?" asked Shale.

She looked up, put her hand to her baby instinctively. Happens a lot with us if we surprises people, and she took the silver piece with some wonder in her eyes, pointing then to a building we couldn't quite see for people, the edge of it in view, lit up and busy for the middle of the day.

There were arguments about. Merchants had moved in with their carts to sell to those who had suffered or lost from what had gone on. We hung about a bit, listening to what the poor were telling the guards of their sorrow and we bought some of what the merchants had brought to give out to those who looked desperate, and we learned more of what had just happened the previous day. Someone called a scapo had been arrested and some other scapo was giving out blankets and food about the Indra Quarter. Seemed scapo was their word for one what led a crew of gangers.

Achi was right that Kailen was in trouble, but trouble had arrived before we did, Agents and Reds and the militia here killing more than a hundred and losing at least half as many it seemed, which give us a clear understanding of which side Kailen must have been on, for if he was on the militia side, there would have been no losses to speak of, given their other advantages.

The rain got a bit heavier then so we made for The Riddle, splitting up and approaching from two ways to better cover the lie. I tagged on the back of a crew that must have worked on the river, heading to the inn for a soak. Inside were a good number of men, must have been up all the last night with whatever work had to be done. There was the usual big fug of smoke from some cheap hemp, probably cut plenty to fit the purse of a tenter or waterman.

We got service quick when they saw our skin and scabbards and they moved away from the serving table.

"We're here about a man stayed a while a few weeks back," said Shale to the barkeep.

He give nothing away.

"Enough fer a room fer a few days?" Shale flashed the edge of a gold coin at him.

The man was shrunken, wiry and tired, eyes furtive, no doubt with years of smuggling and barfights. Gold coins didn't drop in his pocket as a rule.

"Em! Get these two boys some ale. You'd best come through, gents, 'e said there might be a pair of you, what knows the Ditty of Wild Kitty?"

Shale cleared his throat and surprised us both with the rendition:

> All sing for Wild Kitty, those heaving titties that 'braced us
>   in the Hogger's Red.
> A brewer's daughter she drank what Gant bought her and pissed
>   over his sleeping head.

"Hogger's Red'll do," said the barkeep. Must have been the words Kailen needed him to hear, but to hear it again reminded me of the state I was in when I woke with that girl gone the following day.

"I'm Robbo, follow me." Up some sticky, smoke-blackened stairs we were led along to a door.

I looked at Shale as we got to the landing over the stair and he shook his head. Kailen would have been out to us by now.

"This was 'is room. Been aired, all of it washed down."

"Aconite," said Shale, "in the air."

He was right and all. This was a fierce and pricey mix to be on the air now. The base would have masked it for Kailen not to know it, but even so, the room had been aired.

"He die in this room then?" I asked.

"He did, but it weren't the aconite, was a poison he took 'imself to avoid bein' caught."

Shale shook his head and I was the same.

"I'll leave you two then, Em'll be up with what 'e left in the event 'e didn't get to see you or Achi again."

"Kailen kill himself? I'm not buyin' it," said Shale, after Robbo left.

I didn't know what to say. I was angry at us arriving so late, and uneasy with how we were due to be killed but for him, sending his men and saving our lives though his was in a danger he couldn't get out of. I wasn't buying it either, Kailen killing himself, but the 'keep had said what he said and it was as plain as that. It was still as though I'd been punched, and we both needed a moment.

"I need to get out of these leathers, Shale, wound's playin' up an' I want to go see where they put him."

Shale went and stood at the open shutters, beyond which were the big storage sheds on the edge of the docks. Smoke from the buildings that burned down with the brothel was still on the air, whole place felt agitated, bruised.

I give him a moment as I could see he was struggling with the news of Kailen.

Em came in then, a tray with some fresh bread on it, pot of butter and a bottle of brandy. On her shoulder was a big satchel, which she let down to the floor surprisingly easy.

"His things."

"What were his body like?" I asked.

"He was just lying there, like he was asleep. He had this with him too, didn't want to drop it in the satchel."

It was a necklace, a fine rope of silver and a mottled jade stone polished up. Etched in it was an acorn. Not something of Harudan, an oak. I was always curious about it.

"We'd like to see where you put him," I said, "pay our respects."

"You go, Gant, I needs a drink. Can we 'ave this room, lovely girl?"

"Welcome," she said.

We ended up getting some potatoes and onions with a bit of gravy before I got Em to show me where Kailen was put in the world. She led me out past the city wall the slum was against and there were a lot of pits dug up on a hill around there. Where they put him was still raw earth waiting for grass, like a patch dug for a garden.

"What was he like, the time he were here?" I asked her.

"He was good to us, me dad and me. Seemed to care about the people in our quarter. The scapo we had that run it all, Ostler, he was a bit useless, but Kailen would just work with his captains an' they would soon come to him for advice an' though he kept himself hidden, he helped sort out their disputes an' problems wi' the militia and such. He had me runnin' about, and a few others, as he was looking for you an' those others he said he used to go to war with. He had the colour like you an' all. Handsome." She smiled awkwardly and left me on this shallow slope that give a look over the Crag to the falls beyond it, leading to highlands too dark to see as the light faded. Lampers were out lighting up the main avenues and the docks below.

Nobody about knew the man lying here and what he did. For all he took purse as a merc he changed the fortunes of kings across most of the Old Kingdoms and some part of the world over the Sar. I seen so much because of him, though it was a tough life few would look in on kindly. He was fair, and he give us reading and writing and gold beyond the reckoning of all but the highest, more than a generation of all those living hereabouts would ever see, whose dead he lay among. Me and Shale would do right by him, and in what followed I hope he would think we did.

I got back some hours later, as I'd had a couple of pipes where he was lying, and thought about what become of us, and about the crew we were. It was the only family I had bar Shale and my sister, and I wondered about what had happened to the others.

Shale was sitting on a chair in the corner by the shutters when I got back to the room, pipe in his teeth and a strong kannab mix on the air while he played with the satchel straps of Kailen's pack on his lap.

"Not opened it then?" I said.

"Din't want to open it without you were here," he said.

"Perhaps we don't touch it till we get to his estate and his woman Araliah."

He took a long draw at that, nodded some moments later and let the smoke rise over his face. "Would be right she opened it, not us," he said.

I didn't sleep that night, my guts were hurting and I was cussing for finding myself being on the run again after all these winters, when I was too wasted and old for what it was going to mean, leaving false tracks and sentrying half the night wherever we went from now on.

"We need to see who's behind this," said Shale, supping a tea and pushing some cheese and a bit of cooked fish under my nose to wake me the next day.

"Lot o' Post about. Don't know if Gilgul an' his boys are goin' to come back here."

"Bin down the lanes and over dockside, takin' a look about while you were sleeping. There's these scapos, gangers that control bits of the Crag, rackets, all the usual, an' their crews bin gettin' taken down a few nights back, some Reds an' all, bein' killed by someone who was after Kailen. Odd thing was that all these Agents got involved, Reds come in from the districts about as well. But if they were gettin' killed, two Agents were butchered I heard, then who is after who?"

I pushed myself upright on the bed and drank down the tea what he'd brought me, cold and sweet as I preferred it.

"I'm still tryin' to figure out why he's killed himself, why he din't figure a way out when he always could and did no matter what the odds. He lose his flint?" I said.

Shale was making a circle with his shoulder, trying to loosen it. We needed to put our compounds on and get set for the day.

"Flint in't something I'd say Kailen could get or lack. He was different to us, no highs or lows you could see, no more than a night on the soak before you'd catch him draggin' The Prince off with him fer the next purse."

97

"Strikes me there's a scapo that's making a noise in this quarter a day after its scapo got put in jail and no other scapo comin' in for a piece either. Has to have backin'," I said.

"We should go see this scapo then, 'ave a word."

"We'll need a dayer brew. If he got any sense right now he'll have his crew about him while he gets this quarter under control."

"Leathers then, let's get us set."

Day brightened a bit as we headed west of the Indra, away from the river. Em told us that was Darin's quarter, fair few guildhalls there, a few proper houses for those that were running the Crag. Lot of river-wives and alms houses, droop joints and the like were in his slums and it wasn't long before we decided to take a cup of ale in a sorry-looking tavern. It went quiet as we went in there, a few looking at us wondering what we were about I'm sure, khaat chewers and a number with pipes. We drank slow.

Em had told us to look out for anyone what wore a tat of a tusk, guessing a boar's tusk, and that would be one of his men.

Whores come onto us of course, once it got into evening proper. Mercs with our sort of colouring were usually good for a few silver if the service was right, and, as we expected, it was getting the locals uneasy. We made a bit of a show of it, to make things worse, squeezing coins into their cleavage and being easy with the slivitz, a liquor what was popular in this part of Hevendor and a bit sweet for me.

Then a fine-looking woman come over, black gown cut a bit more sensible than the whores with their tits done up too tight. Her collar was open and we saw the tusk on her neck.

"You got these girls all randy with your purses. You've not visited the Crag before?"

"No," said Shale.

"Men of your colour, with the greatest respect to my girls, could be tasting the far sweeter fruit I have in the High Sevens." She leaned in to whisper. "You might be upsetting the local boys a little less, who object to the show of wealth. You're bringing trouble." Then she froze, saw our eyes, felt the heat we were giving off. "You are trouble, you're brewed." Shale held her arm to keep her close. The two girls with us eased themselves up and went to the bar.

"You work for Scapo Darin. We'd like to meet him."

"They causing you trouble, Aniy?"

She looked behind her to one of the boys at the serving table, off-duty militia, still in his chains.

"We're fine, Amz." She turned back to us. "You know I can't just walk up to Darin, I don't know where he is, that's how it works."

"Everyone's a bit, what's the word, Gant, on edge? On edge wi' what seems to have happened in the Indra Quarter. All we wants Darin for is a few words on who was causin' the trouble. Don't worry, lovely, we couldn't give a shit about Darin himself, it's just what he knows. Then we're gone."

"It gets difficult for the good people about if we feel like you're refusing to help us," I said.

She glanced at the belts and pockets full of our field gear. We'd come ready for a fight.

"I have to speak to my cap."

We stood up. "We'll come wi' you."

At our standing up a few of the boys also stood, having seen the whores move and seeing this woman obviously in a situation.

She turned about and saw them all.

"For fuck's sake, sit down, 'less you all want to be killed."

Amz walks over to her, a few more stands up.

"She's not leaving with you boys I'm afraid. You don't really know where you are, do you?"

"Fuck, Amz, these are proper soldiers."

He give her an angry look. "I ain't?" As he was looking at her he threw a right and whipped out a dagger at his belt. Sad really. His right was caught in Shale's hand, held fast, and I moved in, knocked his wrist into his side so he dropped the dagger. He struggled for a moment, but may as well have been trying to pull his hand out of a wall.

"I'm goin' to let go o' your hand," said Shale. "Don't throw it at me again or it's comin' off. Are we good?"

He looked at Aniy, who nodded. Shale let him go.

"Lead the way," I said.

We followed her through the silent tavern, some twitching, most smelling of doubt.

After a word with a boy she passed to run an errand for her, though we both suspected it was a coded message, she led us up a short hill to a leatherer's, a few of them what must have been curriers or cordwiners sat on benches outside after their day, smoking a pipe before heading home. It was one of the few buildings round here seemed made of proper stone.

They stood as we approached.

"Aniy!" shouts one, sizing us up. He was about our age, colour faded a bit, face only a mother could love. Must've been the cap. They kissed and embraced and she had no idea we could hear pretty much everything, on a brew, that was said or done a good twenty or thirty feet around us no matter how quiet. There were other men here, in the hovels about us.

"Send one in and get Darin down and out," she said to the cap. "They're brewed, signal the men behind them."

"No need to trouble yer men behind us, Aniy," said Shale. "If he's in there we can get this over and done with in there."

She turned to look at him, surprised.

I drew my sword. "I can feel you thinkin' it. Don't."

"If those boys behind me shoots them arrows," said Shale, "yer all goin' to get torn up like a joint of ham left in the mud fer the dogs."

The old man give a nod over our shoulder. "It's not just them you have to worry about, you arrogant fuckers."

There were eight in front of us come out of the leatherer's, they were on some sort of brew, hot and ready, and they took up clubs, a few with hand-axes, something soldiers of Hevendor were fond of.

"Darin's busy and you're friendless here. Aniy, go inside."

Shutters opened in a few of the hovels and workshops about.

"Lot more arrows than you can manage, gentlemen. Let's have your belts."

We looked at each other, me and Shale, and took some steps forward as though figuring what we ought to do. Then we jumped. I was at the cap as he raised his club to strike. Shale was past me and at the others. None had masks, so once I'd knocked his club up and put him on the back foot I pulled a sporebag off my belt and threw it at the three nearest me. Arrows come in from the sides, a few from behind us, the fewer for us being among their own, one catching in the leather on my leg. It was a chance we had to take. Shale disarmed the one of

100

them and as he died Shale used him to shield himself from the arrows about. I saw more inside taking some brews. Aniy had jumped back and run to some side door into the shop.

Those with the cap I threw my spores at were quick with masks, but enough had got in them that they were struggling and choking. I got out a knife to help with the parrying as they swung in at me. Shale dragged the body shielding him from attack and swung it in through the door to the shop and followed behind it, having dropped three of them that were stood before us a moment ago. I managed to catch one of those on me, sheared through his arm and he fell quick with the poison. One managed to slice my thigh as I braced for two others coming at me but I didn't feel any weakening so it must have been something our dayer could cope with.

I needed to get inside so needed a gap before someone got a clear shot. I flipped the knife I had, threw it to shift the cap out of the way and got my hand into a pouch of dust to throw it out. It give pause a moment and I took my chance with a couple of blows, dropping a young one, sad to say, while another got hit by one of their arrows and I forced the cap back so I could get in the door.

Shale had already got three more of them what were inside, the scapo stood back with Aniy as they squared off. They didn't look too pleased to see me and how it was going. Others come at Shale but each was put back with ease and soon it settled into them fearing to come at him, knowing that the poison, from a few screeching their last, would finish them with only a nick of skin taken.

The cap fought a bit as he come in after me, but whatever dayer he was on wasn't up to it. He defended well enough but once I forced him to the wall by the door, kicking it shut on those outside, I got him across his thigh then into his chest. Those outside were retching now and some run out from the houses about to help them. Darin stood then, stepping among us.

"Stop, just stop, everyone," he said.

Shale took a cloth from a bench nearby and wiped some blood off his face and leathers.

"We told him that, told Aniy too. None of you seems to want to listen," I said, pointing to the cap going spasmic with the poison, shaking out his last bit of life.

"Just wants to talk to you about Ostler an' what went on over in the Indra Quarter," said Shale, putting his sword back in its scabbard.

He had a leatherworker's punch on him, Darin, and was stood by some moulds. If they were his, he was fine at decorating. I had a pain in my belly then. Though bound up well, the fight had pulled at the stitching Shale done on me a few days back. I sat on a stool to ease it.

"My friend Ostler's been put in jail by the Master and there's some that see my offer of support to those he looks after as . . ."

"A land grab," Shale said.

"Indeed, a terrible accusation and one that requires I be cautious until my beneficence is more clearly understood."

"Aren't you a slippery cunt wi' words."

Brew gives us a short temper for sure. His men were dead or shit scared outside, half of them dead in here. I was angry as much for the pointlessness of it and the attention it was going to bring on us.

"Can you tell us what were goin' on?" I asked.

"Few of my boys got killed, someone after information about an old mercenary, Kailen. Then I get summoned to a Marschal and it seems there's others wants this mercenary too, only Ostler was protecting him. This merc someone you know?"

"He was. We're thinkin' of visitin' those who were after him," said Shale. "Mind telling us who that might be?"

"Some big guildmaster, called Alon Filston, from Issana. Had Agents and a Marschal so I heard, a lot of influence too it seems, to get the Master of the Crag and his men to join with them looking for this Kailen. Nobody seems to know who the other killer was."

"There, wasn't that easy, Aniy?" said Shale. She looked at Darin but had nothing to come back with, perhaps afraid of him.

"Whoever that fucking merc was, he's responsible for half my crew being cleaned out, with you two showing up for him. Pleased he's dead. Might actually get back to business now."

Shale raised his eyebrows. I saw a twitch, but they didn't. His knife left his hand, whipped from his belt, smooth as running water. It hit Darin in the chest. He stepped back with a question forming somewhere in his mouth. He looked over at Aniy, eyes widening as he fell dead. As the others sparked up we tore a few sporebags from our belts. It give them pause.

"Happy to kill every one of you, less people to point us out when we leave," I said, "but we makes a point of not killing anyone we in't been paid to or in't trying it on, though in his case disrespecting Kailen's not something we tolerate."

Aniy dropped to where Darin had fallen.

"She got a good way with her," I said, to those on the brink of joining Darin and their captain. "You could do worse than take a few orders from Aniy. You want to build something what's been tore down, choose a woman. You want to tear something down, choose a man. Right now seems you need a woman."

We hooked the bags back on our belts and I asked Aniy for a way out that wasn't the way we come in. She obliged and we climbed through some shutters at the back and headed down a lane the other side of the hill, heading in a loop south then round and up the river to the quarter where we left the horses.

Took us a bath and a heavy meal before we took saddles to the stables and got the horses groomed and ready. We knew Filston was in Issana, wouldn't be difficult to find him, but we had some answers perhaps in Kailen's things, and a need to do right by his wife Araliah. So we headed down to Harudan, southern edge of the Old Kingdoms, what looked out and had a say in the Gulf of Merea.

Between us and Harudan was Hisca. Not much to say of it. We took ourselves out the way some, finding a path through the stars and keeping low in the days under bluffs and in long grasses far from tracks and roads. Shale had him some fanny on a stop to buy some bacon and bread at a farm, her man out in the fields somewhere. He still needed it from time to time. She was perky for us both but I haven't been feeling it for a few years. Pissing was all my cock seemed to have a mind for lately, even after that savage joy that comes with surviving a battle.

Lots of men would wave it about when they're soaked in blood and screaming at the sky for being alive at the end of a fight. Brews were a part of it. Whatever gets men's blood up seems to get their cock up too as often as not. I recall Bresken saying it got her excited, but she was careful enough of course not to go within the Twenty for some. I was sorry to hear, later on, that she had been killed and all.

Times enough, now my warring days are over, I can't sleep for those I killed that floods my eyes when I shut them, having begged for and got no mercy at the end of my sword. A fair share of women with child, duts of boys and girls, old men, I took them all if a scorching was called for. It don't take long for you to get so as you can just shut off the screaming and begging, but deep down it's still there it feels like, coming back more and more over the years, my dreams getting more crowded and nasty, my killings returning so real I could feel them in my muscles again, their howling once more in my ears. Like most soldiers I need plant to sleep, though my saying it here is for the record, I'm not expecting pity.

Shortly enough we were through Hisca to the Gap of Irudan, a ridge of mountains what were the northern border to Harudan. I'd been that way four summers before, also heading to the south of Harudan where you haven't seen the likes in many places, except maybe what I hear of the Dust Coast and Jua of course.

Harudan got fierce war academies and the high communes. They reckon a magist been seen too in the mountains here. It's rich, with the highlands fertile enough for the commune farms to grow masses of shiel and ska for shipping. It was the heart of the old Orange Empire what give us the measure of our years for historical reckoning. We were heading south to the coast, following the stone roads with the other travellers heading to the main ports at Melradan and Filden's Spur. On the higher land were the vineyards and farms made of the bright orange stone what was mined from the peaks north and you saw through all Harudan.

It was a fine sight from up in the Gap looking south to the far coast and then your gaze tracks west to the mountains you're leaving as the range cuts round. I juiced some luta leaves and Shale helped with the pasting of them under my eyelids. It was the last time I was seeing this I knew, and once the juice filled up my eyes I took my horse up a pass leading off the road and Shale even joined for a snifter of brandy while I rested up.

Being where I could see a big piece of the world always made me feel I wasn't worth a scrap, but the same made me feel there was something fine about that.

It wasn't more than a couple of weeks along the roads and we were at the coast and getting the soldiers or the locals we saw to point us to Kailen's estate, a few leagues past Melradan. There were a lot of estates about these parts, palaces of the orange stone and the blue slate roofs what they got from the peaks of Jua and Mount Hope Province. The Senate and their fluffers had places all about, Kailen's da even, though he never got on with him.

Kailen got the top medal from their war academy when he was sixteen winters, youngest who ever got it. His da was made up, as he told it, thought Kailen would get a big naval command against the pirates or a field command pushing their interests somewhere out east.

Kailen just flat turned it down, said the commanders he trained with, a big pile of the Senate's sons and fuckers to a man, treated him like shit all through it. His da was blacksmith born. The pride he had for his da and ma with getting through was all burned up by the time he was speaking at the Senate as the star of their academy.

I said he was a big reader and strong with his words. He wove them pretty to the Senate, speaking strong about the haves and have-nots, the rules they got and the rules we got that are bent to serve them and keep them in their fine stone halls. The papers rained on him from the Silks, shouting with rage and some even laughing for the bullock's balls he had standing there and telling them about their exploiting of the poor and slaves and such.

His da was burned, his ma as proud as you like, though she a fine young daughter of a Senator. Strange how it was. I think his ma saw as he did what a man could make of himself given a fierce will. His da was born poor but was ashamed for he wanted to be one of them.

Kailen for his part found the fine learnings to be so much mist blown away with swords and arrows of the armies that decided things for real. So he took his learnings and he left to become a merc. But not, of course, just any merc. He wanted to be the best, saw that if you could put together a group of the best swords and pirates and drudhas and the like you could charge a fat purse for them to fix the battle in your favour, teaching tactics to the fat rich aristos who held rank, leading crews to learn a few things to ensure you get the odds for a win. It was about him showing all of them that were born to riches that it meant nothing.

What was less obvious to them was the fact his readings of history, heraldry, family lines and so on was fierce enough that he knew which sides to take, which men had the more belly for a fight, which could be counted on to see it through. That was how we got our reputation for never losing a battle we contested, not even at Tharos Falls when it was us twenty held the line and the line could not be crossed.

We stopped at the gate to the estate. Most of the land about was his, olive groves and fruit and a good bit of common land we saw too for his serfs.

Two stood guard, no question as to being trained by Kailen. You could see the drilling in the posture and balance and how they looked us over as we approached. Their scabbard fixings and sword hilts were well worn with use. I didn't recognise them as being with Achi when he freed us from the Post.

We dismounted and Shale explained who we were. I showed them the necklace and we were through. They blew for a girl to come for the horses. It was remarkable but expected, I guess, how she whispered and got them easy to leave us for the stables. One of the guards walked along the avenue that run up to the villa and we waited at the gate with the other till a whistle give us call to head up there.

A few hundred yards of summer sun away we saw Kailen's wife stepping out from the doors of the house. She had black hair and was taller than most men; hazelnut skin and in a thin jade-blue robe. The indigo dye was rare enough around Harudan, let alone the strain for that colour. She was a rich widow. I haven't seen such a beauty in a fair few summers.

She knew about Kailen though, it was on us fierce.

"Gant. Shale. I'm Araliah." She put her arms around each of us and kissed each cheek in the aristo way. Her eyes didn't flinch but they wetted up enough when I held up the necklace and his satchel with his papers. Tears tumbled heavy down her face, her fist whitened with clutching the chain and she held me again, trusting me to keep hold of her for she lost herself with crying. She was strong smelling of cloves and fruit, her hair was soft like rainwater to touch and I couldn't see how Kailen could have left this woman and this home for anything.

I squeezed her so as she'd come to and, stepping aside and wiping her nose on her arm like a dut, she moved us inside to the courtyard. She took Shale's arm and I followed them through the door. She was still shaking.

As we moved in it was busy with what seemed to be the quarter-master and the farmers yabbering about the cases of oil and marma-lades from the smell of it all. This was all laughing though, not the haggling and vicious yelling of most estates we'd been to. Seems like he brought something of the book learning back here after he laid his sword down. They stopped a moment as she moved through. The quartermaster saw something was wrong but after a quick glance at us he read it right and he ushered the others to continue their work, knowing the time was not yet for speaking of what happened to Kailen.

Through some shutters we were led to the main dining tables, easy to seat thirty I reckoned. We were about to start untying our leathers when she began it for us. Fast and strong with much practice, she took off the wambas and jerkins and found us some of his wool shirts, using these moments to let it all sink in. Shale give me a swift look that showed he was moved by her attentions. It cut him up fierce, her showing us the courtesies and airs what weren't due the likes of us. It was clear we stank from the weeks out and my wound was not doing well. She didn't once scrunch her nose.

She was shaking at the same time though, looking us over, as though some part of us, for being near him, meant him being near. I can't write enough to say what I was feeling.

She rang a bell what was on the table and a girl appeared.

"Cheeses, chicken and three bottles of red from the old cellar," said Araliah to her. "Gant, you're wounded, you look also to be on some Alfra mix. Amahle, could you ready a horse for Stimmy? I want him to leave in the morning for the Commune."

The girl gone, Araliah sat at the head of the table.

"Achi's here then? Stimmy was wi' his crew. They helped us, Kailen helped us," said Shale.

"Someone's bin tryin' to kill us," I said, "and looks like they got to Kailen I'm sorry to say. But not before he managed to get Achi an' some of his boys to break us out."

"He called fer us in the Crag. We came as quick as we could," said Shale.

She had noticed the way I'd been walking through and how I held myself at the table. The travelling seemed to catch up with me fierce and I couldn't keep a straight back. I saw her and Shale pass a look.

"Achi is on another errand for Kailen. He may not even know. He's a good man, I hope I can tell him myself. Let me show you to your room, Gant, we can talk over everything tomorrow. There's a posting I need to show you."

I was grateful. I slept till morning.

To shouts of the wagon drivers moving out of the estate I woke, and saw robes Araliah must have left for me on a chair by the bed. My stomach was nagging at me bad. Shale come in shortly with her and they set about my wound. She didn't flinch at the state of me. Kailen must have not been a pretty sight either with nothing on. She helped a bit but watched for the most part as Shale got the wound dressed and helped with my compounds; knees, elbows, neck and some swigs with water. He knew what I needed all these years and was quick about it, and I did the same for him, as I always do.

"Gant, you look better for the rest," she said. "Stimmy has gone to the Commune for plant. Shale's told me what it is you need and they'll be quick about it when they see my seal." She sat on the bed next to me. "Shale told me also that it was aconite that killed my husband." I give him a look and he shook his head a touch so's she wouldn't see. "I know enough to know that whoever killed him and your old crew must be well funded to afford it. It makes some sense of that poster I was given. Now, put that thing away and I'll find you both some food." She smiled as she walked out, first proper smile, and it took me away a moment.

On the large table we sat at last night Araliah had put out a notice, drawings of men with swords in hand and a coinpurse between them. Kailen's satchel was also there on the table, still buckled shut. The words on the drawing, in King's Common, Juan and Issanaian were:

A sum of five gold coins for knowledge of the whereabouts of any of the vile mercenary soldiers known to have sought purses with Kailen's Twenty. Message to Guildmaster Alon Filston of Ithil Bay. The Post waives its fee.

"That'll explain a lot," said Shale, "because we heard about this Filston as being him that was behind what happened at the Crag. But five gold coins! A lord's ransom that."

"This is the reason I could not use the Post to tell Kailen, though he may also have seen it."

"Where is it from?" I said.

"It was found by one of his father's retinue that was visiting Issana with a Senate party. There were a few posters around the city. This was over a month ago. Kailen had been away a long time looking for you survivors. I expect this satchel holds some answers for us."

Thick slabs of bacon, still sizzling from the pan, were brought in. We were kings at a feast but my eyes could eat more than my stomach could take with pain like stabbing pins as I filled it. Fucking Blackhands. Still, it was warming to see that Araliah used only a knife, like us, to cut the bacon, and her fingers to eat it. She said she enjoyed not being an aristo and she was soon asking for honey to dip pieces of bacon in, which we followed in doing, for it was near perfect-tasting honey, and an ease to my guts.

"We din't want to open the satchel without you opened it first, din't seem right," said Shale.

"Thank you. I'd be happy for you to open it now."

In it we found papers what were correspondence from various quartermasters and the Post and so on where he'd been finding out where we had all got to, the Twenty. In there was a letter from Forthwald confirming our purse down in the Red Hills, which is how he managed to get Achi to us just in time. Letters were in there too from Achi and others of the crew he'd got looking after him and his estate now, all travelling about the Old Kingdoms and over the Sar looking for us.

We saw letters from The Prince and all, what he appeared to have kept a close friendship with and was now helping run some big guild out of Jua.

There was a letter in there what was addressed to Araliah and she took that and read it to herself and left us for a while.

There was a letter to us too. I can't put it as well as him, so have copied his hand here:

Enemies close on me as they closed on us at Tharos. This time I do not have the Twenty. I have chosen and prepared the ground of the battle, however, and for that they will be sorry.

There is a letter here for Araliah that I hope you are honourable enough not to read, but to get to her if you can.

I sent Achi, the captain of my personal retinue who helps manage my estate's affairs and its caravans, south to the Red Hills to find you. I feared you were also a target for these assassins that, from what Achi may have said and from these papers you will learn, have killed so many of us. We dare not assume it is many assassins, it may just be the one, but such a one would be unlike any I have encountered, given the detail of what follows.

I fervently hope this letter finds you alive. I heard you have become legends among the men fighting the Virates on the eastern borders of the Red Hills, on missions to starve out the aggressor on soil that is foreign to him. The Blackhands have too little alignment in their leadership to coordinate the various clansmen to adopt a coherent strategy for war and supply. I trust you have found much success; it is the correct strategy. Alas, you have a new and deadlier enemy.

Harlain was killed in Tetswana, in his royal pavilion in the middle of the Tetswanan desert, every man and woman at the gathering also killed. He was their king, a unique honour for a mercenary like us. Milu was killed in Alagar, another that had paid out and left to be a great horse-singer for a Maiol there (so you understand, a Maiol is like a lord, owns a lot of land and at least one major herd). *Digs also has been killed, in the Ten Clan heartlands, remarkable enough in itself given their hostility. These deaths I had heard from The Prince, who I had stayed close with all these years. He had done well for himself; a partner in a guild, the colour paid out and he moved on with his life. Barring Digs, all of them died with a black coin. I have to presume Digs's was stolen. It was clear to me someone was out to kill us, I can only presume a betrayed purse, though I can recall no particular purse that we betrayed.*

I then learned Kheld was killed in Handar, had become a shipwright and paid out also. I had only heard of his death at the same time as I heard of the death of The Prince in Rhosidia. Whoever has us marked is not short of coin. I went to Rhosidia and investigated as best I could what had happened to him. At the time of his death a servant in the household where he was staying went missing the same day. They said he was once a mercenary, deep colour, had been working in the kitchens for months before The Prince showed up. This was meticulously planned, a most capable assassin. I fear for all of us, so I wanted to get warning to you. In trying to find out what had become of you I then discovered Connas'q and Sho have also been killed, the latter left with a coin, the former's body not recovered. Connas'q, like Digs, was in the field when he was found and killed by Agents of the Post, far from your operations against the Virates. I have to assume the Post is working with the assassin or assassins. Connas'q was running the western borders against the Ten Clan. You may have heard of the incursions that are inflaming both peoples back to full-blown war. However, in seeking news of his death I found out from the Red Hills' Master of War, a longstanding friend from our time in the Twenty, that Elimar had died before this assassin got to them. The Prince told me as well that Dithnir had died after making it home. Bresken, Ibsey, Kigan, Valdir and Mirisham I have no news of. I have found Stixie and Bense and both are still alive. My hope is that you can find them also. Bense is in a jail in Cusston, Jua. I put him there to get him off a betony mix he couldn't afford to buy himself. I think someone's using him, but I haven't been able to establish why. Stixie will be at the Citadels tourney or heading south again for the winter. He has been going through the Old Kingdoms for years, Jua, Issana, Marola, Harudan. Look for the Great Fair of Gesalla in Jua. In Issana there's a city you may remember, Bruinwen, which has its Burning of the Ship festival at harvest time, while in Marola he performs his act with the circus that follows the Secret Willows. In Harudan you'll find him through winter and early spring if not before, but the midwinter festivals are numerous.

Of Mirisham I'm not aware, Valdir perhaps has gone back to Marola, Langer's End if memory serves. No finer warrior than he *has ever been born in that sorry little backwater and he would be a great help to us if he's still alive.*

You may rightly be asking now who I suspect has been killing us all, who we betrayed.

I must disappoint you, for I have no more idea than you. I have gone back through all the purses we ever took as a crew, from our first major success at Lagrad, through Ahmstad, Razhani, Tetswana to Tharos, and then those purses up to and including Doran's at the Citadel Argir. In each we fulfilled the purse, behaved in accordance with it. I can think of no enemy that would undertake their revenge fifteen or more winters after Argir.

It was my hope that Achi would have found you and brought you to me sooner. There are Agents and Reds and the Crag militia closing on my position. I have no means of escape.

You still have your flint, both of you, perhaps now the pre-eminent frontline soldiers in all the world. I ask that you find those of us still alive, for your own survival. Together, it may be you have the means to confront and kill whoever it is has been pursuing us.

That was it. Araliah returned to us with some more wine.

"He wrote of your letter in my own. I believe he's right, you should seek out your old crew."

"I'm thinkin' a good place to start is that Alon Filston. Seems it's to do with him," said Shale. "Perhaps we can kill him an' this will sort itself out. Mercenaries without purses stop killing."

"Might be that this Filston knows of the whereabouts of the others and all," I said.

"We better do some forms, Gant, the wambos an' leathers are bein' mended while we wait for this Stimmy to return wi' our plant. Kailen's got all the cookin' gear an' presses an' such fer gettin' mixes sorted. We're goin' to take a full field spread fer this, sporebags, pitch blocks an' all the usual."

"Stimmy will be some days yet," said Araliah. "You should rest and help a widow to drink her wine at the end of this harvest."

And we did.

*   *   *

I managed to speak to the Scapo Ostler the summer following my father's death. Of particular interest is Ostler's account of Aniy's meeting with the assassin, only a day or so after my father and Shale had, in effect, made her scapo of what was Darin's district at the Crag.

Goran

If it wasn't for this war I don't expect I'd have found myself in love with Aniy. Us scapos have had to work together to get anything done by way of supplying the soldiers that Hevendor is sending with Harudan. She's a good woman, helped me like Kailen did. My time in jail I spent thinking over what he said and what he said was right. I've prospered by it, or I did until Caragula came.

It was only after I'd walked out with her a few times that we got talking about what happened in the Indra, and what happened to Darin with those mercenaries. She told me about the mercenary that came maybe a day or two after, similar age to the others, stronger colouring.

He had come asking after Kailen as well, she said he spoke funny though, nodding as if he was agreeing with his own thoughts, or else holding two conversations with her. I've seen it on some who paid the colour; a few ends up in the slums as they can't keep a trade, drooped out because they couldn't pay out.

She had been burying those that were killed by the other two mercenaries when he approached, at their Remembering.

As he approached it was clear he was on some sort of brew. His eyes were yellow she said, like a snake's. He had a drudha's double belt. She didn't want a repeat of what the other two mercenaries had done, not at a Remembering. Few of us get to see soldiers like them when they're brewed up. She said she'd never forget it, the speed at which they moved, cuts not even bleeding proper.

She had little choice then, telling him of the guildmaster and the Reds that he was paying, to look for those who used to fight in Kailen's old crew.

She knew the guildmaster was from Issana, but that was all.

What she found odd was that after he'd kissed both cheeks in the aristo way on their initial meeting, coming across as the model of good manners despite how he looked, it seemed that everything he asked her she felt she could not do other than answer him. It was said that the magists could wave their hands and things would happen, great stones move or trees grow or even people near death come back to health. With him that was her first thought, that he had a sort of power. I don't think magists had existed of course, least of all ones paying the colour. When he moved away from her she felt as though she had got some of her strength back. By then she'd told him about this merchant and much else she'd rather not have said besides.

*　　*　　*

Snakewood South / Hiscan Road Main route
The Riddle
Blenner
The Crag

Robbo,

    Please relay to our friend.

    I am at Snakewood as instructed.

    Cleark to Zhilma Fellowship acknowledged your request. Took three days to find ledgers from archive for the years 653–657 OE.

    Cleark confirmed that ship, The Wayward Lady, *with cargo including slaves, left Citadel Northsea 653 OE and 654 OE, for The Dust Coast.* The Wayward Lady *completed first journey and reported missing presumed lost on second journey, south of the Knee of Gath'Fen. Cleark recommended I head up to Feirian's Lock, confirm with their archives the inventory for both journeys.*

    The Harbour Master took some persuading, but my purse was adequate for the task. I can confirm the man you asked of left on the second trip. The Harbour Master recalled also that many months afterwards, the ship's quartermaster, man name of Ethin, returned to the Lock. He reported the ship had gone down in a storm after a mutiny. He was the only known survivor. I requested his likely whereabouts but was told he had died the year previously on a voyage to Rhosidia.

    I am returning to the Crag as instructed. I will go onto the estate to join up with my crew if you are not there.

    It seems safe to assume the man you are looking for died on the far side of the world.

    The Magist follow you.

    Achi

Chapter 7

Sand

They told me they'd found me kneeling, whispering to myself and scratching to a bloody mess my scars and peeled skin, all infected by my attentions.

A fishing raft brought me to land. Held up on shoulders, my head spinning from voices I could not have invented, I was borne into a settlement of some sort. I heard children yapping and screeching, waves thrashing a beach nearby and I could smell smoked fish. Black-skinned women dribbled water into my mouth. They were frightened of my body, shaking necklaces and sprinkling some sort of pungent blackened seeds on me.

I had no words they could understand, they had none for me. They pointed at my brand; it must have been clear I was a slave escaped.

I recall waking at different times; I had no idea for how long I had lain in this state. Some cream I never saw made and only learned of weeks later was put on my skin while I slept, to dry and harden like a crust of euca bark. On some other day, I think the morning after I could stand again, the crust was washed off in the sea, my skin raw but fresh, my colours paler under the hard sun.

A few more days passed and I seemed to lose the interest of the children and the groups of men that came and went, trading fish, leathers and spearheads with each other.

They fed me without question, this clan whose name I only learned months afterwards. Their leader put me in his house at the centre of the village. I slept on coarse white-and-black-striped animal skins, from an animal they drew in the sand that was very like a horse.

116

I watched their lives for a short time; the women using needles to place seeds in the skin of their children, forming the patterns of waves and the stars above. Most of all I watched them make mixes and brews, poisons for fishing, pitch to seal the frames of their rafts.

In the nights I found no rest without some brew made from the milk of giant nuts. I must have spoken out loud in dreams, for names that sounded odd on their tongues I would hear in otherwise inexplicable conversations, each name pregnant with some part of my past if only I could reach it. I knew I was from the Old Kingdoms, but I didn't know where, nor of course, how I ended up a slave. From time to time I would mutter to myself; I would be walking along the beach or perhaps helping with the boats and I would talk, tell myself things. One day I told myself there was revenge to be had, though the answer left no echo or trail, no picture of what came before, except what I lived through on *The Wayward Lady*. Somebody had enslaved me and I had to know who. But how do you remember what is forgotten?

I helped with the scribe and his woman that made the parch and the ink this village used, and for my work they gave me the parch to write down what I could remember. I believed that in writing down the things I knew, I would not lose them as I had lost so much else, and if I began saying things that related to memories I could no longer see, I could write these too and hope they would somehow fertilise the barren earth that hid the record of the man I was.

I can only readily recall my waking, as a slave, at what must have been near the start of my slavery, for what I recall begins just before my fingers being broken.

The stinging of my bound wrists woke me, but it was obliterated with the sharp, savage pain of the guards' cocks. I could not scream out of a mouth stuffed thick with wool. Frenzied snorting was my only resistance, my face damp from the tears that soaked the cotton hood tied at my throat, sucked tight against my nose and mouth with each intake of breath. My arms and legs were bound. On a stone floor in a large cage they took me, cracked my bones, left my gown over my back between their visits. Soon enough my fingernails were torn off and as they did it, leaving time between each nail to draw out my pain, they put their lips to my ears to tell me how good and tight I was, tell me the Droop would grind out this fine body after it had taken away the hope.

Then all my fingers were broken, one a day, a break with each bowl of food for ten days. They were clean breaks, I'd be worthless otherwise, but for the days my hands were splinted and bound to my back, I took the oats and water like a dog, lapping at the beaten copper plate on the floor, licking the gruel down to the blue algae of the copper's corrosion and welcoming the mercy of the harosin opia cross that had been mixed into it. The Droop. My eyes rolled back into the grey clay inside my head as each measure flowed through me. I shook with pleasure each time, let my guts go, flooding over my heels. The first measures you give a slave are the biggest, to establish the need and the despair when it fades away.

On another day I had my irons; a giant man, one of the guards named Rygat, held me wrapped up against him as the brand was pressed in, a crescent moon, a star either side of it. I must have belonged to a Virate slaver from out east.

I did not know this place. There were accents familiar to that same and hidden part of me, of those shouting outside; "Twenty figs the qut!" was the quivering reedy shout of some woman, a voice that a pig would have if it could talk. "Hikri Ope!" responded another. "Three risin's fer a qut, best Juan strains only!" Lying fucker. Beyond these the general noise, the same five or so auctioneers flipping from generous, lurid descriptions of the slaves to the almost unintelligible speed with which they then voiced the bids and cajoled the bidders to recklessness.

The little pleasure I had from the measures of Droop was soon destroyed by betony withdrawal. I recognised the symptoms though I could only guess from my colour I must have become addicted to it while a soldier. It was like drowning in boiling mud, a weight pressing me down and down and I became fevered, the cell around me and the snatches of places and people, voices, turning each other inside out so I could not tell what was outside of me or inside. I rubbed and twisted my shoulders against the wet stone floor but the itching of my skin burned me more fiercely than the kicks aimed at my legs and head by the guards. These were carefully delivered blows, not strong enough to put me out into silence. Bound still like a curled-up baby,

I tried to close out the pain, and as I frantically sought refuge in memory I gasped out the measures of countless mixes and recipes I must have once been aware of. Something deep within me was protecting me as best it could.

I kept repeating these over and over – whispering, seeing the words - even when Rygat came for my hole again. More than I could have hoped for, the Droop was forced into me, juiced. I was fucked to sleep.

I was not dead.

I was moving.

My arms and legs were unbound but chained to the bars of a cage on a wagon. The blood from my ankles and wrists smeared the iron hoops, ragged bands of worn skin seeping and stinging. The sun was high but of no comfort as the caravan rattled out of the small town, the memories of why I was there writhed through and against each other, like iron bars curdling and pooling. I was overcome by the rippled stinging and cramps of withdrawal.

Soon the world receded to a beat of light and dark. I took the bread in my splinted hands and the spoons of pigfat to sustain my value, and from a coastline far within me I saw the other slaves in the cart kick or bite me as I thrashed and spat and kicked back at them. I shat as I pleased in the wagon, hoping for beatings bad enough to put me out and spare me my withdrawal, or end me and spare me whatever the years held in wait.

It was the far north. I had no fight for the bearskins they threw into the cart to keep us from dying of cold. The Droop would have forbidden a clenched fist even were my fingers able to obey. Idly from that inner coast I made out the fourteen others in the cart and only the children would have escaped slaughter had I the strength. I found myself thinking through the poisons I would give them, describing the symptoms, visualising them as I did so. I wanted to speak out, goad them, but the Droop decided against it, my thirst filling and swelling my tongue.

In heavy rain I found wonder. The blacks and yellows from the far east huddled together against the icy squalls on which I could now hear seagulls. The rain found no resistance in me, no refusal of its frozen whips. The numbing cold of the streaming water over my head sank into my skull. Drops of ice vanished into my cuts and the swollen bags of my eyes, absolving me.

It would have been Feirian's Lock, Citadel Northsea that the carts rumbled into. Dark peaks scarred with snow filled the west. Ahead the bay was littered with whaling cogs and caravels, the dockside busier still with the ships' masts, their furled sails arranged like battle standards in rows above the sheds on the quay.

I couldn't remember when I last used my legs. The cage door opened and we spilled out into the mud. Spears pricked us as we stumbled forwards to a pen already full, already heavy with the suffocating stink of fifty people and the hundreds more also in pens around us against the palisade.

A woman to my left held a hand up to her ear, trembling like a rattlesnake, her fingers in the pus of some wound she protected. Two children held hands to my right, eight or nine winters perhaps the girl, five or six the boy.

Rygat and two others took the girl from the pen each night and I found songs in the ash of my thoughts that could only have been from my own childhood, which I did my best to sing and hum to the boy till she was returned. She permitted no singing, would not sit but on her knees. He, perhaps her brother, submitted to her severe grooming for his lice during the hours when she fell back from the Droop.

I slept where I stood when the Droop hit me. I dreamed nothing for a while, a silence, that something within me asleep or else had left me entirely. These spells lasted only for its flow through me. The twitching would begin as I fell, its victory against my betony withdrawal short-lived. I stamped and rubbed my forehead against the bars that burned like ice as I inevitably lost control, shrieking with the voices, the figures about me that could not have shared the pen with me, though as real as the bars themselves. The clubs and chains of the guards, the scratching and bites from the others in the pen to silence me, all saved me. I abused them all in return, their frenzy easing the withdrawal, as though some part of my suffering was being transferred to my benefit. My bound hands stopped my bitter urge to tear at my face, to rip my eyes and pull out the world from its invasions. My shivering bones seemed to rub at my insides; I wanted to tear my skin off to get at them. For these reasons I was thankful for broken fingers.

I slept again, then was awakened, dragged out of the pen for the Droop and food with the agits, spasmics, the murmurers. Was I a murmurer now? I got more food than most, the children did too. We were separated out. We were fit for some other purpose than the mines or the drudha fodder used for poisons and other research.

No sooner had we taken our measure we were to follow a line of slaves shivering its way in a knifing wind through high gates and along a track to the raucous sheds of the docks. Men yelled and whistled over the roar of the whipping sails of the ships and cracking of the nails in the planks and masts.

The Wayward Lady was tied up next to a sister ship on this East Quay. It was a large galley of the old black kishi wood, readying for the voyage, the flag the same design as my brand.

The crew moved with the focus of ants about the ratlines and spars. We were marched past the guards, Rygat at their head, lash in his hand. I was stopped before the quartermaster.

Rygat was fast. My eyes were down and my shakes were rattling the chain. The steel ball at the end of the lash gashed my eye as he followed up the knock with a hook that put me on the ground.

"You got some bad noisies in you," he said. "Throw your shit around on that ship I'll open you up harder than a horse could."

He turned to the quarter, "Noisy one, merc got some plant in him before he was picked up. Not worth the grief in my view."

"He's worth his berth," said the quarter.

One more fist slammed me out.

I woke in a pen beneath deck. My hand was being bitten through the bars by some fierce buck long since drawn out to a shadow by his life.

"'Evitt, 'Evitt, I kill you."

His teeth had gone deep, through the binding, and my blood dribbled clear of the holes, running to my fingertips. I pulled my hands back through the bars, forcing my foot at him in return.

He remained there, cussing at the floor where I had let go during my time out cold. The clamour started up with those woken by this agit's calling out.

The hatch was opened, Rygat dropped through it, a ladder being lowered after him for his subsequent ascent.

"You were told."

"He's fuckin' moanin' an' callin'," said one from the shadows behind the beam of daylight the hatch threw at the floor.

A few others sparked up, a one-armed woman of forty-odd winters spitting across at me from the pen opposite the buck's. A pen over from her and it's an old man, croaking away, licking his cracked lips with the drought we all had from the Droop.

I was dragged from my cage into the light of the hatch. Rygat had little use for speaking in making a point, throwing me at two of his boys, who held my arms out. The lash bit firm, slicing fine lines into my back. "More!" cried that voice in me, a pebble of defiance in my gut that I feared and hissed at to stop. The bars were banging and the agits jeered as the whip handle was pushed into me, forcing me up on my toes. Quickly it was brought round and forced into my mouth. He held my nose till I was spasmic. This happened a few more times as a display for the other slaves before the sallow-looking drudhan of this ship mopped out the cuts on my back, cleaned the bite and put a roll of pasted leaves in my hole to hold the blood.

The spitting and jeering continued for some time. Then I rose up the little the Droop allowed and fell away.

I was not dead.

I unravelled. The betony shakes had scooped me out, as though my skin was filled with only a sick grey porridge for innards. More light and dark, silences, Rygat and others ending their night's brandy with the casual fucking and beating of whoever caught their eye in the cages.

I followed, for the long hours rising and falling from their mixes, the rhythm of the timbers croaking and yawning as *The Wayward Lady* cut past frozen bays over the mouth of the Sardanna Straight and on past Ilana's Hood to the western ocean. In the times I was awake I strove to avoid the register of my senses, the horror of my circumstance.

One day I was forced out of some waking dream by Rygat hauling me awake from the pen:

"I told you to be quiet and you wouldn't fucking shut up. Get this hole out of its cage so I can get rid of this stiff."

The pens were banging, frenzied braying, a chant for Rygat, a chorus of desperate sublimation and dark relief for it was not them today. I was on my knees, leaning forward to the floor. I noticed I was muttering, speaking. I struggled to connect to the movement of words, my tongue reflexively fluttering through the sentences. Whatever the voice was it spoke darkly, of subtle tortures, vengeance.

I was pulled upright. The straightening of my back was terrifying. My head lolled like a baby's hanging from its mother's arms.

Rygat stood only in mail leggings and leather deckers. I could only stare into his eyes, perched like eggs on the vast thick cheeks of whiskers that tumbled in ropy locks to his chest. Why was I still muttering?

He held the back of my head and brought a huge fist into my face.

"Do you have something to say? Sounds like you're threatening me then saying sorry to me. You getting the voices now I expect. Happens to some on the Droop."

I wasn't trying to say anything but now I could hear myself, the words bubbling through the blood.

A buckle seemed to unclasp, a light was filling me up from inside. I'm dying, I thought hopefully. Then it passed, leaving a despair all the more vivid for that moment when something seemed to change in me, a concession struck between this body and its suffering and that whispering other, waiting to reclaim me.

The guards were under either arm, ready to support more blows. Rygat was not getting any resistance by which to fuel his rage, his hardness plain to everyone in sight. I could barely see him for the abstract confusion of my disassociated voice. I was bewildered, thinking that this other voice could be me, the me I was looking for. Whatever excitement had accompanied my sleeping disobedience of his demand for silence was dissipating quickly. He picked a girl from a pen and forced himself into her on the gangway; his grunting, her grunting and retching, and my own mumbling formed a sort of chorus then which, in my finding it oddly funny, fuelled the rage of the guards to finish me off. I couldn't stop laughing and laughed the harder for my mouth was still trying to form words.

Unreached by the rhythm of boots into my legs and guts I scrambled to make sense of what I was saying. There was a vigour to it, a defiance I feared and loved. How strong, how fearless had I been that this part of me belittled the agony I was undergoing. I wondered if I could be mad when I was able to realise it so. The drudhan appeared once more and moved in with rags and flasks for me and the now quivering and bleeding girl. I flapped at him as he pushed the kannabic mix to my nose. The wet sugar cane smell warmed through my throat, numbing the rest of the bruises, mercifully stilling my tongue. The agits, seeing their Droop cook, roared for their mix.

I remember I smiled as I drifted inward, for I was rediscovering the sense of my being. I had dissolved but was aligning myself again. This new voice was one of mine.

I was still here.

"For fuck's sake!"

The words were at my ear, slicing through my slumber.

It was a man's voice I didn't recognise, from the pen adjacent to mine. I was slumped at his side of the bars, he at mine. It was too black to see anything.

"What was I saying?"

"You lost a sister, you looked on a man die from poisoned bread and seemed pleased about it. More o' which you won't fuckin' shut up! It's like there's five of you in there, eh."

I touched my chest where her necklace used to hang, then wondered if "she" was my sister and how I knew I once had a necklace. I couldn't place his voice exactly, perhaps from Rulamna or the far eastern Virates from the tongue, as he wove the scraps of King's Common into his lect.

"Who are you?" I asked.

"Seems a merc like you, eh. What's your name?"

"I don't know. They're calling me Sand."

"I'm Harl."

"I . . ."

"You're makin' the most sense you had in days. Your regulars were Betty mixes?"

"Betony yes." I tried to flex my fingers. Less pain. I didn't have the spasmics as much, just some twitching.

124

"You're on the far side, eh."

I wept and then wondered what I wept for. He was right; despite the pain that came with needing the Droop, I was able to hold a conversation.

"How did you come here?" I asked.

"Why do soldiers end up slaves? Never one reason is it. You got the colour of a mercenary, reds are strong so good plant. Bet you betrayed a purse then. I was caught on the losing side of an assault on bandits. Citadels give us a choker for leadin' and half of us died being marched to the Lock. You?"

"I don't remember."

I must have slipped away again. Now it was daylight, the sound of heavy rain drumming above us. The hatch was open as was the shit hole at the far end of the deck.

Five guards watched as each slave shuffled to the hole. Like starved caterpillars, most of the slaves swathed themselves in their brown woollens against the blue and bitter air and shivered the hours away. The hard daylight at the hole pressed the eyes back so's you could not see past its glare.

Then a guard moved to the hatch and started climbing. His boot slipped on a rung as he was half out and he fell. He screamed; a sharp lump of bone was pushing out at his woollen sleeve, a growing stain of blood about it.

I repeated instructions that came out of the nothing behind my thoughts, calling my best in the rasping croaks of the drooper: "Tie rope above the bone", "Knock the man out with opia", "Shear some skin for sewing. Fold back", "Kannabic on the sword and a single cut" . . . on and on I went, repeating it until the drudhan arrived. He started shouting at the guards, one of whom had filled the man up with Droop from a pouch while the other had a knife going at the skin. They pointed at me. The drudhan spat murder and grabbed the arm of the guard who was trying to cut free the skin of the wounded man's arm. Another guard leaped over and pushed him back into the aisle between the pens.

The sword fell, the guard sucked in his breath like he'd jumped into a river, the Droop taking everything else. "Kannabic paste mixing in fireweed or shredded hardhack and boiled water. Sew him up," I continued.

"Rygat will flay you alive!" sputtered the drudhan.

"He saved his life!" yelled Harl.

The drudhan ascended, followed by the guards lifting the wounded man up.

I had no more words, just bewilderment at the lucidity of my instructions. My eyes were sore with being open. Self-pity dribbled into the cracks of my drying out. The bars seemed more solidly iron than they had before, the pen suffocating where once such containment was a sort of cradling. The bones of the ship rolling across the stiffer water of the deep sea droned like the hemp string of some giant bow. My other voice came back, congratulating me, which I was grateful for.

Some hours later I was dragged out of my pen and thrust at the ladder out of the hatch. The light was like a hammer; the wind so cold I felt I was drowning. Above deck I staggered about, splinted hands over my eyes. Rygat stood before me. With a hot hand curled like a wolf's jaws around my neck he pushed me past the mizzen and into the stern castle where the captain sat at a small wooden desk, the quartermaster behind him.

"I'm Captain Cythe, this is my quartermaster, Ethin. You have been given the name Sand."

I nodded as far as Rygat's hand would allow.

"You are a drudha?"

"I . . . I don't know, I have no memory." I glanced up, three guards each with a knife and shortsword, the smell of lovage leaves being boiled. Nobody but Rygat here had the patchy skin of fight-brew addiction, just the usual yellowish tinge of opia. I muttered to cover my confusion, my inability to explain how I could identify plant so easily.

"Some training you had has just saved the life of one of my crew. He's little use now and a mouth to feed but I'm sure he's grateful."

Cythe looked drawn, unnaturally narrow, as though once crushed in a vice. There was a damp sheen over his saggy face, some grey fronds of hair slick against his cheeks and forehead despite the shutters open behind him. Ethin by contrast had thick black hair, the face

126

of thirty summers varnished by the sun, the build of twenty at the rigging. He clearly ran the ship.

"Get Morki in," barked Ethin.

Rygat released my neck and left, returning shortly with the drudhan.

"My guts are on fire, I can hardly move," said the captain. "Morki, what are you mixing?"

The drudhan looked at me. He was risen on some bacca mix. "Uh, kannabic water, leaves of . . ."

"Have you checked his shit?" I interrupted. Why was that so obvious? Trust yourself, I said.

Morki shot me a glance before staring at his feet.

Cythe nodded, cleared the crumbs off his plate and threw it on the floor next to his chair. He dropped his grey woollen breeches to his boots and squatted over the plate, dropping a pile easily, keeping his eyes on me the whole time.

Tying up his breeches again, he gestured for Ethin to take the plate.

"Well?" Ethin pushed it under Morki's nose. With an instinctive convulsion he turned his head.

"You." Cythe pushed it under my nose. A life at war barely remembered nevertheless inured me to it.

Taking up a fork from the table, an awkward process due to my hands, and awaiting a nod, I cut through it.

"There's blood. Some internal infection or bleeding. Witch hazel, tea, but fresh leaves, black-oak bark, shredded and left to soak in the same tea. Should cure it."

"Morki?" Cythe turned on the shivering drudhan, his head shaking slightly.

"I . . . black-oak? But . . . there is some witch hazel, I was preparing a cream to . . ."

"Shut the fuck up and make me this tea."

Morki paused momentarily, a furtive glance at me, requesting the recipe.

"Hot, not boiled water, shred three inches of bark, eight to ten fresh leaves, double if dried and leave it to cool and infuse."

Morki left. Cythe glanced up at Ethin before staring closely at me.

"You've got the skin of a merc."

"Yes, it looks like." His breathing was shallow, joints sore. There was a lot more wrong with him than hazel would fix. The edges of my vision were crowding up with threat; I needed more Droop. I said nothing, keeping the edge on him.

"You've smelled the shits a number have got. We've got a week to port. I can arrange for some time out of your pen if you'll get that mix-addled cum-drinking drudhan to start treating the crew right and the slaves. Each one alive and fit for transport is an extra seventy silver pieces when we reach Janoa. A good bonus on these dyes and spices we carry, though hardly a good use of space. Still, Zhilma knows best I'm sure. Rygat, take him below."

"Yes, Captain."

I couldn't mask the shivers now, my bones bowing like twigs as my muscles trembled and ached for a comfort no food could provide.

Rygat again had his hand on my neck, thrusting me out of the stern castle and onto the ladder to the pens. My gate was locked behind me with the eyes of all the slaves on me.

I waited for him to leave.

"I'm going to make you stronger," I said to them.

With morning, and surrounded by the tools, pots and plant of the drudhan, whatever source there was of this knowledge was opening up as quickly as I could read the labels on his bottles. My hands moved as though controlled by somebody else, or rather, by a part of me yet unjoined to the slave that endured these last weeks.

Heat the kannab resin. Sprinkle into boiled water. Next the larkspur seeds, shredded painfully with my mending hands in a pestle. Then the brugma, from a dusty jar this drudhan clearly knew nothing about.

I let the mix cool as he asked questions sugared with loathing, suggesting treatments for the slaves that mixed lethal quantities of the plant we had, attempting to find me out. I maintained an ignorance, pleading false limits to my knowledge, deferring to some mixes he felt were unorthodox, but were, I somehow knew, foolish.

I nudged the mix forward in a moment where he slumped against the bench cursing the night's brandy.

"One thing I do know is a fix for the afters. This will work swiftly."

He reached for it without thinking, needing something that might clear his head. He dropped the empty cup on the table. Now he would gradually lose his sense of balance while the brugma, if it was still potent, would cause a growing paranoia. The kannab would make him slur, fug his thoughts, the few larkspur seeds would cause a partial paralysis.

"You should take the air on deck, Drudhan, really get that mix working to clear your head." I was delighted at my suggestion.

I had not expected him to die so soon. He was surprised by a deck boy landing in front of him from a ratline at the midsail, no doubt as a joke. Flailing and shrieking from the boy he hit the gunwale, was overboard and lost.

The captain soon had me, the boy and a few others nearby to account for themselves. The boy believed it was the shock of the surprise that toppled him. I suggested that the drudhan's drinking did very little for his sea legs. The captain's eyes were on me, but he was helpless.

"You are our drudha then, Sand. You will have two hours a day to see to the mixes that Morki has a record of. You will also be watched."

There was little time for my satisfaction to ferment upon returning to the drudhan's cabin. Rygat soon appeared, filling the cabin. My hands were in his, slowly being squeezed, the pain forcing me to my knees.

"You're a right sneaky fucker and I ain't fooled. No mistakes with the brews and you'll be tasting mine yourself."

From crushing my hands he balled his fists and battered me to the floor.

Days later we anchored off some Ry'ylan port built into the cliffs and valley of a narrow estuary, the last before rounding the Knee of Gath'Fen and the final stretch to Janoa on the Dust Coast. Rygat took me in chains to the plant sellers. We were north enough that I found the right breeds for the mixes that would support the mutiny I was planning. Rygat would be days dying. I'd be set with the counter prior to tasting his soups and breads.

Since my promotion I'd caught twelve of the slaves at the line where the Droop's prison and the fear of leaving it met. With Harl's help I managed to get each of them some caffin and an outline of my intentions, how I would provide a Droop that would not make them hurt so much; that would let them live a more normal life. Each gave his word to be ready, seeing freedom in me now I'd begun the fearful journey myself from the Droop's nipple, doctoring our mix before Rygat's ignorant eyes.

The part of me that remembered what I had once known had reconstituted the Droop to harness the harosin to caffin powders instead of the throw-wort. It took the shakes away, but we continued to affect the same manners as the wretches still slumbering, those I had no heart to see die for want of size or age.

Finding the crew members took more time. I fixed them some fine brews and smokes to take the edge off their lives. Those with the scurv, the shits or a whore's pox were easy to treat and in so treating we talked and in our talking allegiances and hatreds became clear. The captain too made some improvement, despite he and the rest getting a dormant poison gradually working through their guts and into their blood. Only Ethin, the quartermaster, I left free of the poison. The respect for him was fierce, and he was my best chance at getting the ship somewhere useful.

Over the following weeks there were ten crew I could say with conviction would be happy to improve their lot with Ethin as their captain. It would be enough to get the ship landed and sold somewhere, if they could be turned when I showed them their crisis.

By then I'd had the splints off my hands for good, itself surprising for I recalled so little of the actual time that had passed since I woke and found myself a slave.

It was a warm morning off the Dust Coast when it began. I felt a churning dread and yet excitement at the prospect of killing, painfully, those who were cruellest.

Freed for the drudha duties, I added the active that would trigger the poison to all the brews and also the wine the cook had warming for the mid-morning sup.

I sat on the port gunwale as I counted out the time it took for the food to go down, the pains to show, then the nosebleeds.

Shivering and retching, the deckside crew went through their stock of curses and insults as the waves of agony built. They had too little time to realise I'd killed them to raise a sword or knife against me. Their abuse was inspired.

I moved freely then among those who had taken the poison as they cowered or fell to the deck, pleading with me and crying for help.

"You are all dying! All except Ethin. The sooner you give me your fealty the less crippled you'll be. Those of you who chose to beat or fuck the slaves will die regardless." This other me was warming my bones. I did my best to play along, almost drunk with the success and the power I had.

Ethin and the sailmaster quickly pledged, followed by ten of the crew that I expected would be well disposed to the brews I'd got them addicted to. Ethin went straight for the captain's cabin but I made sure Cythe was never going to survive the active.

Rygat had been eating with one of his guards near the port ladder to the quarterdeck. Within moments of the active being ingested his strength left him. I made sure of his dose. His bellows diminished as he fought for breath, his great bulk twitching. I took the keys from his belt, pushing aside his now feeble attempts to grasp me, and sent a crewman down to free the slaves. It had gone perfectly.

Harl and the twelve I'd got ready for the mutiny led the others up out of the hatch. The light and the Droop brought them to their knees. They looked as lost and incredulous on the main deck as fish.

I gave those who pledged to my mutiny their draught and watched their backs straighten as the mix broke up.

"Expect some violent shitting shortly, to expel the poison."

The girls who had been in the hold went swiftly for Rygat, kicking and beating him as he heaved and twisted away from them.

"Leave Rygat be," I said to them. "His mix is a slow one. You can beat him and finish him now if you want, but you could sit and watch him. He'll die more slowly and in more pain."

I turned to the sailmaster, who eyed me straight despite still quivering on his canepole legs. He was stood with Ethin at the wheel.

"I'm Wilbo," he said. "Got us a new headin'?"

"I want off, freedom for everyone alive. You can keep the ship. Just get us to shore somewhere I can disappear, away from any towns or ports."

"You won't mek land fer forty leagues at least, these lanes'll be full o' the clans o' Gath'Fen. We get past the Hyczies to the midden an' the Shahn's coast you might mek it."

"You know the waters well?" I asked.

He flicked his head up . . . "We jus' need to find a navy Drom'd or som't to stick to into the shallows 'n' channels. Navy boat might keep us safe." I looked at Ethin, for I was thinking this might be a plan they'd hatched to be rid of me.

"He's right, Sand, he's true. These seas are scarred with pirates, a lot of islands about, the Gath'Fen or Hyczika navies might give us some protection if we find them."

I turned and saw Harl behind me. "Harl, give the slaves some knives and let them have the others. Rygat we'll lash to the mizzen-mast."

"I'm to be captain then?" said Ethin.

"Yes, Ethin. I can't sail a ship, these slaves I brought off the Droop mix can't either, they're just bags of sticks. The crew we have left will work for you, the slaves I hope can help us once we've fed them some of the dead crew's rations."

"A good drudha could make a fortune from his merchant; where do you need to go this far from the Old Kingdoms that you want off now?"

"I need to go back." I said this but in truth I didn't know. My conviction resided in the gaps of my memories, its voice had fed all my effort to seek freedom from this boat without my understanding it.

"You need to hope we can get far enough south," said Ethin.

"You sailed off this coast?"

"As a boy. My father was a sailmaster with the Finola clan. There'll be nothing left of us if they get sight."

"You speak King's Common well," I said.

"He got me off the ships, for a while. We'd put in to Farlsgrad, far north, looking for slavers or cargo like this shortly after the last of Kagh's grandsons forced a war with the Shahn and dried up our supply of meat and rum. The merchant cogs and hulks stayed north of the Knee till the war blew over. The Finolas had navy contacts, privateers of a kind. We took their purse on work shaving down the merchant interests that were getting out of hand, without the navy and the rulers fingered for it.

"Few pirates live beyond thirty summers. He made me up to a man of means so I could study for an education, paid for with a bottle of rosary peas from a caravel out of Hanwoq. His crew didn't realise what they were because they hadn't seen them before. He stashed them and freed me with them."

I shook my head; it was a staggering booty.

"We'll do what we can, Ethin, you'll get no more grief from me. I just want off."

I turned to face the deck, slick with the blood and hacked-up bodies of the crew the slaves most hated. They had whimpered on for a while under the artless blades. It was a compelling and delicious savagery. Ethin shouted at the slaves to clear their mess so they could get the deck in order.

It was slow going against some hard southerlies as we pushed on. Ethin cursed me for depriving us of experienced crew but he was the man to keep those remaining tight while we sailed south.

Rygat lasted two nights before Harl and Wilbo begged me to throw him over so they could get some rest from his howling. I found little more soothing than hearing him suffer. It kept my flint up, a reminder to me that I was no longer powerless.

During those two days he did his best to gesture towards the gunwale on those occasions he caught my eye, the incoherent desire to be drowned all that remained of this tree of a man. I approached only to kick him or hit him with a club, until he flinched whenever I approached, even as he begged me to throw him overboard.

Past the main Siczy Island channel we headed for the midden and Janoa. Squalls gave Ethin a chance to try the stronger slaves with learning to reef, course and stow the main and smaller mizzen sails with the regulars.

A further week or so south our luck ran out. I'd been mixing up the caffin Droop for the girls and older slaves when the shout went up from the rigging.

Ethin danced up the ratlines to the top spar where the crewman was stood, and called down. "Looks like clan colours, not navy!"

The sailmaster cast his eyes quickly about.

"Some't else's not right neither," he shouted as I left the drudhan's cabin to join him.

Ethin dropped out of the rigging.

"Two ships, caravels. Wilbo?"

"We cin put some run on wi't wind as it is, but look . . . no gulls, Captain, I'm not seein' fair clouds so some'ts coming, whitecaps read southwest, an' it bin blowin' east all morning, no caps neither."

"Wind's turned sharply then, a storm," said Ethin.

From the deck I could now see the sails of the two ships closing from the stern.

"Man the braces and ready about!" barked the sailmaster, his sparrow frame belying a fierce bark that cut across the ship.

Ethin shook his head imperceptibly, lips tightening, squeezing out the paralysis of fear.

"Lash up and fix up the stores! You don't need telling what pirates do with captured crews. We're dead if we don't head for the storm and dead anyway without you giving Wilbo and me every scrap of your will to live!" He turned to me, past the blame it seemed, setting himself for the madness of an under-crew galley racing for a storm.

"Sand, you'd best get us a fine mix to bow out with."

I felt the boat heel as we gave it full sail, tacking out towards the stiffening swell. I got my belts, blades and rags on and got to work in the drudhan's cabin. Part of me wondered at the surety of my preparation of the belt. It was a certainty I needed, to crush, to bury the nervous wreck I had become.

"Lee-ho! Tack on the header," shouted Wilbo as the crew and the stronger slaves fought the braces to make the turn.

"Still closing!" came the shout from the mizzen-yard.

They were a way off still, closer but surely aware of the danger they were in if they kept on at us. I finished up the flasks and headed out to the quarterdeck.

Ahead the horizon grew dark, the sky lost as its colour and the sea's became the same. The bow was now slapping down on the trough between the steepening waves, the sea and storm turning quickly and savagely on us as if we were mosquies biting the back of a giant.

"Best get the brew round, Sand," said Ethin. He took his share and I dropped to the main deck to split the flasks with Harl. They should be stronger now for some hours; thinking, seeing more clearly. The price on the far side of it was steep, but who now cared?

"Fuckers are still closing!" shouted Ethin over the noise of the wind and sea. "They want to see us right into it!"

"I'm pushin' us east some, Captain; might get us some headland on the Shahn's coast'll tek the belly outa this waves. Get the boys outa the rigging."

"Give the word, Wilbo."

As the minutes went by the fringe of the storm reached us, the bellies of clouds low and massive above. As we pushed into it we lost the chasing sails to shadows, visible only as the ship headed each wave.

Wilbo and Ethin shouted and then screamed to be heard as the wind made the rigging sing.

"Reef sails! Dano, get below and get the pumps and buckets going with anyone able to work! Battens on the foredeck hatch!"

Now Wilbo was cursing and barking at the wheel, the waves were hitting us from beam and bow as the storm forced a contrary pattern on the currents that preceded it.

Each time he aimed to tack and keep at the waves we'd be hit from starboard. Shortly the waves grew to hills, foaming and hissing as the caps blew at us; sheets of rain whipped us from all sides as though seeking a weakness.

Another hour drew by, consumed by us reacting to and passing on the shout to adjust the haul and keep us with Wilbo's best guess of the wave front.

I muttered the names of the old magists still worshipped around this coast and no sooner had I done it we were facing a fierce wave, foaming white, seemingly boiling and at my eye's height on the quarterdeck. As the helm steadied us to hit it, yells went up from the deck crew fragmented by another wave across the beam. The hit took some of the boys on the starboard side off their feet, swinging from the braces, but the loss of control saw the yard turn and the boat heel about. We rode the wave off line and broached as we fell into the trough and into the next wave port side on. I saw Harl get caught up as the main spar tore out the stays and the edge of it hit the wave and break. The rigging whipped down towards deck as we heeled back and Wilbo and the helm fought the rudder to straighten us.

In moments Harl and most of the other slaves screaming and tearing at the wreckage were gone, some of their bodies left rolling about the deck as we worked our way over to cut the ropes that were dragging the piece of spar and torn sail in the water port side. I could just make out the shrieking below deck as the children cried out. Water must have flooded down through the hatch the crew were bringing the bilgewater up from.

"Get those ropes cut, Sand!" bellowed Ethin. "I need two more to get below and keep the pumps working!"

Two of the crew were already hacking at the ropes as I swung myself off the quarterdeck to the port gunwale. In moments we'd released the damaged spar and sail and I held tight to a ratline as we rose and fell.

The helm and sailmaster kept us at the waves, too few of us now to help with a course without further risk to the masts. I had no sense of time, the mist off the waves that hit the bow blurred everything, I felt only the successive moments of weightlessness as we were held by, and fell on the back of, each crest. Soon enough I was called below deck where the boat's dance had thrown a barrel at one of the boys there, smashing his arm. The others were retching and helpless as the first brew began its claim.

I refreshed the brews and sickness mix, did what I could to ease the agony of the wounds and relieve the exhaustion setting in. We couldn't get the water out for want of sure transfer of the buckets as we rolled and shuddered. Each blow brought a yelp from the girls and among the other droopers unable to help us there were spasmic wails and a shouting that I had to silence with the quickest poison I had, for they were distracting the men bailing.

I knew then for certain this ship wouldn't make land; I only then read it in the eyes of the women holding onto the children and the webbing that covered the casks of wine and spices. They were the last of the slaves not yet helping or put to death.

"I don't want to know it if it's coming!" yelled one, her sharp Citadels accent, one I'd grown fond of as I'd recovered from the betony, betraying a rising terror. I nodded, taking her meaning.

From a loop in my belt I took a tin flask. The eyes of the young girls were fixed on the tin, as though some force to stay the storm were within. I collapsed as the galley did into a trough, on my knees before the woman.

"A mouthful each, when it's time, the girls first I beg you!"

She took the flask with a shivering hand and clutched my shoulder. We could share only a nod before I was kicked, one of the boys pulling me to a pump.

I worked the pump as the storm tore at the ship. I was lost in it, I could not say for how long. The brew boiled my muscle and sang in my aching shoulders as I span the handle and drew into the buckets.

At some point we were hit hard, and as we went over some barrels left their webbing and crashed against a porthole, breaking the storm plate, bringing in a thick spray of black water and the freezing wind.

I shouted up for more bodies but none came.

There was a cry overhead, some break visible in the sweeping rain perhaps. Then I saw a tint to the gloom, barely noticeable despite the brew's sharpening of our sight to the blackout of the storm as night overtook it.

"We may have hit its peak, boys! Let's give Wilbo enough to get us to the coast."

With wood from the smashed barrels the porthole was nailed up but other damage had been done. A shout came through that there were leaks aft, sending the sea pissing like a wall of drunks into the ship.

I started up a worksong, called them for all they had as I looked about for a piece of mast or hull that would bear me when it came to it.

Soon we were up to our ankles in water, the bilge full. Ethin was at the hatch. He looked about, shook his head and vanished, shouting up at Wilbo.

Some of the boys started the shakes now, no more brews were going to delay us paying for that first and heaviest mix. The Droop had hollowed out some marrow in me too, I switched to the buckets for a break but we were slowing.

Looking out from the hatch as I passed the water up I saw enough of the clouds to know that the spray off the caps had diminished. More pieces of a yard, sails and rope lay in heaps around the midship. The crew above deck were holding on by instinct. They'd begun their songs to whatever magists might stride out from the land to protect them, the whispering drones of men past taking orders.

"Are they still working?" shouted Ethin.

"Aye, just about, we're paying it back now, I can't stop the brew's claim!"

He nodded. There was blood over his face, his arm held close to his side, protecting a rib perhaps.

"Keep going, buy us an hour or two before she goes under, it'll blow past us by then and we're just going to have to hope the current's taking us in on whatever rafts we can muster. The smallboat's done for, the rest of the main mast cracked when we got hit abeam an hour or two back."

"There isn't an hour here, Captain; it's over."

Five of us only were left with enough strength to pump out the water as it came to our shins then knees. The strong persistent howl had given way to gusts. One of the boys fell down, shuddering and clutching his head. Sometimes the brew's claim was fatal.

"We're going down," I said, stopping at the pump and standing straight, "smallboat's smashed. Take your fill of water; I'll break open a cask now. Find some flasks for it and then find something'll bear your weight in the sea."

I took the claw of a hammer to one of the freshwater casks and filled some skins, throwing them at those fit enough to move themselves above decks.

I looked over at the women and girls as I went to the ladder. They were stood now, shivering and haggard in the seawater.

Some silver-blue of night through the hatch above us caught the eyes of the Citadels woman as they filled up, staring at me as though I might have an answer. She held the smallest girl tightly to her breast, face in a shroud of sodden blankets, bruised arms like sticks around the woman's waist. She then glanced at another, older woman whose sorrow wrote and somehow authorised their fate with a gentle nod, unquestionably a mother at some point in her past.

The young woman held the flask out in front of her with shaking hands and took out the stopper.

"Let's drink, girls, it'll give us some strength."

The Wayward Lady went down at dawn as the sun began warming the breeze over a recovering sea. Six of us were sat on lashed-up casks after the killing over wood suitable enough for rafts was done.

We stayed within sight of each other for a time, but soon enough we rowed our way apart with torn planks, hoping to find the coast before the water ran out. I shook Ethin's hand once before our casks drifted apart, the last I saw of him, Wilbo and the others.

Then I was alone. Sometime after that the water had gone.

I passed out of time on the Droop I'd re-concocted to escape my reliving of what had been done to me as a slave.

I had accepted death on this sea. Its vastness beneath and around me matched the perfect still blue of the sky. Both crushed me against this raft with their indifference, an unknowing of the fact I was alive. What more would a mountain have cared for a leaf floating on a pool on its flanks?

I recalled almost nothing of my old life. A stream of images were there but I could make little sense of them. I woke on occasion and had been talking, conversing with someone, but the sense, the answers, vanished as I did so. The colours my skin had bleached to were my only solid reference that I must have at some point fought and killed as a soldier, though the skin was burned and flaking. I wanted that missing part of me, for comfort, for something to give me strength. This other voice in me knew the man I was, and someone had taken it from me. This I knew, and I held this in my gut; it anchored me, the only comfort I had.

Sometime later I was weeping and singing in the night, silent white eyes beyond count above me. I remembered a boy and a girl I cared for. I knew I loved that girl somehow. There were other faces, a windmill, I was in somebody's arms. I stared into a stream, entranced by the boy staring back, his nose running from crying. Then I was hacking at soil so hard from frost and vivid to my mind I woke screaming and was sick, so unlike was it to the rolling of this featureless, hopeless plain.

Chapter 8

Gant

We left Araliah and Kailen's estate and headed north for Ithil Bay, troubled by what we had read and heard of those of our brothers killed.

There was little grief along the way. Once we thought we were being tracked due to what we put out to give us some warning of the assassin or assassins, though after what that scapo told us we were inclined to think, despite Kailen's view, it was one assassin. The vapours that the titarum seeds give off caused a coughing that give us a chance to do for five what were looking to jump us one night. They were only thieves expecting some poachers or common travellers. The rest of our troubles were because we were mercs, but our silver lined the way with the militias working the lands about us. Times were we'd have seen to them all for stopping us, but the less noise there was for an assassin to get news of the better. We figured we had fewer problems than was usual through Issana for there were troubles north that took the attention of the militias what were normally strong around the borders protecting their shiel crops and such.

I last seen the port of Ithil Bay some six summers previous, on my way up to see my sister that last time I was returning some plant for the hast.

She laughed at me for seeming to exaggerate the city it was, the hundreds of ships there, docked and moored in the wide bay. Men of all colours and speech you could find on the wharves. Some spoke with the chattering of crows and others would speak to you in a way like singing, where a word meant different things if said in a high or a low voice.

It was only in Issana's docklands that you would find such a gathering. Inland was inward-looking and unwelcoming for the most part, few settled from elsewhere without being driven out by the preachers waving their books of oaths that the sayings made famous.

The docks were as busy as I recalled from that last visit. The colours for the guilds from lands and hasts from all over the Old Kingdoms were worn on the quartermasters, chaplains and guildies what run the sheds and set the caravans. Merchants come from far about to feast upon the war Issana was fighting on its far border, against the Vilmorans.

Like all the Issanaian ports there was a strong presence of the Post and the "Greens" of the king's guard; green was the colour of their hauberks as red was the colour of the Post. (Always struck me as odd that the Post would call its lowest ranks "Reds" and yet its highest rank, the leader, was called "The Red" and not something with "Reeve" in the title.) Anyway, Issana's king was a big one for the laws and punishments throughout his lands, but where men land from sea with a need to fuck and do plant, well, he wasn't fool enough to discourage their interest in some well-defined districts away from the aristos and merchants, so he kept the preachers out of Ithil Bay as well.

Coming from the south into Issana past the hills around the south end of the bay, we hit some big camps spread out across the vale that descended into the bay itself.

The camps were proper established which was a surprise given what Issana was like with refugees. Many would've been looking for work on the docks from whatever troubles in their homelands sent them away, troubles enough that Issana was the better option. Here too were the farmers and tradesmen that couldn't get a settle in even the worst districts choking up the eastern end of the bay. The oligarchy was north with the war I'm guessing; not enough Greens about to dislodge these thousands washed up in boats from the west of the Sar or the Gulf.

We passed through the clouds of flies and screaming duts in these nests of tents. This time of day the men were down the docks or else waiting for the dark so as to hunt in the forests and take their chances with the Issanaian settlements whose common it was.

Begging was ferocious, it was obvious we had coin. Our skin was mainly our peaceful route through, for none of them could much use a sword or take a man who was immune to most crude venoms and poisons from the years on fightbrews.

The ragged remnants of the old city walls were still counted the boundaries for the city itself, the remains of the Four Arches still dwarfing the main roads into the filth of the Dens as were called the north part of Ithil Bay. West Dens and East Dens fell with the slopes into the streets of the docks, where the offices and guildhouses were found along with the better taverns. The Greens said nothing to us, mercenaries were a common sight in Ithil Bay. You might not think it but few mercenaries were trouble, most just looking to escape the battle and noisies from the mixes. You don't win purses if you're fighting the soaks and bucks loaded up on shiel or cut caffin.

Still, we heads for the East Dens and looked for somewhere to put the horses and our heads down where the militia might not be looking.

We led the horses through a dark hive of lanes where the droopers and dealers were sunk in their different stupors.

A shouty little dut was throwing a bucket of piss into the lane from a doorway as we approached, bawling at some soak what was blocking his way. It was a fire-blackened inn of sorts, no sign, more someone's own room with a bench for some kegs. Chairs were mostly full of men past speaking to each other, their own voices being company enough for their thoughts between the last fall and the next drink.

"We need a stable, somewhere quiet, payin' well," said Shale to the 'keep.

One man stood and gestured to the others, despite their lack of interest, telling them to stay where they were. He addressed us square on, soaked enough to not weigh the odds on us.

"You in Jaki's patch, boys, you be paying well enough for Jaki?"

Shale had this look about him what he give people, like he was still and cold as a statue. The lad stiffened a bit, put off as he give us a proper look and saw our colour. Then Shale smiled like a girl with a new-sewed dolly, which the lad echoed with a weak and unsteady smile of his own.

"We'll pay Jaki, lad, no fear." The boy got himself a silver coin which fairly staggered him a moment after bracing for trouble. There was a murmur about as it flashed the candlelight on its way to some pouch in his belt. He ran out.

The 'keep took a few mugs out from a shelf. He had a forehead and bald crown so big and heavy they squashed his nose down to lips and chin, fighting each other for space. I don't think he could've looked upwards if he wanted to.

"Will be more back seeing you got coin," he said. "Rum or beer?"

"Boy'll hopefully get us a stable, safe enough if we pays. And rum," said Shale.

"Safe enough if you pays, aye."

He give us a measure of rum and then one of the others in the room starts up, a line or two about some fierce mix he's got specially for what he called his richer clients. Clients is one of them slippery words for sure, as though the acquaintancy was a dependence of some sort. We ignored him till he got noisy, then Shale put him out.

The other lad come back as we were into our second rum, with a man must have been Jaki. Little colour on him from some recipe of a field drudha or a cooker, probably used it to settle a fight before one began as was often the case with us and our colouring. He was trying to put the show on with the leather vest and some long and decorated knives. Blades were oily for sure but no notches or marks from them being punched through wamba or scale, clean grips.

"New into Ithil and straight to the East Dens, my friends? You must not want to be seen. Old soldiers too, so I can trust you to behave."

"Just wants stables, sir," said Shale, swilling his rum about the cup.

"Knocking the boys out in my quarter isn't behaving."

"He were noisy," I said, "pushing on us some mix. I could shit for more than the worth of it."

He wasn't sure what to do. Our colour was too deep, too much.

"Jaki got your stables, I'll keep your horses good."

"Get some rest, Malk," said Shale to me, keeping the names out of it, "I'll see to your horse an' have a talk wi' Jaki."

The old barkeep took me through what passed for a kitchen to a small room, bare but for firewood and the beetles and rats enjoying it.

I rested for the remainder of the day we arrived. My belly was sore from the riding and sleeping out.

I come to when it was dark, the low murmur in the main room was now a bit more thirsty. Shale was stood over me.

"Gant, we're goin' to see some ganger, runs these Dens, might help us find this Alon Filston. How's the wound?"

"Bearable," I said. Didn't see the need to patch it up till the morning and I was looking to get soaked after this meet.

Jaki led us through the lanes and to a plain old door in a three-storey, noisy with shouting and music from inside. Shale spotted a couple of men on roofs opposite. This was a proper ganger then, a lot to lose.

Jaki knocked. The door was opened by a young man, only chest high, but stocky and sober compared to the crowd of women and children behind him dancing to the playing of a mandolin and drum. They were being clapped on by a crowd with their backs to us, most puffing on the long Issanaian clay pipes they did most of their bacca in. Jaki left sharply and we were gestured in.

"I hope you boys would leave those swords with me," said the doorman, leaning in to be heard. He was wise enough not to ask for the belts, this was a ritual about respect and trust anyway. We obliged with the swords and he led us past the revellers filling a fairly plain sitting room and through a roomful of children behind it, who stopped their play to stare at and dare each other to touch our skin. I smiled to see Shale flex his arm as a dut reached up to touch it, sending him yelling and giggling back into the arms of some fine-looking girl in a red gown that betrayed the seeming modesty of the house.

There was a fierce good smell as we followed the doorman down a short hall, to a kitchen you would expect of an estate. Here on various tables were all manner of stewed fruits, spiced and cured meats from over the Sar for sure, lobsters both steamed on boards and alive in buckets. There were many casks and crates of bottles also, and near the open hearth a table at which stood a small bald man who seemed like he was a boy that grew old in bones unchanged.

He had a young girl lifted up in his arms, four summers I'd have guessed 'less she was older but small like him. She was helping to stir a fish stew in a bronze cauldron what was stood over the hearth. They were singing some ditty that had her counting up to ten for the chorus.

He turned and looked at us and the doorman.

"Pat! Look at all their colours!" she said, leaning out from his shoulder to better see us.

"They give their swords, sir," said the doorman.

"That's good. Thank you, Ralim. I'm Lokio, gentlemen. You've caused some sort of stir with Jaki it seems and now desiring to see me on this my daughter's birthday. Water? Brandy?"

"We're fine, sir," said Shale. "We appreciates you seein' us an' we're sorry fer the trouble. We're lookin' fer someone, a guildmaster name of Alon Filston. I'm Shale an' this is Gant."

Lokio nodded and smiled, pushing the smile through his eyes so you felt it, but he was giving us some scrutiny. He cuddled his girl in close and spoke to her.

"Us grown-ups say that these men have 'paid the colour'. Such rich colour suggests they've paid richly doesn't it, my carina? You see that green shine in their eyes? It's luta. To make luta you take a leaf, a very special small leaf, and you soak it and put the leaf under your eyelid, like this!"

He pretended to go for her eye and she chuckled, pushing his hand away.

"What does it do, pat?"

"Well, when it goes onto the eye the leaf and its juice just soak into your eyeball and into your blood. Then you can see like an eagle." She covered her eyes, supposing to stop these eyes of ours prying into her thoughts.

"The nearest drudha capable of its preparation would be in Harudan, the old Orange Empire, and not even your pat could afford to buy it. These colours mean they are very strong men, stronger than all the men in the whole of Ithil Bay would you believe?"

As he spoke he was pushing her hair behind her ears, a fierce love on him. His yellow swollen-knuckled fingers that spoke of a past life as a fighter brushed her cheek, revealing a face that was thin more like it was fragile than sickly, sticky with the remains of fruit.

"Now, my carina, perhaps you could go through and tell Lamptey and Ralim that your pat's not to be disturbed for a few minutes."

He leaned down a little after putting her to the floor so she could put her arms about his neck for a squeeze, then she passed between us and out the door, holding splayed fingers over her eyes.

As the door closed Lokio seemed to sag slightly, but his fine words and manner of scrutiny suggested this may be some act to loosen our guard.

"You really are Shale and Gant, once of Kailen's Twenty?" He moved around the table closer to us, picking up an open bottle of wine.

"Yes," I said.

"Someone's killin' us all," said Shale, "leavin' the black coin. Seems it must be somethin' to do wi' this Filston from a postin' we got hold of."

"There's a bounty, a fine one," said Lokio.

"We can more'n match it fer the whereabouts of him," said Shale.

Lokio nodded, a downward look as he did that spoke of his head in some deep thinking. He turned from us and went to a shelf near the hearth on which his stew was bubbling. There were a few mugs on it, which he took down. He poured out the wine as he spoke. It was wine as good as Araliah give us.

"Guildmaster Alon Filston," he said, "has a spoiled snake of a wife from the Citadels, but an uncommon beauty. Alon lives, understandably for a man of twenty or more ships and plantation interests across Issana, in the West Head, upper hills. An exceptional estate, hosting Issana's great and good regularly."

"You bin then," said Shale smiling.

He nodded. "Yes, I do much for these guildmasters and they do much for me. I deal with the unfortunate circumstances that arise between the guilds and cause their disputes and profit from resolving them. You don't see Greens in the Docklands or Dens where the trouble is come dark, nor do they have much idea how the slavers are supplied so readily. Deckhands, quarters, captains, carpenters, runners, whores and the security of their sheds cannot be managed by the Greens. They are managed by me."

"In't they got the Post fer that? Thought the Greens an' the Post were tight," said Shale.

"The Post looks after the Post." It was a well-worn saying in most lands that knew the Post.

Lokio tried his stew from a ladle while we supped.

"Which estate? There many up there?" said Shale.

"Four gold coins."

"Two," I said.

"Four."

"Four, an' the routine an' places he works in the docks," said Shale.

146

Lokio smiled again, an approving nod I had no hope of telling was true or fake in making us assured of him.

"His estate has the mast of a war galley that was sunk off the coast in his lawns. Easy to spot when you're up there," said Lokio.

I put the coins out from my purse. He held and rubbed one to satisfy himself, then pocketed them smartly, a move speaking greatly of his position given the sum was more than most earned in their lives as soldiers.

"You won't need the routine, boys, I can manage that. If you'll let me finish in here and go and celebrate my daughter's birthday, then you can join me here tomorrow and we'll ride out there. They'll believe you are guards of mine. Once there the subterfuge will be that you have me hostage, and you will release me for leading you to him. I do not wish to know what follows, so long as I am not implicated."

"Seems fair," I said.

"Good. Now, as fearsome as you are, you pale before my daughter if I delay her cake any longer. Ralim will see you out." He give a whistle and Ralim come through shortly and led us out.

Lokio give us a bottle of his Juan wine to leave with and we headed back to the Dens.

I could see Shale was thinking the same as me as we walked through the lanes.

"Din't trust him, Gant, fer all the gold we give him. I'm thinkin' we see where the estate is, got to be somethin' or someone we can see that helps us figure who's doin' the killin'."

"Fair," I said. "He mightn't trick us but he couldn't lose either by sellin' us out. For all we know he could be getting a messenger up there to set something up. I needs me wound doin' but it can wait till we get to some vantage point overlooking the estate. I can scout at dawn if we rides up tonight and you takes watch. If nobody comes we go back in the mornin' an' go with him to find this merchant. If there's somethin' goin' on there then we're prepared for him at least."

"Aye, you should rest up wi' the horses once we're up there an' I'll cover some ground," said Shale.

We set out straight away, getting our horses and riding back up through the old walls and the camps now peppered with fires and the smells of the food got with hard labour or fast fingers.

We looked up past West Head as we rode out of the port and saw some points of vantage in the trees of the high hills beyond his estate, which as Lokio said was easy to spot with that mast and sail he'd got rigged up.

Soon enough we were on foot pushing through the scrub to the treeline that fringed the back of the West Head. It was a few miles' slog leading the horses through a heavy mist filling the euca trees and it caused us much turning about and struggle to get a line up the slopes in the dark.

We set ourselves back from a ridge we reckoned was high up enough and about right for viewing the estates, roped the horses and Shale got to work on my wound.

"Think we might get boar or foxes up here, Gant, I'll trap about an' see what comes in."

Cats and wolves were more my worry with the horses.

Shale moved out and was gone till after dawn. I let my eyes go for a bit after chewing on some kannab and soon enough he give me a kick, and a flask he filled from a stream, to wake me.

"Found ruins of some outpost about a mile over that should give us view o' the main estates. The bilberry an' luta mix'll get us a good look at what's there, long as yer takes a hood. Yer just got to follow the ridge, we'll shift the horses closer before midday. Seen nothing so far to suggest there's a plan against us."

We led the horses across the rocky slopes among the trees. In the light of morning it was easier to see the path for the once used outpost and before the sun hit midday we were at the ruins. The carvings about the beams of the entrance showed the lineage of some monarchy, giving the impression this was of an age before those that ruled Issana now. The carvings were badly bleached and worn, the woods fully drowning the walls, tree roots pulling them to pieces. We were glad for a bit of shade from what walls still stood.

I sat and gave the horses some water while Shale headed up a broken stone stair to the upper level.

"Throw us some o' the mix then," he shouted, balancing on top of a wall.

I found it in a saddlebag and threw it up to him. He smeared his eyes with his usual cussing and stamping. It was a bit like sliding fresh-cut onion on them.

"A fierce sight this, Gant, we got a good look down at those estates. I can see a few people about, mostly Greens, few tradesmen by the looks of it."

I looked about us for signs of boots or ash from nomads or soldiers but it was true deserted, only birds around, riding the winds off the Sar.

I got my eyes juiced and saw good and clear little but what must have been quartermasters laden with books and scrolls, or women from the estates thereabouts, horses dressed like a princess's dollies and colourful silks on their retinues that stood sharp and bright even this far out.

It was Shale that spotted three riders heading up a slope what wound around a few of the big villas, noticeable for they were riding with purpose. The one at the front had a beautiful black horse, brown mane, plaited, must have been much loved by who was riding him.

"Fuck!" said Shale. "Looks like Lokio has sold us out, it's his man Ralim, what took our swords last night. Got a couple with him."

The luta give us a clear enough view of the pair to know it was them. Shale called it right. It was Ralim what was on that horse. They stopped short at some gates of one of the larger houses there, high walls all around, though not high enough for where we were.

A man come out from the main house shortly and Ralim walked up to meet him in the middle of the stone path that went from gates to a suitably grand entrance, showy with the walls all washed white. We thought it was Filston. They spoke for a bit. The man was dressed well enough, a nice belly what come from his living, young enough his hair was dark.

"Lokio fucked up," said Shale.

"We need to get back then before Jaki tells him we in't about at the inn and he gets suspicious."

"We do. Wait though." We watched and saw Lokio's man leave but he spoke to the other two and they rode one way and he rode another, heading northeast.

"We need to get after Ralim, something's bin agreed," I said.

149

Shale nodded.

The seeing mix isn't good for looking close about. I put a rope to Shale to help me as we guided our horses down through the wooded slopes to where we could mount and head back to the roads out of the port.

It was a fair race back to Ithil Bay. We had to hope that if he was leaving Ithil Bay with some message, someone in the fields about would have noticed the horse.

Luck was with us. A slaver's crew and mercs working a wine caravan from some outlying yards recalled the plaited horse and pointed us inland along the East West.

We spread some coin about for sightings and knew he'd fled the highway when some herders pointed across a valley. He was heading for hills, a silvery hint of them beyond the stony yellowed grasslands that give him few copses for hiding.

Eyes juiced, Shale picked him out while we were stopped at a trickle of water dribbling from a sharp ridge what was a feature of this land and that I hated slogging over as infantry.

We give the horses a mix and pushed on. Closing on him was inevitable now.

Sure enough he'd hidden up, one of a few spots we reasoned. He must have seen our following. With arrows bagged and masked up we split and closed to some clusters of trees. Shale signed first.

Horse one hundred fifty west

I knew some action would rip my wound and I was hoping he would spring for Shale. I quickly dropped some swigs of a shiel and caffin mix, hoping the Honour wouldn't be needed with the price I paid for the fall. I was in pain enough.

We fired arrows into the copses we thought he was hidden in. I heard him clear enough after the third arrow.

A moment later an arrow whipped by me not two feet off.

This one was looking to make a fight of it. I signed for Shale to flank and let the mix fill my head. I shut my eyes and only listened. Leather cracked different to wood, hemp different again. He was shifting about some trees ahead, his footfall stirring the grasses that crackled like bacon as he moved. I dropped as the hemp was stretched, opened my eyes and saw the one side of him out of cover. The arrow flew past me and I whistled the call to Shale, give him the whereabouts. Ralim had me spotted and I wasn't quick enough for the approach with this hole in me and no fightbrew.

I heard two bags thump the ground near him, the arrowheads they were on driving them to pieces as they struck.

He was less careful now, beating a retreat from the bags and their dust kicking up into the branches about him.

I moved up with Shale, flushing him out the copse into open land. He took Shale's arrow to his leg, crying out as he twisted over.

"Get hold of him, Shale, he'll do himself!" I shouted.

Shale was on him in moments, ripping off him the fieldbelt and tearing his leathers off to stop him dropping poison.

The shivering and paralysis spread through him fast, standard bitter nightshade, ska base with juberry alka for softening the truth out of him.

"Yer about ta shit and bleed so bad only a bag o' skin'll be left," said Shale up close to his face as he sat astride him. "Yer whole guts is goin' ta fall out an' I'm sorry fer it, but I got this mix takes all that away if yer quick with yer answers. Yer goin' ta share some answers?"

Sun was setting. Poison took all that strength out of him and he was younger than I recalled the previous night, now I took notice of him. I think it made it worse, for he give me the feeling he was only ever in our position as others lay before him begging and yelling, being one of Lokio's gangers. There was nothing he could do against the likes of us though, and he was seeing his life close out already, his eyes wide and throat gone to sand.

Between the gasping, spasms and the hopeless attempt to stop himself from shitting his breeches, he was begging for something, probably us to end him swift. Shale was going through his fieldbelt while the boy started bawling. Fresh drudharch mixes from the Harudan Commune were a fierce experience for whatever end they were made.

His born colouring, shape of his nose and eyes, give him up as a Virate boy, Corob's Dicta or the Redwall, far east.

"Where are you going?" I asked.

It was an eastern tongue that gabbed back. Shale leaped over and put a thumb at his eye.

"Again, you spoke Common well enough yesterday," he said.

151

Lad just didn't know how to react to this.

With the thumb pressing in and Shale fair keen to push it into his head the boy opened up proper.

"Filston's vineyard."

"Is that where we can find him? Alon?" I said.

"Y-yes, I went up to the house on Lokio's order, to find out if Filston was at home. He is visiting his vineyard."

"Lokio plannin' on sellin' us out then was he?" said Shale.

The boy shook his head.

Shale let up and sat on the ground near the boy.

Now the alka was into Ralim's head fierce. Despite being bare of clothes and lying in his shit he seemed to find something amusing, eyes closed and muttering, a smile playing on his smooth shaved face as the fear he had diminished.

"Where's the vineyard, Ralim?" I said.

"Happy Valley."

He was doubling up now, muttering in his own language.

"Hard to tell if we bin sold or not," I said.

"Fuck off, Gant, it's fuckin' obvious we 'ave. Least this way we can get to that vineyard on our own terms." Much as I agreed with him, we soon learned that wasn't right.

He leaned over and with a twist broke the boy's neck.

"I need a pipe, Gant. How's the wound?"

"It'll do," I said.

He packed one and we shared it, bringing the noisies down from our mix.

"That fucker in the Dens sold us up the river. Once we've done Alon I'm goin' back to sort him out. Four gold coins an' all."

He was smiling, usually happened when he was furious, trying to steady his head and stay thoughtful.

"We need to go in brewed up," he said. I nodded. Masks, full rack of mixes. My guts were dreading it and it wouldn't be pretty on the far side.

Happy Valley was a day east of us according to some hunters that we come across a few hours later. Forests of silver oak filled the lands about and we led the horses up through some of it the next day to get to the mouth of the valley.

A dark leather strip of a man, master 'jacker of a settlement of farmers working the oaks and gathering skins about, pointed us to the vineyard itself. I caught a word off him which I took to mean abandoned or dead from my poor Issanaian, along with "river", which we found later and followed as it worked through the slopes of the steepening hills to the vineyard.

We left the horses and some coin with the 'jacker but took care to take away and stash all but the saddles. Couldn't risk anyone finding everything we had if it went wrong and we had to run.

It was a small vineyard, slopes with wild unkept rows of vines what were all over choked up with other bushes and grasses. The river wound up the east side of the yard and around to the north of it, a natural border. We hid ourselves in the trees over the river, looking across the slopes to the villa beyond.

Shale juiced his eyes while I prepped the masks and the Honour.

Shutters firm, paths clear signed Shale, and we both thought that odd with the vines in such a mess. There didn't appear to be any sign of a merchant's retinue and at that point we should have run.

We kissed and drank the Honour, strapped and coated each other's masks, and checked belts, wambas and pads were all fit.

You can't prep for a war alone, and if Ralim was true, then Alon and, we had to assume, his Agents and Reds, would be here. A guild-master that rich wouldn't have any less than Reds or good mercenaries for a guard. I hoped he was here. It would be easy enough to take out his men, and then he was going to tell us what the Twenty were meant to be dying for.

Shale give me the nod as his teeth started to go. The rising was flooding through me, moments where I felt I wasn't stood on the ground at all before my feet took sense of the earth and stones as fine balanced as though I could see with my soles.

We held our belts over our heads as we pushed across the river, its belly high and fast moving.

The luta was a mix blended to work with the Honour. Though it was dark, the juice made it seem there was a strong green moon that lit the vine fields and made the stone of the villa flash like emerald in the summer sun.

We got ourselves in among the vines and stayed low, wondering if anyone was there at this time. I was listening and feeling out for the sentries that would have been posted were the farmhouse full up.

It was then I felt it and I signed for us to stop. The river I could feel in the earth, the sound of it sparkling and hissing in my ears, but there was other disturbance. In my feet it felt like a mist would look to my eyes were it advancing from the trees, a note sat above the heavier song of the river rolling over the rocks of its bed.

Men at villa signed Shale and we crouched as the crack of bowstrings sent arrows at us. It was like a roar around us; one, three, eight men and more coming across the river from north of us and more yet pouring from the house ahead, glowing bright like fireflies to my eyes with their breathing and scuttling through the tangled bushes. They'd watched us crossing. There were a lot more of them than we'd thought.

The arrows hit the earth and vines around us and the spore clouds went up. We were juiced with oak sap and snuffed for the poison of the spores, but a choke or cough would reveal us.

Agents. Reds. Trying a box. Both flanks I signed, as I saw them move along the banks.

Ten fifteen ahead. Five right. Smoke up and burn signed Shale.

We oiled and put out some limebags and shortly the bushes and vines caught and the smoke was up, thick and black for a few yards about us, choking up the runs between the posts. The flames sprung up like fluttering pennants of emerald on this juice. Post Agents took a bilberry mix for night work that would pain the eyes looking on a fire.

We began tracking to the north away from the villa where we sensed fewer of them. Arrows flew into the vines about us, most loaded with powders. We'd get hit or we wouldn't, we had to trust the smoke and fire.

I put arrows out on both flanks, picking off six or seven of them easy as they closed, giving the rest of them pause. The Honour give us the difference between judging where they were moving and knowing it for sure. The world goes slower on the Honour, even the Agents on mixes of their own seemed clumsy. The dying was making a music for my noisies.

Then the first lot of Post pushed in through the vines at us, a few

154

Agents and some Reds. A sharp exchange of whistles called a halt to their arrows. I shouldered Juletta and got my sword ready.

Two come in to our right. One went for Shale as he was nearest to them, the other moved to flank him. Shale was fast, his first thrust was parried but the blow forced the Agent off balance. His leg was skewered and the poison had him screaming as it froze him up and killed him. Shale dropped out of the swing of the other Agent and brought his sword up. It bit through the man's leathers but was enough. He hadn't hit the ground before Shale broke some sporebags out around us, waiting for the next of them to make their move.

Another come in from my left, blowpipe up, a dart stuck to my leather. I backed him up and drew him about and off balance as he struggled to counter. I put my sword through him, feeling the blood and his bones give through his weight on my hand and up through my arm. His life shuddered out of him as his body fell back off my sword. I looked up and saw the green shapes of more men approach. I put another oilbag down to help the vines about us that had caught well. The fire had cut some Agents off from the engagement as they beat their way back to look for a new path at us. The fire hurt their aim too, so they switched to their own powders and bags, a number landing all over this side of the vineyard.

Powder heavy left. Take right flank signed Shale, aiming us back to the river and a run for the woods beyond.

I shot some bags about behind us and we turned and run at some were slowing for a shot at us as we emerged from the cover of the smoke we put about.

I took a dart in my arm, Shale his shoulder, but it was for nothing. Their moonseed-cut was useless on us and had been for years.

First lad we got to, just a Red this one, had a bit too much love for the technique of what he learned. You get in close with those boys, stamping and disabling because they think you'll just play about in the stances like in their training. He went down after I hacked his arm off. Didn't seem to take much to be a Red or an Agent these days, but I couldn't expect all of them to be so easy. I guess they weren't expecting us to be fully prepped. Some choking and yelling went up from where I put the bags earlier as the agave got in their throats and eyes. Three more now were spreading in front of us, one a captain

155

from the looks of his bearing and stance and how he wasn't breathing so fierce as his boys.

Shale forced the engagement. He knew I was struggling for agility with my belly sewn. I moved in against the other two, putting some confidence in them that I'd shown too much of it myself. Then there was a crackle in the vines from where I put the powders and a bow loosed an arrow, in flight seeming to draw the world to it as it made the distance like an iron swift.

"Shale!" I barked as it thumped into his shoulder. It was enough warning that he took the hit and rolled with it, a feint the captain hadn't reckoned. One of the Agents against me leaped forward to force me back to where the approaching archer was drawing some daggers for me. They got a look of frenzy now, these boys, edging in. They were waiting for the arrow to start bleeding Shale out. Shale just worked with it and he's smacking the captain about. Shale matched the moves the captain made, and then he's forced a cut, two cuts and the mix is in the man's blood. Shale sliced his head clean off to the side as his poison give the captain a moment's unsteadiness.

The severed head distracted the one boy who took a moment to figure what Shale was doing. I stepped to him and thrust. His parry forced him off his stance and I caught him swift at the knee, leaving him crying out for the moments he had left, while I rebalanced to face the next.

His brother moved in and got me a blow across the shoulder. It caught in my pads and give me a cut, pushing me back a step as I tried to shake it out of there.

Shale threw a knife between us at the archer with the daggers who was wanting to put pressure on me, a spittle of poison wetting our faces as it come spinning through. It punched through the back of his head.

The boy hesitated now he was alone with us both. He was cut down swift.

We put more limebags to work on the vines about, renewing some cover for movement. Whistling had started up and the arrows were flying again as they saw the fresh smoke billowing out. Shale cursed as he pulled at the shaft in his shoulder.

"Dig this fuckin' thing out," he hissed, "can't use me bow."

We were crouched and Shale got a bag of agave ready as I sliced out the arrow and put a strong kannab and bistort poultice in the wound.

More arrows were ripping holes in the vines and posts about. The whistling was closing in.

Arm signed Shale, looking at where I was cut.

No time I signed.

I gummed some cloth to his shoulder to bury the poultice and keep it tight. They smelled no more than fifteen yards away, leathers folding, less bright through our smoke, but I could see them signing as they stepped out to form a net. It was looking bad for us.

Flower signed Shale, touching his chest where the tin containing his Flower of Fates would be, on the end of a necklace inside his wamba.

Been worse I signed, tapping my own tin for the assurance it seemed to give. He smiled. Eating the Flower of Fates was certain death, it overloads the body, its effect on muscle and bone and blood causing changes too quick and fierce to adapt to. You use it if capture is worse than dying.

Caltrops front left signed Shale, putting thought of the Flower to the side. *I split front, you right for river*. Shale would engage and draw them out to give me a chance to make it.

The air got shifty then and I dropped as a figure crossed the rows of vines before me. He must've been hoping to flank me as I turned to escape. He got sight of me as I jumped at him.

"Got you now, Gant," he said, and I recognised him as he come at me, for it was Gilgul.

"Bit late, you fat fuck, I got me Honour now."

He was as strong as I expected and once I pushed a thrust away I threw myself at him to knock him down but he rode it, and I got a smack in my mouth and he stamped my knee quick. I lost my sight a moment as his punch dizzied me and I hopped back on my good leg to bring my sword about but he was quicker, jumping in, swift with his knee, a blast of pain in my belly.

"Figure I'll keep you busy while my boys cuts your lover up."

He had some advantage, given my gut. I could only parry a moment as I tested my weight on the knee he'd kicked and I tried a few moves, finding his tells. Often the difference between two men good with blades is the read of tells and the training what removes them. One more reason to be grateful for Kailen. He tried to back a bit himself then, buying time while I hears Shale having a tough time of it. I started on him proper then, realising what he was doing, and he was grinning and licking his lips like this was what he wanted, good and aggressive back, finding out what kind of footwork I had on the offensive. He was trying to get me to hit an opening, but the obvious ones were too obvious, for he hadn't fought anyone like me. I let him go a bit then, took him a few moves before he caught up with me, learned I was waiting him out and saving my strength. I caught him at the moment he tried to adjust, a breath where he went to a stance. I'd seen it as we circled, five or six feints and four of them back to his one stance, always a step if his right foot weren't forward, to get it in position. I thrust as he did it, to that side, to move him left, and I went in as he brought his sword over to move mine past him, caught him with a knife to his arm, a quick stab to get the poison in. He had a good high reach with his kick, deceptive with him being so heavy-looking, and he caught me square in the chest, sending me back hard and winded. I watched him as he shook his arm out, the numbing starting.

"In't none o' the usual shit your brew protects you from," I said. "Best come at me while you got use o' yer arms."

He hesitated, as I expected, because he thought I wanted him to come on at me, but what I wanted in truth was his hesitation, and the poison got going quick, because it was straight out of the Commune, fresh and strong. He switched his sword to one hand instead of two, and now it was working on him, making him pant. For Shale's sake I couldn't draw it out, much as I wanted it. I went at him fast and he was game for a bit, but without his full range I soon took his dead arm off and put my sword through his middle before taking a leg off. He was gone.

There was the bang and hiss of steel as Shale was engaging a few of them to let me get out of there. They were hard on him, one back putting darts in him while the others were defensive, dancing out or moving in as he picked which to engage.

More sporebags come in on arrows then, throwing clouds of it up where they were going at it. Staying in it was going to take them all down but some other captain was playing the odds we'd be pacified.

Shale was grace itself, the Honour filled out a strength and balance that come natural. I run to him, no doubt it would be with him I'd die. I could see in the milky green of the world their blowing and jumping about as he used the posts and bushes to split their teamwork, putting caltrops about as he did. He was blowing for air too though, the poisons were getting a grip as the cuts sliced into his leathers.

They started choking as their own spores worked their way in. The fire was picking up fierce too, sweeping our way across the vineyard. The whole place was going up for it was days since the last rains.

Slowed by my cuts I was still drawn to get in among them with my noisies up. One turned as I closed from behind him. He whistled something out before trying to blind me with what powders they use. The luta mix would save my eyes but the Honour give me senses enough I closed them as the powders blew out and I followed his lines from the noise, feel and smell of his moves.

A moment later I saw enough to lure him into a lunge to strike and he hit a post instead. I put my boot into his belly as he tugged at the blade and I jammed my sword into his back as he doubled over.

My throat was rasping a bit now. Those about Shale, Agents among them, didn't have the masks as well pasted and were hacking up and struggling to see. They were man enough to fight on for the Red. One of them stepped on a caltrop as he was thrown back by Shale's attack, which was poison enough to finish him, and the last one on Shale was killed as I joined up and forced him into Shale's blade. I looked about for more when I heard a horn go up, back near the house itself. Some fighting was going on. Me and Shale looked at each other wondering what the reason of it could be, but the state we were in it was time to get out before any more Agents could find us.

Flames were sweeping fast around us. A few more whistles passed about. It was hard to see now and we choked up a bit as we covered the yards to the river.

"You come back. Weren't the plan," he hissed as we stripped our belts again and dropped into the water heading for the far bank.

I hadn't the strength to talk, my head was throbbing as the noisies dropped. The cut on my arm was aching bad, I could hardly lift my belt, much less use my bow. My belly felt wet, wound must have opened at some point.

Arm needs fixing signed Shale, seeing the blood pouring from me as we staggered out of the river on the far side.

We stopped a moment and he worked quick, trying to stifle his coughing. Kannab water to his eyes and then my arm, the pads cut off so he could get to the wound. Some powdered bark on the cut and he covered it off with some soaked cotton strips.

Split. Two miles. North and east. Horses in two days he signed.

I hauled myself to my feet and headed east, making a way through the cool moonlight to the woods ahead and leaving behind the whistling and crackling of the burning vineyard.

I cried like a dut. The fall was more vicious than in many winters. I was curled up most of the next day under an overhang of rock as I paid the colour. I was shitting fierce and sicking up what strips and biscuits I ate. Belly was agony and I was burning up as a fever set through. Shale was somewhere off and in the same state. If we were found now it would be over.

Kailen and the Spike

This is a Rhosidian lord's account of the Battle of Ubetzwan, 641 OE, against a Tetswanan army that had been wreaking havoc along the Rhosidian border. Incidentally, it wasn't until the following battle of that campaign that Kailen came across Harlain and recruited him.

Goran

The Tetswanans had a marvellous general, Orko Trisi, Orko being their own term for a general. Made a virtue of their lack of horse and excellent counters to our plant. He'd mastered us in two engagements, having bolstered his southern flank with Seeyaltans. Bloody awful savages, but fierce soldiers.

I was a captain at the time, newborn to it. Ubetzwan was my first where I had command of some soldiers. Coming from the coast, the interior of southern Rhosidia was murderously hot. The Tetswanans were looking to push back our border to the oasis of Outpost Forty, which you will have heard of if you know anything of Rhosidian history.

We were confident, given they had little more than some light horse. We had near a thousand, good horses from the Alagar, who were concerned about their own border with Tetswana and its aggression.

They were drilled exquisitely well, advancing quickly on our forces as we were organising our flanks. Our general sent our own infantry after some softening up with our archers, but as the line approached, at some command they changed formation, forming a spike, a wedge with, counter-intuitively, some of their best men and women at the front. We learned to our great cost that they had a counter for our dust, for the volleys did not slow them.

161

They rather easily broke the line of our own infantry and split them. I commanded a unit near the rear of our advancing forces and saw that we had little answer to the formation.

Our General called for the flanking cavalry, but their wedge proved to be an effective counter even to that. As our horse hit their middle, aiming to disrupt their formation, their rear troops, being the wide end of the wedge, fanned out quickly to provide a counterflank to our horse.

These rear soldiers immediately started hurling their javelins at the horses held up by disciplined spear and shield formations at the sides of the wedge. Soon enough our cavalry had to regroup and they had at this time broken through our infantry lines and were running at the archers and reserves. Panic set in. I bid my men hold but was mocked and left to either face them and die with courage or flee myself. I chose the latter I'm glad to say.

The next engagement went similarly, an outcome I and a number of other captains were appalled at, for we received no orders that suggested a counter to the spike employed by the Tetswanan infantry. We must have lost near ten thousand men in both battles, six standards lost as well, which our generals were bent on getting back, for the four they'd captured in the first battle were paraded during the second.

Ubetzwan was a settlement built near the strategically important lake on the opposite side of which was Outpost Forty. The rains were due and taking the settlement and holding it would offer us a significant advantage once the rains had replenished the basin.

At this time we were desperate for soldiers of any sort, and the queen, the formidable Queen Vaurn, borrowed from various guilds and brokers to fund the war and the recruitment of mercenaries and more horse from the Maiols of Alagar.

A mercenary, my age, name of Kailen and apparently a Purple Rose winner of noble lineage at the Harudan War Academy, had requested he be present at the council preparing an assault on Ubetzwan.

At first he came across as ill mannered, for with the presentation the generals made of the ground for battle and how we would try to engage their forces using a river as a means of breaking their formation by trying to draw them over it he rolled his eyes and sucked in his cheeks and made a great noise of sighing and shaking his head. The impression of him wasn't helped by his curious appearance, some accident with brews I was told, had skin that looked and felt like wood, most curious. It lent him an air of savagery that didn't sit well with the generals.

"Someone take that pup outside and give him a kicking while we try to win this war!" said our Lord of Kailen.

"You've explained what has happened twice to your army but you present no solution, Warlord," Kailen replied. "Let me present you a solution."

We thought he'd get his throat cut for that; it's happened for less and to men of greater standing.

"I am in sore need of entertainment and a refill of this cup, young Kailen, so please, take the floor; the map and our pieces are yours."

He laid out the first battle much as I have here, and described, as I have here, what the flaws were with our tactics.

He assumed, correctly, that the Tetswanan general had too limited a set of options to engage with our army except as he had done so, for we had cavalry, horse archers and foot soldiers. He explained as well the composition of our arrowbags and the counter that the Tetswanans had. Our own drudhas concurred that his assessment would be broadly correct, for he, and his famous drudha Ibsey, had learned well the plant available in the region, what could be farmed or harvested in sufficient quantity.

Contrary to even my own thought regarding how to engage them, he took the cavalry from the map and replaced each *centa*, that is, a hundred horse, with foot soldiers, equipped with bows, behind a front line of infantry. He then placed the horse archers at the flanks.

He had the stallion's balls to tell us that we would lose a lot of infantry but in return would utterly defeat the Tetswanans if we followed his plan. He proposed also that his drudhas prepare a different recipe for our arrowbags.

Of course, the other flaw he pointed out in the generals' planning was that in holding Ubetzwan, the Tetswanans had no need to cross the river, nor indeed would it present much of a barrier, being dry just before the rains, for all that its banks would make a marching re-formation a challenge if we were on the slopes less than a thousand yards off.

So we lined up as we had previously, at least to the eyes of the

Tetswanans, who saw the cavalry they needed to see, for the archers were equipped with axes and shields, but each shouldered a bow and their saddles were packed with quivers under blankets.

The Tetswanans marched forward, singing and shouting, and in their midst were our banners. Again we marvelled, as they approached us, at how well drilled they were as they changed to their spike.

Our infantry marched out to meet them, my unit and those of my fellow captains that commanded the cavalrymen now on foot were ordered to stay where we were, not follow behind. Our hail of arrows did little to break them, at first, as had happened previously, and they charged at us. Kailen's drudhas had helped our army concoct a mix that would not work immediately, to better support our subterfuge.

Our infantry did their best and I could not have been the only one that suffered for watching my countrymen die as these brave hearts did, for we could not have told them how this would be won if we had wanted to avoid a mass desertion after two morale-sapping defeats.

Kailen was with the generals and through the horns and flags our flanking horse archers were signalled.

He had timed it brilliantly. No sooner had their vanguard broken to the rear infantry ranks the horse archers charged the flanks. We were then commanded to defend our own archers, forming smaller wedges before the offset formations of archers. As their spike slowed to meet the impending assault the horse archers stopped some hundred yards off, out of the range of most of their javelins. They started peppering them with arrows. While their men were somewhat prepared for this on the flanks of the wedge, the arrowbags we shot at them contained powders that even on the breeze of that day required only a small amount carry to be sufficient to reduce our men to weeping and putting on hoods. Their soldiers suffered exquisitely as the powders rose around them.

Their reaction was to push forward of course, where our archers launched more of these bags at their vanguard, once what remained of our infantry fled past us. Trapped between breaking formation to take on the horse archers on both flanks or progressing into those of us who had stayed back to have the space to launch volleys, they broke up. For all that the powders weren't fatal, their men could hardly see, and their captains struggled to control their ranks as they spread out to attack the horse archers, who, as I'm sure you've rightly deduced, were fast enough to evade them and harry them to their deaths.

We lost seven hundred men that day, they lost seven thousand. The standards were recovered, their general captured and their drudhas captured and tortured for whatever they knew.

It is no accident that we would turn to him a few years later, when General Urutz led a column towards Tharos Falls, our whole kingdom under threat.

Chapter 9

Sand

I am leaving the jungle to take my revenge.

I have spent many years here, living a life of research and experiment, in the garden of a magist, ten or more perhaps since I landed on that beach.

While I still recollect so little of my life as a boy, the family I may have had, I have gained the recollection of what happened to me, how it was I became a slave. I will keep this journal while there are still things I do not recall.

I still do not remember my name.

The story of my slavery up to the point I was shipwrecked I had put in a chest in the garden of the magist and forgotten about it. It had been written in the village of the fishers, the fishers that found me washed up on their beach, but the ink was of poor quality and somewhat faded, so I have rewritten it and continue it here.

One morning, already punishingly hot, there was a gathering as four men on horseback arrived in that small community that had rescued me from the sea.

Their command of these people's language was halting. I caught the eye of one as he noticed me emerging from the doorway of the chief's large thatched house. We had both paid the colour, his colourings a mottled gold and brown, which against such dark skin made him and those of these riders that had paid the colour enough look like leopards, though from what place I recall this I do not know. Blacks that paid the colour in the Old Kingdoms looked the more diseased or bruised due to the red and green those fightbrews caused.

We stayed at the fringes while the trade was conducted, waiting to talk to each other. He wore a fieldbelt, so must have been a drudha to these visitors. A skin full of the seeds I'd seen the villagers thread into their children was swapped for some coins and what looked like tea leaves.

The drudha approached me, shortly after tea was passed around the traders, drinking to health.

"I am . . . Sand. I was shipwrecked, a storm," I said, anticipating his question.

"King's Common? Are you from the Old Kingdoms, thamir? Sorry, drudha?"

I nodded. He showed me a fieldbelt of sorts sewn in the folds of his cotton robe.

"Drudha is thamir here. My Common not good. I am Loza."

"I need to get back to the Old Kingdoms," I said.

He laughed. "You are far side of the world, drudha."

He held up a hand for me to wait and spoke to the negotiator in the group, a man who scowled for the entire time, a head like the end of a club. His appraisal of me was swift; a sharp exchange of words with Loza followed. Then he gestured to me as he addressed the village leader.

Shortly I found myself embraced by most of the village, a flask of the milk brew my parting gift.

The thamir helped me up onto his horse. None but he spoke King's Common.

"Are you selling me back into slavery, Thamir?" I asked as we left the village and rode a trail inland.

"No. But drudha without his book is not valuable drudha. I want the recipe you know. You will be fed and free. These people tell me you speak much in your sleep. I will listen to your dreaming, drudha. You dream plant I am told."

"I would be grateful if you would share what you hear with me. It may help me to remember more."

I had not yet seen his recipe book, but as with most of us it would be hidden away on him, coded in a cyca I would have little or no chance of deciphering, particularly without a deep familiarity with their language.

Over the following three days we rode across lands rising slowly from the coast, trails cutting through bleached brown grasses and patches of fig trees and a sort of oak I'd not seen before; bright orange bark that the thamir and one of the other travellers stripped away and stored some of while we rested, presumably to treat stings and cuts.

None of these men had seen hard service, at least none had been paying the colour deeply. The swagger of the men with Loza suggested they had not seen anything like a war. Blooded soldiers lose their swagger quickly.

The milk and rum brew I had been given was quite restorative. I hadn't felt as strong since before the Droop. The brew had a breed of gilead leaf, the tell-tale bitter resin thickening the drink. The rest I did not recognise.

Despite this return of my strength I did not consider killing these men and escaping. I knew too little of the lands around us and the clan to whom they belonged. I saw that Loza had been writing, for he sat over me as I woke, marking his book with the characters of his cyca.

On the evening of the fourth day we approached their camp, a fierce sun casting the hundreds of tents in silhouette at the top of a plateau overlooking a dried-out river basin.

Ten guards walked this approach. Scouts moving in at least three groups flanked the basin and more in the hills about, to judge from the unwise campfires. Escape would not be on foot.

Past a tannery, pens of chickens and the tangy smoke of the settlement preparing food I was led through a wall of stakes to one of the grander pavilions of the inner camp.

Seated at the entrance to this pavilion was a man wearing the first iron breastplate I had seen since leaving the Old Kingdoms. He stood up from a platter of rice and strips of lamb to shake hands with Loza and the trader who led our group back from the coast.

I understood only "drudha" in the conversation that followed. He was not the chief or lord, for a grander pavilion stood fifty yards to my right, but from his bearing he must have been a captain.

He stepped past them to me, pulled back my sleeves, scrutinised my arms and hands, then my eyes, fully yellow with my paying the Drudha's Share. More talking followed and Loza appeared to protest to something. Two guards came for me and I was marched out to the perimeter of the main camp, edged by a sheer drop some twenty yards to the river basin below.

We were followed and watched by boys and girls, most in tobs as was usual in such lands near the midden, some naked.

They stopped short of the dogs that flanked the gate to the compound, the ten of which leaped to the ends of their ropes barking and straining for me. I noticed the faintest scent of a treatment on the gates, poison for the unwary escapee no doubt.

A student of Loza's worked at the wounded hands of some quivering wretch at a bench in front of the shelters. Under these shelters, tied to stakes, were prisoners huddled to shelter from the sun. I submitted to the gestures and prods of swords as I entered one of the tents. Inside were stakes with lengths of rope attached, allowing some movement. Each stake was walled off with a panel of woven hair sewn into a frame hanging from the roof.

My hands were bound and I was left listening to a man in the next partition, the only other man in this tent I could sense, whispering in their language.

I dreaded being put on the Droop again, being submerged, suffocated in its coils. I couldn't walk that road back a second time. Feeling the knotted rope working into my wrists I pulled at them with a fury, wishing my hands severed. I swore and stamped, and muttered and stamped again, in a frenzy at how quickly I was back in chains again. The whole camp could burn if it meant my freedom, I said to myself. I felt betrayed by this thamir and it compounded the air of betrayal that I carried like a head cold.

The man nearby fell silent. The wind blew the stink of festering wounds through from the tortured in their heaps around the posts outside.

My rage then subsided, the surety of this older me worming its way back in more strongly, decades of soldiering working despite me, the advice of a man whose name escaped me, a leader I knew, drawing me out of this agitated reverie. It is better sometimes not to act, he said, the world will act and it is just a matter of being ready for it.

Loza, the thamir, came for me at dawn.

"I am sorry. I could not change the captain's mind. Your colour is strong; you have been warrior he thinks. Dangerous."

"No. This is the colour the drudhas of the Old Kingdoms pay for their experiments. I cannot wield a sword."

He nodded and led me to a tent the same as the drudha tents in warcamps everywhere. Here were men injured in familiar ways, wounds from battle, the cuts and bruises of drunken disputes or rivalries, but the poisons were unfamiliar, as were some of the stings and bites from the creatures in these parts.

The tools for presses were primitive, as was the influence of Loza's faith in what must have been a magist, Lorom Haluim, said to reside in the vast jungle to the east and who had in centuries past supposedly walked among his people. I did not, however, disillusion him on that score. How could anyone believe there were people with the power to change the world when it was as awful as it is?

I was to assist him, earn their trust, share my knowledge of plant. These things I did, all the recipes I could divulge were recorded in his journal, the ones I'd learned on the ship that I had not forgotten. Others he took from my dreaming, as he had hoped, and as he told them to me, hoping I could make sense of the rambling that characterises sleep-talking, they came back to me. I embellished them, only partly correctly depending on the recipe he gave. I put him right on some of his errors as well to further bolster my standing with him.

In between the treatment of wounds and fevers in the medica, I worked with Loza on the field mixes. Aside from the captain who came in to look at his soldiers, Loza's weathered and rather fraught wife would sometimes come with soup and rice while we worked, bringing with her their daughter who proudly showed us her latest weavings. He seemed happiest, however, as I was, alone with his pots, aludels and sand bath and paying the Drudha's Share.

Within a few weeks I was led to the prisoners' compound but not tied to the stake. I used this time to renew my acquaintance with my body and its ability to kill. I had the colouring of a soldier, I watched their soldiers being drilled from a rip in my tent, and I copied their movements, for my own drills were lost to me. These were hard enough at the beginning, as I was recovering the use of my body. It was an attempt both to prepare myself for an escape, but also to recover, if I could, some memory of the past.

I managed to take an interest in the camp through the mutterings

170

and comings and goings of the injured, as well as feigning some sympathy for Loza, for the pressure the captain and his own wife put him under. He translated for me enough that I learned the warlord was readying for a test of borders, to resolve the dispute of more fertile land south with a rival.

We worked long into the nights now on the mixes, traders and scouts bringing greater quantities of ingredients in, the students of the thamir preparing them for us to distil, mix and separate. I now knew my way around the various bottles in the chests; poisons, curatives and the stores of the concentrates for the blade rubs.

Over two hundred men would be gone in two days, forty to stay. The world was presenting me with my escape.

Through a sharp, clear dawn I worked with Loza to pack the horses and fill the fieldbelts of the soldiers. The women here weren't given to much wailing at their men departing; the children, as in all villages and settlements I'd been stationed at, cried. I vowed then I would go within the day, while the routine was broken and men were a few more measures of wine off balance.

I barely caught a glimpse of the warlord himself; Loza alone was responsible for the captains' belts. I watched the men march away southwest, five riders spreading out ahead of them, moving off into thick brush.

The camp drifted back to its duties, the remaining soldiers jostling and laughing with each other while congregated. A whistle cut through them as the watch commander approached, using a black staff bookended with a dull metal lump to force them into a line and to sort them into watches.

The stables were near Loza's tent, four horses left, any one of which would have to bear me out of the camp under fire from whoever I couldn't kill. I had to hope these women weren't trained to wield bows as they were in many of the hasts spread throughout the old countries.

Loza excused himself for something to eat at his own tent two hours after the last of the warband left sight of the camp. Alone, I drank a mix to counter their poisons and a fightbrew, then hooked a water flask to a belt I'd been given to hold up my breeches, worn by other slaves over the years to a state of filthy fragility.

I began to rise, the rush out from my belly, dropping something

171

like white hot, agonising lava into my legs, a javelin of iron seeming to fix rigid my neck as the shell of ordinary thought and doubt burned to a husk. This was a far better brew than I could have guessed, confirming the vivacity of the plant in these parts, a spirit, a note of rawness, that seemed unusual and also powerful, perhaps because so much plant in the Old Kingdoms would have been heavily cultivated in farms to meet the demand of so many.

Also, the absence of powders in their recipes meant I did not need to fashion a mask as I waited for Loza to return. The use of sporebags or dust was unknown to them.

When he did come back he saw immediately from my skin and my movement that I was risen and was planning to escape.

"We can say you could not stop me, Loza."

"They not believe me, would kill me. You work good, you earn trust, Sand. Don't do this."

"I am leaving, so I'll be quicker with you than they would."

He shuddered, shocked by the imminence of his death. He looked about desperately for a knife or some other instrument to defend himself. I caught his raised arm and broke it with a twist, before crushing his throat. I performed this murder calmly, there was some-thing natural about it, something beyond the thirst for blood a brew gives. I understand how strange it is that the feeling of familiarity with myself I craved should be fulfilled so.

I had no time to try to remove his tob to disguise myself. I found a knife on a bench and tore open the tob to get at his journal. I pushed it into my shirt and walked out of the tent.

In the stable I met only a young man. He frowned as I approached, about to question my unaccompanied presence. I leaped at him and knifed him in his throat to keep him from raising the alarm. The horses were stirred, kicking at the ground as I intruded. I fought for some self-control to display to them, approaching them in a way I must have learned from somebody, some way to settle them as I neared.

I recognised one of the trader's horses and put on her reins. I smeared poison on the necks of the horses that remained, enough to render them useless in pursuit in the few minutes it would take to sink through their hair and skin.

I walked her through the small clearing they used for a paddock and led her towards the slope I approached the camp from those weeks previously. The three guards watching this approach were sat talking outside the rows of stakes that marked the camp's outer boundaries.

I mounted and charged the horse past them, holding myself low to it. They turned at the sound of the approaching hooves, only one with a bow, but sharp enough of eye that he loosed an arrow that caught me in the shoulder. It nearly punched me from the horse's back, would have if not for the thrilling strength I'd missed since I last drank a fully potent fightbrew.

A horn rang out across the plateau. I turned northeast and rode across more open ground.

Taking the reins with one hand I tugged at the arrow but the barbs were firm. I snapped the shaft and kept going. The pain seeped through as the movement of the horse ground the arrowhead against my shoulder blade. The brew kept me alive, the wound bleeding only slowly. I ran the horse to death, there was no point in slowing until I had found either the jungle itself or somewhere to hide and trap. Two days' ride to the edge of the jungle, Loza said. I could not be far.

The horse pulled up shortly after the sun had set behind us. We had passed through some trees that skirted a slope. I needed to scale it to get my whereabouts.

Her head bowed as her frame shook with her breathing, her sweat had soaked us both. Then she stumbled as I dismounted. I smoothed her nose down and brought her head to face me. I buried the knife in her skull with a heavy fist. She was too exhausted to react.

At the crest of this hill I fell to my knees. The great star was already risen and its silver light revealed the edge of a valley. Across this great rift enormous trees stood on the vast claws of their exposed roots, the edge of the Hanwoq jungle, an unmeasured expanse that Loza had said no drudhas or travellers had broached the full extent of in their search for a passage to the Dust Coast from the Old Kingdoms in the far east.

I managed to get the arrow out with my knife. I did what I could to stop the bleeding with the few mixes I had. After resting a short while I found a route down and up the other side that I doubt could have otherwise been followed without a good brew or two strong working shoulders.

I passed into the trees the following morning, the climb having exhausted me to the point of collapse.

The huge kapoks, as I later learned them to be called, threw out their vast roots across the earth, so boggy here at the head of this valley that the mist filled any route ahead. I had no idea where I was wandering, except that I needed to escape any trackers that the thamir's people might have sent after me.

With the wound beginning to fester in this humid chaos, crawling now with midges and flies that filled the air, I quickly withered as the brew's claim compounded my thirst and slowed me. After two days my flask was dry. It was a further two days before I found a large stream, hoping that any people that used it might then find me.

Among the ferns and trees that killed my sense of direction I began to realise the strange and fearsome nature of this place. Some of the trees, the natives called them Chicle trees, had bark that wept a gum, ingesting the insects and birds that attempted to feed on the sticky fluid as they were caught in it and dissolved. I fled across the stream at one point to avoid ants each the size of a child's hand swarming over a clearing from a landslide that had felled trees, building a nest from the detritus about them. I saw orchids of the most vivid colours and hoped for a closer look until I felt movement in the vines that grew out across the ground many yards around them, forming wreaths around the bones of animals and at least one man. They gave off a pungent smell of fresh meat. One of the vines split as I approached, some liquid seeping from it that gave off vapours that dizzied me. I held my breath and ran as other vines opened up, though the drudha in me wished to understand better the properties of such exquisite plant. Away from that nest of flowers, my progress into the jungle alongside the stream was then blocked by vast walls of webs some fifteen yards high stretched across the lower branches and trunks of a number of trees. To avoid discovering what lay within I had to double back and find new paths around and over the steep knolls, each a fight against the soft earth and slippery roots.

I had little defence against the mosquies and flies. Six days of climbing and descending these hidden hillsides and I'd only recognised figs and termites for food. The vines gave some water better

174

than the stream's but my hands were raw and swollen from the fine hairs they shed like barbs into my skin as I held them for cutting and draining.

Dizziness and then vomiting began on the seventh day. My shoulder was swollen and the hole wept, thick with maggots. I collapsed against a trunk once more near the stream I'd followed. I came to fully realise my solitude, the pointlessness of carrying on and the knowledge there was no way back. As the hours went by a howling grew in my head, perhaps some infection in my ears. The water chattered as though through a chamber, the damp trees and bushes seemed to be waiting, full of a presence, an intelligence. I could not stop or control this wailing of the things that lived about me, singing their instincts, a discordant orchestration of hunger.

Soon the phantoms appeared; soldiers, some whose faces eluded my focus, others in violating detail, their skin as dead and smooth as beach-worn pebbles. They cast a massive shadow all about them, as though mountains had elected to walk, at once six feet high and ten thousand high. I knew only that I knew them, no names or memories were otherwise tied to them. They weren't welcoming, they were judging me. Thoughts passed between them, frowns and glances betraying a council passing sentence.

The man at their head brought debate to an end. His eyes closed as he stopped above me, closing out the sun, muttering old hymns I sang as a boy. Theirs was a cold wind in this suffocating and moist audience of trees. This was a reckoning of my life by monsters not fit to judge me or stand against me. They stood for a time in that silent confederacy. I did not care to look at them, I had had enough, so I let myself collapse, to die and be free or live to find and conquer the cause of my suffering.

A sweet nutty smoke brought me awake at some unknown time after. I was lying near a fire on a rattan slenka, the mat having bamboo poles at the side and drawn together at one end to facilitate dragging of supplies, or in this case my body.

I itched savagely, but felt cool. It was the noise then that invaded as I shed the doze I was in; the rattling and buzzing, the ticks, chattering and rasps of the insects and creatures about. I sensed someone was near, I heard a spoon tickling a bubbling pot over a fire, then I smelled the broth, a tang of meat.

It is a struggle to describe him for the noise in one's mind and senses when one is near him. As a man he seemed at times forty summers, at other times more than sixty, his frame seemingly built from dock ropes covered with a paper-thin skin. His colour was in places iridescent; scarlet and dragonfly green mottling his skin. It all served to illuminate the close-cropped white hair losing its grip on the crown and a moustache like a shelf of snow on his lip.

He wore only some heavy cotton pants and sandals, a few pouches hanging from a belt. One in particular, when it opened and I was near, seemed to change the air; my hair stood up, a tickling on my arms, and I felt like I was slipping into a dream of that moment, not there awake. At one point shortly after I began to recover my strength he took from it some dull brown powder and sprinkled it like salt over me.

"You have no inclination to ask me of this pouch," he said.

I smiled. Of course I was inclined to ask him about it, but looking back, I never did.

"You live. You must eat."

He spooned the broth into a wooden bowl and stood over me as I eased myself up onto my elbows to better see him and this place.

His eyes were as white as his hair, or as close to it as I could settle on, but he wasn't blind. The lean cheeks and jaw were a firm reference where the eyes and mouth felt indistinct; a paternal look in a moment switched to exasperated or sad. He noticed my scrutiny.

"I'm told my spirit, my nature, is of such power it turns the eye from me. The Etil, whom you shall meet shortly, no longer look, believing it bad luck. It is refreshing to meet someone's gaze."

This amused him, something I felt as much as saw as I took the bowl from him and tipped a sip to my lips.

It was fiery; I coughed hard but continued, savouring the fatty, salty flavour.

He stood back and at once the air became warmer. He smiled; I wondered if a frown played through it but gave up the speculation to finish the broth.

We were in a natural clearing, at the base of a kapok. For a short while I watched him as he picked at and rooted among the grasses here and climbed the trees about with the strength of a young sailor at the rigging.

Loza's journal had been taken, as had the plant I carried with me from my escape from that camp.

"Who are you?" I asked.

"The tribes of Etil about call me all manner of things; beyond this jungle I think I've successfully managed to be forgotten. The name most familiar to you is Lorom Haluim."

So unexpected was it to hear this I believe I just smiled.

"That cannot be. Lorom Haluim is the name of a magist, who cannot now be alive if the legends speak true. And legends are never true."

"I understand. Well, it is my name, I am happy to have saved your life and I am happy to have your company if you are willing to share it."

"I am greatly indebted, and wish no insult. I . . ." But what was there to say. He was the more convincing for not seeking to convince me. His plant, his drudhaic knowledge, must have been excellent to so quickly ease my pain and clean my wounds. His art was easily the equal of my own, from this first experience of him.

"You have paid the Drudha's Share, as an old friend once told me it was called. Your hands and scars tell me you were at some point a soldier. You have burned more recently, I see coca milk was used to heal you, indeed I can still smell it, can you? You are of the Old Kingdoms, and your brand tells me a slave most recently."

"You speak King's Common well for a native of Hanwoq," I said, sitting fully upright now as the broth brought me to.

"I'm not a native of this beautiful place. I did travel for some years about those lands, the Old Kingdoms. I prefer it here, the plant here is unlike any in this world, but I think I might not love it as much had I grown up here. Come, we have a few leagues yet to travel."

He stood and began kicking over the fire, preparing to leave. I stood up slowly and noticed that the tattered shirt I arrived in was gone. I wore cotton leggings similar to his. Sandals also similar to his were on the ground near the stretcher, soles of a kind of serpent hide, straps softer, the skin of a deer perhaps, affording excellent purchase on the damp stones and, I would learn, the tree trunks themselves.

We left the stretcher he had brought, though he untied the rattan and rolled it up. He took up hammer, pegs and the cooking pot and fastened the lot to loops on his belt. I tested my shoulder; only a mild soreness beneath some clay that he must have soaked on. It would later crumble and leave only a scar, no worse than others I bore considering the cause.

The next few hours in the airless wet halls of the jungle beneath the canopy were hard. He seemed unaffected by it, climbing easily over wet rocks as we scaled ridges and slid down their far sides, crossing torrents flowing hard from deep in the jungle with the use of pegs he hammered into the rocks they flowed over, to give us steps. The ways he took I could see were paths of a sort, though to look behind me I could see little beyond the atap and bamboo we had somehow manoeuvred past. More than once he held my arm and bade me stay close as we approached dark thickets of vines and ferns. As my senses hazed the thickets seemed to wash around us, as if we had passed through a clearing, though to look back they seemed undis-turbed. I was feeling exhausted by his proximity, the strange effect he had, but as my mind cleared from his stepping away I saw we were stood in a valley with three natives of the forest, the Etil. They were barefoot, much shorter than either Lorom Haluim or I, with only skirts of cloth, some with stitchings I later learned the significance of. Their colour was subtle, a greenish tinge to their bronze skin, their hair almost uniformly a ropy knotted black. They all wore finely carved wooden links and other fixings to their hair, which gave a clacking sound as they ran, the carvings on them a kind of history of their tribe, their favourite stories and teachings on them, as well as stories of their own that I later learned would be collected on their death.

"Oldor-Etil," said Lorom Haluim, "I know all eighteen of the hasts, as you would call them, of the Etil. These Oldor are closest to me, though I tend all the rivers when I can, rivers being their own term for 'hast'."

They spoke quickly, chittering in part, animating their speech with wild expressions, as though their faces conveyed part of the meaning to what they said. Lorom Haluim responded in kind, much flicking of his tongue, baring of teeth and rolling of the eyes. After a few moments he turned to me.

"I have some healing to attend to, they have some gifts for me, some plant hard to come by even for natives to this place. Come."

I followed them across a stream bubbling over stones and around boulders in a wide valley, the air cooling with the setting sun. A route had been cleared from bottom to the top of this valley, a hard couple of leagues on which, most of the way up, I had not the strength to ascend further until one of the Etil tied a rope around me to help pull me along.

As the plateau widened we broke through the canopy of the trees and I saw something of the endless jungle around. To the west it broke open to the lands I'd escaped from, but all else, the towering ridges and bluffs this hilltop looked up to, was green, fading blue in the mists of evening, shades of further cliffs in the far distance.

Nearby were around fifteen huts, some open at the sides, some with woven rattan panels tied to the posts that supported their roofs.

A group of young men, beeth chewers, chins and throats red from the excess spit of their habit, were preceded by their children, screeching and all baring teeth for their customary greeting. They appeared to have no fear of me, smitten by the returning Lorom Haluim, but I was watched by the men, considering me an intruder. Lorom Haluim swept the children up one at a time, which put the men at ease. I was no threat. Our three companions greeted them and hollered for the beeth.

"Take some, Sand," said Lorom Haluim. "It will be well received, though your guts will say otherwise tomorrow."

I took only a few leaves, enough it seemed to avoid an insult. My teeth began buzzing within moments and it soon spread a tingling warmth through me, my head feeling light, sleepy and happy. I sat down and watched the settlement go through its evening. I was requested to join in some songs of theirs, my attempts to mimic their chatter apparently appreciated. Their women joined the men later, some coming up from that awful climb laden heavy with water. An elder then brought out some flasks of boiled rootmilk they called Bala (said with the raising of eyebrows twice). A swig of this was shortly going to knock me out.

I learned that this was the fourth house of the Oldor-Etil, four of eighteen that lived by rigid boundaries for hunting and farming from other Etil, Oldor or otherwise. Only two of the men present could find a way to the paths of the Seventh and Third Houses nearest to them, the protocol fiercely respected, for any that might invade these lands would not be able to progress without knowledge of the paths and river crossings; this much was clear first-hand this last few days.

They had some sympathy for my having been a slave. I was fed well on tapi root and a very sweet potato I had not previously tasted, both of which would become staples over the following years when animals could not be found.

I must have slept like the dead that night; I did not recall drunkenness. My bubbling stomach woke me. I barely had time to get up and hobble to the edge of camp before a thin stream of shit announced the start of my acclimatisation to their food and plant.

"It is my view," said Lorom Haluim, a little way behind me, "that what we eat and drink contains forms of life too small for us to see without a lense, and that your body takes some time to grow used to them passing through it."

"You have a lense?"

"Oh yes. We should go, there is much to show you at my own camp."

Two days working towards those distant cliffs I saw on my first ascent to the Oldor-Etil would have been one but for the cramps and my weakness. I felt swamped with questions, surrounded as we were by so much plant and so many creatures. He gave a potted commentary on much that we passed. At one point he cursed and dragged us quickly off the path. A patch of flowers grew there, a foot or so from root to stem, large orange leaves and drooping violet petals like a crowd of heads in downcast cowls. As we passed by I felt a severe headache and my eyes watered, weeping for the next hour. Some insects were unaffected, the ingestion of which would in turn reduce the potency of this flower's lethal scent.

There were many such things we encountered, some I could scarcely credit with the effect he had tested and observed as they were prepared for brews or mixes. He had a cure for river blindness, a cure too for deafness in some. On occasion he practised a piercing of the chest with a bamboo needle, its hollow filled with a mix that could sometimes revive one who had shortly died. Usually it was the children that survived such treatment, if at all, but it was astonishing to see.

What passed for his home was the most curious and wondrous place I had ever visited. We had stopped at caffin bushes that grew out of the wreckage of whatever strange trees were there previously. A high bank was to our right, on our left the ground dropped away. Ahead was a thicket of atap. After gathering caffin berries Lorom Haluim led us into the atap where I felt a change; the air was heavier, moister, my sight was sharper, the leech bites less painful. As before, the thicket did not seem traversable, yet we traversed it nonetheless.

We broke through into a wide clearing, slowly rising to the summit of a cliff. It seemed we weren't in quite the same place we'd been climbing. Now, away on my left, was a rocky cliff face, not the edge of a cliff, and from its plateau fell a stream into a pool that spilled its excess below us, for we were also, it seemed, on a plateau of our own, though the view was masked by the heavy bushes, ferns and trees that fringed the clearing.

Here was a garden, a menagerie of plant that was breathtaking and yet defied the order of nature around it. I could see across these many hundreds of yards species of weed, trees, fruit and shrubs that grew nowhere, to my knowledge, west of the Sar. To see each was to know it, to know what it did, and this itself delighted me. They filled tiers of garden terraces that rose up the slope away from me. The light of this place also could not be described, somehow thickened, creamy as on an autumn evening. Yet it was the afternoon in Hanwoq, the sun ought to have been clearly above us, though now it could not be seen, despite there being no cover, for the breeze at this height freely blew through, cooling me. As I walked through one of the terraces I saw beds in large bamboo boxes that contained earth of many colours, from reddish clays to the fragrant rich black of high mountain soil prevalent in Mount Hope. In these terraces were thick bushes of mountain flowers like a rainbow contained, from the exceptionally rare, potent Citadels Blueheart and Basalt Greenhood to the Rulamna Starflower, a rare ingredient in some of the recipes of Harudan, greatly bolstering the healing of serious wounds or as a three-one kannab mix ingested to ease sickness and clean the blood.

Pathways threaded through these tiered terraces, the walls of which curved together to form a habitat for climbers in the spaces between them. Here grew a multitude of ivies and creepers and runners, many I didn't recognise, some flowering in spectacular ways, creating walls, even tunnels like coloured rain as they spread in their curved rows away from me. I passed further into the garden and felt sharp changes in the air as I did so; in one area it was humid, yet another area felt cool, as each of the species of plant required. I saw no mechanism for this, or explanation deriving from their shade or position. Such then was my first experience of the true power of a magist, confirming the legends we'd all read, and legends many determined sacred, of the powers magists had to wreak havoc on the order of the world and its peoples. The sense of power intoxicated me, so long powerless. He indeed had nothing to prove and I had the chance to discover recipes that could be the envy of the world. This garden rendered pitiful even the highest communes. Great work could be done here.

Nearly an hour I had spent wandering this plateau before arriving at his shelter. Supported by two kapoks at its back, the posts at the front of a grand shelter allowed a roof of thatched atap and walls of lashed bamboo to stop the wind from disturbing the drudha benches and the many trays of jars and bags that surrounded them. An old chest also I saw, a monstrous work of lacquered red oak and bronze that I later discovered was the only place he had to secure his scrolls, powders and other supplies ruined easily by rain or damp. A hammock was affixed to posts within the shelter, near to the fire, burning healthily as though prepared hours before, though he had reached the shelter only a few yards ahead of me.

"I've more of these caffin I've dried and cooked. They make a fine brew, good with curried meat," he said.

After untold time living through the porridge or scraps of slavery, this meal he offered seemed almost kingly, the caffin far richer and nuanced for being cooked and ground so freshly. I gave my thanks and he gestured to the hammock, throwing me a pouch of paste for the easing of the swellings and bites of the insects.

"You brought a good deal of plant back with you from your travels, from what I can see," I said.

He smiled. "It's no great effort to maintain it here; it allows me to better understand this unique, well . . ." There was a brief pause. "Enough of that. So, I have made you well. What is it you plan to do now?"

"This place, the plant you have here, as I saw it I could recall it, its potency. I have lost so much of my memory but I know I have been a drudha, I know that if I became a drudha again, here, it may unlock that part of me hidden since before I became a slave. I would be grateful to work alongside you, to help you, to be a better drudha."

Then I seemed to say the opposite.

"I will go back there, to the Old Kingdoms."

Why did I say that?

"Which is it?" he asked.

"Sorry. I, I wish to stay. The Old Kingdoms can wait. I believe it's a problem with plant, using a lot of plant, being on the Droop. I believe that the man I was, he speaks out from that place I cannot remember. I talk in my sleep. I find myself saying things and I'm not aware I'm doing it. Catching myself doing it seems to stop it. I understand if that doesn't make sense."

He nodded. I'm not sure why I said it, but I felt at that moment I should not try to hide anything from him. This would change soon enough.

"What is he like? This other you that speaks unbidden?"

"A good question. He seems sure of himself, and for that he is a comfort to me."

"I read the journal you stole," he said. "The cyca used is common to many of the thamirs who took instruction in the lands about. I saw the recipes and guidance of yours the thamir had added about his own work. There are few I've met with your knowledge and ingenuity. I should revisit the east."

"I am . . . I was the equal of any drudharch. At least, that is the conviction of which I've spoken."

He kneeled next to me, and put a cool hand to my shoulder.

"I have healed you, but your body tells a story of great pain and abuse. Maybe there is plant here that will restore you to the man you were. You have suffered as soldier, drudha and slave. I agree you should stay, I have some things to learn from you, but have much to share. I would gladly give you a new recipe book, for what is a drudha without one? Perhaps it will be the best of all recipe books, a book that could return to the east and bring some hope to those facing the growing storm from the Wilds."

He looked me in the eyes then. I could read doubt as much as hope in his gaze; his aura gave the sense of shimmering water between us. To be this close was to be submerged, memories arising unbidden from the fractures his presence created, voices of others it seemed, images I am sure were of my life waking from whatever sleep my trials had buried them in.

For many hours I drifted in and out of sleep on that hammock, both weary but stimulated by watching him work in this great living library. For the sake of what little I knew and a thankfully lean companionship, I became the greatest drudha of them all.

It took years. I became lost in it, for while so little of the source of the wrong I felt could be known, so the fascination I had with my studies overcame it. The Etil did much of the gathering of our ingredients, in particular that which required the harvesting of animals and insects.

Navigating the lands of each River of Etils took most of a year. This was made easier by the carvings bound to trees through their domains, crafted to spin like wheels in the wind and, through holes, create a howling of various distinctions. The purpose was primarily to keep their dead and other dangerous creatures from venturing too close to their paths and camps, as well as distinguish borders.

I was soon accepted as a companion of the magist, not the first by all accounts. All the Rivers and their Houses were glad of his visit; the children particularly were fond of him, though I was less interested in their games, my visits a formal duty interrupting my studies. There were many months across the years where he was often absent, no mention of where. He warned me of it, demanding I maintain visits to the Etil and replenish our stores.

I had success in my wanderings with some of the Etil where I sought plant he had struggled to find himself. I might recount much at this point of the strange and terrible and wonderful things I saw. The truth of what lay in that jungle matched more than a few of the wilder fancies spun by survivors of expeditions there. It is sufficient here to note the Etil did indeed eat outsiders who came for plant. I shared more than one of those feasts. There is plant that properly prepared can provide the transformation of a fightbrew without the consequent damage to the body and mind, also plant that could make some sense of the chatter of birds. There is a race of men that the Etil fear and that Lorom Haluim has seen but once, cloaked as they are in skin transformed by the long ingestion of a brew, recorded in my book, which gave them the changing colours of chameleons.

I took advantage of his leavings mainly to pursue refinements of mixes useful for war; poisons, fightbrews and most intriguingly the lucins he had developed that were without odour or colour, to be inhaled from proximity to a paste that could be secreted upon clothing or any surface.

I used these on the Etil without him ever suspecting, in particular oil from the seeds of what the Etil called the Hanwoq Weeper. The chief effect was a powerful suggestibility, my proximity with any of the Etil while wearing this allowed me to influence their actions to an alarming degree. I abused it, and the Etil, in many ways, farming most heavily for ingredients to refine this oil and harden it to a preserve. There were many poisons that I tested upon them without their knowing. Rarely were the doses fatal. The challenge was to deflect the sickness or other ailment with good works, so my visits would not be associated with a noticeable pattern of debilitation.

I took little joy from the good works I performed; I could not share the delight that others had from my helping to deliver babies or heal wounds and other illnesses. There must have been something in my past that had made me choose this discipline, beyond a mere fascination with learning how to control what happened to people. It must have been *for* something. While that man in me spoke more and more openly as the years passed, so I struggled to hold to the man I had become, which, for all the timidity and the tremors and awful dreams, seemed a better man.

For a while at least I retained an interest in the Etil beyond their being subjects for my work. I watched a few of those babies I delivered grow through infancy until they could walk and then over the years learn to hunt and gather with their families. More and more, however, I was looking to exploit their knowledge, impatient and savagely thirsty for learning and experiment. I took expeditions with their hunters, keen to learn how they worked in this world, how they trapped and what signs they used to find water or the monkeys and alabs that provided much of their meat. Their women variously gave me time enough to help me grasp some of that curious language, giving me further advantage in my requests of them. I in turn gave poisons that acted more swiftly, smaller doses felling larger beasts, and counters to more venoms than Lorom Haluim ever had the inclination to research.

The recipe book grew month by month, year by year, covered with skins from the alabs and snakes, the recipes written on slivers of leather bleached and gummed together for binding. I learned to make my own fieldbelt, proofing and lining the pockets for the mixtures and powders, shaping its pouches for the blocks and sporebags, With this I went among the paths of the Rivers on my own, and then into the jungle itself, back to those strange and dangerous plants we'd avoided on my first journey into the Hanwoq's heart.

I would have died if not for the Etil. I sought these plants for lucin mixes more potent than those the Etil used to walk what they called their skytrails. I suppose there were as many names for the effect of leaving your body that lucins gave as there were tribes in all of Sarun. But this leaving one's skin I had hoped would help me travel inward somehow. Sometimes I travelled for days, my limbs moved and stretched by the Etil as I shivered and mumbled and lay lost to the world. They gave me water while I wandered and whispered my way through the vales of the mute cold dead of war and sharp vivid warmth of the living, the ones I bled and experimented upon, the ones I saved, those that sang on marches, frosted breath shouting lusty verses, or stripping and dumping their dead into fires or pits as custom demanded. The thamirs of the Etil scratched away at the leathers they used for writing, a record of my skytrails such as they kept for each other and which they used as foretellings. Some of these words, their record of my dreams, brought fragments of me back, the man I was before the Droop, a man others feared, a drudha.

Then, one day, in their recounting of a dream of somewhere cold, a boy and girl that my thoughts had returned to without recognition, they said the word that felled me like a tree, that was my welcome to that part of me for so long the mute custodian of what befell me.

Snakewood.

186

Chapter 10

Galathia

Another letter from Galathia to her brother.

Goran

The assassin sat on the floor at my feet, his head on my thigh, a tear tracing a cold line down to the back of my knee. Out of his leathers he was indescribably beautiful, broken and mended many times over, scars like ridges of sand, lumps like grapefruit seeds left from the poisons he'd been subjected to. Small patches of skin were now cork, a shining purple unlike any bark I'd seen knitted to a soldier, the rest of him a dawn blue bruised with red over stony arms and back and chest.

I could not bear how much I needed him when I saw him, he crying to see me, his first words that he was betrayed and he had come back to find me, to keep the purse fifteen winters later.

They called him Sand. He had forgotten everything, Petir, and everyone but us. He has been tortured and he still seems maddened by it, a slave too at some point. At times he whispers to himself and forgets or does not realise he is doing it, but he is here with me and he's explained everything, he told me what happened at Snakewood.

Last I wrote to you was from the Crag, where we found Kailen dead. We left there to go south to an agreed rendezvous with Agent Gilgul and his men, who had reported having custody of

Gant and Shale. They were not there, but had been waiting for us at our estate as they believed they'd been instructed to do. Laun was furious, as was Alon, at least until they saw the scroll presented by the men posing as Agents, and realised the quality of the subterfuge.

When a ganger, Lokio (a loathsome little man who protects my husband's interests on the docks), notified us of Gant and Shale's visit, Laun and Gilgul marshalled all the Reds they could. It had been agreed Lokio would tell them Alon was at the vineyard. There Laun and Gilgul would direct an ambush of them.

When Lokio informed us that they hadn't turned up to meet him as agreed, and one of his own men was missing, we rode for the vineyard with a number of Ithil Bay's militia and the High Reeve, presuming that they'd extracted from his man word that Alon would be at the old vineyard.

Upon our arrival, Laun was stood with the man who had killed many of her crew, both in Iltrick and then the Crag. They stood with arrows pointed at his head but the man made no move to escape.

"He calls himself Kigan," she said. "He says he's been looking for you for a very long time, that you will recognise him despite the changes the years have wrought. He says he did not betray you, but that he himself had been betrayed."

He began crying then, trembling as I approached them, and he held out his arms to me. It was a shock to see him, now without his mask, but it was him. I was going to draw my sword, the memory of his leaving us, the days waiting and looking for him and that desperate anger coming back strongly, but her words stalled me, his tears stalled me, his breathing catching, overcome with emotion. I ran to hold him and he squeezed me to him, muffled words as I pressed against the belts and felt his face against my neck. "I had lost hope," he said.

We stood together drenched in a warm fog of rain, barely an hour later. We were looking at the aftermath of a massacre. What could be salvaged of the Agents' fieldbelts and weapons was being packed onto a wagon. The High Reeve of the Post for Issana, Jua and

Harudan shivered with rage at the bodies piled before him, a cloth at his nose to fend off the stink of the burned skin. Our retinue of forty men filled the vineyard that was blackened and shining like wet coal.

Laun and her crew were digging the graves of their brothers. They would permit nobody else do it. I felt no less anger than either the High Reeve or Laun at this turn of events but could not betray it.

"Reeve Fisker of Issana shall become Reeve Fisker of Northspur, in whose icy arms he will learn a lesson about the conditioning of soldiers," said the High Reeve, a look of disgust on his face. "Two mercenaries did for ten of his Agents of the Post and all our brothers here. Thirty Reds you trained, Captain. Do you think you should join him? And Laun over there, a Marschal with a handful of the crew she ought to have."

Laun looked up at that, having heard him, and glared at Kigan and I before returning to her work with a mounting fury.

The captain stood to attention in armour blackened with fire, struggling to contain the shakes as he paid the colour, probably unable to do more than nod to his master.

The High Reeve had the look of a man once fat, now hollowed out by age so that the spare flesh gathered at his middle like a soft coiled snake beneath his crimson waistcoat and embroidered dress.

"With respect, High Reeve Albin," said Kigan, stepping forward to better address him, "ten or so Agents and the rest Reds was a reasonable number for two mercenaries of this quality if they had softened somewhat. However, they are still sharp, clearly close to the soldiers I knew of old. You underestimated them."

"With respect, Kigan, thirty men and women of the Post should be enough for two no matter who they are or were."

Kigan gestured to the pile of blackened bodies as a reply, many contorted, limbs spasmic with the poisons they'd been subjected to.

The truth was that I recalled nothing directly of Gant or Shale, though Kigan told me that legend considered both very fine swordsmen.

"We will find them," I said.

"You may indeed find them, my dear, but not with the Post's help," said the High Reeve.

"I have a right to expect more for my gold!" said Alon. "The purse is yet to be earned." My husband stepped forward then, a sweep of his fur-trimmed robe performed without thought, some reflexive assertion of his status. The pursed lips and smirk of a guard stood behind him was ample indication of a terrible misjudgement. My husband has many things, Petir, but culture is not one of them.

"Your Marschal instructed the ambush, Guildmaster Filston. The considerable expense and your influence in these parts allowed you the privilege of such a request," said the High Reeve. "Yet your hundred gold pieces for Marschal Laun and her crew's services will yield the Post no profit. I instead must sink that coin into finding, training and paying for replacements for these men while somehow making sure that the operations they would have otherwise been engaged on do not lose us further income. Eighteen caravans are now without the Agents or Reds that were paid for, on the assurance that so many would make quick work of these greying mercenaries. What must those mercenaries have that warrants such expense?"

"Nothing that would interest the Post High Reeve," said Alon, who knew then he'd erred in challenging him.

"Information is always of interest to the Post; nothing else can be worth the gold you paid. You there, Prennen, you're Laun's man. What names have you been given by your purse to pursue; who are they?"

Prennen stood up from digging and took a breath. "Yes, Reeve. These two were Gant and Shale. The only other names I recall are Valdir, Bense and Mirisham. We seek an old mercenary crew, Kailen's Twenty."

"The name tickles my tongue; I wish I could remember why. Guildmaster Filston, the Post's interests in Issana have been severely harmed by the events here. These men, Gant and Shale, will not face your own wrath unless you deem it greater than that of the Post's. I shall be sure to tell you of their fate, along with whatever information you require of them. Are you sure it would not help you to share this now, in the event of our successful hunt?"

"No," I said. "Goodbye, Reeve, we are most sorry to have caused such trouble to the Post."

"Alon, you would do well to ensure your wife understands the protocols regarding one's engagement with a High Reeve."

"My apologies, High Reeve, she is of a noble family, it is something she grew up accustomed to."

The Reeve looked me over, like a tutor facing the latest in a long line of troublemakers. He affected an air of superiority, but a little wealth and reputation was in his case no more than the sheen on shit. His retinue soon assembled and a guard led him to his horse, helping him up to the saddle with discreet difficulty. Once mounted he spent some moments in reflection.

"Guildmaster Filston, a new Reeve Issana arrives in three days. The Post is always willing to recognise loyal and experienced merchants and I am assured this Reeve will look to continue our good trade with your support. You must consider this purse fulfilled, or else the Filston-Blackmore guild will find the cargo levies and port duties its own to negotiate through Jua and Issana."

A blackwing had arrived at his birdman. Its message was passed to him and his attention moved on in a moment from the yard around us to some new matter.

Alon bowed and turned away from me, squeezing with rage the gloves in his fists, to manage himself in sight of us all. We had learned an expensive lesson regarding these mercenaries who were still paying the colour, still potent with the vigours of battle.

After the High Reeve had left us my husband turned back to Kigan and I where we stood.

"Well," he said, "you are the man my wife has been hunting all these years, the one she said betrayed her."

He muttered for a moment, then spoke.

"I did not. We were both betrayed and I know . . ." – again he seemed to speak to himself – ". . . I know what they did." He looked at Alon and me then, before addressing the soldiers and Reds with us.

"We need to speak alone." He led us away from the others.

We walked the bank of the river that edged the vineyard, smoke rising from the blackened vines still. I confess I couldn't take my eyes off him. It is hard to describe, brother. Everything from his colour to his fieldbelt, its loops, bags and tools, but more how he moved, something I would never have noticed had I not had some schooling from Laun in balance. If he were a crossbow he would be fully notched, his eyes flicking to each crack of a twig or sudden chip of a bird in the trees about us. A terrifying vigour seemed to be a breath away from being unleashed.

"When Laun's soldier, Prennen, spoke the names of those Twenty we have left to seek, I was watching the High Reeve," he said. "For only a heartbeat the final name, Mirisham, stalled him. I'd have missed the tell if I hadn't been considering what mix could improve the blotched skin of his cheeks and how much I could charge him for it."

"Wait, Kigan, you're not telling me why you are also killing the Twenty. These were your crew for so many years."

We stopped walking and he continued talking, though never looked either of us in the eye throughout.

"They betrayed me, it was them, it was . . . it might not have been all of them, but they were there, at the inn, in Snakewood. I met them, then I cannot remember . . ."

He was whispering now and seemed lost to us for a moment, then he continued regarding the Reeve's reaction to hearing the name "Mirisham", as though I had not asked the question.

"Intentions are very hard to conceal on this brew I take. I could hear the Reeve's heart beat more quickly, see the hint of warmth from that blood on his cheek, the eyes lose focus momentarily as he planned a retreat from the conversation, all upon hearing the name Mirisham."

"That would be a brew, if you speak truly, Kigan, which could make us all very rich."

He shushed my husband, annoyed with him, and continued.

"What could that High Reeve know of Mirisham? Whatever he knew of him it wasn't worth your purse to reveal it. If Mirisham's whereabouts were not a confidence the High Reeve wished to share with you despite your widespread use of the Post to find us, then Mirisham must be somehow connected to the Post or its more important interests. It means Mirisham has become somebody important himself, more so than you."

"Do you know where the others are?" I asked.

"I have Bense. He is on a betony mix I have refined enough that there is no question of his loyalty. His lord saw fit to put him in a jail for a spell at Cusston, in Jua, presumably to wean him off it, but not before he gave me Stixie. It was Bense also that told me of Kailen's last visit, the one that got him imprisoned."

"If you have Bense in your pocket," I said, "we should head there immediately; he may know something more of the others."

"Bense isn't our next move."

"Then we must find a way to persuade that awful Reeve to tell us what he knows of Mirisham. You, well, you seem able to do as you please, Kigan; would you do it for me?"

"I cannot countenance it, Galathia," said Alon. "Assault on a High Reeve, if I am in any way implicated, is the end of me, and I trust you, like me, do not wish to go back to a life without coin."

"He is right, Galathia, it is not the next move. Kailen had somehow managed to warn Gant and Shale that the Twenty were being killed. He had warned Bense. His knowing this would explain why he organised their kidnap from the custody of Agents with a fine subterfuge, according to Laun." He clasped his hands behind his back and breathed deeply.

"Kigan, are you saying there are more of the Twenty dead? Digs spoke of this being so."

"Oh yes. I've killed every one I could find."

I could barely catch my breath, a thrill overcoming me.

"Why, because they . . . you said they betrayed you?"

He looked at me knowing I was expecting a response but I could see from his glassy stare and lips barely moving he was somewhere inside himself.

"How well do you know the Chief Levyer of Harudan?" he then asked.

"Kigan, I . . ." I began, but he held up a hand. I wanted desperately to know who he had killed.

"We have time, Gala." He paused, waiting for me to acknowledge this, before continuing. "Alon, the Chief Levyer of Harudan?"

"How is that relevant?" asked Alon, now frowning at the filth on his suede boots and robe from the wet ground.

"Gant and Shale came looking for you, according to this ganger Lokio. They knew they were being hunted, and I believe Kailen told them it was you that was behind the killings."

"Do continue, Kigan, I'm afraid I do not yet follow the thread of your thought." He looked at me in a way affecting weariness. It was his way of hiding annoyance or unhappiness.

"Laun told me you and Kailen had made contact at the Crag, but Kailen had set an elaborate trap. He either knew or suspected your true purpose.

"Now he's dead we must make contact with Kailen's father, the Chief Levyer or Kailen's wife. One or both may be persuaded to help us understand what more he knew of those that still live."

"Should we ride for Harudan tomorrow? To see Kailen's family?" I asked.

"Yes, my dear," interrupted Alon, "I have plenty more coin for you to spend pursuing this. Your revenge has cost a mere hundred gold coins so far and I've learned only that the Post's Agents, a Marschal even, are nowhere near worth the price I or any of my guild have been paying all these winters. Thirty men and women, as Albin said, should have been enough and any right-minded man assessing the risk would have agreed."

"My husband, I'm only glad that Laun did not hear that. You might then have learned what a single Agent can do to a man."

I know what you must think, Petir; I have wed badly. His wealth has been useful to me, he is soft with me, supports me, but it isn't love. How could we expect that after Snakewood, let alone before?

Kigan revealed much of what happened to us, and what happened to him, as we rode south to Harudan. Something isn't right with him, he's paid the Drudha's Share, and with the Droop and the torture he is . . . it's hard to find the phrase . . . he is like a player, convincing enough in his part, but it is an eggshell, with something dangerous tapping at it from the inside.

I put here an extract of a conversation Galathia had with me, of this time immediately after seeing Kigan again, for it reveals much of what had become of Kailen's Twenty, and what Kigan remembered.

Goran

"You have changed," he said, the following night at my estate in Issana. I sought him in his room, while Alon was away at the docks on guild business. I did not want to be away from his bed. Now he watched me from his pillow.

"In the memories kept from me, the images I questioned for truth or dream, you had hair like a gorse bush as a girl, a thicket of orange, every strand stood outwards as though straining for the sun. Now they are becalmed to curls. Still those violet eyes."

"Supposedly lucky, violet. Yet all these winters later I am Alon's trophy."

"It is a contract to both your benefit, and I did not see a mere trophy in the alley at Iltrick."

"Tell me about my father. You say your remembering Snakewood brought it all back."

"Gala, how sure can I be that it is all true when so much of my life I cannot recall, not family or even name until I confronted and killed Harlain in Tetswana. Yet I feel as sure of these memories now as I do of my senses, and that has been a sadly rare feeling these winters.

"I saw your father last the day Kailen disbanded the Twenty, the day we left. I realised at the same time as him that we were ruined and the Twenty finished. I woke up, and the marble floor was so cold it numbed my face, only my cheek warm with my drool. I'd cooked up from a wormwood and poppy oil press. Three measures of leaves to the splash and cut in with raw threaded kannab, a soft three-one twist I was as proud of then as I am scornful of its vulgarity now.

"Around me were Kailen's Twenty. A roomful of mass murderers, naked or else lumbered with whores. They were smiling or drooling in their dreams, bodies of smoke and pleasure as the poem goes, flattened by my mixes. I made little else, and cared nothing for the fact.

"My head still pounded and my muscles and bones woke sharpened, stabbing me all over. I got to my knees and felt around the sheets and cushions littering the filthy floor for my belts, for my nerves. I was paying the Drudha's Share, a lifetime of mixing, testing and drinking fightbrews and other experiments. I had to whisper to my hands, coax them to achieve my goal, the clumsy unknotting of a drawstring and the rub of the betony on my gums and under my tongue bringing me some clarity.

"I worked through the remaining compounds, skin rubs for the sores, kannab salves for the rubs. Then my prickly eyes settled on you.

"Those violet eyes were full of pity. Pity! I couldn't hold your gaze for it; I could see enough what your father's courtroom had become: a whorehouse for men drowning in his luxurious patronage. I had had so little to do with children, nothing at all relating to the care of them, until, for whatever reason, your father saw fit to make me your and Petir's guardian. I could not understand it myself, except perhaps that the fear of drudhas would discourage anyone out to hurt you more than the fear of a soldier, however good. It was extra coin, a sidepurse for me, and I took it with so little else to do. I did not, could not expect you to be so inquisitive, so interested in my work and in my teaching you your letters. For a time I took some pleasure in your achievements, and in the schooling of Petir with a blade and his forms. But I did not expect the pity for the state of me, had not expected, over those months, the questions a child can ask that a man cannot answer. Why did I kill for coin? What was it like to kill? Had I killed any girls like you?" He was silent for a moment, and put his hand to his mouth to disguise some muttering, and I had the sense he was ashamed of it.

"But it was about to end, our time with your father the king. The all-powerful merchants of Citadel Argir had wielded their political rapiers that last year in the dissection of your father's power. They made the court and its judges theirs, they dispensed what justice they saw fit from a guildhall a league or so away from us in the citadel's main square, their bid for power supported against you by the Post. The Post had long coveted a more central role in Argir's trade than your father would concede to them. He stood little chance as a result, given he had no more than respect from the people, where love is required when a test of strength is made.

"So, he was duly strangled in the kind of web a sword cannot break, nor the eye of a soldier see.

"Your family and other courtiers and men of office hated us, for they saw the coup coming and no real way to get away with any of his wealth from the palace. The soldiers we were trying to train cared more for the fires and beer at their posts than the forms and drills, and hated us as well. When the guilds could no longer trap the king in their politics while Kailen was called to be present, they moved decisively in the shadows.

"Soon after I saw you I noticed that Kailen had woken up, staring around us, at you and me. He had pissed himself during his dreams. He gave me a curt shake of his head, clear where he put the blame for merely providing his men, his 'brothers', with the lucins and mixes they sought to escape the boredom of this last purse.

"You called my name and ran over to me. You were frightened, perhaps by seeing so many of us naked. I put my robe on as quickly as I could. I remember hugging you to me; you smelled of lavender, a bottle of it that your father had given to you that had belonged to your mother from years before. Then I took you outside to the balcony and down the steps to the gardens. A cold wind woke us properly. I remember the palace stood high up against the peaks that formed the backbone of the great citadel and overlooked the city beneath us. Perhaps we will go back one day soon.

"You told me that your father, Doran, said you'd have to leave that day. I saw that the guards and the serfs that worked the gardens and the house were not guarding or working. They stood in small groups about the overgrown lawns and beds of weeds and dead roses. They smoked pipes and shared skins. This was the mutiny beginning, but they could not raise a hand while we stood at the king's side.

"Your father loved you, Gala. He was always a fraught man for whom the crown and the games at court were a maze of nettles and debilitating traps, his marriage to your mother an icy union of expedience between fathers themselves colder still."

"She was a soak that I remember only for hitting me or Petir. I wished she'd drown in her goblet."

"She did, in a sense. Well, I heard shouting from the courtroom behind us. I thought the mutiny had started, and we were being roused. Back inside I saw Kailen dragging whores off Shale, Harlain, Kheld and Sho while the others found robes to put on.

"I told him I thought the mutiny was beginning. 'Fuck you' was all I got back from him.

"Moadd argued with him then; Kailen must have said something about disbanding the Twenty while I was out in the garden with you. He said it had been over for a long time. He was right. Said we were no more a fighting unit than some aristos dancing to guitars and trumpets.

"Ibsey had a go at him then, shivering for a fix almost the moment he woke. He moaned because it was easy money and because he was, by then, as good as a drooper. He made me sick.

"Kailen closed on Ibsey and gave him a single fierce punch. Ibsey was flattened cold, the crack of his jaw silenced us.

"Kailen found his mark on all kinds of problems with us, seeming to rise like bile from him, from whatever clarity of our situation we seemed to share that morning. Then one of the boys down the line belched, just as Kailen was wailing on at the shape we needed to find, the jobs to pick up after an uncounted time in the golden silence of the best presses and smokes Ibsey and I could cook.

"It was how our final line ended, that belch. I laughed as he fell silent, for it was oddly liberating. Too long I had been criticised for my methods, too long I took shit from him and the others, treating me like some village cooker. There was an accidental, casual disrespect to that belch. But something had ticked over in his head at that moment and he walked from the court without a word, without turning back. Kailen's Twenty ended there.

"Stixie Four and Bresken lifted Ibsey onto a bench and set about bringing him to. His jaw was smashed and I had to bind it tight and blend his mixes. The rest of the Twenty dispersed. We were all shocked by how suddenly it had happened. Elimar and Milu found a couple of pipes and packed some press to get about rising again. Others, like Mirisham and Valdir, pissed into large carved pots containing exquisite miniature soora trees before leaving to find some food.

"Those two had been the ones I had most friendship with. Mirisham was someone we all looked up to, like The Prince, a few years older and good at talking us down off a bad rise or out of the fights we'd all be looking for when the brandy soaked our good senses red.

"But things about us had moved quickly as I had suspected. Once the king had seen the serfs gathering at the gates he knew that the coup was imminent. Kailen was with him handing out our final purses. We were in armour, belts and swords, waiting in the grand hall outside the king's private quarters. I was the last man in, each of us going in turn to see them both.

"Kailen had not spoken to us since the morning but we all knew it was over. After years of rising and falling, side by side in the front lines, meeting each crossing like we were immortal, we shuffled in and out of the king's quarters barely able to countenance this dissolution, this being bereft of purpose. With hard embraces and few words there was an agreement we might make our way to some lavish Juan planthouse to consider what we would then do.

"In the room, your father and Kailen stood behind the delicate writing desk that had once been the queen's. Dresses of hers were still in piles on the day chairs about his bed and her screen. Mould and moths had disfigured them. A carved wooden dog, a toy of Petir's you might remember, sat on a mantle over the dust of the disused fireplace. The ghost of your mother still poisoned the present, leaving a room that you no longer played in.

"On the desk was a ledger. Kailen pushed forward my purse. I had no words for him. At the end of it he had no words for me either, no acknowledgement of my part in creating his legend. My brews and mixes were the masterpieces of our generation, originals we were able to sell on for many times more than the purses themselves. No battles before or since we fought in the open field left the skin of our enemies bubbling and exploding after the merest splash or cut. Word spread of the Hevendor serfs' uprising ending with a field of a thousand silent men fully paralysed. I watched their eyes fluttering like newborn moths and weeping as their teeth were pulled and other sport had with them by the scavengers descending as the loyalists had ridden away. Kailen took the glory for all my own pride in the recipes.

"I took the heavy velvet purse from the frail table and signed the ledger. It was heavy enough that I looked quizzically at both the king and Kailen.

"'You are the last, Kigan,' said the king. 'Thank you for your protection. Kailen, would you leave us?'

"Kailen didn't like it, gave us a lingering glance before nodding and leaving the room. Your father waited some moments before speaking, a once-commanding voice frayed with pipesmoking and the wheezing of a chest beyond my repair.

"'The uprising will begin in days. A party of Justices, with a charge of incompetence and fraud concocted by the rancid clowns cowed before the Post and that cunt from Eural, arrives tomorrow. The guilds have bought my clearks and stopped their men from working until I am dethroned. My nobles have abandoned me.' I imagine they too were bribed with some of the Welvale land, your birthright, Gala, in exchange for their allegiance. Your father knew he was done.

"I told him his best chance was with us, the Twenty, for getting out of the Citadels alive. He shook his head and moved from behind the table to look out of the mildewed shutters at the colourless dawn.

"'I'll not shame my family further. My brother, Moren, was to be the better king; the people made that much clear to me. He always had a way with Galathia; Petir too adored Moren for his prowess as a soldier. I miss him.'

"Your father told me then that you loved me."

"We did, you know we did." I held him closer to me as he talked. "You may well have had time on your hands, Kigan, but you chose to tolerate us, to treat us intelligently, challenge us to use our privilege. My father never had the time, never made the time."

"Well, he knew he wasn't leaving his kingdom, with his talk of shame. The years, the duty, had aged him. He looked like a man withered by a disease at the end; jowls no longer full of fat and strength, bags of skin settled over each cheek filled with tiredness.

"After a moment's silent scrutiny, meeting my eyes, searching them for something, he bowed his head, a grief rising in him. He was looking for a way out, Gala, do you understand? Despite knowing there could be none. Then he told me to take you out of the Citadel, you and Petir. He gave me a bronze seal, an oversized coin with the royal heraldry.

"He said the most valuable items had been removed from the treasury, the Argir Book, flasks of rosanna pea and henbane wax, flasks of sun's heart preserve, fire weed, emeralds and diamonds and so forth. These were to provide you both with the means to live comfortable lives far away from any assassins looking to end your line. More than comfortable, for I had not seen such a quantity of rare plant as that. He told me I had to present the seal to Alven, his drudha, at Post House Snakewood three days on from that morning, so Alven could then lead us to where the treasure was hidden. He paid me thirty more gold coins for this service.

"'Galathia always wished to see the great Sar ocean,' he said. I was to be paid a further fifty gold coins upon delivering you to Alven in Snakewood. This ought to have secured your passage to Jua. You can see, I hope, why I could not have betrayed you for coin, never mind betray a purse once it was agreed. Not at that price.'"

As Kigan spoke of my father, remembering his words, he had brought him to life for a moment, his last wish for us itself resurrected.

"What happened to us? What more do you remember? When I think of Snakewood, all I can remember is those people in carts everywhere, slaves I suppose, and the windmill where you left us. I don't remember much of our journey there from the palace, just it was dark all the time, it seemed. Cold and dark."

"These days I've described are as clear as any now, up until the night I left you," said Kigan. "This part of my life is part of me again.

"Hours after speaking to the king, I said goodbye to Mirisham and Valdir, promising to meet up with them when my last duty was done, a promise I doubted I would keep. I stood at a small servant's doorway to the royal gardens as your father wept and held you for the last time. I respected him for that, staying to meet his fate head on as a king should.

"You cried your heart out, insisted he join us. Your brother just closed up, a boy now the height of his father, a quiet and helpless rage in him against the forces pushing him into fleeing with a mercenary like me to unknown crossings.

"'Kigan will protect you and I will follow you when I can,' he said. He made such a fuss of your pack and boots, Petir's dagger belt.

"Once you could bear to let your father go, making him promise to meet you again in the plains of Jua, we followed a wall in the cellars to a point where the smallest of catches, shaped like the stone around it, opened a concealed door into a dank passage. I carried you, though you faced me to better see past my shoulder your father behind us as we descended some steps under the light of a torch. Petir did not look back.

"Petir refused to believe he was crying in his sleep, and refused any salves for his blisters as his feet grew accustomed to such long hours walking. You and I spent the nights humming songs as we passed the ruins of old forts and stone outposts that formed the historic frontiers of the Citadels.

"Soon enough we reached Snakewood, its well-beaten tracks taking us into the settlement alongside numerous caravans and carts. A major outpost of stables for the messengers the Post ran, Snakewood was a key hub in the Old Kingdoms slave trade. Seasoning camps and pens for the big slave-trading operations surrounded the main square; forts of high stone walls plain but for the stages set with heavy doors where the slaves were displayed in iron galleries.

"I muddied our faces and robes to better conceal us while we looked for the drudha. My sword, jerkin and pads I gave to one of the beggars that lined the tracks. Both of you would be my children, if anyone was to ask.

"The caravans of slaves, both on the Droop and those yet to be seasoned, surrounded us as we picked our way through the hawkers, singers and other shit filling the main street passing the square. It was as we were passing an exhausted-looking but raucously voiced row of taverns that Alven, the king's drudha, approached us, having followed us from the gates. His experience, as with all long-serving soldiers and drudhas, I measured by his colours and the eyes; his had gone black from the experimental salves and leaves used to sharpen sight. It was for these reasons more than my being recognised that I muddied my own skin.

"We led you through some alleys to the back of the main square. You tried to push yourself into my robe; no doubt this was your and Petir's first encounter with the comparatively shrivelled existence of the labourers and commoners of the world.

"The mill was at the southern edge of the settlement atop a natural slope, with a view to the plains of Lagrad. Alven greeted his former drudhan, now working the mill, with a purse and we were led into the storehouse.

"Alven told me that he'd seen the rest of the Twenty coming into

Snakewood. I thought it would be wise to see which of them were going to Jua and would be willing to go along with us.

"I took a pail of water into the storeroom from the well and washed the mud off us. You permitted me to wash your hair. Then you leaned into Petir and settled back against the wall. I watched you drift off to sleep, his arm hanging over your shoulder, his cheek on your head. It is one of my most vivid and precious memories, one that I had before I could remember who either of you were. He would have made a fine king, Petir, a handsome and strong man that the serfs would have admired. I hoped the wealth and the luxuries of Jua would not destroy him. Between Alven and myself I was sure we could settle you."

"I blamed you for so long," I confessed. "I thought you were complicit."

"You've survived, Galathia, you're strong, brave as well; you got dirty with the world."

"The world has worked me over one too many times. What choice do you have but to fight back?"

"Many don't, deceiving themselves about who really is to blame for their condition. Tell me about you and Petir. Tell me you've seen him."

Her later account of this, presented below, is no doubt at least as full an account of what happened to her and Petir after Snakewood as that she would have told Kigan, so is included at this point.

Goran

The first touches of grey speckled Petir's beard and hair the last time I saw him. This was recently of course, long after Snakewood. He stank from the month or so of his journey from the Wilds north of Hevendor. He had crooked yellow nuggets for teeth, a finger missing, though he had paid the colour somewhat and had grown as strong and tall as Kigan had believed he would. He would indeed have been a beautiful king but for the life we were given. He told me that to see me so grown, so beautiful and him so rough broke his heart, or would have if he had not such stories to tell me of a daughter he had named after me.

This is what I remember of how we got here.

The evening after Kigan left us in that windmill Petir had gone out with Gemayel, Alven's drudhan from the windmill, to look for him. We never saw Alven again either, and Snakewood was so busy, so frightening at night, that we had little hope of finding either of them among the rest that plied their trade with the caravans. Days turned into weeks. Petir's resentment and anger grew, however. Before long he had robbed Gemayel of a harvest's takings at the point of a sword and dragged me south in a cold autumn that preceded a vicious winter. Gemayel had done his best and didn't deserve what Petir had done to him. Raiders had come out of the mountains around the borders of Fort Donag and Lagrad in greater numbers than anyone alive had seen, their own nomadic pickings dwindling as their animals died of starvation and cold among the high peaks. Petir had found passage at the cost of most of the coin we'd stolen, with nomads moving south to the Lagrad border hoping for support from the Lake Ahm clans against the raiders. Extra mouths were unwelcome in the north at that time and we were forced to move on alone, beggars by then. At some point we had crossed into Ahmstad itself. The snows had been, but it had become too cold for more to fall, so we found even less in the way of forage, just the silence and indifference of winter.

It was as we spied on a huntsman a way off the track with some coneys at his waist that Petir had a desperate idea. I was to pretend I was alone and lost, used as bait for any curious herders or farmers, unwary of my murderous brother waiting to ambush them. For a time I was terrified of him, of what the hunger did to him. He threatened to leave me if I didn't follow his plans, and that was more terrifying still. So I would feign that I had hurt my leg, lifting my skirts to show each man a good part of my thigh, and a bruise which he had kicked me to bring out. I had learned a little native Westhill and Laggie from my tutors, to avoid having to answer questions in King's Common. More than once they'd got me under them, despite how I fought and screamed, before he came and killed them for whatever they had on them, hares, fish, eggs, bilt and robes to keep us warm.

The last time we did it, it was a shepherd, his sheep the first life we'd seen in days. But it seemed the shepherd had once had some training; he saw Petir coming at him, knocked his knife away and went for him. They wrestled and fought for their lives. Twice he'd kicked at me or threw me off as I tried to interfere. I saw Petir's knife near my hand where I'd just been thrown and picked it up. He had rolled over on top of my brother and got his hands on his throat, a hacking laugh as he hit Petir's head against the earth. I had frozen, wet myself, resigned to it until I saw his struggle end, his arms falling back. Then I snapped; I went into a frenzy at the thought I'd let my brother down, had let him die and left myself alone. I stabbed the shepherd square in the back, drove it in and tried to hold onto him as he grabbed at me to pull me off him. Petir choked then; I saw him move, fight for breath, wheezing and wriggling away from us. The shepherd grabbed my arm and started to pull me off him. I grabbed the hilt of the knife as leverage and as it moved inside him he let go and howled. I twisted the hilt and he fell forward screaming in pain. Moments later Petir got to his knees, and, with a heavy stone, smashed his head open.

That was the last time we did that. Petir had recovered somewhat a few hours later and we took an arm each and dragged the shepherd to a ravine and threw him into it.

We killed one of the sheep and I told him how to get some leg cuts. He didn't curse me for giving him instruction as he usually would, didn't insist he knew what he was doing when it was clear I was right. It wasn't something that's happened often in my life since, being listened to by the men around me. We couldn't get a fire going with the little wood we found before a blizzard tore through the pass. We had the shepherd's cloak and he wrapped it round us both as we sat against a tree to escape the worst. He told me the story of Ramban's Necklace that night, like he used to a few summers before, his voice quivering and breaking with the severity of the assault, and he still attempted impressions of the lovelorn servant, the princess and the rebellious queen bee. We filled our cups with snow and made our vows that we would die together, and I was happy for a few hours.

Dawn was bright as new steel and when I woke it was to the smell of smoke, a weak fire to do the meat. He had been crying. That was my apology.

After a few hours' walking we followed a path through pines that opened out to a precipice with a view across the southern peaks of

Jua's Teeth to the fabled Jua itself. Seeing what must have been the edge of it on the horizon encouraged us to abandon some caution and push down on to more travelled tracks, hoping to find someone we could beg some food from.

A Post pathfinder unit caught up with us as we struggled through the snow on a track through a pass. All of them were sodden with over a month's travel through Donag, leading the horses due to the ice and treacherous footing. Their red cloaks were blackened and most of them stared at me as though I were a hot fresh ham as they surrounded us.

Their captain, Nielus, was a weary and disgraced ex-Marschal, running the southern Donag routes with this sly band that I soon learned was preoccupied only with their next rise and what lay under my robe. They'd lost a horsehand two days before and killed another while risen and arguing on a bad mix. Nielus was a giant, he seemed to fill the camp, eyes of an owl that kept the boys in order, dismayed at whichever cleark had signed up such young soaks to the Red. He had a stinking oily grey beard and an exquisite leather helm worked around bone horns, a helmet he'd taken from the head of a warlord the Post had had to kill after it had hit a few of their caravans. But despite their complaints that we'd slow them down when they were desperate to collect their pay and get cooked to a stupor, he'd seen how wretched we were. He was faithful to values Alon later told me had long since been renounced by the Post, the Farlsgrad Creed, a code of honour that the Post had when it was less the power it is now, when its reputation was everything, its relations with the people who lived in or near the Wilds making the difference between its caravans getting through or being raided and enslaved. They did little more than mock him for it when he used it to justify them sharing some bisks with us, but they didn't disobey him. There was a respect built on fear, a ruthlessness I never got to see. Petir put me on the recently spare horse and he led me for the rest of the day.

That evening, as Nielus helped me off the horse to ready a camp, he asked if I'd go with one of his crew to help carry some wood. "I'll keep you safe with this lot, I promise," he said. "Sten, take her with you to fetch some wood for the fire."

"She'll give you a hand with yer wood, I'm sure," shouted one of the others, and the crew laughed.

206

"You heard of the word 'impropriety'?" said Nielus.

The man, Sten, shook his head.

"It means touch her and I'll gut you. He'll behave, girl."

I looked to Petir, who was with three of the others and sharing a cup of their shine. He was trying not to look at me, and one of the others put their arm around his shoulder and started singing. I was angry that they were distracting him, playing a game to get a rise out of me.

Sten had me carry the torch as he looked for dead wood and otherwise took his hatchet to branches within reach, leading me away from the camp. He moved through the trunks around me, silently, and he spoke, from the darkness, of my beauty, my red hair being as beautiful and bright as the torch, of how he hoped he could help my brother and I if I helped him, if I was just willing to hold him, for it had been many years since any woman was willing to do it. "I'm not a woman," I told him, but in the silence I heard him breathing, hard and fast, and he asked if I'd lift my skirts for just a moment, vowing not to approach, promising a share of his bacon rinds.

"I want to go back," I said, disgusted with myself for my eyes were filling up and I felt powerless again. He laughed and stepped forward, wiping his hands on his cloak, still stiff.

"You did help with the wood, Manady was right. I might let you touch it tomorrow, seeing as how you can't take your eyes off it." He grabbed it like I'd seen so many of Kailen's Twenty do back in my father's halls, chasing whores. It enslaves them all doesn't it, the cock.

"There's worse than me in that camp, girl, remember that. Don't think Nielus is immune to you either; there's a lot his wife has no clue about, and them others, they wouldn't have shown such courtesy as me to keep their needs to themselves. You don't know how it gets and how hard to show manners out here in these winters running these routes."

The following day he kept in line with Petir and I, asking about us, and I had no chance to tell Nielus what he had done. It was that evening when I refused Nielus's request to help him that I was able to say why. Nielus listened, then said that he and I would collect wood, Sten could tend the horses, oil their hooves. I could see that despite a night's soak that had made him sullen all day, the crew had Petir on their shine again.

"I've got something for you, Galathia," said Nielus, once we were away from camp. He had stopped dragging the slenka they'd made the previous night, which would help us take a bigger load of wood back. "I'm sure that's what that idiot was saying to you last night, but they aren't a good lot at the best of times, and you being around is getting them rowdy and stupid. I won't abandon you out here though." He held up a knife, a short fat blade, the one I keep with me still. He held up with it a small black pouch and a rag. "Let me show you how to use these. Not for show. Never for show. If you use this knife right they should never see it, and this pouch is a paste of poison I made from lobelia blocks that I salvaged from a caravan run went bad. Few counters to it here in the north and it brings a terrible death. We have an hour, and I'll set up camp earlier tomorrow so I can teach you a bit more."

He held out his arms to hug me. I accepted, and was grateful.

"I'm sorry for whatever has happened that you and your brother, both highborn it seems from the way you are, and how little used to the world, should find yourselves in these parts in winter with nobody looking out for you. I'll do my best to get you to our Post House at least."

So he taught me, showed me that if they couldn't see the knife they might assume I was unarmed, but that I must never assume the same, that they mustn't ever get a hold of me if they're wielding a knife or it's over. Above all he taught me not to hesitate; move quickly and savagely were his words, unthink.

In the days that followed, the marching and the hours before sleep, Petir was drawn more and more to the men, who goaded him for being a boy, for being colourless, for not knowing the truths of the sinkworm, a wild opia mix that left him stupefied under my nursings. He grew distant from me, becoming addicted to the pipe, and he began treating me as his servant as much as I became theirs. Nielus saw it, and so insisted that after I'd gathered wood I join him, and he shared some caffin beans with me when I brought him his mixes at the end of the day. He wouldn't join in with them as they cooked, smoked and sang to a flute that their drudhan, "One Knee" Manady, had learned as a boy on the ships. As I sat with Nielus he told me his story over those weeks.

He had a son who seemed to hate having been born to him and his wife, a sister that disinherited him, but a wife who he loved and loved him back, who'd bring their horse and trap up to the Post House from a village twenty or so miles over the border when he was due in from a run. It was a love that had persisted even through his being captured by wildmen, who tortured him, left him with just a few teeth and plenty I didn't see I'm sure, on his last campaign as a soldier for the Donag, his people, many winters before. His brother and father were eaglers, and therefore of a high rank, but he lacked the talent for it. Once soldiering was over through his injuries inflicted as a prisoner he was only able to prove himself useful to the Post, earning tolerable coin for his knowledge of the mountains around us, and their people. Soon he became a Marschal; he led his Reds well, running the routes from Jua north through Mount Hope to Citadel Hillfast with few disruptions for a while. His lieutenants, however, exploited his weakness at administration and keeping account, his trust in them betrayed, many hundreds of silver embezzled before the thefts were discovered and the blame seeming to be his. The High Reeve had a choice between killing him and removing him. His reputation for honouring the Creed was something the Reeve greatly admired, and so his disgrace was engineered to save his life and he took it without question. His wife was there through his rise and fall, their becoming wealthy and then disgraced. They had to leave the heart of Donag society and discovered that life was not as hard as they'd feared at its border with Jua, but instead a deal quieter and more honest.

I think of him often, the love he had that was unaffected by coin or reputation. I doubt Alon's love for me matters more than either of the latter.

My time with them, and Petir, ended savagely. Our luck had run out again, as did Nielus's, but not before Sten's. I did my best to gather wood or water with either Nielus or my brother. Daily I had to retreat if I ventured out looking for plant and saw one or more of Sten's little crew, slipping out of the camp at the same time, hoping to loop around to me. It became a game for them, played under the eyes of their captain and my brother, who by now had decided that it was indeed just a game such as men play all the time with young women. He thought it would teach me something of the world.

Finally, there was an occasion I went looking for berries while they were cooking a rise and I didn't notice the pursuit. It saved my life and cost them theirs. The three of them left camp shortly after me. Nielus was dozing, Petir slumped with the others while Manady cooked. I had found a few patches of blackberries on slopes away from the path and started filling my hat when I realised one of the patches had been picked clean, more than the work of birds. I heard laughter echoing up from the clearing away through the trees and my stomach floated like a feather for a beat as I realised we weren't alone on paths where there were no known settlements.

"Here she is. What a good girl." The crackle of phlegm and Marolan accent belonged to Gerin, the oldest of Nielus's crew, face hollowed by his lack of teeth. He stood with Sten, who gave me a bow.

"We would like a dance, my lady," said Sten, "we'll pay well."

"We're not alone up here; someone's been at these berries," I said.

"Some hungry bears perhaps?" said the other, a nose like a rodent's snout, a chin that receded into his throat as though to escape his face.

"I'm hungry myself, hot cherry pie," said Gerin.

"You're second, Gerin," said Sten. "Boys, get the rag on her to shut her up."

The rodent stepped forward; he expected no resistance. I put my hand to the small of my back where the knife was side on in the scabbard and I tucked it flat so it sat against my wrist, a reverse grip. As he approached and reached out it must have looked as though I had batted his arm away with my hand. He hissed and looked at his hand to see a thin red line running across his palm.

"The little whore just cut me," he said, holding his hand up to the others.

Sten laughed and reached for his own knife. "I can't tell you how happy I am about that."

The rodent shook his head, holding his hand up again. He had begun shivering, his fingers flexing, the fear evident as he looked back at me, realising he'd been poisoned.

"Help me!" he shouted. "Her knife was juiced."

"What's the mix," yelled Sten, his fraternal affection immediately overcoming his ardour.

"Pure lobelia," I said.

The rodent fought to control his breath but he looked to be cramping all over. He started to weep, reaching for his crew who had stepped back from him. I wouldn't see anything work as fiercely as that again until I was at the Juan Academy.

"Drop the knife or I swear on The Red this will go far, far worse for you," said Sten.

"Fucking make me," I said. I had no real idea of the danger I was in. I was flushed with the power of what I'd just managed, sick of the fear and worried still for who might be watching us. I believe a sort of instinct must have overtaken my sense.

Gerin smiled, far less concerned about the rodent. "You know what, boys, if anything, she's getting me even more horny." He pulled open his breeches to show me a modest but stiff cock, some command or wish on the verge of being spoken when his eyes widened at the crack of a pine cone behind me. Without looking I ducked and ran towards them. I heard a bowstring and an arrow hit him in the chest. Gerin and Sten drew their swords but I darted to my left and kept running, hearing movement all around us, whoops of what must have been bandits of some sort. Risking a glance around at the twenty or so that rushed the three of them, I saw I was not being chased so I shouted for Nielus and Petir, screamed to burst. I had got within a few yards of camp before slipping on the loose stones from the cliffs and boulders around us. Petir caught me while the others drained brews.

"Where? How many?" demanded Nielus. I pointed back up the path where the sound of swords and shouting carried faintly, told him how many. No sooner had Petir put me back on my feet Nielus threw a shortsword at him.

"You bragged about your swordmaster and the training you had. Time to put it to use, boy."

"You can't leave!" I shouted.

"He can and he will. Get a brew down you, boy and stay close."

Petir's eyes filled. He looked around us. "There, a dell, see those bushes down off the track? Get some food, water and blankets and get down there, I'll whistle something from Ramban when we get back. Go!" I rushed to kiss him. He quivered, terrified, before Nielus dragged him away. I wouldn't see him for the next twelve winters.

I took what I could from the camp, some flasks, a knife and a saddlebag of bilt and bisks. A short while later I heard cheering, then the camp being pillaged for the horses and supplies. I fell asleep under a woollen blanket at some point that night, told myself stories in my head to stop myself from thinking of him dead and crying and so alerting the raiders to my position.

I woke up to a heavy mist and silence. The bush I was in shivered with my withdrawal, flecks of ice falling like shingle through the twigs. I wanted to know if he was alive or dead, that the last I saw of him would or wouldn't be that last panicked farewell. I had never felt more the younger sister, the little princess.

I was too scared to head back up the slopes to where we were ambushed, to find out if the raiders were there, for I knew what they would want, the more and worse perhaps than Nielus's men. Petir had bade me get away and hide. If he was alive, he might forgive me. It was the middle of the day before I carried on along the frozen path and slowly down towards the foothills of Donag's Boot and the plains of Jua beyond.

I became feverish the next day and despite the air clearing to a drier cold as I got into the foothills and woods of the Juan border I made little progress. I grew terrified of every sound, desperate to find someone to help me and fearful of what they would do to me. The fever grew, magnifying my terror, and I begged for my life to all the magists I had learned of from my tutors until the vivid beating life around me became a clamouring, then an agony in my ears that I could not stand straight from, that made me sick over and over. I retched up what little water I dared try and take until I fell in and out of dark accusatory dreams, filled with fetching and fantastic figures that made a puppet of me until I could bear no more.

I was woken by a man who said I reminded him of his daughter, a hunter checking his traps like those we'd preyed upon weeks previously. He put a bearskin over me and his mittens on my hands, fed me morsels of bread, for my saddlebag had been scattered in my delirium. I remember little beyond the beautiful clean white whiskers of his moustache, protecting his smile from the world. He was thin too, he'd lost flesh and his jumper slumped around the bones of his shoulders. After a small bitter apple, he gave me his walking stick and helped me away to his camp.

212

He had to argue with his camp's leader and his wife to be allowed to nurse me, for the bandits and the winter that had moved south from the mountains and highlands of the Citadels and Mount Hope had brought hunger and its attendant savagery to the borders of the wealthiest country in the Old Kingdoms. If I could give that man all the gold I had I would, for he saved my life and fed me at some cost to his own family and people. It did not last long of course; they had no room for another mouth to feed unless it came with a strong back or a good sword-hand.

They spared me some boots and woollens as the price of my goodbye and gave me directions to the nearest Post House, for I wanted to tell the Post of what had happened to Nielus and his awful crew, and I hoped they would send a party up to the hills to look for my brother. The Post of our nursery tales was as dead as Nielus said it was, or at least had too few of the leaders and numbers to do much more than keep its routes from being overrun completely by bandits.

A sleepy boy, not much older than myself, walked me from the gate of the Post House to an office next to the stores. He had armour on that must have belonged to a man twice his size, with what looked like two arrow holes in it, at the centre of his chest. He asked for my story of the events that befell us and wrote it down. Shortly, a Red came in cussing and took off his cloak.

"Carving up fucking pigs again, Reeve's sold two of ours to some merchant we've got our finger up who's trying to work a contract for tin and he wants one for a spit and the other made into cuts and broth."

"Canny's got you doing it again after last time? He said you fucked it," said the boy laughing.

"You need a butcher?" I said.

"You offering?" They both laughed at me. "Sorry, girl, for you sounds too well spoken altogether for that profession," said the boy.

"Who's this?" said the Red.

"She come in from the mountains, said Nelly's up there with his boys but got done by bandits. You need to tell Canny to put a crew together."

"Give me the pig that needs butchering and some proper blades,"

I said. "If you think you can do better, kick me out. If not, feed me and give me a bunk for the night."

He clapped his hands. "I'll let you sleep with me if you manage it."

I knew they would give me the chance, and as charming as the boy was (I felt he had a good heart) I had to tell him to fuck off, but he took it well and the Red cackled away for a good minute while I gathered my blankets and woollens and pack and followed him through to the kitchens. I had stayed out of my mother and father's way by spending time in the kitchens or with the herdsmen out in the fields, and I'd made a nuisance of myself until they let me help. Over the years I'd learned a lot about the preparation of pigs, cows and birds, more than these Reds.

I asked the Red what he would do about Nielus and my brother.

"Nielus was a good man, we'll get a sortie out for them. Right, here's the kitchen, this is Foddy. Foddy, she's doing the pigs or she's out on her ass."

An old man was hunched over a pig on the ground, sewing it up for the spit. He gestured to the other pig stretched out, mouth wide open as though killed while startled.

The Red left us and the old cook helped me with the pig onto the bench and I earned my bunk with his knives and cleaver. An hour or so later the captain of the Post House came in to tell me that they'd sent a crew of twelve up to find Nielus and the others, confirm whether or not they'd been killed.

I washed my hands and arms in a bucket of water, exhausted, and the cook saw me to a bunk with the boy and two other Reds that were all that was left.

"She is an excellent butcher," was all Foddy said before leaving us.

I was kicked out of my first proper bed since Snakewood at dawn the following day and made myself useful until the Reds returned from the Donag passes, though that was four days later. I helped Foddy with a stew for them and demanded I help serve so I could ask what had happened as they warmed themselves in the main hall. They had returned with the cloaks that all Reds wear, including Nielus's. But nothing else. They spent the night getting soaked and singing and telling stories of Nielus, as well as Gerin and Sten, which I couldn't bear.

214

The captain saw me leave and followed.

"I'm sorry you lost your brother. Nielus's wife will be here tomorrow, same as always. I would like you to give her his cloak. She may understand then that he made a sacrifice for you and find some peace in his death in the days to come."

I washed, dried and folded his cloak myself, ready for the following morning, and I polished his old Marschal's clasp. It was a piece of copper carved into the shape of a Coldbay Tern, wings like scimitars and tail like a pitchfork, chosen as the Post's symbol by the Seventh Red, who had seen them in the north and the south and so was the first to know them to fly so far between the seasons.

Nielus's wife came up the track to the gates of the Post House and started shaking her head, bringing her horse to a standstill some distance away as she saw all the Reds stood in a row outside the gate, leathers and chain freshly waxed, and their cloaks as bright red and clean as poppies. I stood out in front of them, holding his cloak across my arms as I'd been shown.

She got down from the trap unsteadily and held onto the harness as she straightened herself. She strode up the slope and the captain began humming "Brother Red", which the others took up. It always moved me to hear it, and never more than on that morning. She smiled as she approached, the look any good mother would give to a suffering child, for I must have looked dreadful, grey and thin with hunger, damp blackened woollens and the leather boots I was given by that hunter, far too big for me.

I couldn't help but cry, knowing of Nielus's love for her, and I held out his cloak as the Reds became a choir and the captain led them in a beautiful high voice through the words of their glorious and melancholy hymn. The tears shone on her cheeks like gold in the sun, and she shook out his cloak, the breeze catching it, flinging it out behind her, cracking as it rippled. She took the collar and swung the cloak over her shoulders in a smooth strong arc. She clasped it at the neck and took a handful of it up to her nose to breathe it in before wiping her eyes with it.

She looked at all of them as they sang, clasped her hands in thanks and bowed her head until they'd finished. I stood to the side as each took his turn to approach and share a word with her before going into the Post House, leaving us and the captain alone.

"How did he die?" she asked, looking at me; she must have intuited that I was with Nielus before he died, for my presence was otherwise incongruous.

"I was gathering berries, I saw raiders and ran to alert them all. We were ambushed. He, he found my brother and me starving on one of the passes."

"The Farlsgrad Creed," she said. "You lost your brother, didn't you?"

"He saved my life. He saved us both, for a time."

"You are far from home, a Citadels girl by the looks of you, so beautiful."

"She has nowhere and no one," said the captain, "but she's by all accounts an excellent butcher; I'm sure she could find work."

The woman nodded. "Well then, gather up your things. You can keep me company for the next few days and tell me of my husband."

A purse passed between them, some whispered words as they embraced. I had retreated to the gate watching them, but when I came back the captain was gone and she was back on the trap.

"Put your things in the back and come sit with me. We've got some miles to do before we can camp. I'm Sylve." She pinned back her greying hair and reached down to pull me up, which she managed almost entirely without my help, strong sinewy arms from a life's hard work.

She made more of a fuss of me in those few days than my mother ever did. She bathed and washed me, gave up on my matted hair and cut it all back and fattened me up as best she could on cheese and porridge. She had decided to try and find me work and somewhere else to live at a market fair the herders and growers would come to every year in this province of northern Jua.

It was similar to the markets back in the Citadels. Thousands had come to the City of Elden's market. There were the auctions for livestock through to the plays and recitals I could not follow because they were in Juan but that seemed from the players to be as bawdy and lacking in deference as those I watched at Argir, judging by the foolery of those in the fine garments having their breeches pulled down or wigs knocked off. Peddlers and traders from the coast of Jua came up with their cages of speaking birds, mewling puppies and stoic lizards, cookers promised brews and compounds that were miracles from furthest Tarantrea or the fabled Hanwoq and Coral Bay. Sylve bought me some tea leaves that were more common here than further north, which I threaded with some soft kannab. I've made that tea ever since.

I wandered into the livestock market, dominated by those buying and selling for the lords. Much of it I couldn't understand because they weren't speaking Common, but there was a boy not much older than me haggling over a couple of cows that didn't look worth anything.

"Don't buy them," I said. I thought he might have been buying for his family, but it turned out he was working for a Juan lord and his master hadn't arrived, the instruction being to purchase at least five cows.

"Piss off, girl. You lost?" said the seller.

I could read him well enough. He knew full well the condition of the cows; I could read it too in their eyes, the way they stood.

"What makes you think they in't right?" said the boy.

"Teats. Apart from being dirty, which is appalling for cows being sold, a couple look infected, they're leaking. Looking at the back of that one, the haunches are narrow, so you might not have such good calving, and apart from being able to see the ribs on this one a bit too well, I'd say there was only a finger between them, so it won't fatten as well. Shall we look at the hooves?"

The boy bowed his head in dismay, and I got the impression he had just avoided getting into an awful lot of trouble.

"Can you help me . . .?"

"I'm Galathia. Yes." He shook my hand when I held it out.

"You saved me a beating."

"I need somewhere to live. I can work," I said. Sylve did not have the means, especially now, to feed me.

"I can speak to my master. He was due here and I'm not sure what's held him up."

I found the boy some good cows, cost him most of the silver he'd been given, and in return he bought us some bread and some berries. Later, his master, head of the lord's livestock, caught up with the boy and inspected the cows.

"It was all down to her," said the boy, fearing getting it wrong, a pained look in his eyes and his ragged mop of brown hair covering his face as he stared at the ground.

217

"Well, she has an eye, this girl you've picked up. Seven silver is a good price."

"He said you might have a place I can sleep. I can work, worked in a royal palace up at the Citadels."

"Who are you here with?"

"Woman that rescued me. I was abandoned." Strange how I'd lived with it for all this time but only in saying it did I nearly lose control.

"I think we can find a stable for now and I can have a word with the lord."

I found Sylve and told her I had some work as a servant of some sort. She held me, begged me to be safe and gave me some coppers which she wouldn't let me give back.

I left Elden's market driving the cart that they'd brought while they led the cows the few leagues to the Juan High Commune, in the Somskaat region, one of the finest communes in the known world. The woes of my trail ended and I found some peace.

The following years fared better for me. My education made me suitable to write then cleark for the quartermasters overseeing supplies and shipments of plant. I endured, of course, the attention my body aroused in a commune full of men as I became a woman, but in my work in the kitchens I got to know some of the guards, good men who humoured my wish to learn to use a sword, and better use Nielus's knife. I would no longer be defenceless. I wanted to be strong, and I studied drudhanry with the apprentices. During these years I lost contact with the outside world, which had taken everything. I was determined that were I to leave the commune, I would not be afraid.

This being Jua, and this being its High Commune, I found myself at the heart of the Old Kingdoms' most ancient establishment. Jua, along with Old Ceirad and Issana, established the first modern alliance, out of the wreckage of the Orange Empire of Harudan. Others joined and while allegiances came and went, the name for the lands around the east and west coasts of the Sar stuck, for most of them enjoyed long-lasting wealth and stability by profiting richly from trade between each other and south into the gulf over many generations.

Jua's royal lineage and patronage ran further back than that, the oldest unbroken line in all the known lands. The network of royals, merchants and lords that ran Jua now comprised the current custodians of ancient families, legacies and guilds. I toured the estates with the Commune Comprado and drudharchs on the Elevens and Beaches; parties and gatherings on invitation only that brought me in touch with the very wealthiest of men and women outside the Dust Coast. The wealth was sickening, an almost innocent self-righteousness of the culture, for the last civil war was too grand a name for what I'd learned really was a dispute over plant growing among the people, and what constituted personal use. Perhaps it was that I saw in their lacquered pomps, satins and silks the life I'd been denied, but I felt only disdain for the rituals they abided by, poisonous words spat between shimmering fans as the ladies shared their gossip in the pavilions pulled along the Elevens highways between their estates.

The Filston-Blackmore Company were guests of the Post. Their adventuring carracks, mostly Alon's, had found a supply run from Coral Bay delivering strykna tree seeds that fed a lucrative poisons market among all the High Communes on the Eastern Sar.

Forgiven their ignorance of centuries of the Elevens and Beaches' ritualised courtesies of Jua's high families, they attended the feasts, as we all did from the commune, in a fearful awkward silence. Positioned with the drudharchs in one of the minor pavilions of the second Beaches, Alon and I were seated together on a rug.

His courting was boring; he missed few opportunities to discuss his fleet and estate, fewer still the stories of great trades and profits, including the strykna seeds discovery. Those from the commune were amused that he should attempt to woo me so seriously, they knowing how little an interest I showed in the flirting that so many of the boys engaged the few girls at the commune in. They encouraged me nevertheless, and spoke well of him.

That he wasn't fat nor interested greatly in whoring was enough for me, for it was clear that he was a very rich man, one of many the great Juan families indulged. The time-honoured trade of wealth for respectability and acceptance was as widespread here as anywhere, if a little more discreet. I could hardly believe how easy it was to go along with his rather clumsy fondling. He was gentle enough, when I'd agreed to accompany him for a play that evening. For the first time in my life I was with a man I did not feel intimidated by. Quite the opposite. I enjoyed it. He seemed as nervous as I when it came to us sharing a pillow. I felt nothing for him, I'm sorry to say, but our joining ceremony was opulent and I realised that whatever I wanted to do now, his wealth would enable me to do it.

Kigan rose to his knees to kiss me. His body wrote the story of his pain. All his suffering had been for me. His revenge was my revenge.

"You will get back your birthright, if not the book and the plant. You will once more sit on the throne of Argir, or Petir will perhaps. I very much want to hear what became of him."

"He will cure us all of the Old Kingdoms. The world is going to change and he is at the heart of it. There is a warlord, Caragula, who has united all of the wild tribes east and north of Lagrad, Ahmstad and the Razhani Province. Hundreds of thousands of men are marching towards us, my brother in the vanguard, one of his generals."

After our parting on that snowy pass, Petir, inevitably, became a killer. He would not have me say he cried, for he could not look back to where I was hidden, for fear of someone seeing him do so. The raiders had the numbers, Nielus's crew dropping one by one, closing up to each other's backs as they were encircled. Five men stood against thirty and three of those had taken poison enough from their wounds that they collapsed dead as they were circled.

Petir and the last of Nielus's crew laid down their swords before the raiders, realising the futility of their position. At the raiders' head was a man he could now hardly describe for being of such little physical distinction. The man picked his sword off the ground and threw it back at him. A choice was offered with a toothless lisp: die together, or kill the last of Nielus's men and join his crew, his swordsmanship being in sore need. The Red swore by a magist. Petir's sword arm trembled as he raised it, his sharp thrust bearing the weight of the raiders' expectation. He was stripped and made to march naked the leagues back to their camp while the Post's horses were led behind with everything else they owned apart from the cloaks, for they did not need to identify themselves to any of the Post that might come after them by wearing the robes of those they'd killed.

The raiders in that high pass nearly beat the life out of him, and he took on the instincts of an animal amid those cold black ravines and passes. Yet his reading, writing and grasp of Hespen took him quickly to the heart of their chief, too quickly for some. He was wise enough to know it, finding the read of faces once so vital at court among his father and counsellors now vital here.

The first attack he had expected; two sleepless nights with one of the raiders on a hunt to some loose woodlands a few miles from camp. The cold tea he'd sipped from the flask of the other man, whom he'd seen snub him at a meet, was too bitter. He feigned to drink the rest but returned each subsequent sip back to the cup until he could tip it while the man sorted his skins out.

Just before dawn Petir lay still, holding a knife close to his chest, curled up under his sleepskin. He fought with his fear to breathe slowly as the man shifted and got to his feet. In the moment of silence with which the murderous intention sought to mask itself he spun and slashed wildly with his knife. The man was stood over him, closer than Petir had read it, so the knife's point caught the man in his thigh, driving into the muscle there. Petir got up to his knees and stabbed the flailing man's belly repeatedly until he collapsed. He told me it was a euphoric feeling, a moment that changed his life.

Returning a day later with some rabbits and a calf that were too slow for his bow he realised, unlike so many men, that to get anything from the world wasn't to wait for it to act on him, but to act on it. His first real and intimate fight to the death was alchemic; he was surviving.

He made his case with the chief and the others for why he had returned alone. There was no open dissent. As he stood there unchallenged he saw the woman his hunting mate had shared his tent with. She took him from the gathering and to the man's tent, and Petir took his place fully in the camp.

This, he knew, was sure to draw out those others who were jealous of his position. The woman helped as he dug holes and covered them over with straw, just inside the tent. When they came, the first stepped into the hole and fell forward. Up from his skins, Petir killed him with a shortsword as he tried to fight back from his knees. The man behind fled but Petir was after him and shortly ran him through as he caught up with him.

The chief called for mugs of wine at dawn the next day, spoke of being for each other, of the common good they needed in these hard times to survive and prosper. Enough of the respected men in the camp knocked cups with him, burying further dissent through their show of support.

A daughter was born to him the following summer. He knew and loved her only briefly, a baby with a shock of red hair like mine who didn't live long enough for her naming.

The chief of so little outward distinction proved an inspired tutor to Petir in the art of hit and run. He was soon leading his own squad with iron conviction, killing the fighting men of other bands of raiders and the Ahm Plainsmen around the south edge of Jua's Teeth.

Nothing gets noticed like success. The Post was roused by the growing attacks on its caravans. My years with Laun have shown me that it protects nothing so fiercely as its reputation.

The Ahm clans, suffering Petir's contention of their hunting grounds and being defeated in sorties of their own to muzzle the raiders, found the Post willing to supply a plan and the means to carry it out, for their mutual benefit.

They soon entreated Petir's chief and his advisers to meet and discuss what fealty they could pay to reduce the incursions.

Petir accompanied them to a gathering at the heart of a vast plain where surprise and ambush could not be countenanced.

With Post silver and supplies of kannab and skins the arrangement was made.

Reds and mercenaries, armed with the whereabouts of Petir's camp from the vengeful members of defeated clans, moved against them; the camp was burned, his wife and daughter among those who did not escape.

The Ahm clans concluded their talks a day later, leaving Petir, his chief and the other raid captains to return into the trap. Fighting out of the ambush, he fled to the high passes with only two other survivors.

A month later he walked south alone, a gaunt thief wandering through the great wilds of northern Issana before turning east to Vilmor and a king he said was bent on creating a legacy for his sons while instead slowly destroying his father's.

A stint as a carpenter's mate gave Petir some of his strength back, enough that he could once more do his forms and try to prove a way back to fighting, where all the coin and respect was. He became a mercenary, and learned much about the managing of an army, while proving himself fearless in battle. In a few years he found himself at the Virates bordering with the Wild and he found a clan chief, Imil of the Rivershall, and captains that took him in and trusted him after he'd led back forty of their people from a camp hit by Wildmen. He led Rivershall sorties on the hit-and-run work he knew so well and soon the clan got noticed, as much by the hast leaders and chiefs in the near Wild as those of the other Virates clans. He stayed away from the sea; treachery enough among men let alone from under your feet he told me. The learning at his father's feet of the skill at winning minds and brokering oaths took his clan from one of the Third tables to the Black Table in the Reckoning feasts the Blackhand Virate held to debate and empower their common cause, which was sometimes to resolve conflict with each other but more often their common enemy, the hasts and raiders out of the Wild. There, in Rivershall, he soon fathered another girl, paler than her friends of course and with much-admired blue eyes. This child at least he got to keep.

Imil, chief of the Rivershall, flushed with bravado stoked by Petir's successes, was soon overplaying his hand in all inter-clan matters, with Petir too much away at their borders to see the rot at the heart. He returned from a long sortie with a tithe of plant, weapons and a treaty with some nomadic raiders to find Imil executed by his captains and another clan, the Standhals, controlling the Rivershalls. The Standhals were in no mood to entertain the tactics and strategies of a mercenary from the north, hardened against all his good reason by their prejudice. They had a mind to appease the Wildmen more than the Rivershalls had, especially where Rivershall land was concerned. Returning to Rivershall, he was found a day out by a scout warning him that a run of skins expected from his home fort was late, with no weger returning from its aviary.

Bidding his men to continue on, he turned west to follow the south edge of the great forest that bordered the Blackhand Virate. A day later, despite seeing no evidence of raiders, he arrived at the fort to find it also unsullied; no burned buildings, no forced gate and no living thing. Desperately he made for their hut, calling for his woman

Aliam and the daughter he'd named after me. Inside, despite his inks and parches missing, all was as it was kept by Aliam.

At their small table he saw a straw bird his daughter, Galathia, had made with bits of coloured ribbon woven into the rough blonde stalks. He held it, hoping it would somehow still be warm from her hand. He stepped out of their hut clutching the bird, unsteady with grief. Outside the wind had picked up, chilly evening gusts ripping through the silent lanes. At the gate to the fort he'd entered only a short while before stood a giant of a man, a long sword hanging like a dirk, in a plain scabbard, the boiled leather armour soiled, ruptured in places. A short well-kept beard framed a handsome sun-beaten face that looked as though it was chipped from a boulder. His black hair was plaited and woven with dried blue poppies.

"Petir. I've heard much about you. A formidable squad leader, a captain in all but rank."

Petir walked forward; something about this man demanded it. This could be no trap or ambush because it would not befit him.

"Where is my wife, my daughter Galathia?"

The giant appraised him, hands at his hips.

"She is well. They all are."

"Who are you?"

"Caragula. I came here hoping you would return once word had spread about the sacking of this camp." His speech was clear, though King's Common was not his own tongue. His voice was a smooth rasp, as though the words were formed by a blade being sharpened on leather.

He extended a hand, a Virate greeting custom to hold the forearm.

As Petir approached he heard no others besides Caragula's horse, nustling at grasses beyond the gate. They were alone.

Caragula's fingers fully enclosed Petir's forearm, as though he held a twig. Petir said that he may as well have grasped a slab of marble in return. Caragula's eyes shone with a captivating, fatherly lucidity. Petir had to look hard to see a sign of fightbrew in the skin.

"It is good to meet you, Petir, I have a great need for men of your quality. Would you prefer us to speak in Hespen or Common?" He gestured for them both to sit.

"Common's fine."

"I hope you will hear me out and join me as your family have done. More than that, join me to lead far more men than this sad little Virate would allow you for the mere fact of your not being of Rivershall blood. Your blood is nobler than that, isn't it? You are the rightful heir to the throne of Citadel Argir. I believe we can be of a great help to each other."

As they settled, Caragula smoked of Petir's pipe and told him of the great change coming in the world.

"The people of the Wild live barbarous lives, beholden to the seasons, raided and plundered, within and without. Numbers beyond count, along all the borders of the world you know, stretching from the Virates to the Citadels, are killed and worse. The Old Kingdoms were built on our plant, grew and then fattened on our blood, were served by our enslaved. Hevendor, Ahmstad, Razhani, Lagrad, these are lesser provinces the Old Kingdoms shaped and moulded from whichever tribes were greedy enough to take their iron, their plant and their rules. They are mere protectorates with the illusion of freedom, civilisations of straw, yet they are still the armour that protects the Old Kingdoms' cultures and wealth and greed. But what do these Old Kingdoms know of the Wild? Do they know that it stretches east and north many times further than all the lands west of the Razhani clan's? We are, in our languages, history and stories, as rich as they, but our recipes are crude, our fighting men disorganised, our ambition stunted. Yet we have overcome these failings."

They were sat near a small pile of hewn stone. Caragula rolled towards him a stone that was ready for pitching. "Do you know anything of a mason's skills?" Petir shook his head. Caragula took up a pitcher and a hammer, ready to shape it.

"You should watch a good apprentice mason at a quarry. My mother was one of the best, a master. She would look over a stone, feel it, then with a strike seemingly of little strength she would crack it in two, as if she could crack it to the shape she wished it to be." And Caragula did just that. He turned the stone, ran his hand over it and positioned it. Then, with the tools, he smacked the stone as though slapping a fly, and it sundered to a surface almost as level as a pond's.

"Inside something seemingly as solid as this stone was, there are faultlines. The stone represents those protectorates, those lands with their border patrols and their forts and roads. They have laws, some have cities now. Perhaps they think of themselves as the Young Kingdoms. But I know their faultlines, for they are the tribes, like planes in the stone, adjacent but weak. Their histories are the pitcher. I am the hammer. When they break I will unite them anew. When they see the Old Kingdoms for what they are, for what they have done . . . when they remember, then the armour is gone, and we may shape Sarun as we see fit, you and I."

Petir was free to debate at length then, but found reason in all the answers, little in the way of boasting. He maintains that Caragula is a wise leader, with a charisma born of humility and surety, with no little humour. He felt something like hope for the first time that he could remember and I knew when I walked into the Juan Commune how that felt. Like all the other men serving him, Petir found an older brother in Caragula, a brother he then swore to serve with his life.

Kigan leaned forward to move a lock of my hair that had fallen over my brow and nose as I leaned towards him.

"I have not heard of Caragula, but I have not been east since I saw you had beaten me to Sho, and I did not stay for news of the Virates and the Redwall Confederacy. When will this army be upon us?"

"A few months, maybe less."

"What is its number?"

"A hundred thousand or more. My brother tells me a thousand drudhas and plant enough to sustain them on many battlefields are with them."

I thought he would be as pleased as I that things were changing, that my brother and I were at the heart of a change in the order of the world. He whispered something to himself before his eyes came back to me. He smiled, and I wondered if he had just instructed himself to do so, but my need for him rushed me now that the story of my life, my victory over it, was told. I grasped his head firmly, opening my thighs to better guide it to what I needed from him.

Chapter 11

Gant

Shale was waiting where we stashed the saddles before the battle, grimmer than I'd seen him in a long while. He put his arms around me, managing a smile.

"Wound in't that bad, Shale," I said, making light of his affection, but I too was glad to see him again.

"It were a fierce oppo, fierce enough wi'out yer trouble. Din't know if you'd make it. We got to get the horses from the 'jacker."

"I took Gilgul down. Fucker must've bin there with his crew. Made the last couple o' days a bit more bearable at least."

"How'd I miss 'im?"

"You had three or so on you or I'd have give you a shout. I needs me wound sorting out anyway, it stinks," I said.

He was shaking his head as we did it.

"Yer patched up, I found some decent bark nearby, nice bit o' luck fer once. Now we get the horses an' figure out where we're headin'."

"We only knows of Bense in Jua and what Araliah told us, that Valdir were likely in Langer's End," I said.

"It may be Valdir in't there, Gant, but we know Bense is."

"And if we knows it then whoever's doing the killing must know it," I said. "There'd be some fierce Post in Jua and what went on in the vineyard's going to be stoking up some vengeance on men of the colour."

"Old men o' the colour in particular," he said laughing. "I reckon it in't more than a few weeks to take a route through Marola an' find

227

where Valdir is, a warm autumn so far and once winter's in then it's slow," he said.

"We should go see Valdir then. We only bin running the killer's way and not ahead either since he were tracking us. If he knows Bense is alive he might be thinking he'd get the three of us at once," I said. We didn't say it but each was thinking that it must be too much to take on three of us, but he already had accounted for near all of us with no comeback, according to Kailen's letter.

"Valdir always said Langer's End was a shithole," said Shale.

With nothing else said that day we moved late evening with saddles and the bags we had hidden and went for the horses.

If it wasn't quite the shithole, Langer's End was a quiet place with little pleasure in seeing strangers. There was little of the Post here either, which was something. Langer's End was at the northwestern end of Marola, a marketplace for the cattle and grain that were traded inland. It was called The Court by the districts hereabouts for it was a group of landowners what run the justice, though heralds and banners we seen at camps, and some villages suggested some three fiefs were bordered here.

We got some good food for our coin and were shortly pointed the way to Valdir's family's farm, for his da was once on the court so was well known.

The stone walls about the farm and the bit of land it had enclosed were only secure at a few points. I reckoned a lot of those about were setting their own walls with the pieces of this one. The farmhouse was on the top of a rise, backing onto some woods. The thatch was in disrepair and there was a clutter about of broken forks, flails and a cart that spoke of hard times, not least because this was harvest and they should be making the coin now more than later. As we approached I saw a face at an open window, then a woman stepped out, smoothing out a blackened apron.

"It's soldiers, mum," she said, calling indoors. "Expect they's after food." She addressed us then. "We got little food with a bad harvest and two shites for farmhands probably off smoking kannab. I can get you some brin, been baking this morning."

"We were looking for Valdir," I said.

"You found his sister, but he lost an arm. He won't be signing for you even if he was here. You'd best come in. It would have been nice to have word he was well."

She said to tie the horses near a hay cock, which was a kindness.

It was damp all through inside, despite a big fire where the main table was at the back of the room. A fat old dog was stretched out by a window to the front but the place needed more light in it than the two small candles what were sat on the table. Their mother was an old age for sure. She was adjusting a blanket and presently dozed for the time we were there, small like a bird and as free of concern for the plight of the place.

The daughter, herself grey, greasy hair drawn back with a tie, stared for a moment at her mother as though she was another chore waiting its turn. She had a bit of a lith, which softened her words.

"I can't spare you long, the brin there cooling needs running to Picket's and he screets if you're not on time."

"We'll do that for you . . . um . . ."

"My manners! I'm Julir, did you know Valdir before?"

"It were more than fifteen to twenty summers past since we last spoke to him. I'm Gant, this is Shale," I said.

"Oh." She shifted some trays and rags that were on a bench and bid us sit at the table.

"It's good o' you to let us in an' feed the horses, we'll pay well for it. Valdir was a brother," said Shale.

"A real brother would have been a saving here, pat might have been less rummy if I'd got a length and not a soofy." She flashed a smile but it seemed to vanish for lack of strength. She fetched some brin, which was a kind of bread in these parts, from under a cloth on a shelf near the window, unshuttered and giving a view west to woods and open land far off. The brin was a bit heavy, but good with some of her salted butter.

Her hands were scarred, the fingers thick and knuckles swollen from the work. She had no more meat on her than her sparrow of a mother behind her, deep lines on a face that might once have attracted comment. None of us were paintings now though.

"I will take you on that offer to deliver the brin, gives me that bit of time to sort out the cows. You worked for Kailen then?"

"Yes," I said, "we need to find Valdir because we got someone seems to be hunting out the Twenty, killing us off. We want to be sure he's alive."

"He came back however many harvests ago after you all split, said he'd been with one of you, Miri, but it ended badly and that's how he lost his arm. Our pat was alive then, never forgive him for leaving in the first place, his only son. I never forgive him too for a while. Then he's back but pat's still tanning him, about his working the strips, prices he's getting on the barley and such. I begs him to stay but then he's gone, never seen him more sad though he said his true sorrow was in here and what he seen and done." She tapped her head and chewed on some brin a moment.

"So he went to the coast, come back for pat's burying then went again, but he brought a woman with him, her boy too not his. She was fine to look on, suited to him for how she would lift him with her touch. He was happier then and I stopped wishing bad of him. Anley's Harbour is his home now. I reckon he's still working the boats there."

She put a cut of brin on the stool next to the chair her mother dozed on and fetched a jug of her beer for us to sip on. She sat back down and was silent then, like she was alone.

"I have a concern," said Shale, "that who it is lookin' fer us might not spare those who he asks the way of, if yer follow. Bein' family might make it worse in that regard."

I was thinking the same.

"Yer got nobody lookin' out fer the farm if yer gets ill?" said Shale.

"Oh I can't get ill, that would do us with the wasters that want paying for the scratching about they does. Winters don't have to be cold to kill you when you's poor, and there's little here for us if we don't shift this wheat for the right price. Pat's stint at the court was a favour all used up over the years and they's that run it now didn't know him."

I took a bag of coins out of my belt and opened it on the table among the crumbs, all silver, about fifty pieces.

"Thinking you should be considering taking it easy, but somewhere far off where this man or men doing the killing in't going to find you," I said.

She took a few coins up in her hand, not believing it, looking at us both keenly. Then she dropped them to hold a hand each, me and Shale's. She shook her head, beginning to weep. We give her a bit to let it go. Who round here would've seen as much on their kitchen table? It was easy to forget.

"Why?" she said. "Two soldiers coming like this and offering us a fortune like they's got no need of the coin theirselves."

"We couldn't leave thinking you'd be in trouble, and I'm dying besides. I've got enough for what's left of me. Take the coin, Julir, if we don't find Valdir we would've done something for him at least."

She had some more vigour about her as we left and saddled up. Seems the coin wasn't enough to rouse her ma as she slept there all the while. Julir was muttering about repairs for the broken cart at her doorway as she bid us off, though we impressed as far as we could on her the need for her to disappear. Shale took the brin as she wanted and we give the buyer word to drop the coin up to her farm or we'd be back for his reason.

The ride to Anley's Harbour was a couple of days, thick forest for much of it but no trouble other than from my guts. I was slowing us, needing to rest a bit more in the night when we were making our ground quiet.

There were some houses on the cliffs about the harbour that were half hidden in the sea mist that soaked us as we come to it. We walked the horses down a track cut here and there with slabs of stone. It was a cove, a horseshoe of cliffs in which was the bowl of the harbour, two big wooden jetties reaching out. Around the slopes as we headed down were large and small huts each thickening the mist with smoke from busy chimneys. What noises we could hear of gulls, animals and children seemed to lose themselves in echoes.

The big huts for the families give way on the harbour to the terraces about the quay. Here it was fairly quiet, boats being out I guess. The nearest inn was The Admiral.

There were fifteen or twenty in there, a tight run of benches near the fire and the air thick with pipes. There were arguments, chattering and some chuckling that all hushed to the odd whisper as we stood at the table where the 'keep was stood with a buck and an old sailor that sun and the sea had turned into some grey-whiskered oak.

"We're lookin' fer an ale an' a man, name o' Valdir," said Shale.

"Aye," said the 'keep, who filled some big tin mugs as we settled. "No' wantin' to grieve men who paid colour, but what business do yus have wi' the man?"

"Hope yus comes to take him out," said the buck, "then yus all fucks off."

The old man looked past him at us, then rested a hand on his shoulder. "Yus be lookin' at them again, lad, sin the red leather an' quillions o' their blades an' these oils whut no such colour be found abouts. The lad's sorry for that," said the man.

"Don't mind a gobby buck," said Shale, "long as he don't raise a hand."

"Fine ale," I said. "Happy to see a round for the men here."

"Aye, sir," says the 'keep, watching the buck and Shale staring at each other. "Well, at the stone posts yus saw lit on the way in, top o' the rise by the burned out tree yus goes right an' there's a path yus teks to a house wi' a great bell on a post, our summer bell we uses for the festival."

"Winter too," said a soak cheered by the free ale he was waiting on, but he was quickly shushed.

"He's there, wi' his wife, mother o' this one," said the 'keep, gesturing at the buck, who was sulking and staring fierce now at the serving table, a rage in him.

I dropped coin on it for the ales and we drinks up. Outside and going back up the hill a couple of duts running about give us a few cheeky songs their mas wouldn't want them to sing, but they only followed us so far with their begging and they too mentioned Valdir because of our colour and his. The hill was a bit of work this way back, I was sweating and the wound was itching. We got round the lamps and were at his door near the bell, where we tied the horses. Here there were a few yards more of garden than those huts we saw roundabouts and it was kept sharp, some veg growing and a fenced-in run that was tidy. From the house too it was clear a soldier was in it; small place with a strong-looking lacquered door and shutters what were new looking, the sliver of candlelight and smoke of the chimney hole the only sign of people there, keeping out the late afternoon's chill.

I give a knock and Valdir opened the door. He's took back for a moment then shakes his head with a smile growing. "Gant? Shale is it?" He straightened at the sight of us, we embraced and he's grinning. I see he's missing most of an arm.

"Come in, boys, come in! Alina, we got us some guests," he shouted. "I was just feeding her," he said to us.

He backed through the door and we walked in to a warm room spare of much. His woman was there in a grand old chair, something he must have built, but she didn't move. Her eyes took us in, and she started breathing fierce, as though feared or nervous. She made some noises but I saw her lip was drooping, seeming to pull her face down a bit on the one side, a bit of dribble hanging from it and she in no control of speaking. I saw it sometimes on some of the boys we run with over the years and which condition was the end of them as soldiers.

"Alina, my love, it's just some old friends. Sit at the table, boys, I'll get you some stew shortly. Now then, girl, let's finish these carrots and onions, shall we?"

He picked up a wooden bowl from the floor near a chair next to her and he shushed her. Putting it in his lap for balance he put the spoon to her lips. Her one hand was still but the other was lifting weakly, trembling with the effort, though to help or hinder him wasn't clear. There was a bib round her that caught some of the gravy that fell with her spittle, but she made a go of swallowing it and nodding a little. He fussed her, forgetting we were there. After each spoon was taken he would drop it in the soup and wipe her, or fuss with a frond of hair, tucking it behind her ear, telling her the stew had maybe a bit too much salt or did she think the veg was a bit hard or soft. He was bigger now without the fighting, a fuzz of grey about his ears all that remained of his hair and his colour darkened with the years on boats, salt etching his skin deep. He still had those eyes sunk back under the strong ridge of his brows, now as well as those years past they lent him that air of an old sorrow.

Soon enough he was done and she was tapping her good hand, three taps, groaning a bit.

233

"Sorry, boys, she needs to go, I need to get her outside with you here."

"How'd you . . .?" I said, but stopped myself, ashamed a bit.

"It's easy, Gant, I carved a couple of wheels and fixed them on the back of her chair, just got to get her outside."

She give a tap and he nodded, squeezing her hand. She had no obvious grey in the golden hair about her shoulders, and would have been a heartbreaker ten or so summers past, though the struggle since what must have happened to her now darkened her eyes and drew her mouth and cheeks in narrow.

"We come by your sister," I said, when he brought her back in.

"Aye, think you must have. What brings you here?"

"Yer got a fine woman there," said Shale as Valdir headed for the pantry. He's looking at Alina and he give her a wink, which she returned, a flash of warmth run through her cheeks.

Valdir nodded, fetching us a jar of ale.

"Aye, she is. Expect me sister told you the tale of it?" he said.

"Sounds like your da were the same cut as mine when I says I'm off, but I never got back to see him after and I regrets it," I said.

He took a deep draw in his mug, "Pat was on their court and I come back to get me life in some shape. Me colour was trouble but to him also a dishonour. Couldn't stand to look at me. Me sister was glad of the help, but not much help with one arm. She brought me off the brews but I still take some kannab. I hated him then, pat, much as I loved me mattie and sis I had to go. I come to the coast. I needed a bit of the sea, some sky I could lose a bit of me in. Coming off the brews, paying out, was bad."

"Yer sister's runnin' it alone, Valdir, but she's strugglin'," said Shale.

"She was tied with a man, but when we last went to see her, when they put pat in the ground, he was a drinker and workshy. Near broke the farm I think." He stood and went over to Alina, who give a brief nod.

"She wants to lie down for a while. You boys'll take a cup later with us? Happy for you to stop by the fire here tonight if you're passing," he said. I nodded, giving Shale a quick glance.

He took her up on his shoulder, a well-practised move, and he

234

pushed through a curtain to a room beyond where they kept their sleeping mats on a little stand off the ground.

Me and Shale helped each other with our wambas and other leathers, piling them at his door.

He come back shortly and pulled the curtain.

"Wouldn't have her if not for a storm took her husband." He got a couple more jugs down off a shelf and a fat pouch of kannab and bacca. "Was on the boats, four of us out south looking to run some nets and pick up trout or herring. We got caught in a rusher, spun up out of nothing and the boat her man was captain of got caught on the Spikes, which is some rocks we was pushed into on our run back. I made it, many didn't.

"I was lodging at one of the inns down on the quay and her cousin it is runs it, he had me fetch up suppers for Alina and our boy, well I think of him as me own, but then she's just recovering from his pat being gone. The boy, Heldon, never got used to it."

He finished the pipe he was filling as he spoke and give it to Shale, who put his jumpcrick bones to it and got it lit.

"She got men sniffing about after a couple of months, for her man had this place and kept an investment in two of the other boats so had a bit of coin.

"One of the fishers that worked with him soon made a move and she took him in. I would still bring up the odd bit of salted fish but I saw enough to know he wasn't right for her or the boy that he was mean to. Then he's got some of the fishers and workers from about calling and they seemed to be here most times I called up. Her cousin asks if I could put a word in. Course, I call in and they's thinking I'm messing outside what I should be. No brew to swig mind, boys, older and fatter, but I took a dislike to one gobby buck at the door there and puts him out with me good hand. The others comes out and a few got me down and gives me a going over, even took a knife thinking it would do me, but the knife found its way back to him that used it. She looked after me from then on and soon enough here we are."

"What happened to her?" I asked. Might be harsh to ask, but I felt by asking him I'd know a bit more of him in the years since we split.

It still cut him to recount it now.

"Ah she, well, I was bringing the catch off the boat and Heldon

235

comes running down to tell me she wasn't right, had fallen and couldn't get up or speak properly. I run up here and lifted her but she was like this, bit worse than now for she was making no sense."

He took the pipe off Shale and had a good draw, managing himself.

"Those couple of years with her was the finest, happiest. I had no right to them, that make sense? She took good care of me even when all I did, all we did, was and is plain for everyone to see." He held up his cup to drink to it and we clacked and drained them.

"What about you boys?" said Valdir. "Looks like it's been a hard life." We laughed at this. There was a pleasant fug to the air now we were smoking. It was Shale that brought up what we were most fearing to have to say.

"Valdir, we're here because we're bein' chased, Kailen's Twenty are bein' killed. Kailen's dead, Kheld, Sho, The Prince, a load of us, an' we just got out of a trap sprung wi' thirty or so Reds an' some Agents. We come to see if you were still alive an' if so, well, yer dead wi'out you come with us."

"We give your sister fifty silver to get her and your mother out of the farm and south somewhere," I said.

He squeezed my hand with this news, grateful.

"You were tight wi' Miri, is he alive?" said Shale.

He looked at us then, reading us almost.

"Thirty?" And he was meaning the ambush of course.

"They weren't much equipped fer what we had," said Shale with a shrug.

I took Valdir through what we found at the Crag and what happened to us since, including what was in Kailen's letter.

It took another bowl of that kannab to cover it. My head was going soft like hot butter.

He told us then what happened to him and Mirisham. But me and Shale were fierce shocked at his story, for what he said made it more than likely, we reckoned, that it was Kigan, one of our own, what were killing us all.

"Couldn't say if Miri was alive or dead now, but not fussed if it was the latter. A few of us did those Citadel kids out of their shinies, the boy and girl we were protecting for that king in Citadel Argir. He gave Kigan a purse to see the two children right into Jua and set them up there. It was, if I recall right, a balls-out fortune. He always was a bit queer, up hisself, that Kigan. I was for cutting them out of all that gold, as was The Prince and Kailen, so Miri said he'd take care of Kigan and I would have a word with the other one they met with, that king's drudha that had the shinies. I run him off and got the place where the stuff was buried, so, with Ibsey and Kheld fairly risen and not due down a while, and the rest of you had gone on from Snakewood, we thought we'd take it all and disappear. I'm not fluffed with it, but I'm not fucked either whether the boys got a share. I was out of purses with that kind of shine. It wasn't that I wanted Kigan dead of course, but I couldn't care that much for what happened to him either, not after some of what I saw him do. His brews were the best, but he didn't seem to give a shit who he tried his recipes on."

"Agreed. Somethin' weren't right wi' him," said Shale. He was right and all. More than once I caught him putting a drop or a pinch of something on food for prisoners, and in our own cups at times. Saw him once doing it to a bottle that he was fetching for me and Moadd from some Lord's kitchen and I beat him though all the while he was saying it was just something to perk me up. Told Kailen I wouldn't go near him after that, for through the night I was sick and he was blaming it on the wine.

"So this stealing of treasure an' killing of Kigan were all at Snakewood?" I said.

"Aye, Snakewood. Miri didn't kill him though, I think he just give him a dose of something bad and sold him to slavers for a bit of coin. He hated him, and the gold he had and the luxury he was about to have back then, well, Miri wasn't going to let it happen. So we headed west for a bit, needed to find somewhere we could trade off some of the plant and shinies. We split it as best we could. Kailen and The Prince went over the Sar for a while, because we knew they's'd be after us, the guilds, the Post too probably and the other Citadels involved in taking over Argir when that king was deposed. Miri was clear in his head that we could do some more good with that wealth than what those kids would. He was from a place around the east of Mount Hope if you recall and his mother and father was killed when he was young by the raiders there that lived in the passes. We did some work there once, cleaning out hides and camps for that Post Marschal that had the one leg and the goit."

"It were tough is what I remembers, we got almost nowhere with that purse," I said.

"And he was for changing that; saw that if he could clean out those fuckers and set up the old Iron Passes routes, get the mines going too in land nobody could lay claim to, he would turn this fortune to a legacy. It was something useful to do, better than some Juan flesh pit."

"What about you? You went along with him then? You don't look like you got any of that coin or plant now," I said.

"Trouble was, and there's some stories about how we settled that land and cleaned the filth out that could fill a few evenings, once he got it settled and the routes walked by men we could trust, the Reds come sniffing, oil-tongued Reeve and his lickers. The Post was likely involved in what happened at Argir, for Mirisham seemed easy about them getting involved in our operation, and before I could consider a move or something else, he betrayed me much like we betrayed Kigan. Now at that point Miri was administrating, setting tariffs of passage with the guilds and lands around, including Mount Hope. I was out on the passes doing work on the bridges there all over those valleys. It was beautiful. But the Reds had more than they could get over the passes and in no time Miri was putting pressure on the others that were shipping their own goods in competition with the Post and soon I was finding the bandits and thieves had somehow returned. I still reckon they were in the Post's pay. Miri and me had been caught up, the Post must've found us. It was about Argir's money. Anyway, Miri was telling our men to cause some havoc to those 'vans that didn't belong to the Post, along with whatever bandits had come back. I flipped on him when I caught wind of it. He was seeing only the promise of this settlement that was gathering about the mouth of those valleys that was then just a staging post for those 'vans. I hadn't pieced it all together at that point, the last we spoke. With Post patronage he saw a chance to secure the place and I guess become a player in those parts. I'm guessing this was in exchange for what we stole, for I never saw a penny of it after."

He took a draw on his pipe and topped up our cups.

"One escort, when my men were meant to be walking some horses and carts with some families and their wool harvest over the Dockweed Pass, my men turned on them, tipped carts and were going to do worse, getting the women stripped tatty. Two arms I had then," he said, gesturing as best he could what he did, "and I got a slug of brew and took them apart, but with a few on me I took some blows and was on the edge of a drop. I saw a couple of bows being drawn and it was die for sure or jump. I went head over and got broke up bad on the fall. It wasn't sheer, me arm was torn up and hanging off, me ankle also broke but I hit the bottom and was well out of range and somehow left alone. Dragged meself a mile or so before a few miners that were leaving a shift saw me and they took the arm off and strapped the rest. I knew Miri was aware I was going to go against him, and the boys there had no problem turning on me." He took another long draught of his beer.

"I owe those miners my life," he said.

We were quiet a moment, letting the crack and whistle of the fire he had going fill the room. It was always a settling sound. Shale shook his head then, he was figuring something out and then must have got it.

"Gant, what Valdir's said now I think tells us why all this is happening, who it is doing the killing."

"Let's have it then," I said.

"Kigan weren't killed," he said. "And whoever's bin doin' the killing is leavin' a black coin. Us gettin' killed is all about a betrayal of some sort and Kailen himself weren't able to say that there was a purse we let down proper. I have to say it, Valdir, but if anyone's got a grievance against us it's Kigan from what yer tellin' us. Seems like it's to get at you, Mirisham, Kailen an' The Prince, an' I got no better explanation. We won all our other purses an' if there were any bad blood it was wi' him."

"Kigan?" I said. It was hard to take at first, I couldn't see it. Valdir was sucking on his pipe, nodding as he was thinking it through.

"Why kill the others if he was after us?" he asked. "And who in this world could take out Kailen never mind the rest of us, on his or her own?"

"Killin' others is perhaps to find out where you lot are, I'm guessin',"

239

said Shale. "If he took Kailen down alone, by the looks, an' the others, he's on some fierce plant an' has the backin' o' some guild, the Post too. We found out it's some big Issanaian guild, master name of Alon Filston, what put a poster about with a ransom o' five gold for news o' the Twenty. I can see from your look you in't got a clue who he was either, and that's the thing. Why's he want us so bad unless he's bound up with someone like Kigan who would 'ave a grievance? I can't argue that unless we're sleepin' we in't easy to kill, but the kill-in's happened an' I can't help thinkin' a drudha, an' one of us at that, stands the fairest chance if he kept his flint. Look, we come to get you out anyway, we knows where Bense is, up in Jua workin' fer some lord, name o' Fesden, an' yer seems to know where Mirisham is, so we got to get after 'em before Kigan, if it's him, does. Our best chance is gettin' Bense first an' then four of us goes to Mirisham, as he would be closer to us than where you're puttin' Mirisham."

"Would have to be some guild and bounty for the Reds to want rid of the man settled the Iron Passes after a generation lost. It'd rightly be making them the cream," said Valdir, "but I can't leave with me wife this way and me son not visiting us."

We all draws deep on the pipe, knowing what was to be decided. It was well said from Shale, he give a good account of the reasons.

"If he finds you here, Valdir, you're both dead, her son too I expect," I said. "Particularly if you were one of those that betrayed him." I said it like it was Kigan because I was convinced of it.

He was shaking his head, feeling helpless, glancing over at the curtain she was sleeping behind.

"You going to get him, Kigan?" said Valdir. "Maybe we get to Bense and Miri and put an end to it and I can get back. Sure her cousin that runs the inn can keep her hidden if Kigan was to come sniffing," he said, but it was a hopeful, sort of disbelieving tone. I think the danger was becoming more clear to him as we went on.

"We can sort you out fer money, Valdir," said Shale. "Got a lot o' gold an' nothin' more worth spendin' it on." He put a fat purse on the table and pulled out a few gold coins, Harudanian dubloons, pure as they come.

"Su'l's Eyes! You boys kept earning as mercs then? That's a fine spread you got there."

"How many o' these gold coins will it take to get Alina an' that boy safe?" asked Shale.

Valdir laughed, patting Shale's shoulder. Shale was dry, I'd give him that, and it made me laugh too, with the kannab. A shaving of one of them would've been enough.

"I can't say what it means to see you appear on my doorstep. I'm just sorry bad tidings brought you knocking. I'm not sure what use I'd be to you, one arm and years out of practice."

Alina made a noise in the next room and Valdir got up and went in there. She was agitated about something, perhaps was listening to what we said. Presently he brought her through for the evening and we had tea and some of his stew besides. We talked a bit about being in the Twenty too, something I wishes I had more time to tell of. Old men got a lot of stories in them and the Twenty had its share of good. We had to steer from those bad ones for none of us could hold on to each other if we let ourselves think long on the killings we couldn't face the recalling of. His mix helped, and in the telling of stories I saw Alina watching us three, for him though her eyes were most on and for him the tremors of a smile and a look of fierce love. He sat with her and held her hand through it, getting up occasionally to put more wood on or look through our fieldbelts and other bits we brought in. Shale did my wound and Valdir was moved by it, for while I mentioned it earlier in recounting what had gone on, seeing it give him the news fresh again that I didn't have that long.

Then, late on and heads full of moths, Shale and I were lying on his floor by the hearth for that bit of warmth after he takes her off for the night. I hears him talking a bit and trying to choke his crying in their room for a while.

Shale was out getting some eggs from the run as dawn come about. I got the fire up again and we goes through the ritual before putting the pan on. He found some toms too that he added in. I slept bad. I been getting dreams, of me da, of home, and our elders says that's when to go back and go into the earth.

I was struggling with the pain while the brews and compounds worked through me, so Shale too was helping Valdir get his wife up and cleaned up and a dress on while I sat feeling a bit useless.

241

"I got to see our boy this morning," said Valdir as he brushed her hair and put a tie in it.

I nodded. It was done then, and we'd be leaving today.

"I can take a couple of coins?"

"Whatever yer thinks is needed," said Shale.

He was moved again, for us giving him what was such a lot of coin. Then he headed off down to the harbour.

An hour or so passed and Shale was clearing up and off fetching some buckets from the well down the hill.

Valdir come in as we took a pipe and he was shaking a bit, had her cousin with him.

"Good to see yus boys again," said the 'keep. "Alina, me love, I brought up yus favourite pony Eth, thought yus'd come down to the inn on her, see Heldon an' have some breakfast wi' yus son."

I was moved, seeing a man we knew so settled and us tearing it down. He put a sack of things together and was weeping openly now. She was crying too and her hand was moving to follow him as he went about us, trying to get him close, and she was keening but trying too to hold it in for us being there. Shale got my shoulder, thinking straight of course, and led us outside so's they could spend a few moments. We got the horses ready and stood by as they brought her out. In Valdir's hand was his old sword, what he give the name Drondir, which I think in his own speech meant "loyal son", and he had an old robe he must've kept all these years, which he threw to me to put on his horse. I was surprised and glad to see Drondir, for it was a sword much admired among the Twenty, forged as it was by a great blacksmith out of Harudan what had also made Kailen's own sword. We kissed Alina as they put her on the pony that had a fitting on the saddle for her to lean against. She kissed my cheek where a tear was, and I hope even now it was a sort of blessing.

"Yus boys are always always welcome," said her cousin. "We'll keep her safe till yus get back."

"I'll take her down the hill," said Valdir and we watched them walk away down the slope as the first men were about and the boatbells were ringing across the hills.

We were facing a crossroads and Valdir knew it, doubting we'd come back, for what other need was Valdir intending by taking her cousin gold pieces in payment for her safety. I felt then less like we would see it through than I had to that point. Only Shale was fit and we had to find Bense and Mirisham while the Post and Kigan, if Shale was right, were all looking for our heads. I did what I could to keep a face on it, but I didn't think I'd make it much past Jua.

Destination: Candar Prime, Q2 670 OE
Jua Main routed
CONFIDENTIAL FOR THE RED ONLY
Report of: Fieldsman 84
Debriefing of: Alon Filston and Marschal Laun

Messengers have confirmed a number of important developments regarding our interest in Galathia of the line of Welvale.

First, it is reported that Kailen has been killed in the assault on the Crag you were briefed on previously, but before Laun's crew – and Galathia – could reach him. An aconite mix found throughout the inn Kailen used as refuge supports this conclusion. In my view it is likely Kailen chose to kill himself rather than be incapacitated by aconite and subsequently imprisoned or tortured. I would have otherwise thought him to have escaped, but for multiple witnesses to his body being carried from the inn. Marschal Laun is sure that the aconite was placed by the same assassin who was present at Povey's Valley at Galathia's killing of the mercenary Sho, and present also at the massacre of Agents and Reds in Alon Filston's vineyard. He was not responsible for murdering our men at the vineyard. However, he is suspected of killing a number of our Reds during the assault on the Indra Quarter at the Crag to get Kailen.

A messenger from Filston's estate, document enclosed, reported that two of Kailen's Twenty whom Galathia had believed were captured, Gant and Shale, had been taken from the crew of an Agent Gilgul, by men posing as Agents. I enclose their seals and parch as evidence of the skill of their forgery. They instructed Gilgul to leave Gant and Shale in their custody, and then promptly disappeared.

The purse for their deaths was put up by Guildmaster Alon

Filston of Filston/Blackmore, one hundred Harudanian pure. I have insisted that all rosters are double-checked and inventories confirmed in the Post Houses within a hundred leagues of the Crag, but as yet no thefts or other discrepancies suggest any of our own were involved in this subterfuge.

However, as explained in the enclosed report of the vineyard massacre, Gant and Shale have been confirmed responsible.

High Reeve Albin has claimed Reeve Fisker's pin and arranged an assignment in Northspur by way of punishment for what he considers gross misconduct in the training of our soldiers and the resultant failing of the purse to kill Gant and Shale.

Marschal Laun conveyed a concern she believes shared by many Agents that this event will cause damage to the reputation of Agents of the Post.

High Reeve Albin has sourced additional men from Post Houses along Issana East, Issana West and Jua Main to fulfil the contracts the dead Agents and Reds were due to undertake. The necessary reparations to families of our dead are of course in hand.

Find enclosed letters from the affected guilds, variously conveying their displeasure and seeking preferential terms on three caravan runs value seasonally one hundred twenty gold coins for the cost of additional security and delay.

High Reeve Albin has limited cancelled contracts to seven, of those affected by this loss of soldiers to our guild partners.

If, being formerly of Kailen's Twenty, Gant and Shale used the fightbrew known as "The Honour", this will have conferred a considerable advantage over our Fortune Chia at the vineyard. The new brew harnessing the Iliskan ginse is undergoing final refinements for distribution to Agents and should come close to matching the Honour. This will give our Agents and Fieldsmen a considerable advantage over most other fightbrews.

Marschal Laun was present at the vineyard, to intercept Gant and Shale, directing the Reds and Agents against them. What she thought was a third combatant to the rear of her men as they were attacking Gant and Shale, was in fact the assassin referenced above, who we now know to be one of Kailen's Twenty, specifically, his former drudha Kigan.

It is to be understood, given what is contained in the enclosed reports, that his appearance unwittingly created the distraction that allowed Gant and Shale to escape, as his desire is the same as Galathia's: to see all of Kailen's Twenty dead.

Galathia, Alon and Kigan now travel south to Harudan to Kailen's estate, seeking information regarding the whereabouts of members of the Twenty still alive.

Alon Filston's messenger reported that Kigan, being formerly the bodyguard to Galathia as a child at Argir, has a strong bond with her that Alon is suspicious of. Kigan is reported to be a most formidable soldier and a drudha of the very highest skill.

However, as his intentions towards Galathia directly accord with our own ambition to promote her to the throne of Argir, it is my recommendation that Laun be requested to develop an understanding of him and be watchful of him but otherwise take no action against him. It is not clear to her or Filston why Kigan has retained, after so many years, such a strong identification with her. They had not had contact in the intervening time, proven by what the messenger relayed of the details of Kigan's own account of his life, as he had shared it with Galathia and Alon.

His account contains information of singular importance. The report is enclosed within the case, sealed separately, and it is imperative you read it.

It is my strong recommendation that you establish contact with Kigan personally. Suffice to say it is my view that any recipes devised by a man the equivalent of any drudharch using plant from the Hanwoq jungle are of the utmost value. Marschal Laun has been instructed to ask Kigan to name his price for his recipes.

I will travel into Harudan with Laun and meet with Alon and Kigan with a view to seeking an audience between you.

Given their ongoing success in locating members of the Twenty, I advocate sending word to Mirisham of the potential threat. Fort Donag Main and its tributes, as well as Stages three through eight of the Forstway, remain under his protection.

Finally, I have nothing to add to the reports you will have already received regarding the east. It is harvest, winter is coming and this time of year sees Wildmen pressing the borders of Ahmstad and Razhani for plunder of grain and any they can make slaves. While there are reports of some very serious incursions into the above regions, I cannot confirm rumours that a large army of Wildmen has amassed at the Ahmstad borders.

I will proceed with the above plan regarding Kigan until I am informed otherwise.

Chapter 12

Kigan

I put here the continued account of Kigan's journey from the Hanwoq jungle and his subsequent revenge against the Twenty, who he appears to blame in their entirety for his misfortune. These journals were written at different times, judging from the parch and weathering and are Kigan's account of leaving the Hanwoq and beginning his revenge, including his confrontation with Harlain, where he learns once more his own name.

Goran

The memories awoken by Snakewood were welcome. They poisoned the life in this jungle I had taken peace from, revealing a lack of purpose that grew unbearable. I researched, I learned, I used the Etil more and more to prove my experiments and for what end, if not revenge?

The betrayal I had only retained a glimmer of revealed itself so fully that it suffocated me, names of soldiers, men I had known well: Kailen's Twenty. I spent more time climbing and juicing my sight with mixes of great power, longing to be away from that River and the garden of Lorom Haluim. I created mixes that helped me see hunters from Loza's clan near the edge of the forest though I was leagues away. East I saw only trees, all of which, to beyond the horizon, would need traversing if I was to get to the Old Kingdoms as the bird flies. I was caught between the opportunity to discover more, to finish threads of research with tantalising and profound conclusions, and the need to find the

Twenty, who could now be so little match for me. I recorded and drew what I could to aid me. I look back on the later drawings and see a surer hand, almost that of a younger man, compared to the earliest notes and drawings I made shortly after Lorom Haluim found me. The recipes grew stronger, purer. I was becoming the drudha I once was and more. I feared nothing and I learned how to prepare for a war alone.

Soon the Etil shunned me, though Lorom Haluim was not around to see it. They had taught me enough, as had those other nearby Rivers I used covertly to test my mixes on. As with the magist, they would not now look at me when I went among them. It mattered little. My forms were strong, I had nothing left but to prepare myself for the journey through the Hanwoq and on to the world beyond.

When I remembered Snakewood I remembered clearly for the first time a wave to the boy and girl that Petir and Galathia once were, a walk down the hill from that mill to a peeled red door open to a barful of slavers, merchants and Kailen's Twenty.

We drank brandy in that bar, a fine one, for there were only two barrels and we had outbid some table of slavers who had no idea of our purse at that time. I asked who would be riding to Jua and told them of my purse to see the children settled. Mirisham asked of their wealth, the legacy to allow a secure settle for nobles in a land like Jua.

I told them. I am amazed once more as I recall the treasure the children had been provided in that book and the jars of plant, an amazement shared at the time. I recall Mirisham nodding, calmly talking of his experience in Jua, and asking Valdir of his time there, having hailed from nearby Marola. Kailen spoke of the challenge of hiding them during the next few days, others like Milu and The Prince wondered at the gold all that plant would fetch, with Ibsey running the numbers with his stick on the corners of his recipe book. I remember arguing the sanctity of the purse, despite the treasure, a dispute among us over whether I should honour it. I had been paid a heavy purse, and had been set up for the years following, unlike them. Of course the arguments began, for we were soaked and Elimar speculated loudly about how many people I could buy to experiment my plant upon, and had I realised there were laws against the use of prisoners for drudha research in Jua. The others joined in, Sho, Bresken, Shale, The Prince, Kheld, and only Bense and Ibsey had a mind to say anything against them, which caused further dispute. Kailen did his best to quieten us, for the locals were unused to such a group of mercenaries when they were in their cups and sucking on their pastes to get a rise.

I recall some saying they would go east, Elimar and Bresken among them. Kheld, The Prince and Bense planned on leaving that night, forgoing whatever floor they would otherwise fall to when the mixes were going in the brandy.

There was a point where I was given the mix that did for me, left me for dead for the sake of my purse. When that came, who gave me the cup with it I cannot be sure of, though I see enough of their faces at the table, smoking their pipes, arguing or laughing.

I did not, on the last occasion of my meeting Lorom Haluim, fully commit to leaving and had no speech or goodbye prepared. I expect it mattered little to him whether I stayed, except perhaps that I could care for the Etil in his absence. But I had to find the Twenty, who saw fit to turn on me for the treasure I had been given a purse to protect, sacrificing to whatever end that of the children. It wasn't only that the purse bade me protect them, something I could not do; it was more that, since I recalled Snakewood, and recalled them as the prince and princess of Argir sworn to my protection, I recalled that they were something that mattered to me, and in all these years since there had been no one of whom I could say that.

Lorom Haluim had been gone more than a month when I committed to leaving the forest, some ten summers after I entered. I packed as many of the rare mixtures, pastes and preserves as I could into an expedition fieldbelt, crafted from the hide of a tapir. I would journey across the jungle to the eastern side. I daresay nobody had ever, the magist aside, journeyed the hundreds of leagues to the mountain passes that led into the red savannahs of the Ilis'kan Virate.

I left the Oldor-Etil, who, for all their murmured misgivings over my dealings with them, celebrated my leaving with dancing and howling to match their spread of windmills shrieking in the dark. I had, as I say, done much good and they did not forget it even if they were perhaps glad to be rid of me. Theirs and the other Rivers' guides led me a good way to the eastern side of the jungle before their fear of the unknown and the end of their paths left me alone. Understand that these were a good people, living simple lives that were strongly bound up with plant, not the trade or commerce of it that so infected the rest of the world. They gave me peace for a time.

I set off, and with a long knife and a blowpipe I caught and gathered what I could and kept east by the lead of the stars, though many days this required an ascent into the canopy at dusk to get sight of them. The heart of the jungle holds few predators for such prey as myself. It was the approach to the eastern fringe that proved most alarming. I was grateful for the efficacy of the poisons and impetans I had refined, for I had disturbed a giant cat the Etil called Gaju as it stalked a tapir. The dart felled it as it leaped at me, my leap to evade it quicker than could have been managed on the old number seven I prepared for the Twenty. I treated the gouges from its claws and I smoked and mashed into bilt the meat that would have made the Gaju's meal.

Many weeks later my first encounter with a clan of the Iliskan Virate went badly and I was forced to kill three men who saw me for an Etil and thus good for slavery. I needed to get to the coast, Coral Bay having some major ports I could begin my search for the Twenty from.

Hin'ton was the nearest port at the heart of the bay. Ruins of cultures long and recently dead provided the foundations for many of the fortifications and buildings that crowded the shores of the deep channel that made it such a prize for conquerers in ages past. The bleached yellow stone of the port blazed in the dawn as I approached. I walked a track taking farm workers out to the near fields from estates that spread some miles inland, growing beans and caffin of course, but also limes and amla, sought after in colder climates due to their potency against scurve.

Cogs, caravels, skits and the giant junks that plied the coasts of the western Sar and Gulf of Merea littered the sparkling swell off the quays, the vast curve of the bay lost in the early haze north and south.

The ground was paved like Jua, legacy most likely of the Amarot empire, gulleys cut for the emptying of shit buckets that had, through some form of pumping system, running water to progress such matter down to the sea. It did not take me long to find the mercenaries pitching up off transports from the Sar, their bold colours and subdued manner familiar to me. The taller three-storey houses that filled the lower bay seemed by their angles of leaning, shabby tiles and crumbling stone to be something like as drunk and tired of standing upright as many of their visitors and lodgers.

I looked for somewhere to settle among these streets. I followed some mercs, who clearly knew their direction, through the cold alleys the sun hadn't yet reached, to a large tavern called Doxton's Flop.

It fared grandly for a flophouse on the back of mercenaries' tips, but they knew their custom for the doors were open and both barmen and stable hands were stood at the crest of the slope and greeted us with trays of a thick but drinkable ale.

Some shook hands or kissed as was their way, all were greeted in a number of tongues and led inside or led through an arch to stables.

Doxton's had no need of the soaks and their pennies and excuses; food and lodging were mainly for soldiers and wealthy mercs with little patience for beggars.

This ship had been expected. There were only a few others taking an early pipe with their fish or meat when we arrived. Everyone here had paid the colour.

My own colour and fieldbelt were sufficient openers for conversation. I shared a bench with two groups, one sailing in from Whitefall Ithica and another that had been engaged on a Hets'qavar hunter. Both groups had heard of unrest around Alagar and saw the chance for a good many purses north.

I wove a tale about my purses past to avoid the connection with Kailen and also told of my time in Hanwoq without mention of Lorom Haluim.

Few other drudhas travelled alone as a rule for they were much sought after and could command a large purse from almost anyone employing soldiers. No mercenary can resist the chance to share their plant troubles and the bits of recipes they had learned if they thought it would benefit another, especially with a drudha. Without that sharing each might miss some cure for their ailments or some way to diminish what the fightbrews and poisons did to them.

I spent many hours with these men over the following months, listening for news of the Twenty and noting afresh after so long away the evidence of the handiwork of lesser drudhas and how it broke soldiers. One I met repeated himself, forgetfulness and confusion came and went, for which his friend would cover. Others had the spasmics and tremors, for which their companions would help with the separating of coin and other small fussy tasks. Whether for a purse or an oath, soldiers everywhere paid the colour and became brothers through it. I doubt I will fully recover from having those moments where I am unaware I am talking or whispering, as though different parts of me are watching each other, taking turns. These men knew full well the price of the Drudha's Share, and if anything it made my dealings with them easier.

I soon found myself negotiating the price of mixes for various afflictions and the price also for batches of their brews from which I had refined out the coarser and more damaging ingredients. It was repairing the work of ignorant men and the mercs were happy to spend coin on being better prepared for the conflicts around Alagar, with which I could buy better pots, presses and tools. The Iliskans had some familiarity with shiel, but none with powdered ash bark, arnica or guaia, yet nutmeg was cheap here. Little kannab came to Coral Bay but I found supply from Shalec traders across the Gulf, and I began to sell my own mixes at a great profit.

With Doxton's approval, for a fee, I could provide this service which so clearly pleased his customers. I quickly amassed a few hundred silver coins bearing the marks of lands as far east as the Blackhand and far north as the Citadels. With these I bought the materials to craft black coins for the Twenty, the symbol of betrayal of a purse. I was left to die by them, and not one saw fit to stand for me. While I cooked for Doxton's patrons during those months I would ask what happened of the Twenty and it was some time before one who had been wounded escaping from trouble north knew that Harlain, the Giant of Tetswana, was back with his tribe as its leader.

Kailen had picked him up during a campaign north of Tetswana, an engagement on the Hensla Flats where Rhosidia and Alagar had allied against Tetswanans flooding to the Flats from a drought worse than in many generations. He was one of the last of the Twenty to join. Once the infantry had engaged, Kailen led us into the heart of it. The Seeyaltans and Tetswanans were no match for our skill and ferocity, until we closed on the man standing half as tall again as any about him and cutting men clean in half with a scimitar and a deep glorious laughter.

Kailen was as revered by our force as Harlain was by theirs and both sides engaged in the frenzy caught breathless glimpses of their circling, seeing a chance for a single combat and the cessation of the fighting to the old ritual. The lone shout of single combat by Kailen was taken up by all, much to the disgust of captains and nobles themselves a safe distance under cotton canopies.

It happened rarely this side of the Sar and more rarely still once the battle was on and the archers had already trimmed the numbers. The smoke their bows sent and the poisons laced with it drifted about like mist as we stepped away to create the space for the black giant and the squat Harudanian.

"Greeting you, Easterner, how goes your killing?" shouted Harlain above the cheers of exhausted men draining out their noisies.

"I go well, killing many. With my greeting I offer a chance to join with me, the price of your submission." Kailen replied in the appropriate manner, though he spoke haltingly, both men muffled by their masks.

"Black is the night and overwhelms the gold of the sun!"

With that, Harlain leaped forward, a good brew in him, the scimitar swift in its arc. Kailen took only half a step to avoid it and then another as Harlain thrust as he turned about. Both moves, for their lack of connection and counterforce, followed through a fraction and Kailen placed a jab of his shortsword to Harlain's thigh. The next blows and parries kicked the dirt up for yards about them, rumbling the earth, such was the might of their exchanges, but through it Kailen moved always knowing what Harlain would do. The whistles turned to jeering; the men, only a few of his tribe mixed with most from Seeyalta, saw their giant swing more desperately as his inferiority became clear. Only those of us with Kailen wondered if the fight could go differently were Harlain on my fightbrew. Kailen was quicker in thought.

With eight cuts on him from a blade with enough paste to drop horses, Harlain stopped and threw down the scimitar.

"The sun is bright." Harlain bellowed with laughter once more before kneeling in the midst of the silent lines of men now looking about them warily, for many did not know if fighting would continue.

Kailen kneeled next to Harlain and put a putty of bistort to his wounds.

"The son of the Ageh Tetswana honours his family with his strength and joy." Battle resumed the following day, though Harlain had then defected with many fellow tribesmen and the victory was swift.

Each of us was bested in single combat this way, the price, the offer, to join his crew.

Harlain was the best of us, for he saw things simply and spoke them directly, which on occasion was wrong, but no more frequently wrong than those of us who were learned.

I left Hin'ton a few days after hearing of him, buying a horse to cover more quickly the land between.

Tetswana is a hostile place, mostly desert. The horse would be little use beyond its border. A handful of silver coins brought me to the Post's Reeve for the Iliskans, a man more dried out by his life than the sun. He had a caravan in need of a warrior-drudha as it went north with kegs of wine and cases of dried bacca, now much sought after among Tetswanans since they first copied the travellers and caravanners they had spied on and killed.

The Post had secured good enough relations with the nomads of the southern wastes of Tetswana that the caravan found shelter and some hospitality among the goatherds. We joined with two elders a few days into the dunes, both grandly decorated with tats over their bodies and arms displaying the great achievements of themselves and their forefathers. They were the purse for this caravan, funding this gift for the gathering of their fellow leaders who were to meet with those from the neighbouring Seeyalta, a people secretive and primitive like the Etil, but dangerous in this territory. I had little hope of escaping alive if any of them were left alive once I'd found Harlain.

The rub of the Weeper soon worked to my advantage a few days later, the guards agreeing that they should leave their post to question a plainly suspicious kamil herder asleep a few hundred yards from the caravan. It was thus a simple thing to lace the kegs. I took note also of the stars as we travelled. The kamils would be stout enough to carry me out alone from this gathering when I was done.

The eight-day journey passed without incident, a trudge through the dark sands, acacias and orange mesas. We were skirting the vast erg the locals called The Red Sea, towering dunes that shimmered, hummed and moaned with the wind, ruptured here and there by half-buried columns of cities once of kingdoms of which no record or knowledge remained.

Horns were sounded as we wound our way up the path to the head of Sillindar's Table, where once the Tetswanans would consort with her. Two riders came out from a camp dominated by three enormous white pavilions pitched amid thickets of hardy white grasses.

There were eighty here at least, more than half of them the personal guard for the leaders attending the gathering, the rest entertainers, whores, cooks and servants.

I helped unload the gifts in the nearest pavilion, outside of which mansok was being prepared on a series of fires, the smell of lambs and spiced rice wetting my tongue.

Here also were the stone jars of their sour fermented honey, a rich drink over which negotiations and plans would be debated.

As a drudha that did not arrive at the gathering with a party of dignitaries I would have been refused access to the foodstores. Once again the Weeper persuaded the cooks and guards otherwise and I got to work preparing spiced sauces and rubs for the dishes, mixing in powdered strykna and extract from the cassava root for the wine.

The laughter grew with the darkness of that night's feast, the wine was broken open and the soldiers given their rice and lamb. Great pans of the mansok were taken to the pavilions.

During the following hour I pasted my knife and reapplied the aconite, then took a measure of the fightbrew I had created in the Hanwoq. The rise was exquisite. Now I could perceive the words of almost everyone in that camp; their shallow boasts, admiration of the babs and backsides of some of the leaders' consorts, then Harlain, loud like a bull given voice. Around him comments were made about the potency of the sour honey. Then some began to realise something was wrong, a change in tone spreading through conversations about the camp, turning sharply to a panic, shouting that was swiftly strangled. Gradually they all fell silent, food for vultures and dogs. I wondered at and yet also took delight in how effective the poisons were.

I stepped through the muslin of Harlain's pavilion and over the bodies lying on the thick rugs of his opulent dining chamber. As I expected, I could hear only one other breathing.

Harlain regarded me thoughtfully, the man of ten or so years before had grown thick about his arms and belly, the line of jaw once so clear was softened with luxury.

"Agent of Alagar, your day goes well, you have achieved a great blow to my people. Know you would have been welcome, Kigan."

And so I knew my name again. It was a shock, like he'd hit me. In those moments he could have killed me, but I recovered; losing focus kills you, a lesson learned at the academy with sticks and stones and broken bones.

"I am neither an agent of Alagar nor am I convinced of my welcome given what I need from you. You will tell me what happened to me last you saw me, Harlain. All these long years since then have been defined by my suffering as a slave, but the Droop took the memory of exactly who had betrayed me of our old crew. You were there at the tavern. I remember we had argued about my purse, to protect that old king's children and escort them to Jua. Somebody poisoned me, sold me into slavery. If not you, who was it?"

He tried to rise to his feet, but the poison was taking hold. His legs refused to take his weight.

"My day goes badly, my allies' healer brings only death. Your discourtesy in this place dishonours you, no greet and no wrong done?" He shook his head in disgust. "I heard nothing of you, Kigan. South you went to share the gold those snow-white children took from their people, this I believe, but you sit here older in the eyes and leaner with hard work than comes of sitting on pillows."

"Where are the others then? You tell me you believed I had left with the children? Lying to me won't help you, not on this brew. You don't have long, Harlain, the anti-venom is here and I would very much like to give it to you. I was betrayed and I need to know who poisoned me, who profited. You were there, you must have seen something."

He took a moment, his eye on the vial I placed on the rug before me.

"You did not join my songs or share my jars when we drank to our own glory, or you would know my pity now, that you think this of me, an Ageh. We went well, Kailen, Moadd and Sho. I do not remember a farewell to the others. Gold flowered in our hands, the salted edge of life walked. Moadd's great story was ended by an arrow. He fed the grassland of the Dust Coast. All our rivers cut the world's face, until we slow into the lakes of our reckoning. Kailen had reached his lake, and so had I. We parted on the Day of Rains, which would be thirteen rains past."

Harlain caught his breath, sweat trickled over his forehead and cheeks, his hands beginning to tremble. He gestured to the dead around us.

"Wine we would have put in your cup, Kigan, but you put poison in ours. Great hurt and trouble you bring to Tetswana, war blossoms from this poisoning and I have no story that would move the sons of these tribes to believe me otherwise. There was always so little of the spring in you. There is drought enough about this world to challenge our strength, what need therefore to add to it? What could have quenched your drought, Kigan? You must answer that yourself, for I think you will get no ease of thirst from Harlain of the Ageh."

I leaped to catch his hand but was a moment too late. He had drawn a knife firmly and quickly across his throat, falling backward and releasing a broad spray of blood over the chamber. I felt only frustration as I watched him dying, for I had tackled this badly.

I placed the black coin in his hand, stood and packed what mansok I could, salting it for the weeks I would take a kamil east to the Sar. The wild dogs that sensed a feast showed little interest in me as I drove the kamil out of the camp, down through the Ironwoods and scrub towards the Eastmark star. As I rode I tried my name again, saying it over and over, hoping it was a key that would help me remember more, perhaps everything. It did none of that. Sand was as familiar and acceptable a name as Kigan, for all that it was the name of orphans or others that were nameless in the Midden lands about the world.

I picked up caravan work in nearby Rhosidia, moving north to Limao and Handar, seeking word of the Twenty. The best drudhas in these squalorous seaports were no more than cookers running droop joints for the plant-soaked sailors, mercs and pirates that found haven on those coasts. I sought out those of the colour and peddled my mixes in stifling alleys and the backs of bars and whoredigs. With little serious competition for my artistry the mercs were soon seeking me out around the Bay of Alante, Limao's main seaport, where the "unlicensed" found little trouble. It was six months before I heard the name "Milu". I sat sipping rum with two lecherous soaks shipping horses, or "ganneys" as they called them, from Alagar, the ganneys no doubt to end up bearing the Post's messengers on their web of routes through the Old Kingdoms. The two were paying a fine price from their apparently senile Maiol's expenses purse for a mix I brewed to increase ardour, their cocks swollen at the sight of almost any girl with sufficiently prominent babs.

The one mentioned meeting Milu, now working with a Maiol's ganney stables, "Maiol" meaning "Lord" in Alagar, rectifying an apparent weakness in his trade book. They marvelled at Milu's work, as I had when Kailen picked him up as a squire from a prince we had a purse with.

I told them of my longing to see Alagar, perhaps to find a patron there. More rum cemented a promise that I would join them on their return from Issana.

The stink of that bay, situated near the midden where the hours of night and day were equal, gave way to the increasingly lush plains of Alagar as I took my place in their returning caravan.

There are few sights more capable of silencing a man than the herds of free horses, numbering many thousands, roaming the hills and plains of Alagar. The Maiols farmed this stock wisely for their stallions and mares, sought the world over.

The caravan took me to within a hundred miles of the Maiol's estate where Milu worked. I met nobody until I arrived at the estate, settlements forbidden on parts of the great plains over which the herds migrated. I was escorted in by scouts to meet with the men running the estate. I professed my intent to the stablemaster and quartermaster to earn my keep, wishing to learn a trade now my fighting days were done. Once more the rare opportunity to engage a drudha swayed their doubts.

The stablers and fieldworkers were barracked away from the singers and masters. Two days after my arrival I had found where Milu worked. Suggesting I go hunting for betony, a salve of which was good for cuts and soothed the nerve of both man and horse, I headed out across a river and more wooded land to the yards of the warhorses.

I heard his singing as I approached the whitewashed pits, paddocks dug into the ground to allow observers and customers a view sheltered by the grand wooden roof fanning out over the pit cluster, the walls of the pits providing amplification of the songs.

He was alone, the other singers and stablers gone for the day. The air was sweet and dense with the rhythm of his melodic humming, almost chewing the sound with an impressively small songpiece, the same as that of our time in the Twenty. Every singer crafts their own piece, as unique as their face. The song filled the pit that the stallion stood in, its hoof worrying the ground as the drone filled its head. Milu brought his note up and down according to the shivering of the horse, his great cheeks and chest able to hold notes for minutes at a time. Shortly, the stallion stepped towards him, the note lowering until my head pounded. Then he stopped. I didn't realise my eyes were closed. He was looking up at me. He carefully led the stallion through a doorway beneath where I stood.

I coated my lips with the barrier, then the poison.

"Kigan?" He approached from a paddock a short walk away. The Roob brew he took was still a strong one, among the singers' brews, his voice carrying profoundly across the air between us.

"Milu. It's been many years." I smiled, holding my arms out.

Like most of those I'd kill, he was fuller in girth, the skin muddy. His hair only grew in clumps, common with a horse-singer's mix. His neck and cheeks, from the singing, were now a distorted, jowly bag, atop which his features seemed small, like islands clustered in an ocean.

He smiled, we kissed cheeks, which was his way.

"It's good to find you, Milu."

"Kigan, I hope you are here to teach these cookers how to make a six properly. Where have you been all these years?"

He rubbed his cheek and frowned. Harlain's death was ill-conceived. This would be more instructive.

He lunged at me then, understanding what had happened immediately. I stepped back, catching his arm and helping him to the ground as he began choking. We were against the wall of the pit, out of sight.

259

"The paste you felt on your cheek will not kill you, Milu, but it will prevent you from lying to me. Now you're going to tell me what happened at Snakewood, the night I was enslaved? You will tell me if Galathia and Petir were killed."

He held his throat, breathing hoarsely, then mumbling. The Weeper was taking hold. He sputtered as he tried to lock his jaws and press his lips shut between words.

"Nothing, I'm not going to . . . Mirisham, Mirisham carried you out with Valdir. But you were speaking, you spoke wrong of Kailen, always – fuck you – always knew better . . ." He tried to burst from my arms, frenzied and spitting with fear, but had nothing of his former strength. I held him tight, legs around his, squeezing him still.

"Where is Mirisham?" I whispered. "Did he plot to get rid of me?"

"I, I saw nothing of them, you were drunk, they helped get you somewhere to sleep."

"Where are the others?"

He looked at me as I held him, pleading through gasps.

"The Prince is a partner in the Quartet. Kh . . . Kheld is . . . Kigan, you cocksmoking fucker . . . Kheld is a Handar shipwright. He's a good man, you don't need to do this."

"Of course I do. While I lost my memories for a long time after that poison, I've recovered many, enough to remember your revulsion, Kheld's too, to my services, my research. You all took my mixes and all too readily yet when it came to burning the bodies of those that helped me refine them, not one of you apart from Ibsey and Bense offered to help except when Kailen instructed you to do it. My fight-brews and poisons gave you the life you have, and at the end, for that, when my final purse became known, there wasn't one of you stood up for me."

"Is it gratitude? Is that all it is, Kigan?" He was struggling to speak.

"No, it is what the lack of respect cost me and cost those children, that is what you are paying for now. I cannot let you live, Milu, not while there is a chance a warning from you would reach The Prince before I find him." I punched him, his nose, quickly enough he could not react, stupefied for a moment. In stopping him from breathing through his nose he opened his mouth and before he could react I took a thumb of poison from my belt and pressed it to the inside of his cheek. I then took a black coin and put it in his hand as he shook with a creeping paralysis. Now dying, it was only moments before he stopped breathing. All manner of regret escaped him in those last breaths, some girl here at the stable he seemed lost on, memories of his father also, who beat him until he found peace in the singing.

I saddled up the horse he had sung to and left the estate, riding east in the dark. Handar was close, but I shortly discovered the Quartet was closer.

The Quartet was a venerable trading guild that offered the Post its only serious competition on the main Rhosidia to Jua shiel runs. As a Partner, The Prince would be somewhere near its heart, his family connections of high value in the seduction of the nobles and quartermasters that ran such trade across the Sar.

I waited, hiding up in Port Bronso, listening, living off some plain, decent mixes that wouldn't get me noticed.

I dyed my skin and got some more respectable robes for access to the merchants and the officers off the Post and Quartet ships. Beyond a sweltering summer that brought disease and sickness to the streets, the autumn shiel harvests were cut and pressed. On the docks it was the Grandhouse Findel's sigil that adorned much of the cargo for the sloops and junks, and I learned that it was at Findel's estate the Quartet would house its harvest celebration, inviting their fleet's officers and other worthies to a feast.

I trailed a number of the Grandhouse's servants and workers as they left the estate. Of them, the most accessible was a popular old cook, a drinker and card player.

He played cards well, an endless list of tales and jokes of the most lewd kind, fleecing some gilded lordlings and sailors alike while they laughed at a large table in a busy quayside droop joint for those fresh off the boats. I took a seat with a bottle of brandy and spun the yarn of my travels while he took my money. As the evening wore on and the cups took their toll his pile diminished before him, better players out in the night. I had done little to persuade him of my worth in the Findel kitchens until his son walked in, rescuing his father from his familiar vice. His son had river blindness, one eye enough to get him by, the condition giving him a stooped demeanour, as though he needed to get closer to the road to see his way along it.

I told the cook I could cure that blindness, for I had learned of such plant in the Hanwoq. He became serious for the first time, taking my arm for an oath that his son's sight would mean a job at the Findel house.

Later that night he staggered against his sober and serious son as they followed me to a lodging I had with the family of a Watchman. I pressed out the alka in which the compound was suspended and with a warning I put a thumb's worth of it on his eyes and held him while he screamed out. They were to return the next morning, which they did, the son knocking at the house door early at dawn, half dressed, stood tall and hysterical with the clear sight he'd gained on waking. The cook wept and took me with him to the Findel estate and its astonishing marble palace.

The work in the kitchens was surprisingly hard, but after five weeks there I learned a great deal about the Quartet and the living arrangements for the principal merchants' retinue. I knew where The Prince would be from the moment he arrived and had much time to plan that it was I who would take him his meals, persuading the usual maid-servant to switch our duties.

The Prince took a balcony room overlooking a central oval courtyard dominated by an obsidian fountain that could take forty men bathing; grand lawns and giant potted shrubs surrounded it, sheltered alcoves along the walls beneath the rooms for the discretion of guests doing business.

His fish and wine were tasted at the door, as I suspected.

The room, like the skin of the palace, was of fine white marble, blood red rugs over the floor, olika wood chests and a simple bed. He was gazing from the open shutters out to the aqueduct that fed the huge lawns and groves sheltering the view of the palace from the arid hills beyond.

"Your fish, Prince."

It took a moment, then he remembered.

"Kigan! By Sillindar. How are you here bringing me this food? I was promised a most delicious maid."

He made no move to approach me, gesturing me to sit at a small table, where I placed the tray of fish and wine. We sat. I showed him the brand I was given back at Snakewood.

"I gained my freedom when I was shipwrecked, I have had a testing few years since last we met. I work here now. I heard you were visiting so asked to see you."

"Slavery? How awful." He took his time pouring the wine into a glass before offering it to me. He was buying time to think. He was still handsome, still no hair troubling his chin and lip, typical of his people. He left his colour as it would be, the scarlet and green of the old fightbrews gone muddy like Milu's. The oiled hair and embroidered robe, coupled with his scrubbed hands and painted nails, was perfectly of the Rhosidian nobility he had come to court for his merchant. His frame had shrunk with the lack of work, but his voice had a hearty, peaceful sound still. He poured some wine and drank.

"I have had appalling news, Kigan, of the massacre of a number of Tetswanan leaders at a gathering, fifty or more men dead, including our own Harlain."

"He went back to Tetswana then?" I said.

"Indeed. He and Kailen continued on for a while after Argir. I think he lost his 'flint' as we used to say." He smiled and picked at the skin of the fish I'd brought. "But more interestingly, I heard a few days ago through a Maiol we've invited to this feast that Milu has also been killed."

"Milu as well? Killed, not just, well, dead?"

"Yes, it is strange, and Digs also. He went back to the Ten Clan and was found dead there as well. I understand black coins were found on their bodies, Milu and Harlain's anyway."

"A black coin, a betrayal?" I was buying time and wondered if he knew it, for I had no idea who would have hunted and killed Digs for a purpose so similar to my own.

"Yes. It's as well I found you, a great drudha serving me fish. You should be careful."

"I have been brought low. Whatever had been used to subdue me to make me a slave has taken my memories, an ephedra mix of some sort. I can no longer cook. What happened to me, Prince? Do you recall? At Snakewood I was betrayed by one of us, poisoned there and put to slavery."

"I was not there, Kigan, indeed I'm rather overwhelmed to see you here. I'll not say a word of your escape to our host."

"But we were all there at Snakewood, Prince," I said. "I remember enough to know you were one of those most interested in the purse I had taken." This was a subtle mistake, too confrontational.

"Ephedra is an interesting plant, Kigan, as you know. Those who recover, they remember things that never happened, or remember some parts of a conversation or an argument perhaps, and not others."

His eyes flicked about as he tried to see a way through this. I knew he didn't believe me, for he was baiting me. He didn't think I could be brewed up enough to notice but I was on an almost clean rise. He would not yet know himself he was sweating, the first hint of it on the air beneath the jasmine of his hair oil. Nevertheless, I had misjudged the moment again. The brew rose in me. All brews want blood and his subtle slights were stoking a fire I was struggling to control.

"You say you were victim to someone giving you ephedra, and then were on the Droop for many years. If you are speaking truthfully, Kigan, how is that night so clear to you that now you remember me there? I passed by Snakewood of course, but I had a large purse as I recall and a good many better places to spend it than that Post dung heap."

The lie wrote itself in the glance downward as he said it, his hands meeting in a clasp, then consciously unclasped.

"Did I offend you then, Prince, all of you? We both stand as equals in thought and wisdom, we always did, but you are lying to me now all these years are passed. You can hardly look at me. That is some measure of revulsion."

"Equals?" He snorted. "At best you were a sophisticated poisoner, apt to experiment on every person who did not suspect otherwise. I, Kailen, all of us, feared you. I am sorry that someone, presumably one of us, sold you into slavery. If I knew who I'd tell you. Not even you deserved slavery, though you're mistaken if you think I could believe you'd forgotten how to cook. I daresay this wine has a little more than grape in it. I'm finding it easier to talk to you than I am looking to get rid of you. This is a most interesting mix."

"Where might others of the Twenty be? Now we're straight with each other."

He inhaled to shout, realising where my intentions lay and what little chance he had if I was on a brew and he had already taken something I had prepared. I would never flee the palace if he was heard. The filleting knife slid into his throat smoothly, quick enough he could not rise more than a fraction from his chair. I spat into his widening eyes, "Your part in our crew of killers was played with no more quality than my own. We did nothing noble or good, Prince. We killed whoever we were paid to kill, and I was instrumental in our doing it."

I withdrew the knife and laid his head on his plate, his blood pattering on the marble floor. It was hard not to cut him to pieces, my fist trembling to stab him until he was unrecognisable. I would subsequently adjust the lucin in the brew. The sight of his blood, the act of killing, made me burn as though I were in a pyre. After some moments trying to regain my poise I withdrew from the room and through the chaos of the kitchens and pens. I left the estate on a horse and cart, telling its driver that I was to help with whatever he needed.

My father had been a sailor for some years when I was a boy. He brought back tales from Handar of the tribeswomen that took men into the desert to conceive children with them before hobbling them and leaving them as gifts for Sillindar the Great Singer, whose song caused the winds in the dunes. The grand old Simursian West Road was now a sporadic and cracked highway that was lost in the sands and dead valleys of Handar and its border with Tetswana. It took me through to the coast of Handar with little trouble worth recounting here.

I needed only rum at Olber's Gate to learn that Kheld was now a master shipwright at Handar's navy yard, confirming what Milu had said. The labourers I treated to the flasks of rum all appeared to have nothing bad to say of him. He was ever the appeaser in the Twenty when disputes turned to blades. Two nights I spent in the tedious company of these men and I learned he would often stay after his own shift to inspect the work done.

The shipyard itself occupied the eastern edge of the bay, its two great sheds dominating the streets thereabouts. There was little in the way of its security to concern me. I played the part of a labourer with a logging crew that was bringing wood into the yard and the crew thought me one of the yardmen and the yardmen thought me of the crew. Shortly I was crouched in among the logs that were piled and tied near the work-bay where they'd be stripped to timbers for the boats.

A few hours later the yardmen were leaving and the guard changing gave me the opportunity to get closer to the sheds where I could see a hull was forming, the new ship mostly a monstrous empty ribcage supported by a wooden frame. Fitters and smiths were calling and laughing to each other and on the brew I heard them also call to Kheld to join them later for some jars. It was then I saw him, ascending the lip of the wooden frame. He dropped inside the ship's hull.

The frame was easy to navigate after years climbing the kapoks. The newly cut lapstrakes were still fragrant with their oil. I lay on the edge of the hull where the gunwale would soon be. The guards were still in a group under the main gate. I took my blowpipe out and coated a dart in a paste of the Weeper and some red opia.

Kheld was inspecting the beams, groaning as he hobbled on the leg that was wounded at Tharos, the wound that took him out of the front line to a role with siege engines and fortifications in the Twenty. It was a sign of Kailen's softening, for years previously he would have simply let the man go.

Kheld sat to light a lamp he had with him, a gloom now filling the corners and joins of the beams and stanchions.

Shadows waved about with the flame, but he was easy to target. I put the dart in his neck. His throat swelled to choke the cry and as he tried to stand the opia killed his balance.

I dropped down the boards to the keel in front of him. He tried to move from me, a coarse choke all he could manage for a shout. He held the lantern up to better see me. His other hand was without fingers.

"You can speak clearly enough if you don't force it, Kheld." I took some of the Weeper from its pouch and smeared it on his face.

"Kigan?" he gasped. "What is this? What are you doing?" His eyes searched my face, shocked to see me but unable to react.

"Let me help you sit down, we have a little time," I said.

I took a moment to look at him. He was still partly a slender man, limbs of sticks that poked out from a large paunch. He was bald now

266

too and the ocean winds he must have spent years sailing in had carved deep lines in his face. He was slick with sweat, the shock of these last few moments and the dart taking effect.

"Whether you live or die is up to you, Kheld. You must think back to when we were with the Twenty, when it ended and we picked up that final purse from Doran and Kailen. You were there on the night we all drank at Snakewood when I was sold into slavery so that Galathia and Petir could be robbed. Do you remember?"

He shivered, the only movements his body could make as the poison spread.

"Argir, yes, Argir, Kailen broke the Twenty there."

"Snakewood, do you remember Snakewood?"

"That Post House? We stopped there yes, a proper shithole, filled with those howling slaves and miserable croppers."

I tugged back my sleeve, the crescent a blotchy black where the ink had faded.

"Who did that, Kigan? Are you a slave?" Unless he could resist the Weeper, he knew very little of what happened to me that night.

"What happened to the boy and girl, Doran's children? I had a purse, they were in my care."

"Are you killing me, Kigan, blaming me? That was not me. Mirisham and Valdir said they were taking them south." He sweated now, cold with fear. I despised him. I almost wished he had the courage to despise me. Harlain had died far better than this, despite my mistake.

"I was drugged and I was sold into slavery, Kheld. Like The Prince, like Harlain and Milu, you sit here pleading with me that you were innocent, yet you were at the inn, you tell me that the children were to be taken south and you know nothing of what happened, nor did you, it seems, bother to question it. Why should you, when you despised me as much as any of them? But I'm going to be honest with you. I have no interest in you let alone in keeping you alive. I won't play games with you or pretend to befriend you again. I don't have the time or the patience." The rage of the brew rose more slowly in me this time, filling my muscle, pounding in my head as my blood thickened. I was goading him to talk more of the night, to remember more. If he could not remember it, the Weeper could not reveal it.

"I . . . I recall Mirisham said something. You were going ahead, to prepare for their arrival. I didn't see any of you leave."

"That at least makes some sense. Where are the others, Kheld, all of them?"

He took a deep breath, attempting to fight the urge to tell me.

"Where's the antidote, Kigan? A fatal dose with a quick counter for good behaviour was your usual procedure. Why shoot me with a dart? I have a son, a woman now."

"The antidote? There is one of course, but it would be of no benefit to me to provide you with it. I will hear your secrets and I hope you have fewer regrets than Milu."

I sat next to him, put my arm around him and brought his head close to mine, where I could whisper and hear what he could recall.

He knew where Ibsey was, a Post 'vanner in Cassica now, though he'd run horses out of Alagar at some point. He remembered little of Snakewood, believed Kailen had gone with Moadd and Sho west of the Sar, as Harlain had said; remembered only that Mirisham, Valdir, Dithnir, Stixie and he were at Snakewood along with the children and I. Digs and Connas'q had gone back south, Bense he believed had gone back to Jua to stay, no doubt to indulge his addictions. I was sure I'd find him there, but Ibsey was next. I would be lying if I said killing him would be harder than killing the others – because he was my tutor – but he is the one man in the Twenty I had hoped would be dead before I got to him.

Chapter 13

Gant

It was as we were leaving Valdir's village to head off to find Bense that he realised there was a way to get to Cusston quicker than we could have over land. Valdir returned from bidding farewell to his wife Alina, and he was puffing far more than I was from the climb to his house from the harbour, as injured as I was. He'd need to be back doing some forms and shifting some fat if he was going to live through this.

"Been thinking about what you said. If Bense were in Jua and you're hot with the Reds, we could get us one of these boats for a sliver of one of those coins you got to put us in some small dock there, go past Issana than through it."

We thought for a moment, then Shale nodded.

"Good idea, Valdir. Guessin' we'd have to be rid o' the horses."

I was sorry again to be losing a good horse, Lagrad was famous for our horses in all the north, and I felt lost without one for all these years I been away, like all of my kin. Valdir was right though, we'd never get through Issana quick enough with the Post on us. It was certain they'd be looking for men of the colour and all their runners would get word back sharp to the Reeves.

"Alina's cousin can keep them till we're back," said Valdir.

It was done. We took them down to the quay and the inn and left them but Valdir didn't go in for Alina's sake.

Valdir was having words with some of the captains what were putting out and for a few silver we found one what were going up the coast a bit but the crew were up for a longer stretch anyway, chance maybe for some peace from home for better pay.

The *Lucky Margalese* took off and we had a few weeks, winds allowing, to get us to Rillion's Chase where we could put in with little shouting and fuss.

The sailors were curious about us, particularly what we had to do to Valdir, which was to get him on the plant again.

It wasn't pretty. He'd forgotten how it took hold. After the first slug of the Honour he started shaking. Now was the risky part as his head struggled with the pain and the noisies, the killing lust and the changes in his blood what makes the veins pop and the muscle grow. He screamed for it to stop. Shale had to hold him, shouting him down from madness. The others were quiet and stood back a bit as he grew before them, his clothes not loose like ours for when we had to take the fight brew.

"How the fuck did we ever do this!" he yelled. "And how is it this fightbrew tastes, feels like the Honour? Kailen never told us the recipe." He hissed as it burned through him.

"He told Shale."

His legs were all spasmic, shivering as he flushed red, and the green on him from his old colour near lit up.

"He's goin', Gant, goin' under I reckon," said Shale. "Give him his sword, something to hit on."

The captain was watching calmly. "Yus hittin' nothin' on this boat."

"He can hit me," said Shale. He took a mouthful of the Honour, took up his sword and give Valdir his own. He was in a frenzy and went for Shale like he was caught fucking Alina. The boys on the boat never saw two brewed-up mercs go at it and they crowded about the gunwale, as far as they could from the bit of open deck. I saw Shale's reason. The brew puts you in a fury only working with it can conquer. It was easy to forget the speed and power comes with being on the brew. Even Valdir was moving about the deck like a bull mixed with the spring of a deer. Through it Shale got himself a good test, but was still barking orders at Valdir, much like Kailen did to us when we first took it and needed schooling on our form, being a father and torturer in one.

Then come the point Valdir found it funny, Shale's movement so exquisitely avoiding the hammer blows and slashes that, without brew, he was hard to keep track of. We both knew Valdir would be all right and the crew give a cheer and shouted him on as he starts laughing and cussing Shale, the other side of the brew that give a calm now his body was up and all the pain was gone. An hour later and the bit of Honour he'd had started its claim. I asked the captain for a bucket, for it wasn't certain that he wouldn't shit himself as his guts started.

Shale and I kept eyes on him as he slept. His dreams were troubling, like they always were as the brew dribbled out of your head. The captain come over then.

"How long will we be out?" I asked.

"It's goin' to be a few weeks before yus hits Rillion's Chase. We'll get our fishin' done on the way back."

I thanked him and sat with Shale.

"Reckon Bense'll still be there?" I asked.

He shrugged. "Hope so."

"Hard to remember him. Same as all of them I guess," I said.

"Bit too keen fer the rise was Bense. Worked an' fought hard, funny an' all, but the plant was in his bones an' I reckon he's a Drooper for sure now."

"Yeh, seemed to have a sayin' or joke for everythin'. Good man wi' the wine flowin'."

"Feels right to get him though," said Shale. "We all got over the crossin' together an' if it's Kigan doin' the killin', well, it ain't right. He needs teachin' an' I'll be glad to do it."

By the time we put in, Valdir was in better shape on the rise, but was in a lot of pain after each session, his body slowly hardening and tightening itself up with the plant and the work of finding a balance and form with an arm gone from the elbow.

A few silver and fewer words to the quaymaster at Rillion's Chase in the dark before dawn and we were off the boat and on our way without another pair of eyes on us. We headed into woodland past some farms and made a few leagues in the mists before the sun burned it off. Moving then at night we got another week inland without being seen.

Looking to keep our bilt for the troubles we might have getting out

271

of Cusston, with or without Bense, we had to send Valdir in to a cluster of huts for the farmers of a nearby estate, to find some bisks, cheese and meat that would see us to the city. We put on him the makeup that would mute down his colour and he went in as a traveller, looking in need of a rest and supplies. Unlucky for us there were a few 'vanners in for similar reasons and for all the care we took, the watch was out for anyone who passed through. Valdir picked up the supplies but a tail too. We got through that lord's holding and out in the country again, only two days from Cusston.

Shale, always watertight, took some luta and got up in a tree on a hill we were making our way over and he soon picked out the tail; five men, one moving a league ahead of the others, belts on all but no packs or mules. This was likely an assault.

We trapped up about our day camp, which was set in a copse of trees, digging out a few ankle breakers and putting the titarum seeds into the dirt and dead leaves over them across the main approaches. I did the watch for I had to have my stomach strapped ready. A few hours after we made it look like we settled, the titarum seeds must have got trampled for I heard a cough escape one, then another went over as he caught his heel on one of the holes I dug. I quickly put feathers and some rubber we had in our packs on our fire and it shortly give off a heavy smoke. Shale and Valdir woke sharply with me moving about and we dropped some brew. It was silent out in the trees, but with the brew we soon enough picked up their song and Shale signed for Valdir to move with him around to the left of where they were coming in, against the wind, Shale guessing they'd look to move in that way for that reason. I stood to draw Juletta and put some arrowbags about to test what plant they got.

I was expecting Agents again, but they were regular Reds, so it would be over in no time for those poor lads. One of them started wheezing a bit and choking, closer than I was expecting. He moved back, knowing he was caught out, but his sound and smell were strong and I leaned out and took a shot that just caught his arm as he leaped between two trunks. He went down screaming as the poison worked in. Then there was a yelling as a couple of others went at it with Shale and Valdir. That was over quick and all. Shale give a whistle, a code for telling that the two Reds left were retreating. I moved from the camp to better listen for them away from the cracking of the fire and I soon picked them up. Shale was nudging them, of course, being the point of noise they would back from. He was moving in line with me but thirty or so yards off to my left. Valdir must've took off in a different direction, trying to get behind them. I caught sight then as they engaged with him up ahead, Valdir leaping in from their side. Shale dropped one with an arrow, a fine shot judging by how far off we were. The other's on his knees then as Valdir worked his noisies and soon the lad was cut to pieces as he begged.

"We want their belts," said Shale, "an' we should put 'em in the ground so's there's no sign of 'em."

We chopped up the bodies to make for less work burying and were on our way as the moon was passing west to morning. I was grateful for not having to fight, but I did some forms to use the noisies and wear myself out a bit. I couldn't let the wound take my flint, for I knew I'd be shedding blood before it all played out.

With its proximity to the great river Almar, getting into Cusston would have been tough without Valdir, who'd been there a year back. We found a spot on some hills overlooking the river and the city still distant, its old walls receded from its sprawling edge like skirts gathered up from a wave. It was a far grander sight than the ruins of Ithil Bay, for many of the towers were still used, and in the parts of the city in which the aristos were walled, the walls were well kept. The great spires of the old guild quarter shone with their polished slates and white and red stone. About these were crowded the countless rooftops that filled out our view, rising in terraces up the side of Curis Hill. Shows what an influence Kailen was I could remember this hill, it playing a part in the wars out of legend that founded the Old Kingdoms and settled Jua.

"Over on the west side," said Valdir, "where the bigger ships put in, there's a good few places a lighterman could get in quietly. The Rotties, as it's called, isn't where the guild boats put in, too many gangers and they's got enough coin they just built their own quays with the Reds which is further back behind those sheds you can see. I think we could head downriver a bit and pick up a willing barge could sneak us in, fair few of the peat and hide boats put in there, Rotties is where the tanneries are."

273

It was a good shout and we took a day getting to a jetty used to load pigs and horse hide from the lands about. With only four boats docked we stood a few jars of wine for the crews what were camped there near some thatched sheds and got passage to the Rotties from an old scrawny merc what lost his strength with the damage of years drinking cooker's brews. We kept under the oilskins with the hides as his boys rowed in, the stink of the hides getting overcome itself by the beamhouses we passed and their fierce stink of dung and piss. Valdir was suffering with the fall after the brew. It had been years and Shale needed to take care of him the day after we killed those boys to help him get his head back on.

I lifted the oilskins a touch and saw the huge wooden buildings what started out as stores but grew out into the river over us, creating giant sheltering caverns above us, under the roofs of which were suspended walkways, store rooms and offices and all the pulleys for cargo such as ours to be unloaded. I had to remind myself this was Jua, heart of the Old Kingdoms and a great centre for trade over the known world, for you didn't see such buildings in other big ports. There was calling and laughing from the boats about what knew our captain and his boys, shouts in their hundreds on both sides of the river as we slipped into a berth and bumped the wooden posts of the quay. It was afternoon and the main commerce of the Rotties played out here, echoing around us as we got our packs off the boat and helped a bit with the unloading for thanks.

The captain give us a tip on a tavern that might have a few mats and fewer eyes, but like any dens, we had little to fear of Reds among this throng.

Where the massive sheds ended and the dark streets began it was impossible to tell.

We quickly turned out some coins for directions to one or two of the duts what were trying to get their hands in our belts, practising for the eyes I expect were watching them and teaching them. We took some paths they may have thought would see us fleeced by whoever was lurking about, but the men in the doorways or on walkways above us looking down wisely give us no more than a glance.

We got use of a room in a tavern what was crowded by some

towering sheds like an old stone box set against timber cliffs and Shale set about my wound while we had a few jugs. Valdir was quiet, so we just sat with a pipe and let the noise of the bar play itself out and I took first watch while they got their heads down.

It was like that through the next day while Valdir set out to find Bense. Shale and I got a few kannab pipes in to pass the hours, the 'keep bringing us some hams and buttered potato for the grits the kannab gives.

Valdir got back in the evening and had managed to find out where that lord Fesden lived, who Bense worked for, but not much more. It was the next day that he come back with the bad news that Bense was in a jail, though put there by Kailen. Shale must've been right and all, about Kigan, for others that Valdir spoke to there spoke of a man of strong colour, like he was still taking purses, that come to visit Bense, and who had the belts of a drudha. We sipped on a bowl of tea while we figured out what to do about him being in jail.

"Jail's a tower built out into the river, just a bridge to join it to Cusston's barracks. Worse, the bridge joins the two near the top of the tower as the barracks are on a natural hill at the side of the river. It's either through the barracks or straight up the side of the bridge to get at it."

"Fuck it," said Shale, speaking for us all.

"It's on the edge of the Rotties, short walk from here."

"What's he in jail for?" I said.

"Those I spoke to on Fesden's estate said that a man of the colour put him there to get off some plant he's been addicted to. Said he had a skin condition and all, strange to look on. Bense is alive at least," said Valdir. "They must know there's a reward on him."

"But not the same man as Kigan, from what yer implyin'," I said.

"Aye. If they're talking about his skin other than his colour that'll have been Kailen," said Valdir.

"So why din't Kigan kill 'im?" said Shale. "Bense I mean, if he killed the others."

None of it made sense and it give me worry.

"We bin sayin' it's Kigan, an' it makes sense to say it, but whatever drudha it is, it's either the same as what's bin killin' us an' so it makes no sense he'd leave him alive if he got to him before Kailen, or it ain't an' I got even less clue what's goin' on," I said.

"Bense is alive an' he'll know what's what, if we can get him," said Valdir.

"Agreed," said Shale, "we got no answers an' he has."

"Let's break him out then," said Valdir smiling. "Remember Vilmor, and the Fat Princess?"

Shale almost choked on his pipe and slapped his knee, his smile widening.

"She was fat an' all, like liftin' a horse." It was Shale carried her out, yelling at Kailen for a day after, who was merciless about it, the boys all ripping him. Valdir mentioned it because of how it was we got her out of a jail as she was being used to blackmail some lord I forget the name of.

"So you're thinking we sets up a few fires and cause a riot to trim down the guard in the barracks. Then we finds someone knows the routines of the jailers and bribes one to help us get in and get Bense?" I said.

"Seems like it, Gant," said Valdir. "Nobody will expect it or be ready for it and most of the jailers we ever met were droopers, gamblers and soaks."

"Gant'll be glad for a bit of a run round," said Shale, "he's startin' to stink anyway. We need a stable or shed to mix the fire-oil, sulphur, rubber, lime an' pitch, an' some bags an' the routes an' timings."

"Valdir needs to run the bags as he knows it all best. Need Shale with me for any trouble," I said.

I set out for the jail and spent the day watching who come and went, then Shale took the night. Valdir was out getting a run going and renting out rooms along the way. He was going to place a bag at each of the rooms he rented, light it and move on, when the time come for the break. Either fire would catch or just some dreadful smoke, enough to cause panic in houses made of wood and sure enough that would bring the guard in. Then he'd move onto the next house maybe a street away and start something there. While the guards were hollering and a noise was being created we could go at the jail without bringing Cusston down on us.

It was the following evening that we picked a guard who worked in the jail. He was heading from his shift to a flophouse full of sour, wrong-looking whores. I got in there and we sat waiting while his preferred one was finishing up.

"She any good?" I said, meaning whatever one was likely to be his regular. He wasn't much younger than me, wore out too, and a skin condition accounted for the flakes about his shirt and in his hair, and his fat nose was peeling like a Sardanna sailor.

"She's cheap," he said.

"I'm just in," I said. "Captain must've give me some wrong directions. You got an hour you could show me somewhere a bit, you know, richer? I got a purse'll see you right for a finer fanny than what's here? Some good brandy too. I got a few hours to kill and I don't want to find meself up the wrong sort of alley." I said the latter with the rude tone I thought would appeal to him. He give a grin, looked me up and down and he was in.

It was a long night. I took care to draw out the booze and give him the fuck of his choice at a place what were more used to captains and the lits what worked the ledgers for the Rotties gangers and other merchants. I put some ginse-laced rum his way and he was soon in a fine mood. Sure enough he was not too fond of his life. Seems those he worked with were all against him, or were getting the choice of shifts because they were in with the Sergeant of the Guard. He found a lot of sympathy in me and I found a lot of their names and a bit of the routine from him, enough to know one or two what were on the following night if we could get prepped for then. I'm sure he got on no better with his new sergeant when it all settled down in the days ahead, but there we are.

It was dawn when I got back to the room we had. We were ready. Shale and Valdir had put together the firebags and Valdir was with them in the stable we got the use of. Shale had his arrowbags prepped. We slept for a few hours then hung about till mid-evening, ate a bit and packed ready for the run. We strapped up, he set my wound and we took the Honour, then he headed out to bring Valdir up on a brew and I set off for the tower.

I was quick to get under the bridge what joined the jail tower to the main barracks. A few people were about as the docks day shifts were clearing but none would've thought more than that I was seeking

277

some shelter. I was rising good now, it was hard not to let anyone see my shakes as I got into it. There was an old man next to me and a couple of soaks sheltering too, but they were sunk in whatever suffering their mixes brought them. I looked up and Shale was getting onto a rooftop that was some fifty yards off the wall above me. Valdir would be waiting on his signal for the movement of the guards about the barracks wall what would set us off. I felt like I was going to explode as the moments passed, my noisies were building and I was shuddering to get into it, the streets about almost suffocating me with noise and the rich violent smells of the Rotties carrying like notes of a tune on the whips of air off the river I was next to.

Then Shale give the go and saluted me like I was a captain, a smile on him as we kicked off. It was a good but strange feeling to be doing it for us and not some purse.

The first black smoke went up from the stable, a good covering of the oil saw it catch fierce. The shouting started up, screams and yelling from that part. Shale slid an arrow onto his bow and lifted to draw. I masked up and smeared my eyes for the powders. Guards were moving above me, their boots clapping on the stone of the bridge. On Shale's first arrow I moved, tearing up the wall to the edge of the bridge's walkway, just beneath its parapet, then I moves along the side of the bridge, hand over hand till I reached the tower. It was an agony holding myself against the wall with my guts not wanting to work. I smelled two at the doorway above me. The orange of the flames behind me played about the damp stone as buildings were going up like they were thirsty for burning. More smoke was beyond the line of buildings I could see and then I heard doors being pushed open inside the compound, the soldiers arming up and supping brews. Shale's arrows were hitting the bridge to my right where the barracks joined it and the shouting was all to duck and find the archer, then retching and screaming as the powders started in their eyes. The guards above me were cussing and arguing over what to do.

I flipped over the parapet onto the bridge and my sword's out and these boys got no answer because they never been to war and were on some cut caffin at best. I put both over the side of the bridge before they got time to get a word out but I heard the bolts go in the iron door to the jail itself. I swapped to Juletta and now put some limebags over the wall into the barrack buildings behind me. Shale had already taken shots at the barracks and the smoke was now rising up fierce from them.

"Bilby? Slim?" I yelled. "I got word to hold the jail wi' yus, Sarge's command."

"Bilby in't on, who is it?"

Fuck.

"Slim? Fuck sake, Nelis on then is he? Don't thus be a cock. It's fuckin' chaos out ere'!"

Shale had left the roof across the way and ran across to the wall below me, his piercing whistle telling me of it. The bolts started going back on the door and with the first crack of the hinge I put my boot into it and forced them back inside. Shale was up the wall before I had to force the fight, leaping over me and carrying the door in. He dug a swift blade into Slim's chest and through. The other was cussing and fumbling at his scabbard when I cut him shoulder to thigh, stabbing his throat to stop him yelling.

Shale slammed the door and I knelt to get at their keys.

"Slim?" come a shout from below. Shale charged down the steps now some blood was about, and the screaming was iced up with cheering as the men in the cells saw a break.

I got the keys and chucked them down the stairwell at him, keeping close to the door and listening to the Rotties taking to the streets to find someone to blame for the fires that were going off.

Doors slammed open beneath me, a rush of men on the stairs shining with freedom, shaking themselves out and finding some weapons. Shale shouted for Bense. I let the boys out to prolong the havoc with the guards and shortly Shale come up to the passage with Bense before him.

He was a mess, slick with sweat and walking like he was on broken glass. It was likely some betony he was on given how wiry he was in his limbs, but his shark fin of a nose and curly thatch of hair were unchanged all these years. If Kailen wanted him off plant, it hadn't worked. Bense was speaking in his own tongue and reaching for Shale's pouches as we tried to drag him out. Course, Shale was right about him being a Drooper, he just went for whatever pouches he could open on the belt to get himself something to take, with no thought for which he was opening, something only a complete fucking idiot does on a fieldbelt. Sure enough he's got his hand in Shale's bag of agave powders and as Shale feels him at his belt, tugging at it, he rips Bense's arm away and it only causes him to fling the powders in the air. Juiced, Shale and I were fine, but Bense and the prisoners about starts screaming. There's men run out on the bridge to get out of the cloud of powder and some inside screaming and rolling around on the floor. Shale's had to drop down to Bense, who's lying there shaking and spitting in agony, and he has to put him out cold with a smack so's he could get some juice in his eyes and wash his skin off and put a fix in him to bring him back. Then I hears a cry outside on the bridge and sees the men had run into soldiers coming from the barracks and all helpless before them they're getting cut down like duts. I pushed past those staggering about blinded and blistering and faced up to some guards and their sergeant. Seeing me The guards readied themselves and I got to it. Two arrows were launched but I saw them in flight and adjusted my body to let them slip past. Sergeant runs in and tried a feint to draw me in but I could read it in his eyes and his tongue flicking out, both betraying his intent to control his balance for his next move. I let myself get drawn, knowing the likely thrust, and as it come I smashed his sword out of his hand. The moments as he stood making a decision were enough, on the Honour, for me to put two blows together that cut half through his hip and took an arm off. As I did I felt my wound split a bit, a sharp pain causing me to seize up a touch. They weren't sharp enough to make good on it and as they jumped forward over the sergeant's body I was quicker and each of them I moved so's in a blow or two they were open and finished. I cussed for I was going to really feel it when the brew wore off.

The prisoners least hurt by either Bense's stupidity or the soldiers gathered themselves, took to the sides of the bridge and scaled the wall down. We followed them over it. There was no going through the barracks. With some rope we brought I tied it round Bense and I scaled down the wall so's Shale could lower him to me. Then he climbs down himself.

We woke Bense with a pinch of shiel and once he was on his own feet we run through a street that had houses and some stores on fire, with that rubber giving off a fierce smoke that had people running all about us. I heard clashes ahead as groups of Rotties boys saw the chance for some pillage and a go at the guards what I'm sure few of them got much justice from.

We picked our way across Cusston, along the river, Valdir's path being away into the city so's the guard and any militia would move to the hundreds what were fleeing their houses.

Soon enough we found a lighterman to get us over the river and we got to the outlying farms and then into the fields.

"He did a fierce job," said Shale, looking back at the smoke and the glow what were visible even with the Rotties and hills of the upper quarter blocking a direct look at it.

"Hope he got out," I said. Valdir's path was straight through the east edge of Cusston, continuing the direction he was setting fires in so's not to run into the havoc he created.

Bense had gone quiet, being led along and not much caring for the reunion. I pulled us up.

"He's cold," I said, a word we used for when we were out of what we were fixed on and were getting so bad we were giving up.

"What do you need, Bense? Betony? More agave, given you don't seem to care much what's in a belt so long as you can snuff or suck it?"

Shale dug about in his belt and took a thumb of the paste and held it out for Bense. He grabbed for Shale's hand quick, sucking the paste from it and then using his own finger to rub it over his gums. His mouth was working furious to get the rise and it began with a sagging of his shoulders as he started up.

"Bense, we need to move, got to meet Valdir before we can head off an' rest somewhere quiet. Got the fall comin' too, feelin' sick," said Shale.

Bense slowed us, but we had no company as we pushed east a few leagues with some luta to help us see enough to keep up the pace through the woods we were in. It was as the light broke the edges of the sky east that we saw the first of those rising for their day, coming out of a hamlet of woodsmen and 'jackers further on. Shale left us tucked under a ridge of earth while he sought out Valdir. My guts were starting as I fell from the Honour. I was glad Bense was quiet

281

for the trembling come on so's I couldn't have stopped him if he decided to make a fuss. We heard some voices in the clearing ahead. This was a sparse bit of the woods and the men about were getting ready to head out. I heard Shale's song then, a birdcall too precise in its repeating to be anything other. Shortly I heard a call back, similar chirping what were made with a mouthpiece.

Some men from the camp passes by us, dawn now on enough to see them. They were cursing out one for calling rain later that day based on what he tasted of the milk he got from his goat.

Bense seemed to be sleeping, the hard march too much for him.

I shut my eyes for a while, wore out with my shakes. Sometime later it was, as I come to, I saw Bense creeping through the trees to where we were hiding. He was looking at me, smiling, which was curious given the state he was in going to sleep.

"Where you bin?" I asked.

"Nowhere, Gant, been here."

"I just saw you, where'd you go?"

"Easy, Gant, I'm not shitting by the fire am I." He had a bit more life about him. Looking back I wishes I thought more about it, but like I said, I just come to and was thinking as much of my own pain. Valdir I heard moaning then, half carried by Shale who was himself in pain with paying the colour. Valdir fell down next to us and was fighting for his breath. Shale give him a few kannab leaves to suck on and a stick to bite as his first full rise on the Honour and the specials, such as the luta leaf and oaksap, in near twenty winters was being paid. Seemed like the smoke from setting fires got in him too.

We had a smoke while he and Bense slept a bit.

"Got to risk buyin' some food, Gant, we were light fer the prison break but according to Valdir if we're goin' to get to Mirisham we got to get to Lake Issan up the Forstway an' that in't goin' to be easy."

"The folks about'll have something, but we needs horses. Prisoners'll be caught and start yapping about us," I said.

Issan was the big inland lake what cut over the base of the mountains around Issana's and Jua's borders. There was no going over the mountains and no going around the lake without losing some weeks. We needed a boat.

I hissed with a stabbing pain in my guts.

"I got some cotton an' gum while I was out in Cusston, let me sort you out so's yer can sleep a bit," said Shale.

I come to later that day to the rasp of crows and other birdsong that filled the trees in the misty yellow of the waning sun. A child stood before us as we huddled under our skins. He was a dut of six or seven summers, long brown hair and smelling and looking like he'd been killing chickens, his hands, legs and feet dirty with the work. In his hand was a carving of a figure, me, in the wool tunic and boots of a 'jacker or somesuch. The carving was like paper in its delicacy. I had a beard, thick head of hair from before soldiering but a big belly. I was dancing a jig.

The boy smiled at me then and the sun seemed to light him up. It was like he was pleased to see me. He held the figure out, a gift for me. I reached out for it then come to as though I was dozing. Same as before the sound of the birds, but the boy wasn't there. I shut my eyes to see him still.

"Gant, what is it?" said Shale. He glanced about. "What are you cryin' for?"

I didn't rightly know.

Chapter 14

Kigan

I put here the remainder of Kigan's accounts of killing those of his former crew that he could find.

Goran

Cassica was only a few weeks' ride from Handar, though the season made it more treacherous. Monsoons and storms tore through the jungles and renewed the plains of the lands I crossed as I headed back to Coral Bay. It was a spectacular journey as the world about me came to life with fierce splendour.

I had joined the Twenty shortly after I had left the Juan Academy of Flowers, garlanded for work with the agave plant. They exploited little of their kingdom's great wealth and diverse commerce, arrogance the disease of their research, their methods stifling. I brought a recipe book to that academy that had been my father's gift, a book that taught me more than any of the scrolls and parches their drudharchs revered. He sailed most of his life, my father, a keen cooker that filled my childhood with his excitement, experiments and their aromas of the wild world beyond the port I grew up in. I would describe him now but it was one more thing I no longer knew on my recovery from the Droop. I remember only heavy brown hands guiding mine, slicing through roots or helping me to mix up brews he would sell for a few pennies to those who could afford no more. During the months he was away my sister and I ate little but oats, rice and eggs and whatever offcuts we could get from the butcher's with the purse our mother was left with till he returned. Then a knock from one of the other women to tell us his ship was in and we'd join wives and other children rushing down the street to meet our fathers off the boat. Every time he would bring us wood-carvings his shipmates made of the strange animals they saw, and once or twice I saw others he would show my mother that would elicit a shriek of laughter and were hidden away from us. His richly illustrated recipe book was embellished further with each visit his boat made as a factor for the larger Juan galleys, putting in at ports as diverse as the Virates and even the Kremen Run. My mother I recall only moments of, snatches of a long skirt and red hair remain, the singing and humming of old tales with him home. Then the sea took him and she sang no more.

I recall this here because for the little I remember, I miss him, my first teacher. Then, at some point after, my sister was gone. I have one memory of her. I want to miss her as I should a sister, but that part of me, somehow, for being blank, cannot. Her name is still lost, yet I recall us huddled in the bed we shared as children, our breath's mist visible in the cold moonlight that we opened the shutters for, and she would share with me, under our blanket, oatmeal biscuits the baker's boy would give her. We would frantically brush the crumbs out from the bed so our mother wouldn't find out. Another memory I have, of my beating the ground and screaming while my mother pulled at me, must have been at her burial.

I was left making mixes and brews from that book of my father's, to earn a sum to keep my mother and I fed. Word of my work spread. The book my father gave me, with his teaching, secured my future. The book was taken from me at Snakewood, having survived all those years and campaigns in the field. It was the reason I was a better warrior-drudha than Ibsey, who could never improvise as well, and the reason also that Kailen took me on though his crew doubted I would have the guts for their life. I saw no better way to learn the use of plant than to pit myself against the work of drudhas we opposed; no better way to prove my excellence than in keeping soldiers alive against the odds, making them quicker in thought and action, stronger and yet to pay less of the brews' claim when the fall began.

No drudha paid the colour like Ibsey, except Lorom Haluim himself. I was surprised Ibsey wasn't yet dead, for there were few occasions he wasn't brewed up and shouting at the phantoms his imagination had conjured. He had the hardiness and appearance of a wild thorn with his colouring. I should not have been surprised he could withstand the abuse better, but to find he was now working for the Post on a route through the Cassican jungle, no doubt for dye and gum, was remarkable and yet pathetic.

The Post worked the one port where they had built a measure of goodwill, merchants dear to the throne keeping them out of the others for the sake of Cassican ships not being undercut in their southseas trade.

Most ships moored here therefore flew the red sails of Post galleys and cogs. A cooperative captain spoke despairingly of Ibsey, though apparently he managed what few could not in engaging the cousins of the Etil in trade for some dye and obscure peppers afforded only by the wealthier citizens of the Old Kingdoms in preserving and flavouring meat.

I took a path west to the jungle, which may or may not have been continuous in some way with the vasts of Hanwoq. Here at least there were well-used paths that were maintained through the thickets, the tribes heavily involved in this trade, dependent on the Post to supply them the vices they needed. Usually the Post laced bacca with red opia to make it both sweeter and more addictive than beeth. I saw no beeth chewers among these Rivers, but men and women smoked from bowls and pipes made from the hardwoods about them. Only through pointing at my own skin did they know I was seeking one like me, my Etil dialect unknown here.

I caught Ibsey's camp just before dawn, the guard dozing, no more than six beneath a few worn shelters. I put a sporebag into the ground near the ashes of their fire and prepared some darts. I started with the guard nearest to me, killing him. I then killed another that had choked and risen to seek the cause of his pain. As the rest came awake I moved position. They made too much noise for me to need to place my steps like the Etil hunters did. I took one more down before stepping out. It was like playing with children. Before me Ibsey was blocking his nose up and putting on a mask. The others weren't so prepared and he watched them choke and collapse with little more interest than I.

"Ibsey."

He looked me over. He twitched more these days; his head and shoulders behaved as if pinched or stung constantly.

"Well I'll be fucked, Kigan in Cassica and you've grown. What you been eatin'? You're not here to take my purse or my juice. Not either here for my side in Mholcar feathers. Not Post nor bandit neither. So why all this?" He coughed. His chest sounded bad, his voice squeezing out what air he could exhale.

"We need to talk about Snakewood, where we met after Kailen had disbanded us and sent us south with our final purse. This just makes it easier." I guestured to the bodies.

"This ship has to sail, Kigan," he said, gesturing to the packs they would have all been carrying back to the coast. "You don't want to cause the sponsors a heed or there'll be word out. Those lads was likely expendable to you but I ain't to the Post."

"There's nothing the Post can do to me, Ibsey, I disappeared at Snakewood and I've only just come back to the world."

"They did it then, they got rid of you. Let me sit if we're goin' to do this, it's fuckin' early and I need a brew." He started fussing with the fire and sat a pot on it, poured on some water from a flask and put some tea leaves in it.

"Was it Mirisham and Valdir?" I asked. I walked over and pulled one of the dead men away so I could sit nearer to him.

"And the others. I thought they'd killed you. Would've been cleaner, I'm guessing. Good to see you looking so well though."

He sat down, undid his mask and breathed deeply now the spores had cleared.

"Bloodroot, something else, fierce too. You got a tip or two 'bout that recipe? I expect too you've got a tale to tell me?" He rooted around in his pack, took a salve for his gums and forgot me for a moment as it soaked through him like the betony did me back in the Twenty.

"You don't need to know what happened to me, Ibsey. I was enslaved, I escaped, I'm here. It was not only Mirisham and Valdir betrayed me?"

"The ephedra's got you, hasn't it? Can't trust it. Some stalks you press have so much more juice in them and you don't see it brewing them. Surprised you lived, never mind remembered what you have. Well, you were blabbin' about your purse, had the bairns of that king with you, and fine plant like rosary, fireweed and so on. It was a fuckin' fortune, Ki. Miri had us all thinkin' we should be rid of the bairns, bump that final purse and get the fuck out of fighting. A few others like Shale, The Prince, Valdir and that agreed. We all thought it was pointless givin' it to the bairns. Sounded like a fair spark to me that plan, anything to keep on a rise. Didn't think you'd buy it though, you were always a bit of a stiff cock 'bout that sort of thing. Lacked the flexibility."

"It was a purse. We always kept to the purse. We were all tight enough to respect that."

He laughed then, shook his head and slapped his legs. He seemed inured to his spasms. "Were we, Ki? All tight enough? They fuckin' hated you an' I was just too soaked most of the time to care enough for what was happening with those you did your experiments on, so long as we were making recipes that kept the purses flowing. And a purse you say that boy and girl were! It was a fortune, Ki, a true and proper fortune, the wealth of a nation, not a purse. Fuck, what do you want, to get revenge all this time after 'cos you were done out of money what wasn't yours?"

"What did you make from it, Ibsey?"

He chuckled, a stuttering wheeze, the rise making him drowsy.

"You were in on it then, Ibsey? Getting rid of me and the children for the money?"

"Yes, you stupid fuck. I would have got you to lose the bairns. We'd have found a way. I passed out at some point, must've. Next I come awake I was in some filthy little room, alone but for Kheld, and you were all gone. Seems I was cut out too, Ki. I haven't spent years cryin' about it."

"No, you ended up on a Cassica plant run for the Post, Ibsey the warrior-drudha. I suffered the lot of all slaves and nearly died more than once. I've been to the heart of the Hanwoq, worked plant you could only dream of."

He laughed hard then, his hand up as though conceding a good cut in a debate. I despised his ridicule and was now glad he was alive, just so I could kill him.

"Yet you're here in Cassica, Kigan, one of the great drudhas of the age, spendin' his life it seems chasin' mercs over acts of betrayal? Sounds like you should be greet for that turn of events brings you here with a book full of Hanwoq recipes. You look good, Kigan, younger than a drudha should look after the life we had. Fuck, you could make a living like I do just selling flasks of the Honour, though the fulva's hard to find this far south."

He shook his head, risen fully and serene in his account of his life. His spasms were settling to tremors.

"I kept up with Kheld for a while, Milu, Bresken, those came west. Digs, Connas'q, Stixie, they stayed east, went home I expect, plenty of trouble at home for them round the Ten Clan, Red Hills and Virates to make purses out of. Dithnir went back to Tarantrea, never sure 'bout him though."

"What about the others, Mirisham and Valdir? What of Shale?"

He shook his head. "Shale was fierce, so fierce, but him and his man Gant, quiet, too fuckin' serious. Bresken I see regular, she's with the Post and all, Coral Bay, guarding wareshouses. We have a drink and a few pipes when I'm back at the bay. Others are lost, Ki, no word. Say, let's do a fuckin' pipe fer the old days, eh?"

He rolled onto his knees to rummage through a pack nearby, oblivious to his dead 'vanners as much as the pot he'd put on the fire for his tea. He was worn out, the plant had taken more than the Drudha's Share. Like all those countless people who soak too long in their brews and cookings he had a greenish, mossy dampness to his skin, his limbs trembling like a doll being worked by a drunk puppeteer. He had a year or two at best, or would have had.

"I would have taken a pipe with you, Ibsey, would have been a good way to bid you farewell. You'll be dead before you finish it though. Poke your tongue out."

He paused, turned his head slightly towards me, then started shaking it. "You didn't, Ki."

"There was a day you'd have recognised it. You could tell from nose to the air across your tongue what was about you, what a brew had in it."

"Fuckin' aconite." His tongue flicked out a few times to confirm it. He continued to dig out his weed, struggling to control fingers trembling more now. He turned and sat to face me, tears filling the corners of his eyes.

"Give us a flame, Ki, me hands are gone."

I left him and his coin with the other bodies and got back to the coast.

He was right about Bresken. The only woman Kailen had challenged to the duel was working the wareshouses of the Post. I watched her head off her shift, going for the tavern nearest with another of the guards. She was a great swordfighter once, naturally capable with both hands and a match for Sho wielding two blades. One of the memories I recovered from the skytrails I followed in the Hanwoq was her duel with Kailen. It was, apart from Shale's that we never saw, the closest. On a full brew she went in side by side with Harlain, Shale, Sho and Gant and she was inspiring. She wore only the one sword now, and shuffled slowly as though in pain. I followed her and the other guard into the tavern, found a place to stand that I could watch her from. The first two cups were drunk quickly and in silence. They seemed welcome to her. She had become a soak. For a time they spoke, but he left after another few cups. I sat beside her when he'd gone. She was about to tell me how little interested she was in company when she recognised me.

"Kigan? What the fuck!" She leaned in and kissed my cheek. Despite only a few candles around the walls I could see enough of her to know how far she'd sunk.

"Bresken, it's good to see you. I saw Ibsey on his run, I'd come from the south, he told me I could find you here."

"What do you need? Are you looking for work? Do you need me for work?" She moved back from me a bit to better look me over. "You're looking strong, Kigan. You're still taking purses?"

She looked hopeful, perhaps thinking I actually would need her as a soldier.

"I need to know the whereabouts of the Twenty, anyone other than Ibsey that you might have seen." I caught a barmaid's eye and gestured for a bottle.

"Are you looking to get us back together? Are you still with Kailen?"

"No, and no. One of us betrayed me." I showed her my tat.

"That's bad. I thought you were set when you said you had that old king's children, what was his name?"

"Doran."

"Yes, Doran. Petir was the boy if I remember." The bottle came over and I tipped the girl and filled Bresken's cup. She took big greedy mouthfuls, desperate to get soaked.

"Do you remember what happened? It was at Snakewood I was made a slave, at the time we had all just left the king's service, when he was deposed."

"I don't recall seeing you, Kigan, not at Snakewood. They said you were there, Ibsey, Dithnir and that."

"Do you recall seeing Mirisham, Valdir or Kailen?"

"No, I think they'd gone on. Spent a few days there with Kheld. Yes, he said they'd gone on. This is all a long time ago for you to be here now asking about it."

She took some kannab from her pouch and pushed some into the side of her mouth, taking a spitton from the sill of a window behind us. She offered me, but I could see it was threaded, diluted, so she had little money. I am beyond kannab now.

She asked about my being a slave, I gave her some answers. She complained about her lot, her Quarter, the bunks in the Post House, how she made some extra coin with the other Reds when the captains weren't about. The day brews had done for her. Once Doran's gold ran out on some ships she'd invested in with the Post, she took on work for them, but here, so far from Candar and the Old Kingdoms, the Post was little better than a crew of gangers. After causing unrest as part of a misguided captain's decision to try to usurp the Post's position and establish an independent factory, she ended up in jail for a few years and lost everything. The plant and ale she drinks must have done the rest, fatigue in her legs and back, eyesight poor. I had little doubt I could cure her, and even less interest in doing so. Seeing what she had become, more than any of the others, sickened me. Apart from Shale, she was a soldier I could admire, one of the few that I could talk to, that understood the value of the work I did on those Ibsey and I were given to try out new mixes on, prisoners we'd kept alive for such purpose.

I made sure she was soaked before helping her up and out of the tavern, a few hours later. I slipped a knife into her side as I dragged her along a quiet alleyway. I eased her to the ground, seating her against a wall, and leaned close to her face as I did so, saw little in the dark but the roundedness of a life softened with guard duties and drink. She had some bad luck and now she was dead, wouldn't be missed. She led a life more glorious than most, but all of this was simply wasting time until her body gave in. I saw little point in telling her of my disappointment during that night. I doubt she had anything to do with my betrayal, but word could not reach any of the others regarding her having seen me, for The Prince had suspected my involvement in the deaths of Milu, Digs and Harlain. The coin I left in her lap was as much to ensure that if she were found, little would be done by way of investigation, and those that had something to fear would feel it. This purpose of mine will not be compromised, not by a pitiful and sick old woman.

Paying passage on a galleon a few days later, I spent the journey back across the Sar sick with fear below deck to escape the blue and my memories of what had gone before, a pipe of Rosie keeping me under till we reached the Ten Clan harbour of Mousakhor.

It was clear that I needed to find Mirisham and Valdir, of all those that still lived. Without a lead to those two I pushed on east, hoping to find either Sho or Elimar, if they'd returned home.

Despite the corruption widespread across the Virates, trade flourished mainly because these lands had much to export; silver, gold, molasses, silverskins – a supple and very strong leather made from specially bred pigs – and a plant trade that specialised in teas, caffin and ska.

The seas and harbours were contested heavily by the various Old Kingdoms guilds that put in, as well as ships from the nearer isles and the Post, the playing off of which for profit and favour determined the longevity of whatever Blackhand rulers inherited their power from the last incumbent to make one fatal mistake. I planned to settle in the Cull, a vast port I had suffered only once before, sure that here as well as anywhere I could find some talk of the Twenty. However, I soon discovered that this pursuit was already underway when I saw the poster Alon had put wherever his guild's ships put in, seeking news of the Twenty.

My first thought was that I was being sought for the killings that had gone before, but Alon's name on the poster was new. For all that I had lost the memory of, it felt, strangely, as though this was a name quite unknown to me.

Issana was distant, but the poster could not be ignored.

I was readying myself to travel back when I found out that Sho was in Povey's Valley, only a few miles inland from the Cull. He was well known in these parts for being allied with a prominent local ganger that ran his own quay, a minor player.

I have left out Kigan's account of meeting Galathia, as her account is already included.

Goran

I learned also that Elimar had died. I remembered he had family among farmers in the highlands of Corob's Dicta. He hadn't returned to them but they had been told, by some traders who hailed from their region, that he had died in the service of a warlord among the Blackhands. It was a pity, for we despised each other and I had hoped to be able to kill him myself.

I realised I had to go to Issana and find out who this Alon Filston was that was looking also for news of the Twenty. I assumed Galathia, who, masked, I did not at first place, and her crew were just hired killers, when I went after Sho. I assumed they were killing for this guildmaster, and decided not to pursue them in favour of him, as he was so open about finding the Twenty. It was on my way to Issana that I decided I'd search Jua for word of Bense, and I found him easily enough, in the employ of a Lord and much ravaged by cheap-cut betony and other opia. I had thought Bense would be a drooper, but he was worse even than Ibsey, who could at least hold down a crew to a task. It was when I first used the Weeper on Bense that he told me he'd seen Stixie recently. More interestingly, Stixie had told him of meeting with Kailen. It seemed Stixie had stayed in touch with Bense and was intent on telling Kailen also to come. I decided then that Bense should live, that he could be controlled with a two-one betony threaded with greenhead kannab to help me, do my bidding.

Over these last few weeks I have made Bense mine, ensured he obeyed every command I gave him alongside those of his lord, no matter how contrary or obscure mine were, to test his pliability and willingness to betray Stixie, but most of all Kailen; to tell me of their movements, earn their trust. I had succeeded in using the Weeper to make him suggestible to me only, to protect my identity in return for this most addictive of mixes.

Stixie was famed for his bow, the draw of which was strong even for a people whose bowmasters were renowned across the Old Kingdoms. I remember not being able to draw that bow, brew or nought. The composite woods, Ash front and Orange Osim backstrips, had to be worked in as a compound over many months before the bow could reach its full potential. The "Four" he also became known as was for the occasion he put a single arrow clean through four armoured men. These were arrows he fletched of course, to withstand the force of the bow.

Bense reminded me that Stixie visited the annual Hillfast tournament. It brought together warriors from all over. Here was a place a man could earn renown, either for himself or more usually for his sponsor. Over two weeks all manner of single and group combats played out, with the biggest crowds attending those contests that were a fight to the death. Underlying the contests, the work of the drudhas was on show, many representing their academies. This in turn attracted the buyers for the major guilds and lords that were looking to see what new brews could do for their soldiers. I put Stixie at the top of the Bowmaster contests every year I prepared plant for him. The war academies of the Old Kingdoms also continued their hallowed enmities and rivalries here.

Hillfast was a grand citadel that had, over the centuries, expanded across the channel it sided, becoming a great city of the northern Sar, a gateway to the Sardanna Strait I had suffered passage through below deck on *The Wayward Lady*.

Riding in to the Post's lodge I took directions from a Red for the tournament fields, still occupying a great plain to the north of the outer walls. Ferries crowded the shore, men and boys hollering for my custom to cross with them. More still waited at the far side, the usual stalls and gangers, pickers and whores. Everything was for sale, little of it as described. My colour, now the richer and more fluid for the years with Lorom Haluim, spared me much scrutiny or nuisance, but I still kept my hood up against the stinging winds as I followed a now boggy trail and many hundreds of others to the battlefields and pits. As I approached, the deep swell of a crowd's roar blew through us on the road from the pits beyond. The young men ahead of me betrayed their cheap rise and knocked each other about, laughing wildly, passing a skin between them as they speculated on the day ahead. Other mercs walked or rode past me, here to pick up purses from among the various factions and guilds, all of them left alone by the pustulent ex-soldiers now begging for coin and the crack-voiced bards switching their jigs and ballads to those they guessed were native to each passing traveller's homeland.

Now, through the iron gates and inside the walls, it was a rancid cacophony of yelling and music, a swarm of rich and poor slopping through the muddy channels between pavilions flying the colours of their guilds or lords and the wagons of traders, cookers and entertainers that filled the spaces between. Before us rose the stone walls of the arenas, six in all, housing thousands crammed into their galleries and stairwells, screeching and betting on the contests before them.

I heard the thunder of hooves from the nearest of these plainly architected structures, the Citadels never having had among their citizens a great desire for elegance and a flourish to their monuments. I confess I admired this trait, for was not excess of form a sop for the unworthy masses, a cost exceeding that required for the function of the thing?

I passed the hub of these arenas and sought the archers, the fields they used being to one end of the great compound in which the tournament took place.

Drawn to the gasps of those crowding at one range I saw Stixie, his flamboyant white breeches and silver stitched waistcoat stretched and faded to the colour of rainclouds by the years. Still too he wore his preposterous moustache, oiled, curled and itself now a mottled silver. His round felt cap had lost the vivid blue feather that seeing him woke the recollection of.

The bow remained magnificent, a massive rare masterpiece once more a joy to look upon. Having bent his knee to the onlookers he bid some boy eighty or ninety yards off to line up some wooden shields, between each of which was suspended a sack of grain. He played us well, showered with copper for it, bidding us to call for more shields.

Four hung there now and some who had seen him in previous years chanted his name, leading the others.

He picked out a boy from the crowd, inviting him into the range. He gave the boy his bow and bade him draw it. The boy could not of course raise even a creak from the string, no doubt still a crafted twine of hemp and Rivvyroot that few outside the bowyers of his people could master the construction of.

With an entertainer's flourish, drawing a cheer for the lad, he invited any to a silver coin if they could fully draw the bow and a further ten if they could hit the first of the shields.

A strong man, a smith or lumberer from his shape, was pushed and jeered into the range. Against Stixie he seemed diminished. Still he handed the man the bow. It was cleverly done, for the man had no plant about him that could have filled his muscle and made it the stronger.

He took the bow confidently, held it forward to draw and then shuddered and shook as his fingers, first two, then all got the string to move no more than an inch. He looked astonished, then, with the cheering, flushed and gave Stixie the bow, retreating back to his friends. None more stepped forward but a clap started. From a quiver Stixie drew a silver arrow fletched with white feathers. His arrows were longer and heavier still than any I had seen, necessary to withstand the force of the release.

He raised the bow, a subtle tug at the string initially that would not have been needed in his youth, but then the draw, the difficulty of which made his arms stand out with the strain as he asked of himself what only the plant could give.

He held the arrow at full draw, exhaled and let it fly. I wondered for that brief moment if anything had happened, then the first shield split in two, collapsing in on the grain behind it, which exploded. The other bags of grain and shields rocked and split apart, the arrow shattering against a natural rock outcrop behind the targets.

In richer times the carcasses of bulls would be strung where now only these shields were hung. He took the cheers and as the crowd moved on to other entertainment he scolded his boy to help him fetch up the coins before other scavengers took their chance.

He looked up from his knees as I approached. I had flicked him a silver coin.

"Kigan?"

"You are as strong as ever, Stix."

"Kigan, you're alive!" He stood, glancing at the coin before pocketing it, and put a concerned hand on my shoulder. "Has Kailen yet found you?"

"Kailen?"

"Yes, he has sent me word from the Crag. I plan to go there after the single target tourney." We began walking from the range.

"What word, I . . .?"

"Someone is killing us, Kigan, killing Kailen's Twenty. A number of us have been killed: Harlain, Kheld, The Prince. I thought it would be why you had come."

"Does he know why?"

Stixie shrugged.

"I think we should get a brandy, Stixie, we have a lot to catch up on."

He shouted at the boy, who came running up.

"I have them all," he gasped.

"Take two for yourself, find some supper."

"Is that . . .?" I began.

"A son, yes, though by what wench I cannot remember. Some woman brought him to me last year. He has the eyes, I'll give him that."

The vibrant blue that caused such a stir in the days we whored about the world with Kailen remained while his skin and the wild bristles of his brows sagged. He looked weary as the brew for his show started the cramps. His colour was as I remembered, though he marvelled at mine as he took a good look at me in the fading afternoon.

"The world has been kind to you," he said.

His son would have found my purse, beside his father's. I had no hatred for him. Stixie asked no questions or believed still any wrong had been done. He spoke truly when he said he did not join us at Snakewood. Still, I could not allow him to interfere, not given what he knew, and I could not let him see Kailen again now that he had seen me.

Now I would kill Kailen himself, though he would be ready. This was a thrilling thought, an action requiring perfect execution, a test of what I had learned.

Chapter 15

Kigan

It is appropriate now, with Kigan's journals having outlined the story of his life after Snakewood up to the events concurrent with the other survivors of Kailen's Twenty, to continue with his account of visiting Kailen's wife Araliah, as the course of his search nears its end.

Goran

Kailen had done well for himself of course.

The wind was sweetened by the orange groves on his estate as we approached. A number of Alon's retinue, led by Laun and her Agents, had already scaled perimeter walls and were approaching the villa we could see beyond the main gate. I approached the two guards on foot, sword drawn. One blew a horn but it wouldn't matter. They were trained well. It took a few exchanges before they fell choking on the ground with the vapours from the paste on my blade. Our soldiers had stayed back from me for the same reason. No sap or barrier on a mask could withstand it. Only those with the counter to it could resist it.

Ahead of us on the long road from gate to villa, Alon's soldiers were seeing out the men, women and children from the house. Araliah, even from fifty yards, was easy to spot, Laun and the men around her were gesturing at her but not shoving or otherwise touching her as she moved freely away from them towards us.

"You will let my workers go. If you have business of the sort that requires the type of soldier only a merchant would employ then you have business with me. Kailen is not here."

Galathia caught her husband's eyes drinking in the sight of this woman in an exquisite dark green gown that was cut low on her bosom. Her feet were bare, a scandal among his society, and her beauty more than rivalled Galathia's own. Araliah's dark hair was messily tied in a bunch, the more appealing for the loose wisps of it across her cheeks.

"You must be Araliah, so you may not know your husband is dead," said Galathia.

After a moment holding Galathia's eye, Araliah turned and called for her people to join her. They came forward, trailed by Alon's men. The children ran to her, before us, holding her gown about her legs and waist, fearing for her.

"Say the word, my lady, we will do what we can to protect you," said an old man at her side.

"There's little to be done here. This man, he has paid the colour, and richly. He wears a drudha's belt besides. Those with the lady are Agents of the Post. There are none among us could draw a sword and live, especially given how quickly Turan and Ancel were killed. There is no purse for your life, Imbrit, none either for the children or any of you. You must go back to your homes while I understand what this gentleman wants. I am sure this fine young lady and her husband are not his contractors."

They moved before an Agent or any of Alon's men could countermand her, a lady clearly high born and much used to dominion over the men about her. Soon we stood around her alone, the sound of the children calling and crying for her to follow diminishing.

"You have little in the way of a guard for such an estate, my lady," said Laun.

"The others are with our shipment of oranges, making its way now to the coast to be pressed and mixed. Few in the lands about are ignorant of this estate's landowner. Would you come inside, I have wine and hams, the children too have been baking."

"We are not here to dine with you," said Alon.

"Oh, I had not guessed, nor yet do I have your acquaintance. Still, whatever you have in store for me goes none the better for me offering you wine and some hams, I'm sure. Your men at least must eat if their work goes as far as destroying what has been built here."

She turned her back on us once more and walked through the line of clearly lustful soldiers to the main doors to the house.

After applying the barrier I took a handful of the Weeper rub to wipe over my face and hands, her contact with which would shortly make her a good deal more open to enquiry. I regretted this course for a moment, for she was a fine and fearless woman. Galathia stared at me as she dismounted, demanding something to be done about this defiance, though I doubt she was aware that it was Araliah's resembling her own self that galled her. Alon followed behind us.

Araliah brought from her kitchen boards with legs of smoked hams, as well as fruit and jugs of wine. She bade Laun help her set them out.

"It is wonderful to see a woman rise to lead a crew of Agents. There has never been a Fieldswoman, only men, I'm told. My mother is cousin to the Harudanian emperor. I find it wonderful that he maintains he has never met The Red. What power that man must have, that emperors speak such obvious lies on his behalf."

Laun flushed slightly and looked over at Galathia, who nodded that she should help Araliah.

"Were you of the Twenty?" she asked me, pouring the wine into cups.

As she reached over the table to give me my cup I grasped her bare wrist and bent her forward. She did not flinch at this sudden violence.

"Yes. I'm Kigan, long-time drudha to your husband. I would say I'm sorry for what has gone on here and indeed what's about to happen, but you matter little to me except for what you can tell me."

Galathia poured herself some wine, enjoying the moment. Araliah maintained her composure.

"She should try this wine first, Kigan. I don't trust her."

I took my cup, brought it to my nose and put it down again. I saw her smell the air between us, shaking her head as the Weeper's vapours filled her senses.

"The wine smells fine, Galathia. Now, Araliah, did you know Kailen was dead?"

I saw the question in her eyes. She realised that to speak was to speak true, the same wide-eyed realisation Milu had had. She shook her head.

"I need you to say it, Araliah. Did you know he was dead?"

"Yes." Her eyes filled with tears and she tried to pull herself away again. With my other hand I pulled at her hair and brought her close to me, pressing my face to hers, our cheeks together.

"Who told you this?" I whispered.

She trembled, "G-Gant and Shale." She breathed rapidly, still trying to assert control.

"Did you fuck them?" asked Galathia, nursing her cup.

"Gant."

Galathia cackled delightedly. "Was he good?"

Araliah nodded and shook her head, the trembling becoming more violent. I let her go. The Weeper was in her, flattening her will.

"Sit down," I said. With that the trembling stopped and she sat obediently. For a few hours at least she could not shit unless I commanded it.

"Where are Gant and Shale now?"

"They will look for Bense and Valdir. They set out to look for you. The poster."

"Good. If nothing else their attempt to free Bense will deliver them."

Tears rolled down Araliah's face. She was still attempting to control her words.

"Where is Valdir?" I asked.

"Kailen thought he may have returned home to Langer's End, Marola."

"I see. I have no idea where that is, but the Post has some use in that regard. Laun, we must get a message through to the Post to that effect."

Alon was carving up a ham. "Why would they go after Bense if he's imprisoned, in Jua of all places? After the vineyard anyone with colour will be stopped and questioned."

"Loyalty. All those I've killed that I spoke with still felt something for the Twenty. Gant and Shale are on the run, as much now from the Post as us after recent events. They are looking for answers, to understand who it is that is killing them all. They may be hoping Bense and Valdir know."

I turned to Araliah. "Do you know where Mirisham is?"

"No."

Alon continued speaking through mouthfuls of the honeyed ham he tore at on the table in front of him. "Will Bense feel that loyalty, should they get to him? Thirty Reds couldn't stop them."

"He's broken, Alon. Even before I began my work on him he had long become soaked on the Harosin. I switched him onto a betony mix of such potency I have effectively bound him to me. If they get to him, he will do what he can to let us know where he is. If not, I also have a man watching the jail Bense is in. He will get word to us if they attempt to get at him."

"We must find Valdir then. There are few left who can know of what happened to Galathia's wealth."

"Of course," I said, "though we may spend many weeks hunting him if the Post are not successful during our journey out of Harudan. I recommend we instead go to Bense. Gant and Shale know where he is, as do we. We may therefore find they come to us if we wait at Cusston. I suggest too we leave here immediately. The obvious loyalty her serfs feel for her will no doubt lead them to the nearest officers of law. Have the horses killed, it will give us the time we need."

"Laun, can you do this for us?" said Galathia.

"Of course. Tofi, Prennen, let's find Midgie and Omara. We'll torch the stores, split and cover a circle of two leagues around this estate, burn these people's homes."

"No, Laun, please," cried Araliah.

"Only the homes, woman. We're the Post."

She left with the others.

"There is another reason to go straight north to Bense, rather than spend time trying to find Valdir over west," said Galathia. "Something I wasn't ready to share with Laun. I need her with me until such news travels to the heart of the Old Kingdoms and the Post call her in. We don't have much time. This letter was delivered to me yesterday. It's from Petir." From a fold in her gown she produced it, worn and mottled from damp and travel.

"You know that he is with a warlord, Caragula, at the head of a vast army. That army marches for the Old Kingdoms. It has begun. They were amassing and ready to march from deep in the Wild to the Vilmorian border when he wrote the letter and they mean to head for the Citadels. The Old Kingdoms are finished. I want my revenge before such chaos engulfs us."

"The Post is also finished then," said Alon. "Excellent. Nothing would please me more than to see them cut down. The opportunities for my guild will be boundless. I trust we will be great allies for Caragula."

"Don't underestimate the Post," I said. "Too few on their thrones and cushions in the Old Kingdoms credit it enough for their wealth and security. Of course there will be many of those kingdoms and provinces north and south of the Old Kingdoms that will also be gladdened by its demise, for it has them on a leash, but it commands more men, as far as an army goes, than any other. Besides, if Caragula's army is as large as you say, Galathia, word will get ahead of it."

"I disagree, Kigan," said Alon. "If the Post represents all that's wrong with the Old Kingdoms Caragula will end it, if he means to do what Petir leads us to believe."

I would have corrected Alon's perception of the Post at length, had Galathia not cut us short. The success and the organisation of the Post, its ability to reinforce, to control routes in and through hostile lands, if these were harnessed properly by The Red, Caragula would have a far harder task without their support.

"The birds that fly west, warning of this army, will not greatly outpace them," said Galathia. "Who will believe those at the borders, no matter how impassioned their pleas. No army of any great organisation or discipline has ever come from the Wild, not in a century of winters. This is their greatest and most decisive advantage."

"Plant over iron. They will perish," said Araliah, who found herself able to speak freely if she spoke truly.

"Araliah," said Galathia, "go to Alon's men. You shall pleasure them all as they see fit."

She stood unsteadily, as though sleepwalking, all colour gone from her face. She slipped off her gown and walked haltingly from the dining hall to the main door.

"Alon, would you like to join them?"

"No, Galathia, I . . ."

"Oh leave us. Your drooling has upset me. Ensure she dies in the next few hours, with whoever else chose not to leave the estate when she gave them the chance."

He stuck the ham with a very pretty dagger and took it outside. A bustling and swell of laughter filled the corridor outside.

Galathia stood and closed the doors as the cheering started.

"I shall be on the throne of Argir in a matter of weeks. The thought of it wets me." She came and sat on the table in front of me and lifted her skirts to better spread her legs.

"Don't be gentle."

Kailen

They told me I couldn't see her body.

But she was brilliant. She had saved us.

My Araliah.

I had been kept in the cellar of The Riddle, a dead ganger filling the sack that went into my pit in the Crag's graveyard. Em and Robbo pulled me feet first out of the narrow pit under the flagstones of the cellar, a concealed breathing hole keeping me alive. I had been lucky; too few, in its secret history, have understood how much to take of the mix I cannot here record.

Coming out of that death-sleep took four days. I came awake within hours but was not able to move. Men have gone mad in those days, but I never lost the certainty that my strength, the mastery of my own body, would return.

It was many more days after that before I could manage a full meal, but it would be many weeks before I could do the Forms.

When eventually I was well enough to ride for Harudan it was too late.

They wouldn't let me see her body, nor tell me why, but their faces were revealing enough. Turan and Ancel were the only full guards on my estate. Araliah had sent the others away. I only realised why much later. The two men were buried near the burned-out husks of their own homes along with those others that, according to the survivors, put up a resistance in defence of their homes.

Jawen, the estate quarter, looked for instruction. He needed none, his recounting of the work being undertaken proved my judgement of his competence in managing the estate. The house was being repaired, stores distributed, hands secured from nearby estates to help with the work. Merchants were sent to secure the materials needed to house my people and to find horses fit for work.

The children of the estate had made flower sticks and fruit baskets for her, which they put in piles around the plot where she was buried, on a knoll that looked over the orange groves. We had our coupling rites there, though our families would not come.

None would blame me for being away. That burden was my own. Those who had killed her came unannounced. She had left no note, or message. I chose to leave her and the estate to pursue the answers to whoever was killing my old crew, when first I'd heard of the black coins. I chose the Twenty, I chose the past, over her.

There was a Harudanian playwright, born of common stock like my father, who wrote a play, *Trials of the Orange Giant*, a thinly disguised satire on the old empire out of which the republic of Harudan rose, and it was his masterpiece. The Orange Giant was a legendary soldier, the play his life, and he returned home for the first time in years to find his own wife buried (as the Orange Empire, indebted from its wars, found its people dead from drought and the corruption destroying it):

> This earth's embrace, the purse for my soldiery,
> These sons also stand apart,
> I killed a thousand men, I did my duty,
> For war I starved your faithful heart.

Who watches the days and weeks bleed into the months and years, each kiss goodbye tallying silently for this inevitable reckoning. The deceptions grew with the months I was away, as my ambitions found their zenith. Only I can weigh the worth of those hours, the purse for my soldiery. It is not a judgement I can bring myself to write here. It's in my blood and it fills my heart.

I took lunch and a pipe with Imbrit, the day I left. He had lived on the estate before I took it over, having managed it also for the previous owners. He told me it was a guildmaster, a drudha and Agents of the Post that came. The guildmaster's wife was bone white, long red hair, a Citadels woman. He asked if I would kill them. It would be the least I'd do. I had all the information I needed.

Chapter 16

Gant

Bense was better with some more betony and some bread and veg we got from the settlement. Valdir was quiet, he was dreaming bad, had to be settled with more kannab.

"Found out there's a stables o' the Post not far off Forstway, about three leagues north if the men here are true," said Shale.

"We trust them?" I said.

"They get a shit price fer their wood an' the eggs they has to give free or the Post got other settlements it can go to. One of 'em said the Post's bin jittery lately, they're hearing news of some army comin' out o' the Wild."

I nodded. "Guessin' we'll find out soon enough."

"You got some thorns going after the Reds, boys," said Bense. "Easier ways to get a few ganneys, easier still to just walk it."

"Post horses'll get us further faster," I said. "Fuck the Post, they can't touch us."

"You might be dying, Gant, but I don't plan to. Too much sweet B and too little time," said Bense.

Shale shook his head, miffed. "You got all the B yer want if you can put yer mind to helpin' us get to Mirisham an' sort out this mess we're all in. And anyway, who was it that were givin' you plant and had stopped wi' you, according to those on that Lord Fesden's estate. They said you had a drudha lookin' after you."

Bense give that slow easy nod that droopers had to stuff they didn't want the hassle of. He was once a ganger that ended up in fighting pits in Jua. His record drew them in from leagues about, master of a spear. Looked like all that power was gone and we had need of it.

"Saw Kailen of course, he came and looked to feed me up. Always trying to fix your problems, isn't he? See's what he thinks then you all got to go along with it. Put me in prison, that fucker did. Not even my captain. The other they must've seen was Stixie. It was him told Kailen where I was, but he must've meant well. I didn't have a drudha with me."

"You saw Stixie? How is he?"

"He's a good man, a good man. Always finds time for Bense he does. Drops me some B when he stops in, a friend he is to me, not like anyone else came knocking all this time."

"What you bin up to all these years, Bense," I said.

"Don't recall half of it. Came back to Jua after a few years. Couldn't take the brews any more. Our purse was pretty good so I got myself some land. That was hard, lot more than I thought, never slept so heavy. I wasn't much for running a farm or anything though, but the gangs was good easy coin, so got into that again. Somehow I ended up getting approached by that Fesden and took his coin, just for standing about looking pretty. Then I'm in jail, Kailen trying to save me. I guess you're here because he wants you to save me and all. Where is he? Ho, Shale, I'm old enough to manage my own pouch."

Shale put the betony pouch back in a skin on his belt and give Bense a rub of it from his finger.

"Yer fuckin' kiddin' me, Bense. How's yer eyes now. Skin still looks a bit sore from where you was dippin' into a pouch o' pure agave, never mind yer nearly got us killed."

Something was a bit off with how little Bense took care of what happened to him, but then droopers have little interest in their own interests, it seems.

"Well, he in't goin' to try save you any more. He's dead. Kailen's dead. We think Kigan killed him and he's going to kill you. So, we're goin' to get those horses from the Post, take some Reds' cloaks to make out we're Post too an' get up Forstway. They need to be paid fer that dance at the vineyard. Need to find you some proper swords an' all," Shale said. "We got to get back on the forms an' some sparrin'."

I nodded. He was right in a way. Been worrying too much on

running and hiding, not on what would be unexpected to them. Wearing the Red would help keep eyes off us.

The Forstway was the old Juan highway to Lake Issan, legacy of Amulith, eighth and wealthiest of the Seruat, according to Bense, who recalled all manner of the wars in these parts, sparking off the learnings Shale and I forgot when we were at the academy here. I was never for the scrolls and what made Jua great and all that. His rambling filled the hours as we passed the smashed or vine-choked monuments to this or that forgotten lord or general, or he called out ruins of forts what were Issanaian from their invasions. Even Mount Hope, what Jua had as the enemy on its other border long ago, he could tell their walls or stone, even the names of some of the nearby places what the Forstway signed, "Mantha Sul" and "Mantha Cree", where "Mantha" was their word for fort.

On our first sight of the Forstway we hadn't expected to see a line of what must've been many thousands coming south. Shale juices his eyes for a better look from a hill about a league or so off and tracks a column of about five hundred soldiers and their wagons forcing everyone else on the road into the verges as it pushed through. They were at a fierce step going north. Coming south was a march of refugees, a sight I seen often in my life but not in these numbers, a dazed trudge of folk shedding dead or dying like lepid skin on the verges and the grasses about. Begging, fighting and sorrow was the chorus of this weary column. Post were still about but were more interested in the 'vans they had to run. Blood was getting spilled as the desperate attacked them.

We agreed I should get to the road and see what's going on.

The starvation was desperate to see and getting close there was all the stink of disease and filth what went with such a mass of folk. I was shortly surrounded by one group of men past caring about my colour. One had to die before I got a handful of coppers to shower them with. I moved away quickly along the line. All these refugees were Vilmorian. The insignia and tats on some of the soldiers showed allegiance to a few of the Houses that made up their royal court. There were many wounded and either hobbling or led on carts. These men had lost a battle and not long since. An old man stepped in front of me then, put out a bird's-claw of a hand, wide green eyes popping

310

out of a small dried-out face. I understood enough Vilmorian to greet him.

"'Nab or coppers you can spare? My greatson's sick," he said. He gestured to a boy of no more than eight winters, pale as fleece, shuffling along on his greatfather's arm.

I leaned close to the old man and pressed a silver coin to him.

"Should feed you and the boy at Cusston," I said. He nodded and reached up to clutch my shoulder in thanks.

"Why are you on this road? What's happened in Vilmor?" I asked.

"Caragula. Vilmor is his, now sure as I stand." He stopped the trudge we were going at to keep in line and moved out of it with the boy, some urgency on him.

"If each blade of grass in these fields around us was a soldier, that is the army Caragula leads. These Old Kingdoms are at an end. Get over the Sar while you can."

"Caragula's a name I in't heard in a very long time. He were a boy then. Where is he headed?"

"Everywhere. He's going to be everywhere. He's got the Wilds hasts united, must have. There's Post runners and vans from east all on this road and further south I'll bet, running to tell their masters the trouble coming. More still overtook us before we got to Issan. The Kingdoms is warned now but they don't stand a chance."

I bid him farewell and headed back across the plains to the treeline where the boys were at.

"Don't know what to do, boys. Looks like there's a war comin', man called Caragula, if you remembers that purse we had well over twenty winters ago goin' into the Wild on the Razhani borders. Seems he's now a warlord an' he has a horde comin' across from the Wilds through Vilmor and, by the sounds, Razhani lands too. I still wants to get to Mirisham an' figure out how we stops Kigan, but we'd be heading into it. More than that I wants to keep goin' an' find me sister. Lagrad borders the Wild. I got to go an' see what can be done."

"We got no way o' knowin' what's over the water, Gant," said Shale. "We push on. Has to be a fair head o' men to cause this. Not seen the like."

Valdir was nodding, Bense was looking miserable and not saying anything. It was killing Shale to see him like this.

"Bense! Sorry we got you out, brother, yer should've said if yer'd prefer bein' killed by Kigan."

"Easy, Shale," said Valdir. "We haven't been in this all these years, we're both coming to terms with what's going on with Kigan."

"I don't figure it," said Bense. "Kigan was tight with me. I saw we had the best plant. His and Ibsey's mixes were better than a fanny pissing brandy. Figure Kailen never did give him enough respect."

"Kigan was slippery in my mind, yer forgettin' much of it," said Shale. "You might've bin stupid enough to agree to take whatever he was puttin' together on his bench, if you even knew he were doin' it, but those prisoners in the custody of our purses din't get a choice once he give a few quarters an' captains coin enough to try some plant on 'em."

"Name a drudha did it different, Shale," said Bense.

"Fuck, Bense, Ibsey din't."

"And who was better for it? We all knew he was carrying Ibsey. Kailen sold Kigan's plant, not Ibsey's."

"All right, lads. Square it off," I said, trying to close off the bickering. "We might be on the Honour in a day or so, need to get the lay on the land about the stable and what routine it has. We best rest up."

"The Honour? How'd you get the Honour when none of us did?" said Bense. He looked confused then, proper troubled by something.

"Gant said that Kailen give the recipe to Shale," explained Valdir.

"You must've sucked him good then Shale, for none of us learned it."

Shale looked to the ground then, close, I could tell, to giving him a beating. "Gant, tell me why, if he's about as much use as a cotton sword, we're draggin' this cunt with us?"

"It's just a bit of lip," said Valdir. "He'll get his Forms sorted."

So the stables we were hoping to raid, that the Post had off the Forstway, had a few more men in than we hoped. To be clear, it was more of a compound. A high wall round it for seeing off casual thieves hid a better guess at their number. Still, we reckoned we could go in dry if they themselves looked to be, which is to say without brews and masks. We decided that with an ambush it was unlikely even the guards would be on full brews so we prepped for the spores and dust and a three-one caffin, and our need of their horses was more than worth the risk if it helped us get to the lake.

We followed some runners coming off the road at about the place we were told the stables would be and found a big old track leading to a clearing where the compound was. Could have been ten or twelve in there for all we knew.

With numbers of the Post likely to get worse before better with what was going on north we agreed to go in that night. Bense was useless. We put him through the Forms and even Valdir, himself struggling for more than a few minutes at a duel, was whipping him. We would've been sending him to his death if we put him in that compound on a Red, or worse, an Agent.

Rain was rolling in heavy as we got strapped up and took the caffin mix. Bense was past us, tucked somewhere over the hill east where the road rose out of these trees and onto a clear stretch what bridged a long valley.

Shale and Valdir spotted the guards in the treeline doing the perimeter, I had to get the two gate guards with Juletta, two quick shots, both tight on the chest so's they wouldn't get a yell out.

Guards were huddled about a brazier in the doorway of one of the gate posts of this old sentry fort.

I couldn't stop my breathing for minutes at a time like on the Honour, making shots easier. I did my best to control the bit of rise we had from the mix.

They were turned away from me at the fire they had and first shot had to be through the back. I drew Juletta and she bent like an aristo's mistress, the arrow true. The moment the other saw his mate struck he looked out at the trees and there's that moment of seeing me and deciding what to do, but the next arrow was in flight and he was too slow as it caught him in the ribs as he made to turn away. I rushed over and I took a red cloak, putting the hood up and then dragging them across the mud to the side of the gate where they wouldn't be seen by the men within. I stood at the gate facing out, in case a guard inside was patrolling. It was lucky the wind was picking up, for Shale and Valdir got at the guards what were sheltering in the trees and took them on. I heard the sound of boots and then, over the wind, some blows, a grunting from one or two, then a shout. Shortly a door in the bunkhouse what sat in the centre of the compound was opened but I didn't look about upon hearing it.

"Yilsen, what's the yap now?" said the Red.

I raised my hand as though to acknowledge him but didn't turn about. I needed Shale because this was about to go wrong.

"Yilsen, if Messe's gone for a dump, get him. About time you switched out. And a Yes Sir would be the right thing to say."

Shale and Valdir crept up along the wall across the gateway from me. I nodded as Shale drew his bow, and we both turned into the gateway and shot the Yes Sir. We dropped bows and ran for the main bunkhouse. There was a commotion inside as we got to the door, a shout for masks, but Shale threw in a dustbag and I waited. Valdir headed about to see who else was there and killed some stabler out with the horses. Shale moved to the side of the building and there were two jumping out to escape the dust, fair with blades for the time it took him to kill them. Then I heard Valdir engaged on the other side of the bunkhouse from the doorway so I got around to help him with the man on him. Valdir remembered enough though; a thrust from the Red, he squatted and drove through under, and with a crack and a shudder the boy went down. There were a few Reds then got out the door of course but we returned for them and they weren't a match for us dry, dying fairly easy.

Inside the bunkhouse there's the room with their beds on frames could fit twenty, warm with the fire they had going. We took off our gloves and wambas and had a few apples and the fried potatoes they were eating, which was a blessing with winter starting up in these parts.

I went into the office itself, small room off the side of the bunk room next to the stores and where Shale was rooting about on a big battered old desk.

"Road's bad an' when we burn this place down the Post'll be hoppin'. We should get the Reds on, give ourselves some orders. Some o' these letters are showin' this army's rollin' over Ahmstad quicker than anyone can respond to. Hard to believe the Wildmen were capable o' this sort of action." He nodded then to the wax pot and parch on the desk.

"Valdir, what's your words like, your writing?" I asked.

"Fair," he called, from the main bunk room, "did a good bit these last few years for me boy and the association of the fishers."

"I'll get the best of the horses and get us packed up," I said. "Go and get Bense." Shale nodded. Valdir got to work on the papers and was soon putting together a mission for us from what the letters contained of the Post's business hereabouts.

Unless you were top coin you didn't wear a red robe for that was what the Post wore and you either didn't want the trouble of being mistaken for it or didn't want the odd lusty Red thinking he could beat on you for some sort of deception you might be trying, for it wasn't unheard of that men would thrive under the pretence of being a Post 'van and then just vanish with the goods entrusted to them. Needless to say it wasn't the first time we wore the Red, for or against their cause.

Shale got Bense to help with putting oil over the outbuildings. I'd seen off the horses we didn't need and Valdir and I stood with the mares would take us up the Forstway to the port.

The fire soon drew its greedy arms around the bunkhouse and the shelters they had for feed. We rode out in the dark to cover some leagues, keeping away in the fields from the lines of people nursing each other along the road, past camps where music and singing were, as everywhere in hardships, fortifying spirits.

Issanaian soldiers under watch sang a song of work as we rode to the outlying huts of Meddyman's Harbour. Hundreds of them were digging out the foundations for stakes while the camps of 'vans that had brought carts of lumber spread around a hundred fires and a few thousand men, most soldiers, that were undergoing some furious drilling as we neared. Issana was beginning to respond to the threat of this Caragula.

The wooden stakes were used too for funnelling people in and out of the harbour, and pens had gone up where, from the looks of that which I experienced previous, those who passed through what had a problem with conscripting were being held until they joined up or starved, men separated from family and all the crying and shouting that it caused.

With the camps come also the merchants and slavers and wanderers looking for a turn in fortune, and the ships and boats from over that vast inland lake what skirted the mountains were like darts jammed tight in the mouth of the harbour. Further across the shore either side of the harbour were the pennants of Issanaian watches, catching the icy winds of this bright day while the soldiers around them were trying to keep back boats landing on the banks about. Issana weren't famous for its welcome.

I kept having to stop and shit though little come of it. Had to mash my food 'less the bits I ate were like glass going through me. Bense did fuck all but smoke his pipe while Valdir or Shale were dressing me or mashing up the bilt and biscuits we took from the Post in some water. It was hard to not show I was feeling a bit sorry for myself.

We come to the lines of soldiers and there's a Red there looking at us sharp, only twenty or so summers but wearing one of the more fancy pins what kept his cloak about his neck. Rank in the Post was measured out in how fancy those pins were, and when you got some shiny in them like a ruby or such then you were a big deal in the land about.

He stepped out as we dismounted and led the horses in.

"The Reeve's commanded all Post refrain from taking routes northward, particularly across the lake. The lands there are at war with a horde of the Wildmen."

Valdir spoke, having devised our story with what he found in the office of the stablehouse.

"I am Rilbin," he said. "Our purse and seal take us to the northern shore only, cured leather from the Abelmar brothers, as well as a summons for the brothers themselves, to flee this very disturbance before it descends over Issan. You are aware of their importance?"

The lad stuttered briefly. Valdir had played a deft hand for we saw from the books kept at the stablehouse that the Red what normally ran the southern shore had been taken ill a lot of late, a man much older than this colourless boy that put on his fierceness with inks and hair three copper hoops long. "Just the northern shore? How much leather awaits?" he asked.

"We can walk it back on horses, fifty or so hides, but we'll need a cart too if we're to move the goods and brothers back to Jua. You are instructed to arrange this if it be within your power."

Valdir produced a scroll with the stablehouse seal, a letter mostly completed of the same purpose that bred our deceit's shape and manner.

The boy nodded to us. "Leave these horses, we'll get them to the stables, I'll send a bird over to arrange things for your arrival."

We were waved through to the harbour itself.

The streets were almost too blocked up with refugees to move against. Mothers and children what lost each other were making the most noise, so many desperate that they'd even push for Reds with colour like us for a few coins. I was more generous with the Post's bag of coins than my own I'll admit, so threw a few coins at those I saw that seemed like they had lost the strength for the fighting of those begging. Shale had to leave me with Bense while he and Valdir went about the taverns looking for a captain mad enough to head back out across the water.

Course, it wasn't a captain that was mad enough, it was a da that was desperate enough. Hearing of the coin we had as Shale was shouting out our purse at the bar, he soon come to see us, asking for some of the coin up front to get some of the food what was now commanding a lord's ransom. The hunger was getting people killed around us.

His name was Pavey, his wife and a bab, two brothers and their duts all on his riverboat what had come down from Ahmstad. We got a bit of food and some ale to ease their worry, the purse taking care of the remaining doubts they had to look on us.

We kept the story up about the hides as Pavey put his sail up and we helped oar out of the harbour. Pavey and his brothers were Ahmstad men. He said what clan but I've forgotten it now. This was a country where men were born with a sword or mace in hand, bordered on my own homeland of Upper Lagrad. Soon as their borders were hit the call to arms went up and he answered, missing his bab's birth, him and his brothers riding out with the men of their settlement to join the legions what were so recently exercised by the madman running Vilmor.

They had marched maybe four days he said when he saw the soldiers coming the other way. Ahmstad's legendary Third and Fifth Cohorts had joined with the Eighth and Tenth and a few thousand more men besides to meet the threat. Now men of those Cohorts stumbled past them, exhorting them to return to their families, that Ahmstad was lost.

Lost! Pavey and his brothers could hardly believe these glass-eyed veterans but for the burgundy leathers. They were routed, the horde supposedly countless, many more than a hundred thousand men they were told.

Bense thought this was a lot of shit, seemed Pavey was inclined to agree insofar as he kept on with the hundred or so men what were answering a summons at Fort Iras. But Iras was burned, the smoke they could see from a few leagues away. It was hard to believe it of course, and it was troubling for so few of the Old Kingdoms had a standing army like what Ahmstad was forced to have on account of its position against the Wilds and with its war with Vilmor. If men like this were being routed then things were bleak for a lot of innocent folk in the lands closer to the Sar.

They found one soldier still breathing, who was led in a ditch near the fort. He'd cut through his own infected leg with an axe but it was a bad job and the killing of him. He told Pavey of the horde that come through, a few thousand seeing to Fort Iras, and as they fought for Ahmstad they were watching tens of thousands just marching by, drilled like no horde of the Wild he'd seen.

I asked Pavey about Lagrad but he knew nothing of it, I was worried about my sister of course. Closer I was getting to home now, even though we were after Mirisham, the more I realised I wanted to see her before I died. Pavey was good enough to give us some furs to help against the winds that blew us over the lake. I could do little oaring, a few strokes and I was struggling. Couldn't put my face on it, I just laid in with a few crates while the others put to. Bense was made to do some of the oaring; Shale would have none of his cussing over his condition, telling him he was needed for what was coming.

For all that, it was a fine few days now I look back. Pavey and his kin were good men and we had a few brandies in the nights on the water and some songs that Bense surprisingly had a clear memory of, leading us through the Ballad of Ribby's Cove and the countless verses of The Doom of Hedler. Pavey's lot had songs where the tune was the same but the words were theirs, a common thing in the armies I took purses with.

Now we were coming to land at the northeast edge of the lake, a roar almost like battle itself grew as we approached. The Issanaians were not in control here, not enough of them, with the thousands coming out of Ahmstad and Vilmor. As we looked for somewhere to land that give us a chance of getting off the boat and north without a fuss, we saw more and more refugees seething over the slopes of the hills about the harbour. They made most of the noise; a starving misery and scattered violence breaking out throughout like some vast creature at war with itself. The younger men would be eager recruits for building the palisades and ditches that would give them some bread and pennies to help their kin as the Issanaians prepared, too feebly on account of what we heard, for the horde as it come south.

We were grateful for some rain as we drove the boat ashore, giving us a chance to put our hoods up without it looking fishy. We give our thanks and some coin for the trip and helped as best we could with the mob what descended looking for passage south, our colour and the red cloaks enough to bring a bit of fear and discourage those as might have tried to take their boat. It was a fierce profit and I hoped Pavey had the sense not to have come back here again when Caragula did send men south to secure the lake in the days after this story's told.

"We needs horses," said Shale as we pushed past the crowd.

"Do you know where we're heading?" said Bense.

"Valdir does," I said. "But we needs horses."

We asked of some of the Issanaian conscripts where the Post House was and we got pointed to it. We had to shove our way through and at one point draw blades to part the mob that was about the square. The dead were everywhere, some wept for, others piled up for the wagons that soldiers wheeled through the streets. We pushed our way across the square to a guard of Reds about the gate of a fine big stone house set in a bit of garden. Must have belonged to someone important here years past.

"Valdir," said Shale, "you trys yer story 'bout those brothers, how we needs horses fer the hides. The moment it's goin' flat jump in. Bense, Gant, you go straight for the horses an' we'll take our chances headin' out from there."

We walked up, five on the gate and I saw two more at the stable, one grooming a horse and the other watching us. Six horses. Our route out was obvious but crowded.

"Didn't think we'd see any more come this way," said the one guard stepping forward, grey and dour enough he was running the house or was otherwise too backward to get up the ranks. He, like the other four, wasn't of a colour to suggest they'd been soldiers of much experience.

"Morning," said Valdir, "one of you boys is Novik?"

"That's me," said the grey.

"Got a seal here from Rilbin, we're to get the Abelmar brothers and a load of hides and horses to put them on. Did you get the bird?"

The grey looked back at his men, who were eyeing us.

He looked back at us.

"Who are you? You're no Post I've seen running the Lake."

"Lot of the colour for runners," said one behind him, as tall as Harlain, though he was skinny like sugarcane, stooping a bit with it.

"I would like to spend some time sharing a cup or two with you brothers," said Valdir, "but the boat that brought us in isn't going to wait long with all these refugees."

Novik broke the seal of the parchment and give it a read. He took his time. I give a casual look about but I knew which one of them I was going to kill, had the olive colouring of a Juan, hand on the pommel of a shortsword. I think they sensed something was amiss and the moments were building to it.

"Here," said Novik to the one that stooped, now stooping further to see the parchment, "fetch the brothers." Novik give him a look, a squint of his eye that told me all that was needed; the parchment wasn't up to the subterfuge.

"I'll go with him," said Bense. Shale was about to fuss over that but I stepped forward and gestured back to our right where the main bit of town was. "What are the Issanaians doing about the refugees?"

"Nothing to be done with this lot," said Novik. "Rilbin was due here two days ago with news of what was to happen to the house here." Novik I think was happy to play for time. I was hoping Bense was taking out that Red and returning.

Shale was distracted, keeping an eye for him. Valdir took out a pipe and was offering it to the Reds here, looking to settle the nerves all round and set us up fairer for a surprise. They moved forward for a pinch of bacca and a draw but it was becoming clear to all that it would only take a word or shout to start it, them waiting on Novik, us waiting on Bense.

I turned half away from them, to see where Shale was looking. He signed with his hand, against his belly where they couldn't see. *Do we jump?*

Yes. Count five when you see Bense

As I looked back, Valdir dropped his pipe and drew his sword, stabbing it deep into the man he was stood next to. He yelled "Kigan!" and went for the stables. We drew our blades and closed on the Reds that were packing their pipes. I smacked the Juan's sword out of his hand and ran him through. I brought my blade up as the Red with him thrust his at me, clipping it away. I stepped forward as it went past my side, kicked his leg and stabbed him as he fell off balance. I turned as I made for the stable, only then looking to see what kicked Valdir off and I caught a glimpse of Kigan and Bense and a couple of Reds running towards us, pushing and yelling at the crowds that had stopped moving as they saw our scuffle break out. Bense was Kigan's man then and I cussed, burned with seeing it. Kigan drew out a blowpipe as he come towards us. He looked older than I recall of course, but lean, a savage intensity on him and he was brewed up, dropping those men in his way with his boots and fists a precise flurry.

Shale dug about in one of his pouches as we ran for the stable, Novik having given him little trouble. Valdir was untying reins. I stopped, pulled Juletta from my shoulder and put some arrows into Kigan's crew, hoping to slow them down. Kigan dropped a shoulder as the first flew in, going past him. The second hit a Red, he was brewed up but not like Kigan, I ain't ever seen the like for I wasn't sure how my arrow missed him, like it passed through mist.

"Gant!" yelled Shale. He'd pulled horses out for us. I ran to him. Kigan shot a dart but it hit me wamba. Valdir tore out of the stables on his horse, turning tight past the wall and yelling at those in the street to move for their lives. Shale threw a sporebag at the ground in front of the remaining horses in the stable and he followed me out as we fled after Valdir, away from those running at us. We spurred the horses and we ploughed through those not able to get out of the way, the horses clearly of a temper to keep on even without reins. Not knowing if the horses were jumpers we stuck to the street and soon picked up to a gallop as fewer people about got in our way. Cobbles give way to a muddy track as we rode north.

"Fucking Bense!" shouted Valdir as we fell into a line across the track as it ran through the bald fields where wheat was recently harvested. "He was Kigan's man all along."

"How? That's what I can't figure. Must've bin lyin' to us," I said, for it didn't make sense to me after us getting him out of the jail. It made me think again about that moment I woke up after our escape at Cusston when he looked like he'd been off somewhere. I closed my eyes and it cost us all and I was sick about it. I'm still sick about it and I got no way right now to manage this feeling.

"Got to 'im before he was put in the jail I reckon," said Shale, but he didn't say it as though he was sure. "We got fuck all supplies an' we're goin' to be tracked before day's out."

"How far to Mirisham's town?" I said.

"About three days' hard ride," said Valdir, now shouting over the wind as we got up over a hill and were galloping across what was left of crops hereabouts. "Our best chance is to get into the mountains but I don't know if there's a way without we slow and sniff about. Look, if something happens and we don't all make it, or we're split, we're looking for a crevice high in the side of a hill, leads in to a passage. Got to crawl in some spots, but goes up for a few hundred yards to a pass that you follow for a good couple of leagues. I made it good myself. Then you come to a door, no other way to it. Hands and knees all the way under Mirisham's walls to a basement in an old building in his citadel."

"Tellin' us where the crevice is might help, Valdir?" said Shale.

"There's some heavy wooded slopes rise above the remains of a statue, last I saw it, a statue of Sillindar and some children playing at his feet. Statue's in open fields, hard to miss, especially if you got some leaf. You look directly west from it for the rise you head up to find the crevice."

I had the sweats, my belly was flared up again and nagging at me. I had a bad thirst on and wanted some betony mix. Each thump of the hooves sent a spike through me and I put up with it for a few hours before I pulled up gasping for my breath.

"I'm sorry, boys, it's hurting bad. I'm going to be a burden."

We had stopped in a dell. Shale got Valdir to mash me up some fruit with water from a stream nearby and he went to see if anyone was about the plain behind us. He thought he saw someone far off but they got out of sight.

"I in't running no more, boys," I said, "something feels wrong in me, not really taking on much food, the last few brews have done me."

I was hoping they'd leave me hid away and just get on and warn Miri. There was a lot of cussing and shouting about it. Valdir stayed out of it, for the most part. Saw the sense in what I was arguing but Shale was as likely to be persuaded as the tide.

"We should make a stand," he said. "I can't see as how we can escape 'em if their trackin's worth anything. We should be lookin' fer some ground that'll give us a shot at puttin' an end to it. Sick o' fuckin' running."

"I think we can push on, Shale," said Valdir. "We're close enough with a hard ride on these Post ganneys, we might yet make the crevice and by the secret way into Miri's."

"You won't go faster than the pigeons or crows or whatever they uses round here, Valdir," I said. "Word'll get there before we do; bribes, lies, we'll have a bounty on us doubled over with what Shale an' me's got from the vineyard, never mind these stables we become fond of raiding."

"I says we push these horses hard then leave 'em if there's a spot near, a hill wi' good cover. We traps it up and makes a stand," said Shale.

"We can, you and me," I said. "Plain you in't for leaving me an' getting the job done, but Valdir should go, he can ride, we can slow them down an' let him get there. Shale, I don't think I'm goin' to make it."

He give me a slap then and he put his arms round me and called Valdir over too.

"I in't leavin' you, Gant, nor Valdir. It's just pain, an' we got betony for that."

Valdir too put his arms about our shoulders. "Gant, you boys saved my life, that of my wife too, I don't doubt it, and that's enough for me. This isn't a purse. I can dig us some ankle breakers and use a sword. On a proper brew I might even kill someone before theys kill me." He give a smile, which was infectious. I was fierce glad he was with us.

"If you aren't going to leave Gant, then I'll go with the plan that we make a stand. Miri can look out for himself. I'd rather die with you than die with him."

A slug of brandy, and me with a dose of betony, sealed it and we pushed on.

Shale got his eyes juiced and as we neared dark we hit a big river coming down west out of the mountains. It offered the chance for us to slow them tracking us if we could get the horses upstream in the river. Hereabouts the long toes of the mountains might give us somewhere to hide or ambush. As we got the horses into the water and went upstream we were heading into a steepening valley, wooded and strewn with boulders and stones and the like. After a few hundred yards the channel was sheer rock on either side, the river dropping from sixty or more yards above.

"Valdir," I said, "lead the horses back to the mouth of the valley and let them go, drive them north if you can. Shale and I'll get the lay of this place and where'd be good to position ourselves. I think this might do for us making a stand."

Recon was hard in the dark but it seemed the north bank of the river was the better, being narrower and giving the advantage of less cover on the banks for any that would be trying to approach from the other side of it.

I couldn't tell Shale at the time of course, but I was afraid for us, for me not being able to acquit myself well as a soldier, for we both believed they'd sniff out we were in this valley. Sure we'd put a few traps about but really it was about the brew and the bows.

"How's it lookin', Gant?" he said, meaning my wound.

I shrugged. The cotton he put on it was damp, it was going bad and the skin were dead round the edges, like cheese but stinking worse. The bark wasn't taking.

"We should've got more maggots on it. Cutting it might help but sewin's another matter. Need a bench, proper drudha. Yer goin' ta make it home, Gant, trust me, I'll spread Kigan over this valley when I'm done."

"I in't going to be much use digging breakers or setting thorns up. Did you see him? Kigan?" I asked.

"Yes, din't look as old as we do. Had a fierce look on 'im. I 'spect he's got some fierce plant too. We got to expect he knows what we're on given he cooked it up himself back those years, an' he knows our methods, well, some of 'em."

I sank back on the grass for a bit, the soft and even noise of the waterfall closing my eyes. Something of that sound reminded me of Milu singing for a boy what were burned all over and dying, back in a raid we did for a purse I don't remember the story of. It wasn't a burning that was called for, more an accident during that raid. Harlain it was that pulled him out of his hovel, smoke coming off his skin what were black and red like lava, screaming and shivering for he couldn't move himself but it must have caused him agony. His mother overcome her fear of rape and sits with him, probably wishing she could die with him.

Milu comes over and he gets a slug of his mix and gets his cloak to put on the boy, then he starts with the breathing and the horse singing, but just the one note it seemed, though he made it like it was a harmony. The boy was stilled by it as the sound shook through all our bones, filling the ground about us. The note of it seemed to get richer and lighter, your ear thinking it changed but you couldn't tell when or how. He kept it going till the boy was dead, who was still all the while, taken out of his suffering.

"Gant!"

I come to. It was night now, Shale must have kept watch and I'd been out for a few hours. I heard the footsteps and it was a few men.

"Shale! Gant!" hissed Valdir. "I got some men with me that know you."

We stayed silent of course. Then another voice, less wore out, carrying a bit in the night.

"We're Araliah's men. Achi at your service once more."

We stood and stepped forward to the figures, four in all with Valdir, moonlight picking out little of them beyond the waxed packs and helms. Soon as I saw one was much bigger I knew it was Stimmy.

"Achi?" said Shale, moving close to him, turning him to the moon to better see him.

"The same." Shale locked arms with him and the others, telling them how welcome they were. He looked back at me and nodded, the edge of a smile there. Their arrival was a fierce lift and I looked up a moment to send over the winds my thanks to Araliah. She give us respect then and hope now. I walked over and locked arms too.

"She sent us after you," continued Achi, "some days behind and you weren't easy to track. Found his family," he said, pointing to Valdir, "sister, wouldn't say a word but his mother let it slip. Then at the harbour we asks about and the boy that didn't want to be called his son sold you out, told us that sailors had dropped you up at Rillion's Chase and so it was." He turned to his crew. "This here's Stimmy and Hau that you met already, and Roin, your cooker for what's to come." They were all about thirty summers, Hau almost the opposite of Stimmy, skinny Virates lad, though he had a pack twice the size of Stimmy's. Roin was chewing bacca, peaceful eyes though that would be otherwise misleading, head shaved to a stripe as I'd seen a lot on the boys out of the Red Hills. He had the drudha's belts.

"Who's after you, because there's a big crew following behind us and I'm worried that if they saw us, shifty as we were, they'll know you got company?" he said.

"Kailen give us a letter tellin' us we were bein' killed off, the Twenty that is," I said. "It was only findin' Valdir that we guessed that it was one of our own, Kigan."

"Kailen's drudha?" said Hau. He whistled and shook his head. Achi give a glance up at the sky then, I think also unable to believe our bad luck.

"I'll be taking you through the plant we got," said Roin, "but of all the men you got after you, what did you do to piss a drudha like Kigan off?" He said it with half a smile on his lips, for when you line up against a crew, you're really lining up against their drudha. He spat a bit of juice from his chewing and slapped me on the arm.

"We in't got a clue ourselves," said Shale. "You in't as sorry as we are either but yer a welcome sight the lot of you an' yer givin' us a lick of hope where we had none otherwise."

"All this chatter's not getting the field prepared against the likes of him," said Stimmy. He took a half-handle shovel off his pack and eased the pack off. "Captain?"

"Stimmy, you're right of course," said Achi, "get these boys on

326

some trips and breakers and when you're done, Roin's to prepare arrowbags. We're waiting on a whistle from Danik spotting up there. Got a man up there as well, Wil, both fierce archers." He pointed to their spots on some rocks high up overlooking the south side of the valley, a good view across the hills to the lake. We hadn't seen any of them surrounding us and couldn't see those on high now. Stimmy, Hau and Roin headed off.

"Could have done wi' you boys when we were breakin' out Bense," said Shale.

"Araliah told us to keep you safe from ambush, not help you burn a city. This man Kigan and his crew weren't far behind you," said Achi.

"Did they get to Valdir's family?" I asked.

"Unlikely, not before us given what passed. We've been with you since Cusston, but if Kigan's who you ran from yesterday I don't think he could have come from Marola, not without he flew."

"Do yer know their strength?" asked Shale.

"Stimmy was tracking them. Kigan's got Agents with him, Reds too. You say he killed most of the Twenty?"

"Yes. Kailen train you himself?" I asked.

"Aye."

"Any of you beat him one on one?"

He smiled. "What do you think? Look, seems as though you're making a stand. Good plan and good spot to do it. We tried to take down whatever birds came out of Lake Issan but couldn't get them all. Post will have men ahead."

"What news of this army?" I asked.

"We know as much as you. I think reports from the borders of the Wildmen making an incursion never causes a stir on the coast, but the more news they'll be getting, the more they'll know what's happening. I expect the Post's spreading it about the Old Kingdoms as we speak, so it's about how quick they can mobilise . . ." He was interrupted by a whistle, Danik giving a wave, a shadow against the silvery stone of the cliff. He signed down.

"Danik's saying there's about forty men must be with that Kigan. We got a few hours. The boys and I would be honoured if you took command."

"Shale's your man, pulled my arse out of the crossroads more times than I could count," I said. "Sorry I in't going to be much use prepping the field."

They nodded and Shale started off into the trees with Achi to go through their tactics.

"Some kannab, Gant? I got no betony." Valdir sat and packed a pipe for us. "You and Shale always were tight, couldn't see him taking me off to Miri and leaving you holed up somewhere. It'd be leaving you to die in your state."

His kannab mix had a sweet taste, something like apple, a smooth draw that settled me a bit.

"I just wanted you both to have a better chance. I'm dead anyway, Valdir, you got a wife and he got years left."

"I didn't think I'd be getting back to her, not deep in here. I took those gold pieces for her because I knew it."

I nodded. I knew it too and was glad he did and could say it. "Why then, Valdir, why come at all? We give you warning though I guess we din't give you much choice either."

"Kailen summoned you, you went. What wouldn't we do for each other, now as much as all those summers gone in our prime? How many times did we cover each other at a crossroads? It can't be counted. A bit of me wanted to see Miri again, see what had become of him after being so much a partner with him in the settling of his homeland. Before he was turned by the Post we built something special, we gave his people hope again. Then you came into our house in this fine armour and beautiful fieldbelts and you look strong and you're rich. You showed me the full colour of what I was, someone fierce, a younger man. It's hard to say what I mean but I'd been years getting fat and I'm a fisherman, a deckhand. I suppose I felt somehow forgotten."

"You're in love too. We in't got that and I in't seen a woman look so much on a man with want as she did for you."

He smiled, though his eyes as always seemed to tell a sorrow mixed in. "You're right, I am in love with her and wouldn't change it. But we're in his debt, for everything. Neither of us could do otherwise."

He knocked out the pipe we'd done and pocketed it. We didn't have

328

any fine words as he prepared to leave and give a hand. He clutched my shoulder a moment, then used it to help him get up.

"Get some rest, Gant. It's good to be at your side again, brother."

I ate something but I was sick after. I dreamed of being in Lagrad, my sister calling me, so loud once I woke with it, thinking she was in the tree above me. The only thing I craved of the dreams that came and went as the night waned were that in them I was whole, though all else were horrors that over the years I committed. In another dream I was at the water well again and those men that survived the drop were screaming for their ma.

It was daytime, mid-morning. We expected they'd find us, though Achi's men used the river all the way in so there was a chance Kigan's men still believed there were only three here from their tracking. I knew Kigan wouldn't come in at night, it offered us too much cover.

Kigan's men would've had fieldbelts he'd mixed that were more potent than anything we had, but Achi's man Roin had give us plant from the Harudanian drudharch that was improved over what we used for sporebags and the like. We been on the same Honour mix all this time, but Achi's boys were using one that had a cleaner drop, which was a welcome fact to me. They had some seeds mixed with a syrup they give us, said Kailen got them from an emporium in Rhosidia. The syrup made a difference in what followed, give us a chance against Kigan's powders, and I wished I had known of it previously.

Achi's crew were drilled tight by Kailen. Hardly bore saying but there we are. Achi could've made the Twenty I'm sure, his boys all up to the job against the Reds, a tight crew to watch.

We heard the bird chatter increase and knew it was them, tracking up the valley. We were spread on the north side of the river. Danik and Wil were high up, juiced and by Achi's account fierce shots. The rest of us were spread with the intention that we give a position away so's they'd believe us three were at one spot, then wait for them to move like a net around it, at which point they hits either traps or else gets ambushed by the four others working in pairs; Roin and Valdir tucked up tight nearer to the waterfall, Stimmy and Hau in the river, under the water and breathing through reeds.

Of course, it ended up a fucking bloodbath.

Me and Shale got brewed up and put on masks and specials. Achi had a leaf mix were better than white oak for the eyes that would help with the smoke out of limebags and stop some of the aggravation from the mustard and whatever else was powdered. We were tucked behind a couple of boulders that had a sight through some trees to the river and a clear view along the valley on this bank.

There was a shout then, echoing heavy but had to be "Masks". Another one moments later and he was howling out before his scream was muffled. They'd found some traps. A breeze had picked up and the trees were whispering it. There's more bird calls and then Shale started signing behind his back, for Achi's benefit. It was hard to feel their movement with the water flowing, it had a strong song, but soon enough we could smell them like I'm sure they could us.

Three or four we saw moving out of the trees south and towards the south bank of the river opposite us, looking over in our direction. Achi and Shale were signing, there were five approaching on our side of the river too, downstream of us. It was these we had to drop, to push them over the river and encourage them to form their net. The five moved straight past Stimmy and Hau what were hidden. Wil would put an arrow into the water near them as a sign we wanted them up and at it.

One of them stopped the others as he saw a trip that he was meant to, stopping where we had a clear shot. Arrows dropped three, the two with shields we made sure of while they had them lowered, and of course they ran around the wire to the wooden spikes were dug into holes there. The spikes got one, slowing him enough to take an arrow from Shale and then the other got poisoned as another arrow sliced his leg. He was doing his best to keep his noise down but he was an easy kill. Course, as Achi moves to get the shot there's a voice from further along our bank and the arrows started flying. We tried to put some smoke out about our position and we emptied what caltrops we got before us. Then we heard their chain as they no doubt heard our leather, but Shale give a chittering sound for warning and put me sharp against our boulder. There's a splash on the far side of it, some sharp smell and the faint breath of flames. My skin was itching at once, Shale signing for us to move back to some trees nearby. Achi

330

put some arrows through where the men come from, limebags that sparked more fire up. It was dry weather in these parts and the trees were going to catch.

We had nothing to counter whatever was in their lime, it was like a frenzy of fire ants on me and I needed a good slap to get my head clear and some oil poured over my throat and face that'd clear it off and coat my skin. If not for the Honour I might've lost a bit of flint at that point. Whatever Kigan give them was more than a match for whatever we had.

More arrows come over from the south bank, the breeze was a fucker for this, spreading their dust about. Achi looked up at Danik and Wil, who were giving signals about positions when they thought there were no eyes on them.

Full hoods, one minute said Shale, counting on them holding off that long for the powders to work into us. We lay against the trunks and counted, listening and feeling for them. There was a disturbance in the water, two, three. I heard those advancing on the north bank, iron armour, Reds. My brew was right in now and I was trying to control my breathing, every piece of the world about me craving attention. The faint whip of arrows and the crackle of air as they flew past us proved they were going heavy on this poison. They followed close enough behind the volleys that Kigan must have give them some plant that made them immune. They were looking to end it quick. At the minute's end we stripped off the hoods and looked about. As I did I nearly got an arrow, hearing the crack of the bow on the draw. We're pinned proper, so Shale signed Achi to give word to his boys above us. Danik and Wil lit some big oilbags what they had heavy slings for and these got hurled down at the positions where the arrows been coming at us from. As the bags blew out amid trees and the grasses we leaned out and put some arrows of our own about. I heard two caught, stabbing breaths and slapping each other to get the flames out. I just missed an Agent who ran for the river near Stimmy, another one what were too quick on his brew. Stimmy must have tripped him or he tripped on him for Stimmy broke the surface and broke his neck before jumping for the bank, his bow in his hand. Hau stayed, which was to make a difference shortly.

There must've been a few more on our side of the river for I heard

Wil putting arrows down where Stimmy was, about twenty yards off. Danik was dropping all kinds of heavy bags on the trees and riverbank south of us to spoil their view over the water. Brewed up at that height it would take a fierce marksman to land an arrow on Danik, specially as he had a buckler on his bow arm for arrows what might come his way from below.

Achi broke cover and ran to support Stimmy. I give my eyes a squirt with some oil and then could see Stimmy was engaged hard against a few of them, a crack and ringing of shields, axes and blades.

Me and Shale tried to pick out the movement among the trees on the south side and put in sporebags where they looked to be hid, to protect Achi's run. It was coming back with interest though, limebags and all, forcing us to move about. We moved towards Stimmy and Achi. I didn't know if I could take Reds out in a melee, for all the noisies. Fire was catching good now, smoke making it harder for us to see about. Shale signed for me to keep my bow trained for a shot in the trees on Stimmy's oppo and he hit the earth and started crawling along. I had to trust the boys high up would have the river covered enough for me to ignore it, but the powders were getting in. I could hear Shale choke some and unstopper a bottle. Despite the oil my eyes were starting up bad. I could see only shadows moving about in the trees ahead. I knew we didn't have a spear among us so as one of them, covered by a nearer trunk, stepped back to throw one I put an arrow in him. Above me there was a whistle and crack of twigs as an arrowbag blew open over my head. I ran forward, catching Shale just as he rose to join the melee on Stimmy and Achi.

The stink of paste was strong, like sticking your nose against a diseased dog.

Achi was at it fierce with an Agent under a tree now burning and filling the air about with smoke. Like us he was only in leathers, relying on his skills and his brew. Both of them had sword and axe. I heard "Five!" and it come from one of the men was on Stimmy, shouting over the river in a panic that there were more of us than was bargained for. They were Reds; shields and platemail and a two-hander, Kigan knowing some heavies would test us what used only the broadsword.

We closed in, hoping that their own men would be some cause for hesitation from their archers.

Stimmy give a toothless grin as the Reds closed up but they were clever, moving back towards the edge of the river and into the open. Wil saw the problem and dropped firebags on the trees between us and the shore to stop them and mask our melee from the archers over on the south bank. It was the crossroads for us though, so we just went straight at them. I went at the shield bearer, a scorpion stance swinging down. He brought his blade up but with more speed and force than I expected, pushing me off balance. It did for him though, for he thrust out his shield to put me down but I was falling back and saw the opportunity to kick the edge of his shield, driving the top edge of it into his face. My noisies took over and I brought my blade in at head height. By instinct he parried but he was dazed and with a kick he was open and run through. Shale was having more trouble. This Red was highly skilled in the two-hander. I threw myself at him and Shale took his head off. It flew past me and the eyes met mine for a moment as it did.

Poison not working, Reds on Kigan brews not Post brews signed Shale as we found the cover of a tree. Achi nodded, rising from the body of the oppo he'd got to grappling with.

Cuts not slowing them. Fierce plant

We can't stay in powder and fire signed Shale.

Achi risked scaling a bank behind us to get sight of Wil for some tell of their positions over the river. He couldn't see him. He looked over to Danik.

Wil down, Danik pinned. They're coming

My throat was raw now. Whatever Kigan was using was clogging up my mask, my head was pounding with it.

A tree near us caught and started burning. Over the river there were flickers of orange and the crack of branches we could make out through the smoke, a lot of trees burning over there from the big oilbags.

A number of men started crossing the river. This was the last play. They must have thought we were the full number, in this one spot. Achi signed for Stimmy to take his bow up the bank, see if he could thin them out now they were in the open. It was a rush though, they were running, a few straight at us from the other bank, a number of splashes further along either side of us. Their net.

I heard Stimmy's bow. He got some shots off but a sharp grunt told us he'd been hit. I risked a glance up at him, see if I could do anything for him, but he was led against the bank he was on and he was shaking violently, a grimace as he dealt with his paying out. He give me a look then, a salute and a sign for how many he saw, doing what he could for our crew in the moment of his death. I signed it to the other two. Achi shook his head; we were feeling dizzy, fuggy with what powders were getting in us. Kigan's plant was the difference. If not for the plant Achi give us that was new out of the Harudan commune we'd've been dead already, even accounting for his crew's help. I leaned out to get a look at the numbers and their arms and saw Agents and Reds, Kigan still nowhere about, no doubt biding his time, waiting on the odds to shift. Then arrows come in from our right, from up near the waterfall, hitting Kigan's men as they crossed the river, Agents dropped first. Roin and Valdir saw their move and Roin was shooting at them with a fast, steady flow, while Valdir slung limebags with his one good arm. He was wild on the brew and it was a good feeling to see him tall again. He kept with Roin, who was quick and true with a bow, calm as a cow. The Reds realised they were flanked and picked up speed to get to our side and some cover. I signed we should make our move now as they hit our bank.

I took up a shield, two or three winters since I last used one in the field, but good for bad odds. Three of us ran at the men who were meeting us head on. I was hoping at least this would stop us being targets for the bowmen over the river. A few of them had turned to go after Roin and Valdir, but there were still ten of them coming at us. Shale and Achi flanked me, off my shoulder so's I could cover them with the shield. Reds were hurling caltrops in, some knives. One hit Achi but his leathers held and it clipped off him.

The first Red was looking to buy a moment for his brother to get to my side but I went in with the shield, twisting with it to push his sword out. He was quick to roll it up to a roof stance, but he wasn't much practised, too formal. I caught his thigh with a thrust and stepped in to crack him one with my head. His nose broke open. I dropped to my knee as his sword come down, stopping it with my own and then bringing my fist in to smash his balls flat. An Agent come in shield-side. He struck down at me with a scimitar while I'm on my knee, his hand digging about in a heavy pouch, something of Kigan's to put me out no doubt. I launched myself into his legs, rim of the shield out. The blade hit my lower back but near its hilt, which dulled the strike. The rim of the shield hit his knees and he had to step back. I swept my sword in and took his left leg at the shin. In the gap his movement created, his brother behind him put an arrow into me. I tried to twist as I saw what was to happen but it went in at the side of my wamba. He's drawing the next one quick to end me when Hau must've risen from the pool, putting an arrow through his head. Being hidden from the opposite bank by a boulder, Hau put two more arrows through those he could get a shot at as they pushed Achi and Shale back from me. Knowing this was going to be a fierce poison if the arrowhead was coated, and Hau having dropped the oppo on me, I stopped and kneeled and yanked the arrow out of where it was lodged. Edge of it had cut through and I had to thank a magist that it didn't go in proper. I got the guaia over the wound, poured on the salts and pulled myself back to a tree for protection, seeing a fair scrap being edged by us, though the brew these men were on was something beyond the Honour. It was only our skill and experience, much as Shale said it was back in the Red Hills, that could make the difference over men younger and so much quicker on whatever Kigan give them to drink. The men fighting Shale and Achi were cut down between their blades and Hau's arrows, and Shale moved off to help Valdir, now engaging with those were on the other side of their net. Achi give a yell and ran to Hau, trying to warn him. I looked over and saw he'd risen to take some more shots over at those bothering Valdir, his focus on the shots complete and so not knowing there were two more moving in from downriver behind him. Hau were cut as he heard Achi and turned to engage them and then, as Achi come in at one, the other killed Hau off, the poison swift in freezing him up.

I wiped the salts off the new cut I had and put another lump of guaia on it wrapped in bistort leaves. I was out for a moment as I did it, like my head was underwater but my insides were frying. This was plant like I never saw before, to wrack me so with just a dribble of it. I vomited and dragged myself a bit more to the tree, shield over me.

The fire was raging over the river, I couldn't tell how many were there or where the flames were moving the oppo to. Then I saw some come forward into the river so I give a yell for what it was worth.

For a short while swords went at it. I was dead if only one of them came upon me, but I worked the arrow wound, though my fingers worked as though I was instructing another's hands, no more strength in them than a dut's. Shale come back to me then, patted my shoulder and whispered. "Finally botherin' wi' the guaia then, Gant? It in't good, Valdir's paralysed, can't move, not dead but barely breathin'. Lot o' smoke but we can't risk gettin' to 'im. Danik's shootin' again an' Roin too, got good positions with the firebags pushin' a few of 'em, probably Kigan too, further up the valley."

Achi crept over to us then and dropped his mask. His skin was bruised, blisters where it was exposed. He was barely thirty summers, would've been a great commander, for the brew give you a sense of fear or doubt on soldiers and he had none.

"You boys have a clear run out of here, or we're all dead anyway. I doubt any got east of us to cut us off so this is the best chance you'll get."

"We should all get out, I'll get Valdir," said Shale, making to move. Achi put a strong hand to his chest to stop him.

"He's not coming back, Shale, we got nothing could get him moving. We promised Araliah we would keep you safe. What her and Kailen did for me isn't a story I'll get to tell, but we swore and do for him what you always did for him. Magists watch over you and we'll do what we can for Valdir."

With that he was gone.

Shale nodded and cussed to himself, took a deep breath and dragged me up. I didn't want to let him down. I tried to walk but the poisons and wounds had me a mess, not the first time I left a battle bawling with the pain of it, but truth to tell I was crying for leaving Valdir and all, who I wished I had kept up with, who had paid out but was back in.

Achi called it right, lucky for us. Danik must've been prepped to put his firebags down the river a way, to cluster them further up the valley.

I heard little beyond the fires blazing, saw nothing on a glance back but a choking pall that hid the valley and the endgame playing out. We hobbled north as the Honour Achi give us made its claim.

Destination: Candar Prime, Q4 670 OE
Jua Main routed
CONFIDENTIAL FOR THE RED ONLY
Report of: Fieldsman 84
Debriefing of: Guildmaster Alon Filston, Kigan

Received your instruction.

Met with Kigan. It is unlikely any purse could be found to persuade him to give up any of the recipes he may have picked up from Hanwoq. He cares little for anything but Galathia.

He seemed to be on a day brew for the two days I rode with them. He had a heightened awareness of the world and the presence of those around him, as well as their tells. Be most guarded in your demeanour should you get audience. His colours are a vivid and quite unique blue and red. I witnessed his forms the morning I left and they were exceptional. He should be considered the equal of the best Fieldsmen, but with potentially superior plant.

He has agreed to an audience with you in exchange for my providing the whereabouts of Mirisham and he seemed to know of Mirisham's importance to us.

Met alone with Alon Filston as they travelled to Cusston. Alon was in a highly agitated state. It is clear to him that Galathia is betraying him with Kigan, and that he is losing status with his own retinue. Kigan and Galathia are constantly together.

He is unable to seek redress with Kigan for obvious reasons but it is clear that Kigan appears to be a formidable man to be near. Galathia also has little interest in appeasing Filston, though this is in part in relation to a sense of anticipation regarding her reintroduction to the Citadel Argir. I reiterated the importance of his efforts in securing Galathia in Argir and the bearing that would have on the relationship between the Post and his guild, Filston-Blackmore.

I also conveyed to Filston how important it was that he ensure Kigan and Galathia arrive at Mirisham's, that The Red himself will be there to meet Kigan and ensure he no longer interferes with Alon and Galathia's plan. He has been told to take advantage of the Reeves' hospitality along the route to Cusston to allow The Red time to arrive and prepare for the meeting. He has also been told that The Red desires he and Galathia remain allied and happy in the coming years.

However, he confided information of the highest importance regarding the problem in the east. Galathia's brother, now a warlord among Wildmen for Caragula, has taken Ahmstad and marches on Donag and Issana. You are aware of the horde approaching the Old Kingdoms from missives my brothers will have sent from the Wilds, Ahmstad, Vilmor, Lagrad, confirming those earlier rumours. Her brother has been in contact with her regarding their movements and their intention to take the Citadels and control Lake Issan, perhaps even Mount Hope Province and Fort Donag if he is any strategist.

They will be there in two months or less.

Filston expressed his concern regarding our ability to ensure we can resolve matters in the face of this horde. I could say little but that a war council of the Old Kingdoms is being formed and that a strong Argir with its rightful ruler was good for Argir and all civilised peoples. I shall travel as per your instruction to escort Hiscan and Marolan dignitaries to Jua and provide them our intelligence.

On behalf of my brothers I apologise. We did not investigate the recent period of calm among the settlements and Post Houses that border with the Wilds, nor investigate the reason for the highly successful period of delivery along the border tributes. These constitute unusual activity at least as well as excessive trouble.

Chapter 17

Kigan

Here Kigan recounts events from Cusston through to the aftermath of the fighting in the Donag valley.

Goran

I blame myself for what happened in this valley. Perhaps I could not know we were being tracked or observed ourselves by men Araliah had dispatched. Why didn't I think Kailen would have a resourceful wife? A further mistake, for as pliant as I made her, she would not answer a question that was not asked after I'd got the Weeper into her skin.

Her men had only the Honour. It started making its claim from the engagement after a few hours and they made a final stand on their desperate second rise. I expected nothing less.

We had left the burning ruin of Kailen's estate for the Harudanian port Mothmarun, Alon procuring passage on a Juan cog's ballast leg from there to Port Fortuna.

It was as we travelled there that a Fieldsman for the Post introduced himself. Fieldsmen are the rank of Post between the High Reeves and The Red himself, representing him, for only Fieldsmen, and a very few others, know his identity. Fieldsmen are given free rein to operate in the Post's interests wherever they see fit. Where Reeves are renowned administrators and negotiators, Fieldsmen are that, but also, as the name suggests, excellent spies; they know many languages and are highly skilled warrior drudhas. It is rare one introduces themselves, but this Fieldsman has taken an interest in me. Presumably Laun has spoken of me, who I am and what I want for both myself and Galathia. I cannot fault her loyalty. Indeed, inducing an interest in those members of the Post higher up, that must know something of Galathia, accords with my aim, and sure enough this Fieldsman offered Mirisham's whereabouts, confirming that he had indeed gone back to the borders of Fort Donag, working with the Post to keep routes open through the mountains. In return the Fieldsman offered audience with The Red, the Post's desire being to understand better the plant and my recipes gleaned from the Hanwoq.

The thought of the Post having recipes sufficient to give their soldiers a decisive advantage and consolidate their power throughout the Old Kingdoms was abhorrent to me; for all that it can glue kingdoms and confederacies together, it is greedy and corrupt. Feeding it to grow further is in nobody's interest.

The Fieldsman was eloquent, speaking of the Post's "important role" in keeping the peace across the boundaries of kingdoms for the benefit of all the peoples that relied on trade for their lives and families. The Post, he told us, was a civilising force that could do great work, to bring further peace were it to have access to more potent recipes. He asked if I'd thought of the contribution I could make, as a drudha that had been to the Hanwoq jungle; floated before me the idea I could find an "unparalleled opportunity" for research in a high-ranking post at their academy on the island of Candar. It would have made no difference to him my recounting of the countless incidents of their involvement in coups and other acts of destabilisation of those powers not amenable to giving them what they want, not least of course their involvement originally in deposing King Doran, the cause of all the woe in my life.

I cared only that he gave us Mirisham, the additional benefit being that Cusston, and its jailhouse holding Bense, was on our path to him. I agreed to a meeting with The Red. It would be interesting if nothing else. I was told that we should meet at Lake Issan, from where he would accompany me north to the town Mirisham was now mayor of. The Fieldsman left us the morning we boarded the cog.

A week or more from Mothmarun and we arrived at Cusston, entering the city as Lord Hesskan, in whose domain Cusston lay, led the memorial service for those who were killed in the fires. The charred bones of the joists and frames still smouldered as we rode past them to the service where I was told the Reeve would be.

In silks that nearly matched the lord's for their colour and splendour, Cusston's Reeve of the Post watched as the mayor and captain of its garrison spoke to those gathered about. Rotties and slummers oiled the commercial interests of the guilds and they needed soothing, not least to stop the attacks on the captain's own men. They must have spoken well, for there were shouts and cheers of agreement, predictable calls to solidarity and the encouragement of grief to bleed out the rage. There was no mention of arson, only the forthcoming beneficence of those looking to stave off further riots with bread, blankets and wood.

With Alon and Galathia I waited for the service to finish. She must have sensed in Alon a resistance to what we were doing, and so far north as well from the heart of his business interests. She flirted with him, fussed with his robes and teased a smile out of him, necessary for what was to come. It was obvious to me my presence had caused them far more damage. He snubbed me whenever he could. He must have known we bedded whenever there was a chance, but what could he do?

The tracker that I had watching the prison and Bense had left word at our inn that there were four at least heading north. Valdir must have been with them. I had no doubt they had started the fires to create the diversion necessary to get Bense out of the jail.

The Reeve would have the men and the stables necessary for me to catch up with and overcome them. He would not, however, discuss anything with me without our party join him for a banquet he was holding for various Cusston worthies and visiting dignitaries, which he made Alon out to be one of.

As soon as those present at the tables had sated themselves I pushed aside a whore who was seemingly stuck to the Reeve's ear. "Reeve, I have news both of the fire here and the vineyard."

He was almost white blond, tall like a Rulamnan. The Juan sun suited him for his darker skin, reddish with a mild intake of brews, made him a striking figure. At fewer than thirty summers and already Reeve Cusston, this was a man with ambition and thus ripe. He kissed the woman and told her to fetch them another bottle.

341

"Remind me, it's Kigan, isn't it? You're with that guildmaster?"

"Alon, yes, of the Filston-Blackmore Company, and his wife Galathia. One of your Agents, Laun, travels with us."

"Yes, Marschal Laun, she served me very well shortly after I was promoted to Cusston. I trust you aren't still searching for the mercenaries that so grieve us? I have heard of a crew of Reds killed only twenty leagues from here that I suspect they are also to blame for."

"We are sadly bound up with the fate of those men," I said, "for I know why they have come here and burned so much of this city and know where they are headed. They have kidnapped a brother of mine. They mean to seek out a man called Mirisham." It was obvious he was not aware of our conversation with the Fieldsman.

"The information you have will be much appreciated and sufficiently rewarded when you share it with us. Would you accompany my scribe to his office where we can make good this arrangement?"

I admit I struggled to keep an even tone as I considered the hours that Valdir, Shale and Gant were gaining in leagues on us. I recalled then how Laun had buried the bodies of her fellow Agents and gestured for her to join us.

"Marschal Laun," said the Reeve, "an honour to meet you once more." He waved his hand for the whore to fill our cups on her return, before dismissing her.

"Marschal, I mentioned to the Reeve that we are seeking out the men who killed so many at the vineyard at Ithil Bay. Marschal Laun and her crew buried every one of their brothers in that vineyard, thirty in all as you know. In our revenge you will find a most willing Marschal of the Post instrumental in its execution. I respectfully suggest that our desisting this pursuit, particularly given the calibre of Laun and her crew, would be the least successful approach for all of us. The man they have kidnapped is loyal to me, he will seek to pass me a message of their heading if he can, to a tracker that only answers to me. Right now I know which direction they are going and you do not. I do not doubt that you noted, in your High Reeve's report of events at the vineyard, that they had plant exceeding that which the Post gives its most elite soldiers. I made those fieldbelts, I was their drudha for more than fifteen summers. I can supply fieldbelts many times more capable than your best and can counter their poisons and fightbrew. Unless you can muster fifty Agents or more Reeve, I believe you need me almost as much as you desire delivering their heads to your superiors."

Laun began to petition him with a passion bordering on insolence. He raised a hand to silence her.

"Please, Marschal Laun, there is no need. Kigan, I believe the Post's prestige would be greatly enhanced by presenting Lord Hesskan with their heads. A caravan arrives with a few good men later this evening I'm told. I shall have birds sent . . . where?"

"North. Lake Issan."

"We have orders not to send anyone north at this time. There is word of an army from the Wild, though I'm surprised at the instruction, as the border countries normally deal with those savages quite effectively. I believe you're more than capable of executing this task despite this. You will need assistance with preparing the belts?"

"Just the use of your benches, I fear the required skill does not exist outside the academies." I admired the attempt.

Eighteen Reds and two Agents joined Laun's crew and Alon's men. Birds were sent out with instructions for the Post Houses ahead to watch for and detain the four. They would be heading up the Forstway to Lake Issan. It couldn't be long before news of the full extent of Caragula's army came to Jua and put this whole pursuit at risk so I pushed for us to leave that night. Alon, naturally, was reluctant, but Galathia spurred him and his men to consider the future, already sure, indeed glowing with the knowledge, that Petir would return their throne and her place as a princess, if not queen, of the Citadels. Alon's promises to smooth her way to the throne may well have worked, but she didn't need him now.

For all the maids that waited at the Reeve's lavish banquet, all eyes were on Galathia; her knowledge of commerce and her husband's dealings, the green dress she changed into that was taken from Araliah, all conspired to win an urgent departure, much to the dismay of Alon's travelling party I'm sure, for few of them would have eaten as well as this while working for Alon.

The following day the food they ate would have my own mixtures in it. They now lived or died by my whim.

I faced Valdir, getting up close to him, savouring a most subtle shade of fear in his skin.

"Haven't you killed me yet?" he said.

"I haven't finished with you."

He'd had a bad day once I'd brought him to. Paralysed where he fell when the arrow caught him, Achi's men couldn't reach him with our archers waiting for the attempt. We finally shot his archer at the head of the valley, making our run to the north bank easier. I led the remaining Reds across the river to end the resistance Kailen's men were putting up. There were a few arrows shot at me as I took the lead, but none could find me, so slow they seemed in comparison to my sense of them on the brews of old. Achi and his men must have taken some poison before engaging with us. They fought well for men thinking and reacting more slowly than those with me. I finished them myself, my cuts putting them into the state Valdir was in, except they then died, one final trick played on me, one I could have done nothing about. They were loyal to the end.

"What more do you want of me, Kigan? Bense? Bense, you cowardly plant-addled cocksmoker!"

Behind me, curled up in an oilskin, Bense stirred, groggy with his Harosin mix.

"Bense, Valdir is annoyed with you. You betrayed him."

"You're like a child," hissed Valdir.

Bense sat up, nodding as though it was expected rather than because he understood the question. He wiped some drool from his cheek and was struggling to pull some thoughts together into activity.

"I, have you got any tea, Ki, I need some tea to drink, that's it." He stood, shivering with cold and the fall as the evening spread through the valley. Only the high peaks retained the last carnelian red of the sun on their crowns.

Valdir was sweating, the flushes coming on hot and cold, his body beginning to shut down. The whole valley will soon drown in the noise of his agony.

"It must have been a good purse, Bense," he said. He shook his head then, convinced of the pointlessness of conversing with a drooper even as he said it.

Bense hung a small pot over the fire that Alon's remaining men sat around. They were concentrating on ignoring what was going on. Few men had the stomach for torture. It was music to me.

I leaned into Valdir's ear as he hung, limbs bound, from a tree.

"Bense is on a Harosin mix, cut with some peyot. I've added a little extra to it. He'll die at about the same time as you, just more peacefully."

"Bense, you're next! He's going to kill you with your next pipe you drooped-out fucker! It's in your mix."

Bense scratched his head as he squinted at Valdir.

"These mixes are good, Valdir, the best. I gave you to Ki, I'm useful to him. He kills you and the rest but he sees me right. Man of his word is Kigan."

Valdir shook his head as he looked at me, then hissed with a spasm. "Well played. And when you've killed all of us, Kigan, what will you do with yourself?"

"I shall see what use I can be to the new master of the world."

I said it confidently enough. I thought of Galathia as I said it, but the thought of adopting a cause, the thought of a purse or obeying someone that I might fulfil their ambition left me numb. I knew I could not follow the will of another. There was so little of me left, gnawing at these thoughts; of faces or names or stories, not able to sort them into the right arrangements. I could recall the memories were there, that I had them, but not what they contained. This was work enough, this occupied me, more so as I returned east of the Sar. My bones carried the indifference in their marrow now, indifference to all but that girl and her brother. A life with them in a land of pines and ice? I thought of the jungle then, its fierce noise and the solitude of Lorom Haluim's hold pulled at me.

"Why did you do it, Valdir? Why betray us?" I asked. I did not have a lot of time, or rather, he did not.

"Because I couldn't give a shit about you, your willingness to deliver that last purse, the richest of them all; two children into the wealthy arms of Jua. Mirisham it was decided it differently. He thought you were tight with him, tighter than you were the rest of us. He found that hard to believe, that you wouldn't be persuaded to take the wealth on offer, because of how much you loved that girl and her brother. We were looking at a purse that we could pay out on, no more crossroads for men like us getting old and damaged. You put them before us, your crew." He managed to look up at me then, and smile. "So Kailen, Mirisham, The Prince, Moadd and me, we took your fucking jewels, the coin, the plant and the recipe book. We sold it and we split it and we spent it. I ain't sorry, except that we didn't kill you back then."

He nearly got what he was hoping at that moment, for my knife was in my hand in a moment and I was ready to gut him. I could hardly breathe for hearing it, to finally know.

"Do it, Kigan, don't be weak."

No.

"You betrayed a purse. You know what happens, Valdir."

"Your purse, Kigan, not ours. I see the difficulty you had. You killed enough children in your time, orphaned more than you could now count, we all did, though how many of yours died in pursuit of your recipes? But they were none you knew, so it's easy to see them like animals, not children. You don't remember it, do you? That night in the tavern in Snakewood?"

"I remembered some of it, the ephedra took the rest."

"Seven or eight jugs to the wind and you're telling us about the wealth that had been smuggled out of Argir. A royal recipe book and jars of henbane and jewels and so on. You went on about how you were going to set them up in Juan society, you, a warrior-drudha, a man of the colour, in that society. We laughed ourselves ragged, how could we not?" He bowed his head and panted as his guts were burning. With a gasp he lost control of himself, a sudden, sickly sweet smell and a curdling sound as his bowels emptied.

"You were saying, Valdir?"

"Fuck you. Here now and back then and ever since, fuck you. You would have lived in the luxury required to introduce them to Juan high society. The rest of us? The rest of us had fifteen gold pieces, no drudha to mix the plant needed to fix what other plant did to us, except to pay through the cock's eye at an academy. We were heading back out onto the battlefield. We wanted more than that, those of us listening to you shooting off. I wanted more and what was stopping me was a man getting self-righteous about some spoiled children after all those years poisoning and abusing prisoners with his plant and the many children among them. Pity on a whim, pity for a purse, is no pity at all."

"Fifteen gold pieces is fifteen gold pieces, earned, like all of you earned it, because Kailen could manage a battlefield and I could furnish you with brews to make you legends. Your lack of gratitude is pathetic. Doran chose me for that purse, and none of you. You feel aggrieved, you stole my life for it, but once I'd accepted it, it was none of your business. You are paying the price for your greed now. But let us talk of betrayal. It seems you also were betrayed, Valdir, for here you are, dying in a valley, abandoned by your remaining friends, far from your wife and son. Gant and Shale fished you up beautifully. What was the bait? That I would come for your family? I had no idea where you were. You might have been the only one to escape me."

"How did you know of them? My family?"

"We spoke of it earlier, before you passed out. You've been singing, a verse or two about the path to Mirisham's township, a verse or two regarding your lovely wife, a cripple now though, a lonely cripple." He spat in my face, bucked and strained against his bindings, frenzied. He spoke in short, weak breaths.

"You might yet win this purse you've devoted your life to, but one evening with Gant and Shale makes a lie of this petty abuse. We took one last chance to pay what we all owed Kailen and each other. I'm only sorry I'm not there to see Gant and Shale finish you. Goodbye, Kigan."

He would have said more, but was reduced to a muttering as his eyes rolled back and his head fell forward to his chest. With death a few hours away he would say no more. His nerves were about to catch fire while his muscles decomposed. I tucked the black coin into a pocket on his belt and turned to the men around us.

"Return to Meddyman's Harbour. Galathia and Alon have gone to meet her brother Petir, whose army is heading for Fort Donag and Mirisham. It is better you don't join back up with them; the fewer there are in their party the less attention they'll attract."

"You're going alone to this Mirisham?" asked one of Alon's men.

"Better that I do. Petir's army is days away, and the township of Mirisham's is a principal target, a gateway to the high mountains and Mount Hope itself. You shan't be much use to Alon there and we shan't catch Gant and Shale before they get there because if I know them, the horses and your man guarding them will be dead."

347

He tried to hide his relief, his crew avoiding my eye, nodding and staring at their cups. I took up my belts and sword.

"He'll start screaming shortly. Don't kill him, just leave."

I set off along the bank. It wasn't long before I picked up their tracks. There was blood. One of them must have been badly wounded.

Chapter 18

Kailen

Midgie loved Laun. She called her name over and over as she staggered back to the hollow where Alon, Galathia, Laun and what remained of her crew set their camp in the early evening, on the edge of some deep woods just inside the Ahmstad border.

I had the good fortune to meet Midgie once. Well, we couldn't meet properly, but I watched her as Laun was going through their drills and forms, Midgie always looking to her, asking questions of her, fussing her. Now, as she was falling unconscious, falling to her knees, her arm was outstretched for Laun, who came running to her while signing for Omara, Prennen and Tofi to spread out around Galathia and Alon and ready their bows.

Omara drank his brew and rubbed his eyes with some luta oil to try and see better into the twilight of the trees around them. He took a dart to the neck, staggered as though drunk before falling to his knees, hand to his face. He shuddered, spasmic, and fell still.

"Laun," hissed Alon, "do something."

She glanced briefly at him, a vicious look. I called out to them.

"If you'll hold your arrows I'd like to step forward and speak to you. Midgie and Omara are not dead. They're just sleeping. It wouldn't do me to be killing Agents of the Post."

They whispered among themselves, but Laun it was had the final word, demanding they allow this, arguing that they'd all be dead if that was my intention.

"Step forward," she said.

I stepped out from a tree trunk and walked down the bank towards

349

them, my hands behind my back, for I held something I did not yet want them to see.

Needless to say, their faces dropped, and Galathia shook her head.

"We killed you," she said. "I kicked your dead body."

"It cannot be you," said Laun. "I . . . I don't understand. I saw you dead."

Laun kneeled next to Midgie, checking her pulse to confirm I spoke truly. She was wary, and looked behind me.

"Don't make a move, he isn't alone."

"Fuck, Laun, they won't draw if we engage him now, we've got him," said Tofi. He drew his sword and ran for me, his hand drawing out a bag from his satchel, no doubt powders as I was not masked.

"No!" shouted Laun. He had made half the distance when an arrow went through his raised arm. He dropped his sword and fumbled in his belt for something to put on the wound. He fell forward mumbling, in the same state as the other two.

"Allow me to introduce myself. My name is Kailen, I once ran a very successful mercenary crew. Our last purse, as Galathia knows, was for her father, King Doran, of the Citadel Argir.

"Now, because it's necessary for Galathia to understand what's going on here, and because you'll give me all the time I need because you think it will help you concoct some way of escape or retaliation, I'm going to explain what happened to King Doran, Galathia's father.

"Doran had a problem. The Post had strengthened ties with the Citadels surrounding Argir, for the use and maintenance of routes through their territories. Key to all of those routes south is what the Post calls the North Passage. The North Passage goes through Argir. Perhaps you can see where this is going."

"Yes, Kailen," said Galathia, "I knew this much, Kigan told me, Alon told me. Caravans cannot go around Argir without passing through Upper Lagrad, which is too dangerous, their nomads a constant threat."

"Did you know there were guilds south of Argir that also suffered. Those guilds numbered four: Walling Trading Company, The Quartet, Kursmeier and Filston-Blackmore. They too needed someone ruling Argir who was more amenable to the Post's proposition, namely, that everything would go very profitably for everyone, Argir included, if that troublesome king could be ousted."

I paused briefly, to see how Galathia took the mention of her husband's guild. Alon stared at me, shaking his head.

"Alon?" she said.

"Galathia, this has nothing to do with me, how could it? It . . ."

"Stop it. Don't insult me. Keep on, Kailen, you're clearly enjoying yourself."

"Alon, you don't need to listen to her any more. She can't hurt you now, so you can admit that you've been involved in this since you were made a guildmaster. You've known for a long time."

Galathia leaped for Alon before Laun could stop her. He barely got a hand up to stop her, but he appeared to be no match. She'd got her hands around his throat before Laun tore her off him and slapped her. Alon was on an elbow, holding his throat and coughing.

"You are a mad whore, a selfish mad whore I will no longer tolerate!" he gasped.

Galathia was straining to get back at him.

"Get control of yourself, Gala, this isn't going to help you," hissed Laun.

"Laun is right, Galathia, and I take no enjoyment in this. This is a reckoning and it's important you understand what is really going on, because it is going to help you in the months of reflection to come. The Post approached the nobles and guilds of Argir, to persuade Doran to relent on his unreasonable stance regarding the Post's proposed treaties. And he would not relent. So they, the Post's allies, starved out his resistance, and that of the people; they pillaged, stores grew low and the riots began. Fortunately for the Post, and unfortunately for you and Petir, it found enough nobles able to secure the militia and put a puppet in charge.

"The ringleaders of this coup perhaps expected that your heirlooms; the plant, the Argir Book; would be theirs, but who could foresee Doran entrusting it all to one of my mercenaries, Kigan. Needless to say, they have hunted for the book ever since. You can trust a mercenary with a purse, but the treasure of a kingdom?"

Galathia approached me then, halting abruptly when she heard the draw of a bow from behind me. "You are wrong, Kailen, Kigan was betrayed. Doran chose the right man, a man loyal to Petir and I, who has continued to seek those who betrayed him without the knowledge

I was alive, to find your scum crew and kill them, until our common purpose brought us together. When he finds you this time he's going to gut you like a fish. There will be nothing you can do, as those you once led have all found out. He has a coin for you." Laun stepped forward and put her hand on Galathia's shoulder to stop her coming closer.

"There will be no repeat of the Crag, Galathia. He failed to kill me then and will fail again. Kigan was little loved among my crew I'll admit; he deceived me, he deceived us all. I did not do enough to curb him then, did not look into the evidence or the accusations of his experiments, those men, women and children who were forced to drink his mixes, trial his poisons, dying while he made notes in his book. Indeed, I looked the other way, truth to tell. I believe all the truly great drudhas do not become so without these sacrifices and we benefited handsomely from the awful things he did for many years. There is much I'm not proud of, much more that my failings have cost me. But to learn then he was to run to Jua with you and all that wealth? That he would not, with such wealth in his hands, remember us? Five of us decided against it. We split the wealth, the Argir Book you'll see soon enough.

"Well now, the Post, your uncle and those four guilds all looking to extract their share of the plant and the jewellery that was taken, went looking for it. They eventually found Mirisham and Valdir, just north of here, settled among Mirisham's people, building up the reputation of his tribes, arming them and winning back land they'd lost. The Post left Mirisham his life in exchange for his share of the wealth not yet spent, and the use of his routes through Mount Hope. He had done a splendid job. He got rid of Valdir, as part of the arrangement he made. He would do nothing to jeopardise what he'd built with his people, and Valdir fled penniless. Some summers later, the Post and I found each other."

I turned and nodded for my companions to step forward. There were two, standing twenty yards either side of me.

"Just three of you?" said Laun. Then her eyes widened as she looked more closely at the woman to my right.

"If there's only three then I'm brewed, Laun, let's go!" said Prennen, dropping his bow and drawing his sword. "I'm in the mood to slice this arrogant fucker to pieces."

"Laun, kill this piece of shit and my deceitful cunt of a husband and you can have one of his ships," said Galathia.

"No! Stand down, Prennen, can't you see, she's, she's a Fieldsman? That's a Fieldsman's formal dress, I saw it once, in Candar."

I held out before me then what I was carrying behind my back: an old waxed leather satchel. The stitching was lost in places, the strap thin, soft as silk from wear, the leather almost black with centuries of treatment. I unclasped the buckles and lifted the flap, then dropped the bag and held up in my hands what it had contained.

Both Prennen and Laun took a moment to register what they were seeing.

"You're The Red."

"Yes, Laun, I am The Red, and these are both Fieldsmen. Fieldsmen Seventy-seven has been on duty, so he has no formal dress, but Fieldsman Eighty-five came from Candar directly at my behest and she has done so for just this. She has carried the shirt here."

"Your wife told us there were no women that were Fieldsmen," said Galathia.

"We shall talk of my wife soon enough. There was much, sadly, she didn't know. Prennen, see to Tofi, Midgie and Omara, give them some salts. They are not deeply asleep. You know how to treat the arrow wound. It will have done little damage."

Laun could not take her eyes off the small shirt, a child's shirt, blackened with long-dried blood. It was the Post's greatest relic. As I spoke to her I folded it into a square.

"Marschal Laun, you have led your crew on forty-four assignments, and took part in thirty-eight others as part of Marschal Mesch's crew. You have served with distinction, not failing to deliver the required outcome on any of those assignments. In the killing of one hundred and seventy-three across those assignments you have led, you have led your crew also with distinction, not least in the operation against the Jinzy Gang that plagued Strinmore's Heights in the Ten Clan, which killed forty-seven Reds and six Agents prior. Your crew respect you and would die for you if you gave the word. You have been willing to question orders and suggest alternative strategems where you felt a better outcome for the Post could be achieved. These are essential qualities for a Fieldsman. You understand that I am here to give you a choice, and you know what that choice is. You have earned it with this final assignment, the protection of Galathia, winning her trust and friendship. You have performed exceptionally well. The evidence is plain in Galathia's face. I need no more proof.

"You see, Galathia, despite losing your family's heirlooms, we, the Post, nevertheless benefited greatly from securing the North Passage through Argir, until recently.

"There was no doubting your family's line treated the people of Argir fairly and had maintained peace for a long time. Corruption sprang up, nobles at court feuding and vying for the Administrator role we made in your family's absence. Immigrants moved into Argir's borders from Lagrad, sensing its weakness, and as the court tore itself apart with conflicting alliances fractured along family lines of many generations, our problems multiplied, and your people clamoured and challenged us and demanded their royal family back.

"Fortunately, my predecessor believed it was important to find you in the event of this outcome and had for years harvested reports of red-headed girls from the Citadels matching your age, you being the more distinctive of Doran's children. Then you appear in the Juan High Commune, and from there we needed to ensure you were safe, we needed someone who could be with you constantly, a guard of course, but someone closer, more a husband."

"No!" she screamed. Laun grabbed her arm as she lunged again at Alon, who flinched before her, his head bowed. She screamed again and again, swore at us all, pulled at Laun, kicked her and spat in her face. Gradually she collapsed to her knees and sobbed. Laun kneeled with her but did not let her go.

"Your husband has proved to be a most loyal ally to the Post. We have shared much success through collaboration on so many routes out of the Old Kingdoms."

I wavered for a moment, seeing vividly the small patch of freshly turned earth within which Araliah lay.

"But unfortunately for all of us, because of my position, you had no idea what you were doing when you went to Harudan."

"Kailen, I . . ." began Alon, but the words died as it all dawned on him. It was clear to me that he remembered her, remembered what had happened.

"Do you know Gant fucked your wife?" said Galathia.

"If I know my wife, she fucked him."

"Laun was there. This sly bitch was at your estate as well. What will you do to her?"

"I know, Galathia, and I can see what you're trying to do. Laun never forgot her duty to the Post, nor would I have expected otherwise, in the circumstances, while she was paid as the Post. But she didn't kill Araliah. She didn't kill anyone on that estate who didn't put up a resistance. You, Kigan and Alon, however, despite my wife not being of the Twenty, despite her telling you everything she could, you saw fit to kill her in such a way my own people would not tell me how she died. I implored them of course, and they would not tell me, though my quartermaster and our personal servant Imbrit wept while they refused me. I can imagine many awful things, for that has been my life. But she deserved better. This reckoning is for her, irrespective of its effect on the Post's interests.

"Now, Laun, before I take my revenge on Alon and Galathia, let go of her and step forward. I need you to make your choice. Will you walk the Hiscan Road?" I held the folded shirt across my palms.

Laun took a deep breath and stepped forward. She looked at Galathia, at her men, and then back at me calmly.

"I will walk the Hiscan Road," she said.

"What? What are you doing, Laun, what's going on?" said Galathia. Fieldsman Seventy-seven raised a hand to silence her.

I kneeled before Laun and held up the shirt for her to take in her own hands, reciting the vow, specifically for Laun, which would have been said by the first to hold the mantle of The Red, long ago. "We serve each other. May the blood of my son make strong the blood of my sister, to protect those that are in our care and deliver to them reward fair for their toil. This shirt I keep, for the Post was born with his blood. On this shirt we pledge to bind nation with nation, and we honour those that die for that pledge. You are Fieldsman Ninety-three and you will walk the Hiscan Road."

I stood again, with the satchel, and took from her the shirt, gently, for she had gripped it tightly and had not realised. She was weeping, her head bowed. I stepped back and Fieldsman Eighty-five stepped forward, in her hands Laun's new leathers and fieldbelt.

355

"Please," she said, gesturing for Laun to undress. Fieldsman Seventy-seven helped her out of her Agent leathers and then Eighty-five helped her into her new ones. She shivered through it, it was plain that she had grown attached to Galathia. How else could such subterfuge be effective?

"You do not need the mask today," I said, "for these Fieldsmen you may know, though there be many you will not.

"Eighty-five, your duty now is to take Galathia back to the harbour and there, with this seal and purse, seek passage over Lake Issan and onto Candar Prime." I walked forward and stood over Galathia. She stiffened, and I sensed some deceit or defiance about her.

"When the time is right you will be Queen of Argir, assuming your brother sees sense. We shall find out how much he loves you when he learns you are my hostage."

"I'd rather die than be your puppet. Your pathetic ritual, the lies about binding nations when you cow them and control them for your own profit, you make me sick." She rose and tried to push me away, her arm flicking out towards me. While she moved quickly, my dayer helped me read her intent, see the knife tucked against her wrist. I ducked back and spun to her side.

"Nielus taught you well." I took her arm in a lock and tore the wristband holding the knife from her. She yelped but I held her to me, her arm bent so close to breaking that she dared do no more than breathe, her defiance momentarily drained. I whispered to her.

"The blood of the founder's son made strong his own blood and through it he forged a company for the ages. You tell me these are lies, but I can say only that if you look past yourself, you will see your people, as all of our allies see theirs, as I see my own people, my Reds and Agents and Reeves. The blood of your people makes strong the line of Welvale, your blood. You would see them get the peace they crave, for their children, for their toil; the freedom from bandits and thieves and thugs, the coin they need for the skins they cure and cut, the plant they grow and harvest, the iron they hack and purify from the mountains. If you love your people, what matter who it is you ally with but that they can provide you with the means to help your people thrive? Think on this in the coming years. You and I do not matter. To what extent we can make a difference to the majority? That matters."

I released her arm and pushed her away, then turned and walked up to Laun, now dressed in her new leathers. All who are born are born suffering. She went to bow but I held my arms out and embraced her.

"Just make me proud," I whispered. "You may hold the future of the Old Kingdoms in your hands, along with your fellow Fieldsmen, as we face up to the future this new warlord from the Wild presents us with."

She stepped back to Galathia who was rubbing her arm but otherwise downcast.

"Now, Alon, Galathia is still necessary but you are not. Unlike your wife, you did not meet Captain Nielus. Sadly, I did not either, though Fieldsman Sixty-eight told me that he excelled with the knife, kept the blade so sharp he often achieved the compliance of his targets by demonstrating only its sharpness on a length of bamboo." I took Galathia's knife from its strap.

Alon stood and ran to his left, scrambling away to the safety of the trees. Fieldsman Seventy-seven, in a conical straw hat and long loose robe as you would see commonly worn on his people in Corob's Dicta, lifted his iron blowpipe and hit Alon in the neck with a dart, sending him sprawling.

Seventy-seven dragged Alon back to the centre of the hollow, near the campfire. He was dazed and whimpering. He tripped Alon flat to the ground, kneeling on his chest.

Taking some short wooden stakes and twine from his pack, he then staked Alon to the ground and cut away his woollens to bare his chest and stomach. Alon was calling for Galathia now, who shook herself free of Laun but did not otherwise move, waiting. He started offering us money, all of his wealth and estates, and of course begged for mercy.

I dipped Galathia's knife in a pouch on my belt, kneeled before him and began. He was wide eyed now, his breathing coming in short gasps, and he cried freely. He could not lift his head up to see what I was doing, for his throat also was pinned to the grass.

"While I complete this, I will tell you what is happening to the Filston-Blackmore guild. You have seventeen ships currently sailing short hauls to ports across the Sar, three more heading around to Western Farlsgrad, Ryylan and Rulamna. When they arrive your crews will be paid off and your cargo turned over to the respective militias to fund that payment and profit that militia. Your ships will of course also become the property of those countries.

"You have sixty-four caravans travelling to thirty-three destinations. All of them will be taken similarly. By the time I've flayed you, your brother, Diens Filston, will be strangled in front of his family. Thiek Blackmore has been decapitated already and left at your headquarters at Jua. Well, outside them. We've killed everyone we found there and burned it to the ground, so your guild is finished. I say we, I mean the mercenaries I hired, because this has nothing to do with the Post, though I suppose the Post has benefited. This is my own revenge on you for what you did to Araliah, nothing more. I will have my revenge on Kigan in good time. Galathia, well, her blood denies me the chance of giving her a simple death, at least until she is no longer useful. Ahh, there we are. I've managed it all with a single cut."

I paused and held up a large flap of skin that had covered his chest before throwing it behind me.

"There, you didn't even feel it, did you? This is an exquisite knife. Now, you may have guessed I'm dipping your wife's blade in a potent clove oil. It's why you can't feel a thing that is happening. In an hour or so it will start to hurt, and it will continue to hurt until you die, whenever that is."

I looked up to Galathia and Laun. Galathia was weeping, her fury overcome.

"It is time for you to leave, Galathia. I hope you understand better now what your position in all this truly is. We will either put you on the throne of Argir in due course, or you will also die, and for your part in the death of my wife, you will die like this, at my hand. Fieldsman Seventy-seven and Laun, Fieldsman Ninety-three, will come with me to see Mirisham. We will no doubt see Kigan. I very much hope so. Fieldsman Eighty-five, would you take everyone else with you?"

She helped Prennen bring the Agents awake, whispered in their ears as she did so, aligning them to what had transpired while they slept.

"Fieldsman Ninety-three, your full induction will take place at Candar Prime, after we have found Mirisham. From there you will walk the Hiscan Road. When that journey is complete you will find a way to serve and when you do, I will find you again."

Laun embraced her old crew, stood also for a moment before Galathia. Before she could say anything Galathia slapped her, turned and left with Fieldsman Eighty-five. I looked down at Alon.

"Let's do the arms now, shall we?"

Chapter 19

Gant

I must have slept, maybe a few hours. Like where I started this journal I'm in some trees and the air's like iced clay on my face. Shale's about, hasn't slept proper in days. I know if I move it'll hurt. He give me some plain betony last night, stupid to be taking it like that but it give me rest and anyway, I didn't have much longer.

"I bin dreaming again," I said, "that time Mirisham had us loading those stinking dead sheep onto the trebucks and you puts his fieldbelt and sword on one of them and he watches it sail off over that river. I can see him now laying into you."

He was setting the saddle on the horse we kept of those that belonged to Kigan. "I were lashed fierce fer that," he said, smiling. I dreamed too of my ma, following her and the goats with my sister up Ravell's Pass, past the burned-out fort nobody'd go near for fear of disturbing what was there. My sister said she heard men singing to her, but the magist that come to the war academy in Jua put us right on the matter of ghosts.

"Let's go, Gant. Eat this an' let me do yer rubs an' that fat gut yer got."

The birds started up, thrushes and sparrows I recognised as Shale led me on the horse at a brisk walk in the shadow of the near peaks. I was in and out of sleep as I rocked with the horse's gait, Shale looking back every so often for signs we were being caught.

"Hope this statue of Sillindar's as obvious as Valdir reckons," I said.

We ate some bisks, honeyed as well, from the saddlebags of this horse. Kigan must have still been involved with Alon for such a luxury. The sun took the edge off the breeze, but offered little more as it got smothered by some low cloud out of the north. Shale kept up a good marching pace and I joined his chant to help keep him going. Each time I tried to get down to march with him he was ratty with me, telling me he needed me ready for the climb to the passes Valdir spoke of.

We both hoped he'd got out of there with Achi, for Kigan could work his plant in ways even us mercs couldn't watch. We didn't say about it, so we both knew each was sure they were dead.

Later that afternoon we saw a farmstead, tucked into a hollow beneath the wide rolls of hills we followed; a few turf-covered buildings, what looked like cow byres, and with his eyes juiced Shale saw some mountain leopards just as we heard a cow giving off an awful shriek.

"Anyone about, Shale? Surely not if those are leopards."

He took his bow and made a few hundred yards. He put a bagged arrow into the enclosure, aggravating the leopards. He gestured me forward and I drew a sword as we closed on the homesteads and barns.

The noise of flies and stink of the dead animals hit us first, then we saw it was a calf, lowing and thrashing about with its back legs torn and useless. The rest of what we smelled was a more organised slaughter. The leopards fled as Shale put arrows into one and about the others.

"Not seen one o' those in near twenty winters, not this far out and in the plains," he said. I dismounted as he put an arrow in the calf's head to silence it.

"Look in the houses, Gant, I'll get us some cuts off this."

Would've been eight, ten families hereabouts, byres enough for maybe forty or fifty head and the sties too. The stink and the flies were in one of the byres. What was left of most of that herd was there, slaughtered for their meat. Most of the tools – spades, cleavers and the like – were left lying about.

From the doorway of one of the houses I saw enough to confirm they all just fled quick as they could; some fine carved figures on a table, a chest open with some fine linen in it, useful for bandages I reckoned. They were probably on the Forstway, escaping the horde what had come to the edge of the Old Kingdoms.

Outside, Shale was washing the calf's blood off his hands in a water barrel.

"Plenty o' straw an' wood about. I can get a fire goin' an' cook up these steaks so we can be on our way."

"They took the salt," I said.

"We sees Mirisham in a day if Valdir's directed us right, no need fer it."

Meat was good in my mouth, blood and the burned flesh like hot bark, but I was soon needing the betony to cope with it as it hit my gut. I didn't want my steak cut to slivers this time, thinking it had to be one of my last proper meals.

We used some of the linen to help my wound and I got back on the horse and we're off. We didn't stop but for an hour or so that night. He took some of his snuff and I'm sat shivering and crowded out of the moments and the world about me by the memory of things. Seemed like my head was sorting through it all, like a dut tearing through a bale of hay looking for a hide-me. Shale wasn't for hearing what I remembered. I was hoping he'd get a bit of sleep anyway. Most of what I was seeing was from before we met, clan tourneys we used to have in Lagrad, when I was the pride of my da. Some of those boys I beat were probably leading the clan now, settled with women and boys of their own, probably old enough too to be running their herd.

Dawn come again. We found ourselves climbing steadily. Shale had a strong luta in his eyes, looking back and hoping there was a sign of Valdir. Soon enough his attention was drawn east, away from the range we tracked. He thought his eyes were tricking him, then he thrust the luta at me.

"You should see this yerself, Gant."

I got a flake of the luta leaf pasted up and with his help slipped it under my eyelids. I never got on with it, like sand over the balls of my eyes till the leaf melted in. The light gets unbearable, like the sun moves closer in to reveal the secrets of every blade of grass, the channels and ridges of bark on trees hundreds of yards away. But beyond that, a sight that give the source to a sound I hadn't otherwise noticed. Six or seven leagues off, on the plain below us and north of us, the land itself seemed to move, a river's shiver under a gust of wind.

"How many of 'em yer reckon?"

362

"I can scarce believe it's an army." As I stared it got clearer, catapults and carts muddied the shimmer of arms on close marching men. The closest I ever saw to this was what the both sides mustered in full when last the Ten Clan and the Red Hills tried to end each other, and that was fifty thousand added together.

"We needs to find that statue," he said.

We were looking for something less obvious than what we found, looking too much at the bare rock of the near cliffs and gorges. Course, what you see on luta that looks close is probably a league on if you could see it with plain eyes, but the statue itself was away from the near hill a few hundred yards, not at the mouth to a pass.

The scene was carved in relief on a stone some ten feet at its widest and the height of a man. Sillindar the magist was taller here. I saw him once before, the subject of a Juan artist, a portrait of his what hung back at the Academy's main hall. There, of course, a bit more Juan was painted into him. I preferred this rendition, a fur coat and a mandolin, a mass of duts playing about his feet and crawling over heavy fur-lined boots.

Looking over it to the mountains we saw a steep, muddy slope to the treeline.

There were two natural gorges, with one only that we could follow.

Here we let the horse go and took only a small amount of food. Little need now for more with what was coming behind us and to the east. It was here too I left Juletta and my quiver. I couldn't draw her true no more and the climb would be hard enough. I could barely do it I loved that bow so much.

Going was hard initially, I had to stop for breaks and holler him back. My guts were a bag of broken glass. After a few hours we were on a stone ridge and had breached the main skirt of trees that filled the gorge and the high slopes out to the plain we come from. The horse was grazing far below us, how an ant would now look at my feet. The going was less steep here but the stones were slick with frost like white stubble and treacherous underfoot.

Just as the ledge narrowed to nothing, we shook our heads for a moment fearing this was not the path. We saw another ridge above us, a short climb up the rock face. Shale give me a lift to get a hold and with a bellow I managed to get up there, a path barely a foot wide against the sheer rock. Shale climbed up swiftly and took the lead again but we were more pressed here, wind trying to pluck us away from the rock face and tip us down.

"Havin' fun, Gant?" he said with a chuckle. He knew I hated heights. The luta wasn't a help neither, for anything you looks at up close is just blurred-out shapes. We were away from the east side of the peaks now, our view being the immense ranges west to Mount Hope, a blue sky painful to look at, almost as fierce as the sun itself.

There were points where we turned into the rock face and just spread our arms to better keep on the broken lips of stone that had wore away with time. He kept telling me to calm my breathing, for I was panting like a dog in a desert. It grew wider again as it rose to and past a cave, a crack in the rock little bigger than a man. Shale had put a few torches together at the farmstead and lit one and threw it in. The gap was tight and it didn't go far but showed signs of being worked, a smaller hole further in with barely the gap to fit your body.

To get in the crack we needed to bend backwards and shuffle sideways. It was only eight yards but a struggle, the ridge of rock grazing our backs was cutting into my wamba as I squeezed along its edge. We couldn't fit with belts and such on so had to tie them to our legs and drag them behind us.

There was the sharp smell of bat shit and a rustling above my head as I dropped onto my hands and knees, up to my wrists in it and the roaches that lived on it. We put our belts back on and started crawling. It was warmer and dry further in, nothing about but whatever things brushed over my hands as I followed Shale.

Shale cussed a bit as he went, wondering when we'd get out, for the black of it was so much that, perhaps with all the luta we'd used, my eyes seemed to see shapes, the palest things dancing before me. It was hard then to know if it was real light ahead. Then we come to forks in the passageways and we cussed, for Valdir must've thought he'd be here to tell us this, having only told us how to get here.

More than a few times we didn't know if we'd make it out – easy to lose your way, go down the wrong path and die in the dark. Men on less plant wouldn't have made it, but we had a day brew that give us sense enough to taste the sweet air showing us one path or the other. We were some long hours in when Shale confirmed proper light, marking out a doorframe. There was cooler air now and the growing noise of winds beyond.

The door give with a modest tug and, battered by a far colder and stronger wind than was afflicting us earlier, we looked out and took in a view north and east. Ahead of us was an exposed ridge, to the right of us we could see Caragula's army on the plains below, a carpet of locusts blackening the ground, a smaller stream of which was going south to the lake by the looks of it.

"We got to move swift now, Gant. If Miri's town is ahead, that army'll be there and on 'em before we gets a chance to see 'im."

"If he's still there o' course."

"Aye, well, if he in't then we get out this way an' all an' figure out what's next, but if Valdir spoke true about it bein' his home, he in't goin' anywhere."

"He betrayed Valdir. How do we know he in't goin' to betray us anyway?" I said.

"We're doin' this fer Kailen, an' because Mirisham was as good to us as any in the Twenty, one we looked up to. He wronged Valdir for sure, but much as we looked out for that shit Bense, and for the same reason Valdir come along despite what happened wi' Mirisham, we owe Kailen, above it all. I don't need no more reason than that. Would've bin good to have this chat down on the plain though, eh, Gant?"

I laughed and threw him a punch.

"Worth it all fer this view," I said.

It was getting dark now. We pushed along the ridge, five hundred yards I've tried my best to put from my mind. There was a doorway the other end. I guess that either door were not visible to anyone but birds given how they were situated, and they protected the runs thus from the worst of storms.

The descent was steep enough that we needed Shale's torches to keep moving at a good pace and not fall over the stones and ridges that marked the work that was the least Mirisham's labourers could get away with.

At the bottom, a few hours later, it levelled out to a short but much wider passage ending in another door. It was blocked on the other side, moving a few inches before hitting what looked like some crates. Shale started banging the door itself against them, hard enough in the end they toppled in. We were in a basement room, the mortar was damp, the flagstones mossy. Around us were crates and a few steps up to a door which was locked. Someone's cellar, it must have been. From beyond we heard the sounds of shouting. The army must have begun an assault on the town.

We found a spade and Shale smashed open the door into a workshop, a big shop for carpenters. The shutters made it hard to see but now the screams were louder, chaos outside. There was a thump as a fireball hit a building nearby. The trebucks were finding their range. This was going to get ugly if they were after scorching the town flat.

"A carpenters's in't a good place ta be if another one lands on it," said Shale. "You ready?"

I nodded and Shale smashed at the lock, opening the door out to an alley. To our left there were people running our way from the fire what were roaring out of the row of houses nearby.

"Who the fuck are you?" A group of boys, no more than eighteen, twenty summers, is stood with jugs of ale and each armed with some sorry-looking blades and clubs. The tavern across from us was noisy with shouting; someone giving orders we couldn't see. A boy stepped up, his mates going quiet. "I said who are you?" The boys dropped their jugs and readied their weapons.

"We're mercs lad, Mirisham hired us. You know where he is?" asked Shale.

"Yer lying," said another. "Let's take them, lads." They were hesitating, our colour was obvious.

"Where'd you come from? There more of you?" said the first.

"A passage down in that cellar, and no. If you'd seen the fifty thousand about to break down your walls you'd get out now," I said.

"He's full of shit," said another lad as the mood turned against us, "and besides, this is our home, and we'll fight to our last with the mayor."

"Then you got more to worry about than two old men," I said, pointing up.

There were more fireballs coming over, each making a high and sort of peaceful arc, deceptively slow. It was like twenty stars falling.

We broke left from the workshop before the lads knew what to do and rounded a corner to where the first fireball hit. The smoke was thick about us. People were forming a line, I guess a well was near. More of the fireballs landed about. Pigs started screaming as one hit their sty, throwing its oil over them and the stable what were adjacent. We headed down the street, past the line of people waiting for the water buckets. Some woman was shouting for her girl and her husband what were trapped in one house as the thatch caught, another girl was crying for her da to get in for their dog, a moment before the roof give. I didn't give them more than a few moments such was the fire.

As we come to the end of that row of houses, I saw the well and some stalls in an open bit of road ahead, then I heard the roar of a fireball just as it hit the roof of a lumber shed to our right. I yelled at Shale, who dived in the door of the nearest house, kicking it shut as the oil from the ball exploded over the street about. Some people were caught and the smell of skin burning come indecently quick to us. A number of those trying to save their homes had been hit.

An old man and his daughter were crouched against the wall opposite us. She had a poker in her hand, her da a carving knife. He must've been a tanner by the smell of the place.

"Where's Mirisham?" asked Shale.

"Don't tell 'em," he said to her.

"We in't the enemy, they won't need to ask when they gets in," I said.

"Shush, fad," she said to him. "He's at the town hall most like. You help him, he's a good man." She pointed in the direction we needed as she said it.

I walked past her to open the door that was opposite to the one we entered, a stables ahead of us across the way, part of an inn and run where the animals were wildly smashing themselves at their fence to get away from the burning pitch. I heard a couple of men trying to get the horses out into the paddock, them kicking at the boards of the stables as its roof caught.

I stepped out, well was right of us, people arguing over where the next bucket went that was being hauled up by two men. "Head over past the well," I said, but Shale give me a shove. I stumbled forward and the feathers of an arrow whipped past my ear. I flapped my hands at where my bow should've been as I tried to rebalance and Shale was

367

there, bow drawn, facing back down this row of houses. He loosed an arrow and I saw Kigan some forty yards off. He moved fierce quick, twisting his body to let the arrow fly past him. I wouldn't make the cover of the stable.

"Took yer time!" shouted Shale.

Shale and Kigan both had arrows drawn and ready. As Shale shot I made a move and Kigan let fly at me, dropping to his knee as Shale's arrow come in at him, passing over his shoulder. I weren't so fast, no brew in me. I buckled as his arrow hit me shoulder. Shale shot again, again Kigan was too fast. As he nocked again to finish me off he was hit by something, a puff of smoke about his face. Then a man jumped from a roof near him I hadn't seen, strange straw hat and a gown, something that looked like a staff. A woman then come up behind us, a scimitar in her hand, dressed in a Post uniform I hadn't seen before, blood-red and dark blue jerkin, baggy cotton leggings and fully masked and brewed up.

"With me!" she said.

"Who are you?" said Shale as she pushed us out of the street, leading us to behind the stables. We saw briefly that Kigan and the other man with the staff were fully engaged, Kigan being given a tough time.

"Doesn't matter who I am, I just have to get you to Mirisham." She got the arrow out of me quick and slapped me about for the fuss I was making. All the while Shale was watching the other as he fought Kigan.

"You're Fieldsmen," he said. "Sillindar knows what Fieldsmen are doin' here. We're goin' to need the Honour, Gant. We should go after Kigan then, three of us, if yer as good as yer friend there." I swigged the Honour and Shale also took a slug. The woman with us tore off the shoulder of my wamba and jammed guaia in. Shale shooed her off and took over strapping my wamba back up.

"Orders are clear, we go to Mirisham."

The poison and the Honour hit me together. I must have passed out for a moment. I come to and both she and Shale are dragging me along the ground.

"Get me up!" I yelled. I was sick of feeling useless but the Honour was starting up and I was dreading what it would later do. At least it give me some strength.

They hauled me to my feet. My left arm was numb, useless.

We headed to the side of the inn, opposite the paddock.

"What's wrong with him, his stomach?"

"He's dyin'," said Shale. "Wound a few months back. It in't no good. Though it would be good to know yer name, as yer help is most welcome."

She hesitated for a split second. "Laun." Shale nodded and we clasped forearms with her.

I was on the rise now, nothing could withstand it. Shale's teeth were rattling, like he was freezing, all of us looking about for Kigan or the other one what went at him. There was a run of alleys ahead, across the street from us and going in the right direction to where the hall ought to be. A deep thump echoed over the houses as a ram went at the town's gates. The noise of the infantry beyond it grew with each run the ram made. At the same time then we heard it, felt the air, a hiss like a snake rearing up.

"Arrows! Get inside!" bellowed Shale at the people out in the streets, cruel advice given how Caragula had ordered the assault to burn the houses first. There was a slow recognition on those about us as we ran over the street, pointing them to stand against walls as we headed to the nearest alley and into another house, barely noticing the woman in there who give a scream as we did. The volley was vast and as it landed on the roofs and against the stone it sounded like the sea itself come crashing down on the town. Some weren't quick enough from the wailing we heard. They were quickly drowned out by the sound of the attack. The horns went up, filling the sky. The walls were being rushed.

"We need to get to the town hall," said Laun to the woman, stood in front of two children. "Quickest way?"

She took a breath, must've thought we were going to do for them. "You head up the alley, past the runs of the butcher there and you see the square. It's there."

A big cheer at the gate told us they were through with the ram, there could've been little resistance left.

Shale nodded he was ready so we opened the door and I stepped out, facing back to where Kigan had been.

The arrows were so thick on the ground our boots were cracking on them, a carpet of sticks across the mud.

369

As we moved out there was a shout ahead, militia were taking up positions near what looked like a mill, beyond the alley. We were spotted. Shale wasn't thinking, he just started shooting; they were in the way and we couldn't see Kigan, far the worse threat. Laun also started shooting. I put my mask on and put some bags out in the alley behind us as cover, giving them word to mask up. A few of the militia dropped, others were shooting back. They weren't trained, no brew, most of the arrows missed anyway. Now the smoke was about us from the limebags and the powders'll give Kigan pause. We ran at these men, though to say I was running would be to stretch it, and we could see the town square in the gap between the mill and the butchers, hundred or so yards off. There were about eight men, they charged in, it was dark enough I guess they didn't see our colour. As Shale leaped at them an arrow come from behind me and into the eye of Shale's target. I grabbed the nearest man as he come in, disarmed him and spun him. He took the second arrow for me. Another come in and grazed Laun, though her movement made it obvious she was trained thorough. Shale didn't need a warning after the first shot. He turned about, risen. In't no fear in him when he was risen.

Shale dodged the next arrow. Two more militia fell but the alley was thick with my smoke, these shots were coming out of nothing it seemed. The rest of them lost their flint as they saw their mates get cut down and they retreated into the mill.

Kigan walked out of the smoke, lowering his bow. Managed a good look at him now, only the one belt slung across his chest and over a shoulder, but he had the pockets and pouches about his tunic, travelling light for a drudha. He was wearing only cloth armour of some sort, or a fine enough leather it looked it. He'd shaved his head, like us, just a few lines of white stubble under which was a rich blue and red, not seen colouring the like: vivid, summer colours. His eyes were yellow, lit up by the fires about us, even through the wax he had over his face and mask. Whatever mix he was on, it grew him a fair bit, veins popping out on his neck and bare arms, again waxed with something that helped give him such colour, and patches of bark here and there what had grown into his skin, repairs for old wounds. He was fierce lean, like he was still twenty summers, trembling like a plucked lute string.

"Find another boy to shield you, Gant," he said. "Perhaps one old enough to have lost his fig this time."

The lumber shed by him was catching fierce now with the wood in it, cracking and booming as the pine and the oil barrels went up. He didn't flinch as the place collapsed yards from him.

"Who's first, boys? Shall I do Gant quickly? Or shall I kill the Fieldsman with you. The other one was clever enough with his staff for a while."

"Try me, Kigan, yer plant in't goin' to make the difference between us," said Shale.

"Shale, I see your sweat from here, the flicker of your eyes as you weigh up where best to engage me. I hear the sound of five men behind you hissing at each other to find some courage and jump the injured one. Eight children, three men and six women are crying within forty yards. A son is beating his father to death in that inn, the open shutter on the first floor lets me hear his dying words. You have nothing that can bring you square with me."

I got some bags out of my belt.

Kigan shook his head. "Gant, you were never the sharpest on the rack. You're as good as dead judging by the smell of you and the poison that's in you." The battle at the gates was getting closer, the metal clack of men in armour running into the streets, a host of voices shouting for surrender.

Shale looked over at me. He tore off his necklace what had the Flower of Fates in it.

"No!" I yelled. "No, Shale, you can flatten this cunt without it." It was more that I wanted some chance he should outlive me than that he could kill Kigan, more that I couldn't face being alone. I had no doubt he'd kill him, none till it began. I didn't see the point of him killing himself.

"I'm grateful for yer help, Laun, but I need you to get Gant into the town hall, find Mirisham."

"Laun is it? One season you're killing the Twenty, the next you're saving them. The Post is a fickle creature, isn't she?"

"What's he sayin', Laun?" said Shale, not taking his eyes from Kigan. "You need killin' too?"

She sheathed her sword and reached for my arm.

"I am no threat to either of you. You will find your answers in the town hall. Come with me."

"I'm goin' nowhere, friend," I said. "I can't be saved. You can see I'm dyin' and it'll be here with him. Get Mirisham safe, you don't want to be around if we're takin' our Flowers an' without your help might be Mirisham won't make it, and one of us must. It can't be for naught. If yer willin' to help us then help him."

I reached for my necklace, but it wasn't there. I looked over at Shale and he couldn't meet my eyes for a moment, then looked back at me, his now full of tears.

"Why, Shale, what the fuck, when did you take it?" And it must have been when they were dragging me after Kigan shot me, when he did my wamba.

Kigan strode forward. Laun looked at us, tried to grab me but I roared at her to go and she left, unchallenged by the militia. Now I could see Kigan was shining and ready.

"I'm sorry I din't get you home, Gant," said Shale. "I hoped I would. But we were never goin' to do him on the Honour alone an' you in't in a fit state to help. Now get out o' here somehow, get home, an' speak well o' me." He give me a smile and it said all the rest to me that he might have said. He'd weighed his chances up against Kigan of course, there was little of the gambler in him. The Flower of Fates was a soldier's way to go out. There was nobody in the known world could stop Shale on the Flower.

He took it out of the tube, a small thing, its four petals unfurling in a riot of reds, oranges and purple, the stem black. Then he ate it, so he was set.

Kigan shook his head. "It seems it really will end here. I would have killed you more quickly than the Flower, but it's your choice."

Kigan rushed us, a mighty leap from where he stood that had him on us in a moment. Shale met the first blow and returned it, but Kigan was indeed fast. Both jumped at each other, looking for a short violent end to it, but neither was able to outmove the other.

Kigan's poison was seeping through me, I struggled to move and find a way to help.

I could see that Shale was moving him away from the square, rarely conceding initiative from the stances due to his stronger technique.

Gradually they moved back to the cluster of alleys that we come out of. Shale was visibly shaking as he tried to manage Kigan's ferocity and the Flower's claim, building as it was on the Honour. Kigan was simply that bit quicker, for the time it took the Flower to get hold, catching Shale in his side, again on his face, a vicious welt, other cuts slicing at his wamba. Shale give little back. What advantage he gained from his technique and guile was pressed back with Kigan's speed and strength. The plant he was on was an order above anything in use in the Old Kingdoms, but the Flower recognises no poison, and so that at least wouldn't be a concern for him. Each clash of blades and bodies would've broke lesser men apart. Then Shale managed a kick using Kigan's own momentum that sent him flying some fifteen feet back, the Flower now finally into him. Kigan was back up in a moment as Shale leaped in to strike, a feint from a near impossible position off balance, and it was Shale that got thrown at a wall so hard the mortar cracked. I give nothing for the honour of a duel, fuck that. I was aiming to find a way in myself, to do something would throw Kigan off, but I was hobbling, struggling to land caltrops or disrupt Kigan's movement without that it would hurt Shale somehow. Truth was they were fighting on a level beyond what I witnessed even with Kailen, a speed of body that was close to matching the instant of thought and stratagem.

A shouting come up behind me. There were men, I think the last of the town's militia, coming back this way to defend the town hall. A couple come at me, seeing me injured. Some men emerged from the mill, they told the militia to back off, knowing it was death. One didn't and with the Honour strong enough I ripped him open in moments, sending pieces of him flying yards about. My eyes were going in the dark about, the fires blinding me as they were getting more intense. I was losing grip of my senses. A group of the militia then rushed at Shale and Kigan, thinking they'd close them off in the alley. It seemed as though they paid no direct mind to the militia as they continued their own duel. As they come in they were dealt with, each who got close enough was battered by blows they had no hope of countering. I put some bags down around us to ward them off, and as the dust rose they scattered.

Shale was moving to a smith's workshop, which was burning. He must have seen some advantage in it, something that must be affecting Kigan though there was little to notice even on the Honour. Their movement, each adjustment to balance and weight, anticipated multiple counters, as though they were each fighting off multiple enemies. The blades were exchanging nicks and sparking so much that it was hard to see, but the Honour in my eyes, enraptured by what played out, seemed to reveal each moment of their engagement, each possible outcome of a maneuver becoming real as my mind caught up with reading their fight, like many Kigans and Shales were fighting each other in the same instant.

Kigan was working harder now though, a thrust hit, slicing his leg, but he slid in through it, a calculated risk to drive his fist at Shale's throat, a blow that would've felled a bull had Shale not dropped to the side of his foot, balancing in a way I scarcely thought possible, to land rapid blows to Kigan's ribs. With a kick Kigan was away from him, under the eaves of the burning joists of the blacksmith's outhouse.

Kigan got a blow in that took Shale's sword out of his hand. He dodged the kick Shale aimed at his head but the dodge put him also in reach of a spear stood on a rack. He took it and closed on Shale, using it and the sword to force Shale back. Some slates fell in then as the joists give a bit. Shale took two slates in mid-fall, throwing each at Kigan, who parried them, in the moment of which Shale snatched at a knife and shield, using the shield to drive an advantage again, trying to force Kigan into the smith's living quarter, which was aflame. The spear was soon useless as Kigan fought in the doorway, but he still got another cut to Shale's arm as he took advantage of another moment he was out of position.

Shale was bleeding more than he should've on the Honour, Kigan was bleeding a little, the thigh the main cut. His poison was ignoring the Honour's hemlock bark that thickened the blood and made it scab quicker. Seemed that for all the potency of the Flower, Kigan had something in his paste even for that.

Shale threw the shield and pushed Kigan into the room. They were lost to me for a moment, fire and smoke pouring out of the shutters next to the doorway. It was Shale that come flying out of the shutters to the side of the house, his leather smoking and his skin burned a bit. The spear followed. Shale must've seen it for he somehow jumped his body from the ground and the spear flew beneath him. Kigan leaped after him but Shale was crouched in stance. Kigan stopped, took a breath, dousing his sword with the poison in his scabbard. Shale took some wood from a bit of shutter what flew out with him that was smouldering and pressed it on his cuts. The Flower was strong, he was almost lit up with it, a steam rising off him like you saw on a horse'd been galloping. The pain didn't register as he seared his cuts up. I saw he didn't have his sword so threw him mine.

Kigan took pause, was about to say something, but as soon as I realised he was hoping to buy some moments knowing Shale was starting to lose himself, Shale was back at him, knowing the same. I didn't see him yell or rage at Kigan, he was everything Kailen taught us to be, working the enemy into positions he could make cuts. Once, twice he cut Kigan with the knife, the sword used as a distraction. Kigan was more passive, counting on the moments between each engagement and stance to have the Flower win it for him. Shale kept on, his aggression scoring more and more, though it was at the cost of blows and cuts to him. They didn't matter and Kigan knew it, he was caught between taking the fight to Shale to get the most of his speed and strength on his plant, or slowing it down to bring the Flower's consumption of Shale more into the reckoning, at the cost of Shale having the initiative.

Fire arrows come flying down the street. I turned to see soldiers and the town's militia clashing at the far end of the main avenue that went through the town to the gates. Soldiers were putting these arrows into the mill to get it started and into houses and workshops to drive out those hiding. A number come running, twenty or thirty that kicked in doors and were bellowing at the people inside, others marshalling groups of people what had surrendered. A number of them come over and I put down more powders and caltrops, mixing with the haze of the smoking oil what was fogging the town. My noisies were pounding at my head, I was sick with the Honour in my guts, I knew I couldn't fight them. I turned back to Shale and Kigan. The smithy was burning fierce and the roof had now collapsed. Kigan had just put Shale off balance, his sword getting an inch or two into Shale's side as he span off it. Kigan used this moment to run for the smithy. There was a large roofbeam that had part collapsed. He danced up it through the fire to the remaining bit of roof, leaping over to the next building. Shale was after him, a few steps behind. I guessed Kigan thought the slope and the unsure footing of those tiles would give him the advantage.

I could do little but watch. I held my guts as they cramped and give me grief. Above me the two kept at it, both measuring the inches they had to tease the advantage and make a decisive move. Shale got into dagger distance, under Kigan's high guard, and got its point into his shoulder. Kigan smashed Shale's nose open with the pommel of his blade as he brought his fist across. Shale's footing give a split, but he was audacious in dropping forward and threw his weight from his standing leg and barged Kigan across the gap of the roofs and onto his back on the next house. Ki's knee took Shale's weight and lifted him off, giving him leverage to beat him further, three rapid punches, and I heard Shale's jaw crack from where I was stood. Shale then stuck the knife into Kigan's side and twisted it about. Kigan twisted himself over and they rolled down the roof, clattering down the tiles and off onto the ground. Shale landed and moved away to get into a crouch. Then he clutched his head and cried out. He was breathing hard, drooling some, blinking.

"So it ends, Shale," said Kigan, pressing a paste into his stab wound. Kigan was in a state himself, his skin dark with blood, his leathers glistened with it. Both stood swaying like drunks.

About us I heard a final clash of the militia and Caragula's infantry. I was at the edge of the alley and I was shivering, Kigan's poison playing havoc. My one eye was fuzzy, I was going blind in it. The guaia was helping but the poison was spreading, one of those that paralysed.

Shale stood up, trembling. The Flower's effect would keep getting stronger till the body couldn't take it and collapsed. He looked over at me. A nod for his farewell. His leap into Kigan was decisive. It come from no obvious readying of his limbs. He covered the eight or so feet as though thrown from a trebuck himself. Kigan was backed to a wall as Shale attacked with a speed and power that was unnatural, his joints cracking with the frenzied blows. Kigan moved as he could but had no way to adjust his feet or balance with the wall at his back. Then he managed to counter a blow, spinning a parry to take it over his head, Shale's sword breaking against the stone. Kigan stabbed his blade into Shale's chest. But with his sword arm now free, ignoring this mortal blow, Shale took hold of Kigan's throat and brought his knife again into Kigan's side, four stabs almost too quick to see. Shale inched forward, the knife held in Kigan to steady himself as he pushed himself into the sword in his chest. Kigan did his best to push him off but the knife decided it. Shale's headbutt smashed Kigan's eye socket flat.

It was over. For a few still moments both men were locked together by the blades they had stuck each other with. Shale's head was bowed at Kigan's chin. He still twitched. It was Kigan then that moved, pushing Shale back off his sword and gasping as the knife come out of him. Shale fell.

I tried to stand, keeping him in the focus of my good eye. Kigan was quick at putting some bark in the biggest of the knife wounds, spreading on something that seared his skin, hissing at the blood and clogging it up as it bubbled out. I hobbled over to where he stood.

He held his side, shuddering. I looked at him up close, the yellow of his eyes shining bright against the blood and mud he was slick with. His brew was making its claim, he was fighting to control it as he dropped. He shook his head at me. I wasn't sure if it was a warning or him just saying he didn't want to kill me. He tried to raise his sword but had no strength; it quavered before the tip dropped to the ground. I tried to swing for him, but the pain of it caught me, and he ducked out of the way of it and hit me back, knocking me over.

Without my sword, almost too faint to stand, I could only watch him leave us, limping out of the alley over to the butchers and the town square beyond.

I got to my knees to look at Shale. He wasn't right; his face, the muscles maybe, were misshapen, still a fever on him, like he was about to start burning from inside out. I took his hand, hot enough it somehow made it worse. Though dead, he was still warmer than me.

How do words in a few lines like this go over a life with any force or true reckoning? A whole other life we had outside of what I've managed to write in this journal, beginning as it does at the end for us both.

To say a good friend and brother he was for forty summers would be the lip of it. Anyone who knew anyone they loved for forty summers, kneeling with them as I was now, would know the recalling of what bound them, how swift and subtle those memories rushed in and by. I remembered us as fifteen summers first meeting as we shared mats in the Academy. He was of a dry humour then, we both were, somehow brighter and happier I guess before the fightbrews changed us. I remembered us holding each other while the first fightbrew we took give us such terrors and agony in our bodies we thought we'd die. All those years since I can see him in those moments when I stood at the end of a battle hoping he didn't fall, and the joy to catch sight of him stood over the wrecked and steaming bodies on the field, raising his sword to me each time, to which I'd reply. I remembers too being stood at his side at Tharos as that horde come at us, all my brothers with me and the one I loved most, ready to work through them with me, a calm on him like he was watching some sunset, not the end of the world. He give me the belief we would see it through the crossroad. I find it hard to remember a time when he wasn't with me, making us a pipe or a fire when on the trails, or mending my wamba, for he was fine with a needle.

I can't get at these feelings with this quill. I just wish he was here now that's all, holding my hand in my dying days.

Buildings had caught all around the alleys and a cluster what belonged to the guilds along the edge of the town square were also burning. It was an amber smoke, lit by the burning town, that hid me as I passed through some chicken runs and some grain stores to the square. A hundred or so people were gathered there, some militia among them. It was hard to make Kigan out, a shadow flickering, walking unchallenged between two of the militia stood at the town hall itself. He had dropped his fieldbelt before them.

As it got clearer on my approach I saw the town hall was still unharmed, a building after the Citadels style, plainly cut from large and fine blocks of stone, some rough-hewn pillars supporting the roof that reached out to cover a raised platform at the entrance, steps up to it on all sides. The doors were grand enough, fifteen feet tall, one partly open. The militia stepped forward as I approached. It was clear to them I wasn't trouble.

"I know Mirisham," I said, "Kailen's Twenty."

The lad there, soot covered and face streaked with the tears of some tragedy he'd just seen, nodded at me. He was about to indicate Kigan in respect of the Twenty but I gestured it was unnecessary.

"Have my knife and my belt," I said. "I means him no harm." I struggled not to slur, I couldn't feel my face, tongue was stinging and it was hard to swallow. I dropped my belt on the ground.

I felt my legs give and he stepped forward to take my arm and bring me upright. It was an effort to walk with the poison deadening me. Thankfully it took some of the pain out of my belly too.

"Tell him his people need him," said the boy after me, once he'd helped me up them steps.

As I entered the hall two were fleeing, a heavy voice bellowing after them. One had Post robes on. I realised the voice was Mirisham's. He was a mountain-caller as a boy, had a bit of the horse-singer about him. His voice could shake you through if he chose to sing.

The space between rows of benches that was normally reserved for those facing court was full of tables, covered in maps. About the floor and on the benches were huge bronze candle stands, their light a small orange pool only in the middle of this huge hall.

Kigan was leaning on one of the benches, shuddering with the effort. Mirisham come to him from the tables. He caught Kigan as he was about to give way and fall. Kigan's sword was on the floor. There'd been no struggle and it didn't look like a subterfuge either. Mirisham looked up at me, then he looked back across to a figure dim in the candlelight.

"Kailen, get his other arm, let's sit him down." Kailen? The man himself come out of the shadows there, like a ghost in a player's tale. I couldn't believe it. Kigan too stopped at this and looked up. Behind Kailen was Laun, but she didn't move.

"Kailen, let's sit him down."

"Kailen!" I shouted. "Kill him! Kill that fucker what just killed Shale in the street, or I will."

He looked at us both and shook his head before going over to help Kigan sit at a bench.

"He's dying, Gant, we don't need to hasten his death, least of all I don't. I want it to last, and you can barely stand anyway. Sit with me, we'll watch him die together."

He nodded to Laun, who come over to me then and helped me to a seat near the tables, opposite Kigan. Right then I didn't think I was getting out of that hall, I had a fever starting and I was getting a bit spasmic.

"Heard you died, Kailen. I were sorry fer it too, Shale were an' all. We come to the Crag when you summoned us, quick as we could." I stopped, thinking of what had happened the last few days, my last words with Valdir, and Shale just then. "I'm glad to see you alive all these years since Argir, fierce glad," I said.

Kailen sat next to me, heavily, a burden on him. Still, he put his arm about me and touched his head to mine, pleased to see me. Then he gestured over to Kigan, what were slumped next to Mirisham, blood dripping to the floor from where he sat.

"Kigan tried and failed to kill me. I took a mix that made me seem dead and it worked. But while it saved my life it cost my wife hers and all I've built since being a mercenary. What do you say, Kigan?"

"She was a broken-up bag of meat at the end, when Alon's guards had finished with her," Kigan leered.

"Not Araliah," I said, and I looked at him, fierce sorry for it. "She saved us; Achi and Stimmy and your boys come and . . . look, just fuckin' end him, Kailen." He'd balled his fist but his self-control took over, the calm he could put on that was what made him the difference for all those years among the leaders of mercenary crews. He put his hand on mine then.

"Achi's crew . . . They were good boys." He was quiet a moment, staring at Kigan, who was struggling now, fumbling uselessly about the pockets on his tunic for plant to help himself. "But look at you, Gant. Still a strong colour, taking purses all these years. I'm sorry for Shale and so help me you look done too. I'm sorry all this came to pass as it did. I only tried to warn you and keep you safe. Now you're all dead."

"You got nothing to be sorry over either, for we'd have done no different than come at your call, me, Shale and Valdir. I know you wants him to suffer, but just stick him an' be done with it. I don't care for his sufferin' for it won't ease mine, but I still want to see it before I'm dead meself."

"Shale's killed me, Gant, I'll die soon enough," said Kigan. A pool of blood, for all his drudhaic work, was dribbling into a crack in the stone tiles of the floor by his boot.

"I didn't know if I would see you or Shale here," said Kailen. "I put these Agents I hired out to look for Kigan, but I needed to stay here with Mirisham in case he got through. If I had any idea you were out there I would have come. Valdir didn't make it?"

"No, Kigan killed him an' all, in a valley a few days south, along with yer man Achi an' yer crew what Araliah sent after us, thank her."

He closed his eyes and had a deep breath. When he opened them they were full.

"You took everything from me, Kailen. I've taken everything from you." Kigan coughed and spat some blood on the stone at his feet.

I hadn't seen Kailen in so long and like Kigan he looked somehow younger and better than he had a right to. He was in leathers, full belt. His hair he kept the same way as he always had, close cut, plain, and it was still dark, which was a surprise. Mirisham sat with Kigan across from us. He'd eaten well over the years, chest and belly like one big barrel. His hair had grown long, streaked through with grey and the big round nose still commanded his face despite his neck and cheeks filling out like a squirrel's.

"Kailen here told me that you, Kigan, could not be dissuaded from looking for me, no doubt bent on revenge, while you, Gant, have a bounty on you a king would trade his kingdom for, killing a bunch of Reds in Issana I hear, then more in Jua near Cusston. The Post isn't what it used to be, eh Kailen, but you'd know better than me."

"We din't get so soft as you all these years, Miri," I said. He ignored me. I was bitter, and didn't feel much like talking.

"What happened out there?" said Kailen to me.

"Are you going to tell them?" said Mirisham, looking at him. Kailen was assessing me, seeing how bad I was, and he give a stern look to Mirisham regarding whatever his question was about.

"Shale took the Flower o' Fates," I said. "Seems Kigan's got plant beyond any of us now an' Shale made the odds an' did what he had to do. If yer Agent had a straw hat an' fighting staff, he's dead too. Laun, she helped us but we shoo'd her in here to look out for Mirisham, for I din't know you'd be here." Word of the manner of Shale's death had given Kailen pause.

"Been many winters since I saw a man use the Flower. You became a remarkable drudha in the Hanwoq, Kigan, and a finer sword than I had known if Shale, on both the Honour and with a Flower of Fates, could only kill you at the cost of his own life."

"Had that army of Caragula's been his target, I daresay he'd be waist high at the gates now and drawing them on," said Kigan, though not meaning to make much of his own skill by saying it.

"Your mistake was not killin' him when you had the chance, Kailen, back in Snakewood. That's what Valdir said an' it's true as we sit here," I said. "You fucked up, you an' Miri an' The Prince, sparing his life an' now we're all dead more or less."

"Do you have a command under this Caragula then, Kigan?" asked Mirisham.

Kigan shook his head. "Petir does. Do you remember the name?"

"Indeed, your seeking me could only have been revenge for what we did to you. Remarkable that that spoiled boy lived to become a captain of Caragula'."

Kigan looked up. "Not a boy any more. We both came back to end you."

"Well, I'm not going to sit here and wish it could all have been different. I didn't care for you enough then or since. You were a vicious, self-interested bastard." He said it with enough conviction, but his shoulders dropped a little then. He rubbed tired eyes before folding his arms on top of his firm belly.

"Valdir told me some of it before he died," said Kigan. "How you, him, Moadd, The Prince and Kailen all stole what was the children's, betrayed the purse. What did you do with it all?" he asked, adjusting how he sat from some sharp pain he must've felt. His voice was thick with muke in his throat.

"It burns all around us, it lies dying or dead in the streets, it is rounded up for captivity by the horde outside and it stands afraid in the square, waiting for me to offer its surrender to this wild pig that covets the sty of the Old Kingdoms. It's a fine irony that Petir is looking to revenge the theft of his heirlooms and yet is in the midst of destroying what they built."

Mirisham stood and went to one of the tables on which were unrolled maps and other documents. He took something, a book or a box maybe, hidden in some oilcloth.

"I know what you've become, Kailen, but I never spoke to you since we split up all those years ago, not until I got your letter. You may remember that I hailed from the mountain people who lived here, in the passes and the plains about, surviving off the edges of Issana and Vilmor and Jua. You decided it was over for the Twenty as the guilds had decided of King Doran, all those winters back. Fifteen fucking gold pieces and little but more bloodshed waiting, unless I wanted to eke out that purse in a slum for the twenty winters I thought I might have had left.

"You, Kigan, were sitting there with us in Snakewood, on top of thousands of gold pieces tied up in that treasure. I thought of the hasts I grew up in; the brothers and sisters of mine still in the Aldenvale here, but hunted as slaves or else thieves when the want of food was their only crime." He sat back down again, facing us, the thing he had he covered with his hands.

"As a child I listened to my grandda, never tired of it. He told me of the Sixway, the old routes of the mountainers that run through from the vales hereabouts across to Mount Hope and from there of course down to the Sar itself.

"Bandits run out our hasts, gangers that did too for the Post. The Post made its name for making the Sixway viable, doing what the kings and guilds about could not. The Post used to stand for something brave and good, wearing the Red every boy's dream. Well, Mount Hope was exporting heavily with the routes east and west open, but this just drew the mobs in. They thrived and soon grew in number, which we suffered for. I remember my da, he got me up by my scruff, my legs dangling, held me up with a single arm, kissing my cheek and that of my ma. It was an ambush our hast had planned, fighting for the valleys and hills we'd grown up on. He didn't come back. Ma sent me away when I started learning to fight with whoever I didn't care for and the pits became a good place for a boy to work out his rage.

"Hast Fathin, my hast, these people, I visited once or twice in the Twenty. Gave what I could but they lived like animals, dressed in skins and sunk fully, as is the way, with the view that it was all they deserved."

"So you reclaimed the Sixways," I said, "hires a crew with your bit of that wealth and goes on a spree and brings your people home."

"I did, and this is Fathin, home to mine and those other hasts that were dispossessed of their old lands. This is what Doran's gold built; good commerce, a livelihood for hundreds of men and women, craftsmen and merchants. Trade builds on itself and those in the farmsteads about themselves thrived with supplying this citadel. Despite what then happened with the Post coming in having learned I was one of those that had taken Argir's wealth, I stayed, because as long as I had paid out, and I was alive, my people were what mattered. I'm sorry for Valdir, wasn't anyone but the Post's fault, but they kept their word. Tell me young Petir would have done as much, for as many."

Kigan spat some more bloodied muke on the flagstones before Mirisham. "Glad you felt ours was a price worth paying. What did my life compare after all, the suffering visited on me? I can't say I'd have given a shit for your hasts, Mirisham, but I would not have betrayed you."

"Tell yourself that, Kigan, if it helps you die straight."

"We all paid the price, Miri, Kigan killed us all to get to you an' Kailen," I said. I turned to him then. "I expect you killed all the rest of us?"

He shook his head, a quiver of something like amusement across his face. "The ephedra and the Droop took my memories, just pieces came back to me all these years. I recovered a memory only recently of most of you being there with me in Snakewood. Most of you knew what Kailen, Mirisham and the others had planned and you did nothing. I didn't, for a long time, know it was these that had sold me into slavery, not until I found Milu, Kheld and Digs. I could not afford any of them warning you, less still let them live for their part of it. Everything had been taken from me. I was saved only by Lorom Haluim, saved as somehow Galathia was from her awful trials after Snakewood, and it was she that killed the rest, her own revenge on you in accord with mine. All of you are killed or dead except for we who are sat here, about to die ourselves."

"You spoke of Lorom Haluim, the magist?" said Mirisham. "You are

384

one of those worshippers that hold to some set of sayings or way of life?"

"No, he saved my life in the Hanwoq jungle. It was by his plant that I gained the strength to pay you back."

"He speaks truly, Mirisham," said Kailen. "I recently read an account of his time there. His recipe book will now be the envy of all the world, as it is the cause of the end of ours."

Kigan was about to say something to that, as if there was some import in it. And I wasn't aware of what that was until afterwards. Hearing that Kigan had met with a magist was incredible, almost a trick, but it was a strong explanation for his plant.

Mirisham took a moment to consider what Kigan had just said. Some part of him probably didn't think it was more than a tale.

"So if you had the secrets of a magist's plant, how is it your poison hasn't yet killed Gant?" he asked.

"He was wounded before I found him in the streets outside. I would have said he got it at the vineyard, but it smells like a special Blackhand."

"Crossroads job," I said. "Blackhand sauce, a few weeks before we got word from Kailen the Twenty were bein' killed. Din't get me guaia in it an' now the skin's dead an' me inside's a mess your poison is finishing."

Kigan nodded. "Shale did for me before I could get to you. He was the threat, not you." He give a hiss then, coughing, his breathing a watery rattling now. He looked me up and down. "If the special's in that deep you've got little chance. I've got something here though, in this pocket, blue tube. Mix a thumb's worth with some boiled water and flush out your wound, then drink the same till it's gone. Of course, I see no reason to give it to you."

It was so quiet then for a moment that only the spitting candlewax could be heard, the fighting outside done. Like Kailen I had a moment where I'd have put my last breath behind a knife in his throat, but it passed quick with a flush of pain that I nearly passed out from.

"Your father would have thought differently, Kigan," said Mirisham. "For him, plant was an ease for the sick and dying, not a weapon, not withheld for revenge."

"What could you know of him?"

Mirisham placed the object that was in his hands on his knees and he unwrapped the oilskin. It was Kigan's old recipe book, taken from him at Snakewood. We'd all seen so much of it those years we'd been together. He give it to Kigan.

"Your father never used a cyca to hide what was written, he never kept his recipes a secret from others. It saved a lot of lives, your recipe book, for that reason. In your father's hand we read only cures and plant to ease pain and put things right. So much of that book that is by your hand is poisons. Perhaps if all you drudhas were like your father there'd be a lot less suffering in the world."

Kigan held the small pigskin-bound volume gently, running quivering fingers over the stained skin, the colour of mottled wood. He opened it at the first page and gasped. I couldn't see much in the light; drawings and sketches, some were beautiful renderings of flowers and their roots, others seemed to be simpler drawings, a child's, all squeezed around faint writing crammed onto the leaves. It was the book of his lifetime as a drudha.

"Her name was Ilina," he said. "Ilina." He was lit up, tears filled his eyes. He was remembering it all, like the memories were real enough to shake him in his seat, and he addressed us then, all around us and what was happening forgotten, as though it was still years ago and we were sitting telling stories as we often did, though he struggled to tell us with his weeping. "She was my sister. She fell from a dry-stone wall we would play on, hit her head on a stone and it was bleeding fiercely. She was still, wouldn't wake. I ran down the hill behind the rooms we stayed at, Vargas Lane. And the hill was Speaker's Hill, yes, Speaker's Hill. We all used to play up there in the foundations of that gatehouse to the old fort. I ran for him to come, he . . . I can see him now . . . he ran, he was brown and scarred, he'd been washing himself in the barrel, my da. He had his belt in his hand and he took quick, mighty strides, left me behind. Some others were there, but when I got there he had taken her head and got an ambin out from his belt, squeezed out its juice, which stopped her bleeding, and then it was a simple kannab leaf, then another. He'd kept them in a solution of black bistort, it's here on this page. And then he put a pinch of euca over her nose and she opened her eyes shortly after and held up her arms to him, as though she knew all along it would be fine, because he was there, this big smile on them both as he lifted her up and spun her round, the boys and girls around me cheering him and joining in because when he was off the ships he was always good to them with limey sticks and apples. They all loved him. I held her hand as we walked back to our rooms, wondering what it felt like to save a life like that, how it must fill your heart up to see people get well because of something you did. The rest of this book we wrote together."

He forgot us for a time, lost in his da's book and the discovering of his old life what he must have forgotten in the years since we last saw him, and what the ephedra must have took from him.

Some men come in then and said a captain was there to talk about Mirisham meeting Caragula. Mirisham thanked them and bid them leave.

He stood again and straightened himself, though one hip wasn't allowing him his full bearing. He took a cloak from a bench behind him, some gold needlework in it from the looks, a judge's cloak. Kailen stood with him.

"You did more for your people than any man. Hast Fathin will survive, Miri," he said. "I came to get you out, brother, to try and save your life. I would still do it if I could. I know you have a secret way, from this hall."

"I don't think so, Kailen, for either myself or Hast Fathin. If Petir heads this army then I had better die with some dignity out there. I can offer him nothing that would save the lives of my people except my own. It'll be good to die for something more than a purse, eh?"

They embraced, then Miri straightened himself and Kailen helped him with his sleeve buttons, for he had them folded up.

"There's an old slenka in my quarters you can take Gant out on, you and your Agent. You can take the secret way." He pointed away to a dark corner. "From this chamber and down through the hill behind us is a passage hewn to join an underpass that mountainers had carved out a hundred or more summers ago. I expect Kigan's plant will give you time enough, Gant. I shall encourage Caragula to demonstrate at length his greatness and so do what I can for your escape." He kneeled then before Kigan, whose head was bowed and didn't look up at him. "I'll see you buried, Kigan, with Shale, unless it matters to Gant." I shook my head to say it did not, for there was no getting him home to his people. He looked back at Kigan then, who hadn't moved. Mirisham looked at us both, me and Kailen, and give a nod, his hand scratching Kigan's head, somewhat fondly. Hard to say why at that moment it was right. He was dead, Kigan, died there with a last memory of his da, a memory of love, of all things. Mirisham moved past the table to the bench I was still sat on.

"For many golden years we fought side by side and that should not be forgotten, for what do they sing of us mercenaries, those that, not being of us, could not understand us?

> With gold in place of pride or blood
> No honour's vow nor noble good
> No song shall long their deeds proclaim
> Their sacrifices all in vain."

He dropped into my lap the blue flask that Kigan said would help me, kissed my head and clasped my arm in farewell as he passed outside, whistling the tune what went with those words.

Tharos Falls

When twenty men held the line, and the line could not be crossed.

Kailen

It was said we saved the Old Kingdoms that day. Were they worth saving? At the time I cared far less about the answer than I do now. The Virates, the southern islands and the Redwall sent armies north to fortify their borders to the Red Hills and they sent navies across the Gulf of Merea to invade Cassica, all because the Old Kingdoms had been exploiting them so hard and for so long that they snapped. Plant, slaves, gold and steel left those lands under the heel of Old Kingdoms factories, protected by their own navies and their superior brews. It was centuries of exploitation, yet the Old Kingdoms were deaf all the while to their pleas for help against the Wildmen. This drove them into a union for the first time in their histories, for civil unrest was spreading and it would only encourage the Old Kingdoms to exact even more punitive contracts to reduce their risk. Enough was enough.

A war council was formed, but, crucially, was manned by a number of truly great generals and sea lords. They secured the Hiscan Road at their borders, stopping all caravans. In the southern islands they amassed a large navy in secret and launched an assault both on Cassica, the far side of the Gulf, and then raids across the Gulf itself.

When I came to hear of all this, it was obvious to me that if the Virates meant to control the Gulf, the Old Kingdoms would have a big problem. Word then spread regarding the invasion of Cassica, and that's when I became really interested. If they took hold of Cassica, and could push into Rhosidia, a much larger and richer neighbour, the Virates could start controlling the Sar, and the world order as it stood could very well end.

So, we sought a purse in Rhosidia, because of its superiority as a force, at least by my reckoning, as well as a chance for a free run at pillaging in such a plant-rich land as Cassica, a great opportunity to make a fortune and give Kigan and Ibsey a chance to develop further our recipes.

With the welcome the Cassicans gave the Virates army – they too had long been exploited by the Old Kingdoms – their land was quickly taken and at little cost, which had a direct bearing on what happened at Tharos Falls. We went south to the Cassican border with the Rhosidian army.

The border to Cassica was mountainous, and with haste being a paramount concern – in order to destabilise the Virates forces before they could significantly fortify and reinforce – the Tharos Valley and Falls were the main and quickest path when going between the lands and was thus the Rhosidians' only option.

The Rhosidian general, General Urutz, gambled on the Virates army not having had time to fortify the border around the valley. His scouts passed out into the plain beyond the immense waterfalls and reported no sign of the Virates forces. He ordered his own forces through in order to make good the valley for the Rhosidians and from there move on south to the interior of Cassica.

The Virates warmaster, Warmaster Jaon, had, of course, prepared a trap. Its ingredients were exquisite: a local populace either vanished or up to the subterfuge that nothing was amiss, giving our scouts no immediate cause for concern; a far larger force of cavalry than Urutz and even I could have anticipated, many times larger than Rhosidia's own; and quantities of strykna, a very potent poison, I would have thought impossible to acquire, much less bring to bear in its purest form on this battlefield.

Jaon knew exactly what he was doing. He deserved victory and would have achieved it but for the quality of the Twenty, and in particular, the inaugural use of the Honour.

We were in the van, with Urutz and about four hundred men. He took the idea of leading literally.

Jaon waited for us to pass into the plain, our infantry following in a column, some eleven thousand men and women, with a thousand horse at the rear, for much of Cassica was jungle, and not amenable (all the more remarkable and astute on Jaon's part, for what followed relied heavily on his own massed cavalry).

By letting most of the column through, there would be too many men to retreat into the valley should we get flanked. The roar of the hooves in the hillsides about gave the Rhosidians little time, and we were duly flanked both left and right, the Virates cavalry coming in near the Falls and the mouth of the pass behind us, cutting the column off, leaving many thousands of us out in the plain and most of our own cavalry stuck in the pass, unable to form up. The horns blew and Urutz started commanding those about us. His value as a ransom was huge, so he needed the protection of his main force, not to mention lead it, which he couldn't do at the front of the assault, for I knew full well as the horses rode in behind us at the column that the next assault would be at us in the van, their hope being to create a pincer, front and rear, crushing us between them. I wasted valuable time persuading him to leave, but kept his bannermen with us to trick Jaon into thinking he remained in the van. At some point later I found out he had been killed, but perhaps his influence was enough to have made some small difference that would ultimately count for us.

Gant

Kailen saw the danger to our general and he had words with his captains to get the general to fuck off back to his main force and give them some order and leadership, and to try and repel the horse that come in at the flanks behind us.

We were disorganised from being in a column, none of us on brews barring a few scouts on dayers, so time was wasted with getting brews and mixes down.

Soon as the flanking was happening we saw on the ridge ahead of us that sickening sight of even more horse, which started then pouring down at us, for we were in a bit of land not unlike a plate, its edges raised up all around a bit. This was the cleverness of their own general, this many horse where we didn't expect it. They come straight at us of course, so's the column would split at the front I'm guessing, and in so doing smash us apart and rout us.

"Ibsey! Kigan!" shouted Kailen. "Get that brew out you've been working on, get it round the boys and give what's left to anyone willing to take a swig. If it's as good as you say we're going to need it!"

Because our plant was better and more valuable than most we kept it on a couple of packhorses that come with us, so it was all in the van. Ibsey went for the packs to get the flasks out.

"We got a replacement for Liberation Jack?" said Elimar. "Do we know it won't kill us, Kigan? You tested it on any kids yet?"

Kigan walked over to him with a flask and threw it at him. "Take a good slug and pass it around, you mouthy cunt, you should be fucking honoured."

"Oh, boys, Kigan's telling us now it's an honour to drink his and Ibsey's new brew." He wasn't stupid though, Elimar, he knew it would be good, he just didn't get on with Kigan.

"Quick about it!" roared Kailen as we heard their shouting and horns. "Sheltron! Spears Fore!" By sheltron he meant infantry forming into a square, archers in the middle of it being protected as they got their arrowbags out into any oppo advancing on us. I got a big slug of Kigan's new brew down, give it to Shale and he passed it onto Bresken and Kailen and the others.

"Ibsey, I need a Roob," shouted Milu, and from the packhorse he took out a long and heavy horn of bone what had to sit on the ground and was made for spreading and increasing the sound he made. It was carved in a twist that give it some extra noise. The Roob was a brew he took that give him his full range as a singer, and he had a rare power in him that give his songs a force that caused horses fifty yards about to quail and throw their riders.

There was clashing then to our rear as the commanders across the rest of the column behind us tried to bring their shields and spears to bear on the rushing horse while the bit of cavalry we had in the plain was looking to organise itself and try to counter.

I saw, behind the hundreds of horse charging at us from the front, a fierce army, a huge line that just kept growing as they marched into the plain. Among these were bowmen, and, we were soon to learn, slingers, as well as infantry.

The Honour hit me then, think I barely had time to cry out for how violent it felt, how it gripped me in a jaw and near shook me about. With the screaming of our own men and theirs, and their horse charging like a dark and massive wave, I was almost overcome, like I couldn't breathe because my heart was hammering at my ribs. I took my spear up and stood it in the ground for the assault. In moments the horses broke on us. I got my spear into what I could. I was stood behind Bresken, who held a shield before us and was throwing bags of powders up that were likely to set the horses off as our mix weren't something they were conditioned to deal with. I managed to bring down one, then two horses, the second having jumped over the first and behind us. Arrows finished it and its rider. We were at it, bellowing and full of madness. This fightbrew of Kigan's give me some big noisies and I was causing them all kinds of trouble, sticking a load of them with our poison what put them down and made their riders screech. Dithnir, Kigan, Valdir, Stixie and the Rhosidian archers with us started putting them down and they were laughing, the thrill of being faster and surer something I too was feeling. I didn't feel like a man no more, I felt like something else, something bigger. We kept the square mostly but around us cavalry was getting in. Kailen was shouting for the captains to bring the square in or he was directing archers and running about where the line was breached and mopping up with a savage grace. He give a shout to Milu then as we struggled against their steeds what were kicking at the shields and by their weight pushing us back and fracturing the lock on the shields we had.

Milu was risen then and blew into the horn, now they were close enough, and the sound was this shattering, screaming howl that give us all pain but their horses squealed, kicking up and throwing their riders as they twisted about and tried to get away. It broke their front line and sent those behind them into chaos as well. A cheer went up at this, but there was still much of their formation intact as they'd been able to engage at our sides and the Rhosidians and other mercenaries with us were having more trouble, most of them not getting the Honour in time and making do with their own fightbrew.

Kailen was asking us to retreat all the while, not to push on, hoping I guess like the other captains and General Urutz to get into formation again with greater numbers from the thousands that were in sheltrons or otherwise in disarray behind us. But there was little hope for the Rhosidian army. The flanking cavalry was causing havoc.

The cavalry what were still at us on the front line retreated given the mess its horses were causing the infantry trying to move in. Milu's horn was a bother but the other singers weren't having as much luck, so few were trained and conditioned like him, another advantage of Kailen's in this regard, giving us an edge in this one of many ways against those not prepared for us.

Kailen

Of the four hundred or so of us in the van, the charge must have killed half of us, but many more of them. We had formed sheltrons and ours held well enough, but many others were less able to with-stand the charge and were broken. There were two good captains with me and enough discipline we could close our square and move back-wards, trying to bring men in to bolster it from those other sheltrons broken and routed.

We were dead in this plain, and the pass we'd come out of, as Jaon well knew, would effectively be a wall. The flanks attacking the rear of the column succeeded in their plan by not waiting for the full force to come through, so that the dead would impede those scrambling to get back up the pass and so create a chokepoint that blocked and trapped us here and most of our cavalry back inside the pass. We had no other choice but to move back and attempt to open the pass again, but as I looked back at the success the Virates forces were having, Rhosidian soldiers being routed and cut down everywhere, things looked grim.

Ahead of us then I saw men advancing in place of the cavalry charge we'd withstood. These were archers for sure, though I could

394

see slingers among them, huge numbers. I shouted for hoods as it was obvious we were going to get smoked and I called our banner-man's mate to trumpet the instructions I couldn't otherwise shout while I was masked myself.

They brought horse archers up to fifty yards to do what damage they could while the slingers hurled some big bags of strykna at us, all along the front lines of the remaining sheltrons. Soon as the first hit, Ibsey shouted it was strykna and the boys went into a covering drill that allowed them to apply oils while their mate kept the shields locked, switching back as they did so. Still, it was too much strykna for many in the front line, and soon arrows were finding their way through and the shield wall was breaking up.

The horse archers, no doubt fearful of Milu and the other singers, retreated and the regrouped cavalry went for our sides this time, trying to avoid our front line where they believed Milu would be. The shel-tron's order had been damaged, and though the trumpet sounded for its tightening, the poison was doing its job of breaking up our forma-tion. Another captain with me was keeping the archers directed well at breaches to the walls of the sheltron, directing fire now to our flanks as this regrouped cavalry came in and I moved to a flank myself to encourage the men there while sending Milu to the other flank to call for the readying of spears.

They hit us this time with more success, breaking through on Milu's flank, while I did what I could to stop many getting through our spears and at our archers that we were protecting in our hollow. We were in all kinds of trouble now, and while my boys there — Stixie, Kheld, Dithnir, Connas'q, The Prince and Valdir — organised a smaller circle and achieved remarkable success taking down the horses that came through, many men had been cut down while others were collapsing from the dreadful effects of the strykna. For all our hoods, masks and oils it was the potency of it, its purity, that broke us up so quickly.

I looked about for Ibsey and Kigan, but they were already trying to get to as many as they could still strong enough in order to give them oils and the Honour where they hadn't yet got it. Cheers were going up then behind us, where the fighting was a wide open melee between the Virates cavalry and infantry and the main part of the

Rhosidian column that bore their brunt and were now fighting each man or woman for themselves. The cheers went up among the Virates soldiers as a cavalryman had got a banner of the general's and had tipped it upside down. I looked back at the opposide side of our sheltron that had been hit hard by the cavalry there. I feared for Milu and the men on that flank, but I saw then that the captain who had been directing our archers was now focusing their fire at the horses jumping through. This captain was organising rallying cries with trumpeters to bring Rhosidian soldiers from the other smashed sheltrons into our lines. I learned later his name, and saw sooner how well this bull of a man fought with those two large scimitars. He was the last to join the Twenty.

Warmaster Jaon, who must have seen the Rhosidian banners being turned over, took it as a good signal for a decisive blow, for without them there would be nothing to rally to, and he sent his main infantry against us. Many of his cavalry that had earlier flanked and broken the column were reorganising behind us as well, for now ours was the only Rhosidian banner that stood, a few hundred of us around Urutz's own bannerman, while the rest of our army was chased and harried as it fled for the Falls.

Gant

There were some moments to breathe while their infantry began its advance on us, holding their form and trying to navigate over the dead horses what numbered in their hundreds.

"Fill your scabbards with the hogweed mix!" shouted Kailen. "Arrows and bags! We've got to break their formation!"

He had words with the other captain, who we learned soon enough was Sho, and Ibsey give him some flasks of the hogweed aconite mix. I could see Kailen's reasoning. The hogweed would send them mad, or blind them. If we could get it over them, to any part of their skin or into them, then even a blow which didn't deliver the aconite strongly enough should have got them hopping and unable to keep their discipline. I never come up against it in a fight, but Kigan had put it on me so he could try a cure for it and even a drop on my skin was enough to set me off. Then again, few could work it as pure as him, so it was unlikely the Virates soldiers had any hope of countering it.

"Hey!" shouts Shale next to me. "Kailen! They got a banner, three lines back. Get in at the front with us, we charge on the point they're gettin' over their dead horses an' I'm goin' fer it."

Kailen nodded, had his sword and a small buckler and he tucked in to my left, Shale then next to him and Bresken to my right. He put word back to Sho to keep the square, for we couldn't hope to meet their entire line and couldn't risk them getting around behind us here at the front.

"Harlain! Fall in beside Gant and Bresken, we're going for the banner on Shale's word!" said Kailen.

Harlain come in next to me. "We run into a great wave, Gant, a handful of pebbles into an ocean and we expect it to turn." He slapped my back and readied himself.

There were a good few thousand against a few hundred, and they a hundred yards away now, all horns and buzzing with their noisies what were making them speed up a bit, and as Shale called it, their line lost a bit of shape as they hit their own dead.

"I'm thinkin' that if you throw yer pebble hard enough, Harlain, yer give even the ocean cause fer doubt," I said.

And so Shale it was ran out, as he was always leading the front line when he found himself in one, and with the horns sounding as Kailen and the rest of us followed him, the bags went over us from the thirty or so archers and slingers in the hollow of our sheltron.

Course, the Virates boys didn't expect it, that us pebbles would go looking for the wave, and we hit them hard. Harlain cleared me some room with that big scimitar of his and a hand-axe in his other hand. Two at a time were getting hit, or smacked into each other, and he put a mighty fear on them, knocking them about like a bull would. I got to work tight with Kailen to my left as the lines broke up. The five of us kept a tight point and Shale it was driving at the front through to their banner and trumpet men, who had nowhere to run with those pressing up behind them all gritty for a fight. He cut them down hard. A few cried out seeing that we were after the banner, but by then Shale had killed about ten and, throwing his shield into them, took up the banner from the man he'd killed and fair hurled it back into our lines where one of the Rhosidians spun it upside down and got a roar from the men about. The bags were coming in too of course, and as the powders got up and the pastes working there was panic across their lines. Many about in the ranks of infantry we couldn't reach were stumbling and others blinded and tripped over each other and caused havoc on those advancing around them. Seemed like every few seconds there was one of Stixie's big arrows coming in too, protecting the wedge we had formed for Shale to reach their banner, and each arrow was like a short spear, knocking men clean back, smashing open shields, three or four at a time. On any lesser brew, or with any lesser archer, his shooting, as well as Dithnir's and Kheld's, might have been a danger. We closed back up in the confusion and slaughter, Kailen and Bresken flanking Shale so he could move back, and we edged back then into the main front line of the sheltron as the greater force moved at us, against which of course so few could never overcome.

Shale called it well, for the banner cheered us no end and the Rhosidian drummer we had with us took it and stood alongside Urutz's bannerman and the two were like a big fuck you to the horde. We made the line again and Kailen left us to command, with Sho, our flanks and rear to tighten the square.

"Horse!" shouted Mirisham, only moments after we'd locked shields again, his voice carrying well across the fighting. He was gesturing to the rear of the sheltron. We were sore pressed as it was at the front, but he was on a flank organising the Rhosidian boys there that we'd brought into our sheltron, doing little more of course than replacing what we had lost from the Virates infantry pressing around us. The cavalry what had scattered the column at the mouth of the pass had got itself in line and was coming for us, too few Rhosidian soldiers to withstand them.

Kailen run up to Harlain then, so he could lipread what was needed. "Harlain, take a spear, get to the rear with Bense and Moadd and sort those spearmen out, because their cavalry's looking to pincer us again!"

"I shall claim a banner, Kailen, for they gladden our men to see them!"

Kailen had commanded us then to keep edging backward, and so for a time there was nothing to do but keep the discipline, keep killing, and hope there were some in the pass beyond the Falls that could help us.

Kailen

The land rose gently to the Falls. We were maybe a thousand yards from the mouth of the pass when the cavalry came at our rear. Sho I instructed to form a loose wedge from the men who made the rear line of the sheltron, something that could shield Milu and their other singers who we'd managed to get on his Roob, though it made one of them pass out for he couldn't manage his breathing once he took it. I pulled Harlain back there to ensure our spears were set firm to meet their charge.

I commanded as I could and ran the lines with Ibsey and Kigan and two Rhosidian drudhas, telling the wounded who could do so to move back behind the frontline and get their wounds done. The drudhas' focus was our archers of course, for it was plant that would make the difference now, not muscle and steel. Rhosidian drudhas were a lot of shit sadly, but they took direction well from Ibsey.

Seeing the number of horse now charging the rear I went to the back line and took up a spear with Harlain. As I joined the line the cavalry hit the wedge and Milu let loose with a vicious screaming from the horn that was an agony to their horse. I called Bense and Moadd to me and with Harlain we made a run from the line and into them. The Honour gave us the agility to deliver cuts to as many horses and riders as we could while we ran, for the poison would do the work and we were after another banner, one of Jaon's oldest I learned later, which sits proudly at the gate to the Rhosidian king's palace to this day.

Harlain was magnificent; on the Honour, with his great strength, he was spearing horses and, incredibly, forcing them over onto their sides. Three he took out this way and, seeing his moment, smooth as water, he took aim and threw his spear, catching the bannerman we were after hard in his breastplate from thirty yards. Seeing the banner fall sent another shout across the line behind us and I could feel in the earth the rippling out of this change, the power of these men, of Milu's thunderous singing and also the fear now in the cavalry as they

399

fought to turn about and retreat to regroup, the momentum lost for hundreds of yards around us.

As I'd hoped, there were men in twos and threes about the plain between us and the Falls, many wounded, that were trying to move back as we were, but on seeing the cavalry break against us and a banner go down they stepped up, found bows or weapons around them and ran to us, a vigour in them, shame as well perhaps, that this van could rid them of.

Then came Jaon's last play, another astute manoeuvre, for he could see well enough from his position behind his lines what was happening, and he saw that although our sheltron was withstanding his forces, we were dying, his weight of numbers picking us off one by one. He had his own guard push through their lines, two elite units, one coming at us head on, the other making for our left flank. I called out for arrows to the flank as I saw what he was up to, trusting the boys in front to keep shape and take them out.

"No bags or arrows, Kailen!" called Stixie. I looked skyward a moment. So it would end here.

"Blades then, fall in with me!" I shouted to the archers. "Captain! Sheltron in! Form a single line! Trumpets! On my signal, and only on my signal, blow for a charge!"

Gant

We doubled up on the Honour. We had no choice now, for they kept coming at us and we had nowhere safe to go. Kailen collapsed the sheltron to a line, so that meant a final stand, for it wouldn't be too long before the cavalry that we broke to our rear would regroup to charge us again. I looked back a moment when I was freshing my blade with more paste and there were no archers, so they must have run out of bags or arrows. About twenty yards to our left then I saw some Virates soldiers break through, and to our right some more. Kailen called that there were some specials coming in and it was what give us a nudge to take another hit of this brew and hope it wasn't the death of us, though of course at the crossroads there was no real choice anyway, was there?

I called for us to tighten up and pulled Shale out of the line to join me and go at the men pouring through to our right, what were busy slaughtering those about them with ease. It give them some extra puff of course, seeing us break. We charged at those that come through, and sure enough they were well equipped, quick and cautious, better soldiers than what we'd faced to that point.

We got among them and though we shouted for our own that fought among them to run back to us and reform a line, they were getting taken out. I had to hope that their horse wouldn't regroup again, but with infantry breaking through, they'd be doing it now through their own.

Those Rhosidians holding the line on our left were broken now as their specials come through and they were closing to where the Twenty were. For all that Kailen must've been over that side, their general must've himself ordered a flanking knowing we couldn't do much while he pushed at us from the front with his best soldiers.

We got Sho and Digs with us then, who must've seen we were beginning to struggle; four of us stood strong and the second rise hit me like a spade to the face, and the world come to life fierce then. I was lost to the noisies and the Forms as we killed all that come at us. I never felt such a thing ever in my life again, being as strong as I'd ever get on the best brew I'd ever take. The Rhosidians around us were falling, their brews up and Ibsey and Kigan not able to give enough of them a second hit of the Honour. These Virates boys were much the better and quicker and we started taking blows, yet it was Kigan and Ibsey's plant what saved us from their worst effects for they knew well what the Virates used and had prepped as much before we sailed for Rhosidia.

I heard Kailen calling for Shale and me then and I knew that his flank had collapsed. They moved back in to join up with us again, and it was slow going but soon enough, stumbling over the dead of both sides, I found myself at The Prince's side, who was a credit to himself for we all knew swords weren't his strength.

Then Kailen at some point must have give the shout for a charge, for the trumpet sounded it, and there couldn't have been more than fifty of us left. It give us a moment's pause for sure, while we realised what it meant, that we weren't fleeing today, that the crossroads was upon us and this was how we would go out. Harlain and Shale went at it and we fell in tight. We focused on their advance at the

401

point where they'd put their best men, meaning to give them a fierce tale to tell of Kailen's Twenty, and we brought them to a halt by doing it, their infantry behind closing up and their room diminished. We were quicker, stabbing and parrying, leaving the paste to do the work for there were too many others trying to catch us with their own weapons, thrown or otherwise. A pile of bodies was building up and it slowed them even more. Then The Prince took up a warsong with Milu and we all took it up and with a glance either side of me I saw that as we stood our ground, it was us twenty in a line, including Sho, and just the bannermen and drummer left behind us, and us in a half-circle around them, defending the banners we'd won. They planted them then as we had stopped retreating, and they joined us in the line and they died and all, but we knew that the Virates army's best men had mostly been killed and those left were struggling among their wounded and dead to get at us. Their force spent itself, their song stuttering, no flow to them, and they hesitated and stopped believing they were going to kill us. On the Honour it was like something I could taste it was so clear to me. I cannot count how many I killed.

Shale and I were at one end of this line, and the line held and the minutes passed, though I couldn't have been the only one thought it was going to break.

Soon enough, Kailen was barking sharp commands at intervals, for us to run at them, to upset them from finding a formation to better press us or put bags into us. There were enough of them that it was a matter of time only, and with a sudden easing of their assault from a blast of their horns we guessed it; they were hoping to drain out our brew.

Horns then started up from the pass, maybe twenty. They were clear and loud, a distant cheer then at our backs like the wave that Harlain had spoke of. It brought tears to my eyes then, the sound of hooves, of the Rhosidian cavalry that had been pressed into the valley now breaking into the plain to force a rout, followed by the infantry that also rallied there.

They come past us at a gallop, five hundred horse, but enough, being fresh and with so many of the oppo worn down with our poisons and their own brews, that they broke their lines open, and maybe three hundred infantry come behind them, the last of the Rhosidian army from the valley.

By then the Virates men had lost their flint. They couldn't break us and so it was word spread far and wide from Rhosidia in the months that followed of Kailen's Twenty, who had stopped Cassica being taken and Rhosidia, and in so doing saved the Old Kingdoms at Tharos Falls.

Goran

I will leave the last words with Gant, my father, telling of how he came home to us.

I wanted him to know that I was his son, but Aunt Emelt forbade it. She said he didn't deserve the grief that would come of knowing her deceit, not while he was away, and knowing that if others knew, then our status in the tribe, her status on the council, would be ruined. I know my father would have wanted that least of all after what happened.

When I saw him, being drawn in a cart by my patron, The Red, and Fieldsman Ninety-three, I respected the wisdom of my aunt in the above. He had hours to live it seemed, but survived nearly two weeks more to tell his story, such as it is written here.

It is far warmer here in Harudan than in Upper Lagrad, where my father went into the ground. I'm not used to the sun and my fair skin burns pink and has earned me the name "Goran the Salmon". I am Kailen's ward and his quarter has been teaching me that which is necessary for me to know to one day run this estate and manage its groves and other interests. The children here leave flowers every rest day for Araliah, up on the hill. Imbrit and I weed it and keep the flowers there. A small oak sapling is also taking root, which will be a shelter in years to come for my children, says Kailen, but I am no better than a fish out of water for conversation when Jesca comes by and it is her that I would have those children with. Kailen has yet to come back, being at war.

The houses hereabouts are rebuilt. I have helped to oversee the work. Kailen insisted the main house be done last, once his people had their homes.

Aunt Emelt spared him as little as she did the council with her views, while he was at Lagrad, in this case my being a suitable ward for him, to give me an opportunity as the least that he could do for what had happened to Gant. I think he respected her fiercely for it, her direct manner, and she'd taught me my letters well enough he could not really refuse her. In every way that mattered she was a fine mother to me. Kailen agreed that she excelled also in her work on the council. Introducing himself as a Reeve and introducing Laun as an Agent, I have no doubt she saw him for what he really was and was clever enough still to ensure that our tribe and the Post would not have cause to fall out with each other. In return for some caravans of whatever the council needed, mostly weapons and plant, we would let them through our territories and give word of any of the movements of Caragula's forces.

I can add little more to round out the story. That my father was a man to be proud of, in a life where there was much that many would be horrified by, was more than I could have hoped for. He never forgot his home, and despite how things went for him after his wound in the Red Hills, he might not have managed to come back at all had he not been given Kigan's blue potion, plant beyond any in the Old Kingdoms, the price of which was his own awful life after Snakewood.

Epilogue

Gant

We took Kigan's recipe books and Kailen would soon crack his cyca for the Hanwoq Book, as it would become known I'm sure in years to come. His plant bought me time enough it seems to put here what become of Kailen's Twenty, the end of us remembered at least, for we ruled the world like kings for a time and our story would have been its own sort of history of these lands had I long enough to recall it.

Kailen hoped some good use could be made of them recipes, perhaps the most valuable in all the lands with what Kigan learned in the Hanwoq jungle from Lorom Haluim, who had known of Caragula's coming.

Kailen too it was that insisted I write down this account, for we shared much on the way back to Lagrad. We got there along the quiet ways what he and Laun knew and I had a lot to ask him as we went along, the salve what Kigan give me doing a fierce job with the pain and slowing down what was inevitable.

I was curious, of course, of that one thing Kailen said in Mirisham's hall.

"Valdir told us you were in on the thing at Snakewood," I said, "but I was curious that you knew so much of Kigan and what he was up to, in particular what was said about that magist."

"Let me go back a bit then. I invested much of that wealth we took in some ships, hoping for some good returns from importing spices and plant. The returns were spectacular, so I kept investing for a few years, until I met my wife Araliah. But I was doing little else. I had lost touch with Mirisham and the others, or should I say we avoided each other for a time because we knew we were being looked for, and

I kept up mainly with The Prince, with whom I had some of my shipping interests. Shortly I owned ships of my own. Trading, the nature of commerce, became interesting the more I learned of it. I began to understand better the ways in which the struggle for power in the world, being the struggle for plant, shaped the way so many countries made peace and war. Through it all I had dealings with the Post, and many High Reeves.

"It satisfied me for a few years to become a wealthy man, to move in those circles. If I had not I would not have had the gift of Araliah's love. But if I'm honest, Gant, I sought to achieve more than I had with the Twenty. I wanted to do great things, not just win battles, but change the world somehow, see about making it better. The Reeve of Harudan, High Reeve Kilimar, filled in much that I didn't know about the Post, a power that always fascinated me for how it was able to influence so much of the world. I understand the hate for the Post, how we all believe, as children, wearing the Red means one thing, then we grow up and learn it means another. Everyone knows at least a bit of the Farlsgrad Creed. Now it was that I had time and money and I had, thanks to Kigan I cannot deny, paid out and was still able to do forms. I stayed strong.

"The High Reeve put a message through to The Red, recommending me for a Fieldsman position, avoiding the usual route of becoming an Agent. My achievements, our achievements, were still well enough known, so I became Fieldsman Seventy. In turn then, some five years ago, I became The Red."

He laughed at my reaction, for I was fair staggered. "Fuck, Kailen, you're The Red?" And I laughed too, for why would anyone think they could know or meet The Red, yet all the same I should not have been surprised, for no man I knew was more qualified for what the role must require than Kailen. He was a fine military thinker, a leader what inspired me all my life, with him a good drudha and scholar as well. It was like somehow the puzzle made sense, not of the events themselves but that, of course, such a man as he would not settle for the respect only of other soldiers. No king or purse would sing our praises as Miri rightly said. Kailen believed from his academy days on that he could change the world, and there was no better man for making that than The Red. I was glad, and told him so.

I looked up to Laun, who was riding the cart what Kailen had bought us once we were in Lagrad territory. "Bet he's as hard a master on you as he was on me."

She nodded. I could almost hear the smile.

"So Mirisham's comments must've cut a bit then," I said. "We've all bitched at the Post."

"Yes, Gant. The Post is in many ways not the Post that Mirisham remembered. As a boy I recall seeing my first Agent, riding with Reds that had brought into Harud a caravan that had come over the Hiscan Road. White lions were in cages and I saw my first elephant, for they brought a circus at a time when the Ten Clan was in chaos between the rule of the Afagi and Tosak, and the Hiscan Road was as dangerous as it had ever been. The caravan was intact, but many of them, the Agent included, looked like they'd been in a war. They were an impromptu parade, the red of their cloaks and banners lit the white-washed streets up like fire. They were inspiring, adventurers. Now we are entering a dark age with this warlord Caragula. The Old Kingdoms are ill prepared for it. We have to be inspiring again."

He stopped himself, took a deep breath and adjusted my blanket. "I should not eat up what time you have talking of what the Post must do, and what I should do for it. Its concerns are far from my mind at the moment."

"You don't talk of Araliah," I said.

He smiled but it was brief and weak. "No. I was away and should not have been, because I had learned the Twenty were being killed. I was away too much, but if I could have known what Kigan was doing, and more what he had become, I would have hidden her away, I would have done something. I became complacent and I'd lost my flint. You had come to the Crag, you answered my call, but I did not know what I was up against, and my plan there had failed. I had to take a mix to fool Kigan that I was dead when it was clear I had greatly underestimated him, but it fooled everyone. I had no way to tell you of my deception without risking its discovery."

"That bargirl must have known," I said.

"Of course. She was a Fieldsman, the barman an Agent." And that too was a surprise where, again, it shouldn't have been.

"She, Araliah that is, sent yer men after us, to watch over us an' help us get to Mirisham," I said, "though we had no idea until we got to that valley where we confronted Kigan an' his crew. Achi were a great captain, he could have made the Twenty. I wouldn't be here now but for Araliah an' yer men what come to help us."

"Achi was a good man, and perhaps neither of us would be here if not for Araliah, for if Kigan had met me and not Shale, well, I had not the plant to make the fight about technique alone. Her saving you saved my life. She was a strong and brilliant woman." He took out a flask and we shared a slug of brandy. "I dread going back to the estate. I can think only of her buried there. Yet two hundred men, women and children depend on that estate. I haven't the heart for it."

"Add to those two hundred the millions facin' what is a great war," I said. "No man is better able to outwit or lead soldiers against that horde than you. The Old Kingdoms needs you, it needs the Post an' all, an' it seems from what yer sayin' that the Red could come to mean somethin' again by havin' this horde to set itself against. You were always for a way to test yourself, leave a legacy what would show them silks back home in Harudan what one of its greatest sons could do. You don't need me to add to what those millions would say if they were in this cart now, but if you owes me anythin', an' you don't, you could start by helpin' in whatever way would keep me tribe goin', and me sister alive, an' do somethin' for those what helped make your life good with Araliah. Help 'em all get a force an' match this army in strategy if not numbers."

"He's right," said Laun, and we both laughed at it for she hadn't said a word all day to that point and no more than a handful since we left that town hall.

"As Shale would put it," said Kailen, "'I'm fierce glad', fierce glad you're with me today and that I got to see you again after all these years. I've got my enemies in the Post, however; it's as riddled with factions as any kingdom. But enough! Tell me some more of Shale and Valdir. You said there was a promise I had to make regarding his wife and his sister."

Some days later we come into the camp what my tribe had for the summer months.

My sister Emelt, hair grey as snow gum bark, was there to greet us with her boy Goran. She was now on the council and so, whether they cared or otherwise, run the council for all their sakes. Goran was grown, tall and strong like his grandda, and one what would break hearts too. He was more a man of letters than a man of arms and I was pleased.

Emelt led the council in making welcome an Agent and a Reeve, as we made Kailen out to be, and we left much of the rest out except that I had taken the arrow and had come north to die at home and that Shale also had not made it.

I was bad now, and slept more than I was awake, and in these last days I think Emelt, Kailen and Goran spent much time together.

Kailen give her Kigan's old recipe book. It was known in the lands about as the Fathin book for the years that its recipes did such good that it had made Mirisham and his people rich and respected again. I reckon Emelt would make a good settlement with Caragula for the book and with it a future for the hast here, as Kailen believed it would in giving it to her.

I can see from this bed, through the open flap of the tent, the vast Ordago plains, the westernmost of Lagrad's lands. I rode over them as a boy, the thump of my mare's hooves flying so fast over the wind-pressed grasses my heart was near torn out of my mouth, a searing and wonderful cold whipping at my face. All these memories, of my ma and da, playing with my sister, come back now, mixed with my dreams as I was dying. Nearby, the chatter of our camps hadn't changed, nor the smells of the pots, or chill in the rain, or children screaming and racing past the tent, mothers after them for want of something, woollens as I recalled what my own mother worried me over.

Shortly, Emelt, Goran and Kailen come in with the men what would undertake the ritual we did for our dying. We all cried a bit and each come up in turn before the men got started. What I said to Emelt and what she said to me I'll keep. Goran could not speak for crying and I could only wish him well and to keep on with his letters and stay away from brews and swords and the like.

Kailen come up to me then, as the men prepared the bowls.

"It's an honour for me that I don't deserve, that yer here for this," I said. "I could only wish more for Shale to be here, that would be all I'd need."

409

"The honour is mine, Gant. I never fought alongside a finer front-line pair than you and Shale. You were the finest swords I'd ever faced."

I am about to be washed and fed the Charin by some of the council, what will ease me to death. Then I goes in the earth near my da and I gets to be part of what feeds our people, part of these plains with all my tribe, holding up with our hands our sons and daughters above us.

Acknowledgements

I'd like to thank those friends who read *Snakewood*'s early drafts and gave me the encouragement all novices need. I'm looking at you Rhian, Steve Warren, Ceri Llewellyn, Adam Bouskill, Lewis Boughtwood, Becky Sillince, Ian Smyth, Sean Murray, Dave Fillmore, Charly Hulme, Chris Bravery and Ross Stanton.

I'd like to thank my agent Jamie "I don't love this book" Cowen for his passion, guidance and hard yards getting the manuscript ready for submission.

Jenni Hill and Will Hinton, my editors at Orbit, with input from Tim Holman, have given me fantastic support, doing what great editors do – they shook both me and the manuscript violently out of our comfort zones until *Snakewood* became significantly better. Also a thank you to Joanna Kramer and everyone else at Orbit who have made *Snakewood* presentable to the world!

A first novel is more of a life's journey than any other. Along the way I had an English teacher at Barry Boys, Mr Andrews, who thought my wanting to be a writer was a sound ambition, and so fuelled my love for words. Also, a special thank you to John Singleton, my Creative Writing lecturer at the then Crewe and Alsager College, who took a chance on me after some desperate begging to join his course. He opened my eyes to a wider world of fiction and a deeper scrutiny of my awful prose than I could have hoped for. This book only exists because of his faith.

Finally there's my mum and dad, who have been inspiring me all my life.